Artifacts

Artifacts

Mary Anna Evans

Poisoned Pen Press

Poisoned Pen Press

First Trade Paperback Edition 2005

10 9 8 7 6 5 4

Library of Congress Catalog Card Number: 2003100077

ISBN: 1-59058-180-6 Trade Paperback

Poisoned Pen Press
6962 E. First Ave. Ste. 103
Scottsdale, AZ 85251
www.poisonedpenpress.com
info@poisonedpenpress.com

Printed in the United States of America

Dedications

Artifacts is dedicated to my family. They have never faltered in their faith in my work, even when it seemed that no one would ever read it but them.

This book is for my husband, David. Thank you for your blue eyes, your sweet voice, and your unwavering support.

It is for my children: Michael, who is always the first to read anything I write; Rachel, who is so generous with love and moral support; and, Amanda, the only seven-year-old I know who would even try to read a book like *Artifacts*.

It is also for my sister Suzanne. She has been my mainstay during so many crises, and, occasionally, she pays her older sister the compliment of asking her for advice. And it is for our parents, Irvin and Lillian Sellers, who gave us a home full of love, books, and music. Nothing on this earth could be any closer to heaven.

Acknowledgements

I'd like to thank those who were kind enough to review *Artifacts* in manuscript form: Michael Garmon, Rachel Garmon, David Evans, Lillian Sellers, Kelly Bergdoll, Bruce Bergdoll, Mary Anna Hovey, Leonard Beeghley, Nan Beesley, Tom Beesley, Brooke Beesley, Brenda Broaddus, Diane Howard, Bruce Evans, Toni Evans, Bette Halverstadt, Bill Hutchinson, Jennifer Johnson, Angie Stewart, David Reiser, Ned Stewart, and Rick Sapp. I am also grateful to James Hirsch for his insights into hands-on field archaeology; to James Dunbar for his underwater archaeological expertise; to Diana Tonnessen for her editing and marketing skills; to Chip Blackburn, captain of the *Miss Mary*, whose delightful tour gave this landlubber a notion of how a Gulf island dweller would live; and to Craig Ratzat, the flintknapper who told me how a stone tool might be used for close-range self-defense. All these people, reviewers and consultants alike, brought an array of expertise to the task, from bow hunting to sociology to boat handling, and the final book has been much improved by their comments. The remaining errors are all mine.

I'd also like to thank my agent, Anne Hawkins, for her gracious and able assistance; my editor, Ellen Larson, for her accurate and insightful contributions; the cover artist, Eleanor Blair, who had the talent and skill to bring Joyeuse to life; and to Barbara Peters and Robert Rosenwald, two publishers with the vision to try something new and the ability to make it succeed.

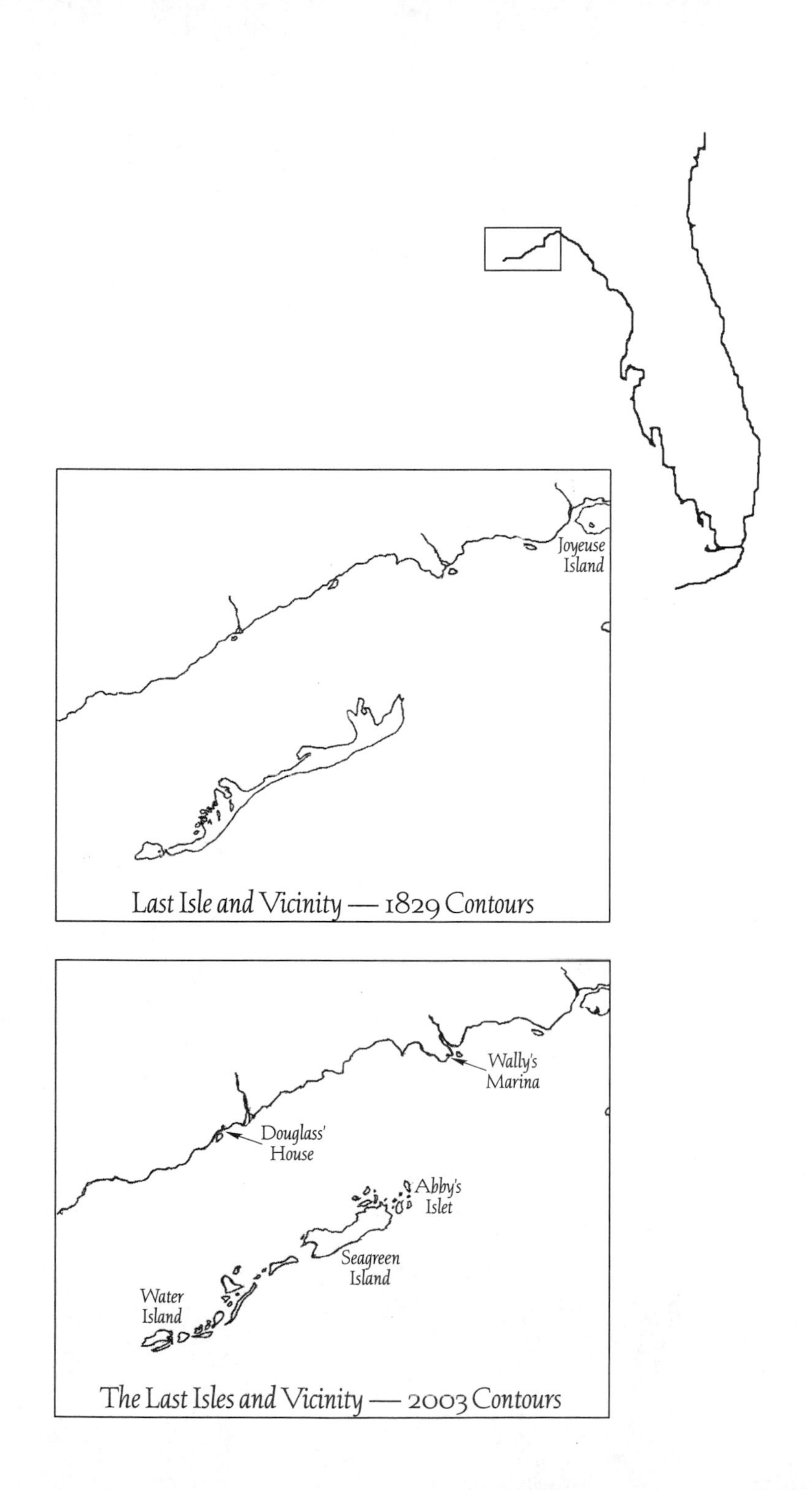
Joyeuse
Island
Last Isle and Vicinity — 1829 Contours
Wally's
Marina
Douglass'
House
Abby's
Islet
Seagreen
Island
Water
Island
The Last Isles and Vicinity — 2003 Contours

Prologue

There is no record of the name that the island's native inhabitants gave their home. The Spanish paused there only long enough to kill and plunder. Any name they gave it did not survive. The French stayed long enough to christen it appropriately—Isle Dernier. The English, though accomplished at empire building, were not original thinkers. They merely translated the French name into their own tongue. English-speaking Americans knew it only as Last Isle.

Nature was never kind to Last Isle. It was inundated by hurricanes time and again; each storm surge trenched further through the land, leaving it broken into pieces that over time acquired names of their own. Some of those pieces can no longer even be called islands.

Around the turn of the twentieth century, cartographers renamed the remains of Last Isle to acknowledge their plurality. Current sea charts no longer show a Last Isle. Instead, they warn mariners wishing to explore the crystalline waters off the Florida Panhandle to beware treacherous shallows around the Last Isles.

Long ago, life on Last Isle was idyllic. Its natives had no need of agriculture, given its abundance of fish and shellfish and waterfowl. Unfortunately, people whose lives are easy attract the attention of people whose lives are not. Their isolation had long protected the people of Last Isle from invasion, but the barrier of distance fell before the European conquerors in their tall ships. When they arrived, the massacres began in earnest.

Before the Americans finally wrested West Florida—and Last Isle with it—from the Spanish, the slaughter had tapered off. There was no one left to kill. Then the slavers auctioned their human wares to the local planters and misery returned. It took a great war to end it, one that touched even this tiny, remote spot. But despite the Last Isles' primeval beauty, ugliness is not yet vanquished. Its old trees have presided over centuries of killing.

The Last Isles are even now an attractive haven for a killer looking for a place to conceal a crime. No witnesses to murder lurk there, so far from civilization. There could be no more convenient place to rid oneself of an inconvenient corpse. With such a history, it is not surprising that the past and its bones sometimes surface. It would be more surprising if they did not.

Chapter 1

Faye Longchamp was digging like a pothunter and she hated herself for it. Pothunters were a bare notch above grave robbers. They were vultures. Once a pothunter defiled an ancient site, archaeologists could only hope to salvage a fraction of the information it had once held. And information, not artifacts, was the goal of legitimate archaeology.

Pothunters, on the other hand, only sought artifacts with a hefty street value, and to hell with egg-headed academics who condemned them for trashing history as they dug. There was no more precise description of what she was doing; therefore, she had sunk to the level of a pothunter. The fact that she was desperate for cold, hard cash did not absolve her.

A narrow beach to her left and a sparse stand of sea oats to her right were all that stood between Faye and the luminous turquoise of the Gulf of Mexico. Since pothunters couldn't excavate in the open, in front of God and everybody, they worked in places like this, patches of sand too small to have names. Not a soul lived in the Last Isles, and the island chain paralleled a thinly populated stretch of Florida Panhandle coastline. It was a good place to do work that should not be seen.

Looking up from her lucrative but illegal hobby, she glanced furtively over her shoulder at Seagreen Island. Its silhouette loomed like a dark whale cresting in the distance.

She knew how to excavate properly. During her abortive college career, she had tried to learn everything about field technique that her idol, Dr. Magda Stockard, could teach her. Even ten years later, working as she did on Seagreen Island as a field supervisor under Magda's watchful eye, she still learned something new every day. And she loved it. She loved sifting soil samples through a quarter-inch mesh and cataloging the seeds, beads, and bones that stayed behind. She loved the fact that every day was a treasure hunt. She would have worked for free, if she could have ignored her inconvenient need for food and shelter. The paycheck she received for painstaking work performed amid the heat and the humidity and the mosquitoes was always welcome, but it was insufficient.

Her work on Seagreen Island was legitimate, but it disturbed her nonetheless. Unless Magda's archaeological survey turned up a culturally significant site, there would be nothing to stop the developers who wanted to build a resort there. The lush and tangled vegetation topping the island would be scraped off to make room for a hotel and tennis courts and a spa and a couple of swimming pools. As if Florida needed more swimming pools.

This islet where she stood was too tiny to interest developers, though the government had found it worth including in a national wildlife refuge. It was really no more than a sandbar sprinkled with scrubby vegetation, but Faye's instincts had always been reliable. The Last Isles were once awash in wealth. The wind and waves couldn't have carried it all away; they must have left some of it under the sand, ripe for discovery by a needy pothunter. A tiny bit of that dead glory would pay this year's property taxes. A big, valuable chunk of the past would save her home forever.

Home. The thought of losing her home made Faye want to hurl her trowel to the ground in frustration, but doing so would require her to stop digging, and she couldn't do that. Something in her blood would never let her quit. Faye did not intend to be the one who let the family down.

Two eager archaeology students had volunteered to stay behind the rest of their field crew on mosquito-infested Seagreen Island. Tomorrow would have been soon enough to catalog the day's finds and mark the next swath of dig spots, but these two were too dedicated to their work for their own good. If the student archaeologists had cleared out on the stroke of five, they could have been enjoying Tuesday-night sitcoms and beer with their colleagues. Instead, they were conscientiously digging their own graves.

The sun kept sliding toward the Gulf of Mexico, and the red-haired girl kept squinting through the viewfinder of her surveyor's transit. She barked directions to her partner as he slowly—so slowly—placed one flag after another in yet another nice neat row. They checked and rechecked the grid of sampling spots, careful to ensure that everything was exactly as their supervisor had recorded in the field notebook that the young woman clutched like a bible.

The young man, standing in the shade of an ancient tree, twisted the surveyor's flag, yelling, "Hey, Krista, there's so many roots here, I can hardly get it in the ground."

The young man grunted as he pushed the flag into the soil, ignorant of what lay beneath his feet. The base probed deeper. It struck something horrible, but the young man and his companion remained unaware of it, so they were allowed to continue breathing.

Faye knelt at the edge of the evening's excavation. She'd put in a full day on Seagreen Island. Then, after her colleagues' boat was safely out of sight, she'd worked nearly another half-day here. It seemed like she had displaced half the little islet's soil, and her biceps quivered from the strain. She had been so sure. Her instincts had screamed, "This is the spot," the moment she dragged her skiff onto the bedraggled beach. This was a place for buried treasure, a place to dig up the find that would change her life. She still felt that electric anticipation, but her shovel had turned over nothing but sand.

The aluminum-on-sand groan of Joe's flat-bottomed johnboat being dragged onto the beach caught her ear, but his presence didn't disturb her dogged work. She hardly looked up when he said, "It's about dark, Faye. If you ain't already found anything worth digging up, you won't be finding it tonight."

Joe was right, so she ignored him.

He tried again. "Faye, the day's gone. Come home and eat some supper. You can try again tomorrow."

Faye continued to ignore him.

Joe sighed, glanced at the last scrap of sun melting into the Gulf and squatted on his haunches beside her. "Okay, you want to dig in the dark? Let's dig in the dark. You got another one of those little hand-shovel things?"

Faye could steel herself against displaying her emotions, even on those occasions when outbursts were expected. At funerals, Faye was the competent one who made sure that the other mourners had comfortable chairs and fresh handkerchiefs. She grieved later, alone in her car, undone by the sight of a woman sitting at the bus stop with her head cocked at her mother's angle.

Sometimes, when forced to carry on long past any sane person's breaking point, she found herself weeping at dog food commercials. Now, since she no longer had a TV, she was denied even that cheap outlet, so she was defenseless in the face of Joe's chivalrous offer. The sudden tears surprised her.

"Why are you crying? Don't do that!" Joe cried.

Faye, in her state of emotional upheaval, found Joe's panicked squeak uproarious. She dropped to the ground, laughing.

Joe bent over her with his brow furrowed in confusion and demanded, "Why are you laughing? What's wrong?"

"I'm laughing because you think I'm an idiot for digging in the dark, but you're willing to be an idiot, too, rather than leave me alone with the sand fleas."

Joe put his hand on her shoulder. His solicitous tone did nothing to quench her giggles. "And why are you crying?"

Her giggles subsided. "Because you're the best friend I ever had."

Joe brushed his ponytail over his shoulder and looked at the few stars bright enough to penetrate the early evening haze. "Aw, Faye. Smart, pretty girl like you—you're bound to have bunches of friends."

"No, not many. You don't know how hard it is...." She swallowed the suggestion that Joe wouldn't understand how hard life could be for a child who wasn't really white or black, who didn't fit neatly into any racial pigeonhole at all, because she knew better. The bronze tint of the skin over his high cheekbones said that Joe Wolf Mantooth knew all about it.

Whether he knew what she was thinking or just sensed it was time to change the subject, Joe took the trowel from her hand. Humming in his monotone way, he aimlessly moved soil around the bottom of the pit Faye had excavated. They both heard the muted click when the trowel struck something that wasn't rock, nor metal, nor plastic. On their hands and knees immediately, they saw the object at once. It was the color of the sand that nearly buried it, but its sleek, gleaming curve attracted the eye. Faye, instinctively falling back on her archaeological training, reached into her back pocket for a fine paintbrush to work the sand gently away from the surface of this human skull.

Joe jumped up, saying, "We have to go home and get my stuff, Faye. There's a lot of things I need to do."

Joe believed in the old ways from his skin-clad feet to his pony-tailed head and Faye respected his desire to consecrate this old grave. He fumbled in the large leather pouch that always hung from his belt. "I've got tobacco here, but nothing else. I need to go home and get some food, and a clay pot to put it in. And some coals from my fire and some cleansing herbs for washing. Faye—"

Faye held up a hand for him to be quiet, because she was busy assessing the skull's archaeological context. It was unusual to find a burial like this one, one unassociated with other graves or signs of human habitation, but it wasn't a complete aberration. She'd read that Choctaw warriors killed in battle were buried by their wives on the very spot where they fell. The burial had to be accomplished without disturbing the corpse, without even touching it. As Faye brushed sand away from a sizeable fracture radiating from the skull's temple, she wondered whether she was the first person to touch this man since his killer had bashed his brains out.

"Faye, let's go. This guy's rested here a long time and we've disturbed him. We got to help him rest again. It's the right thing to do. It ain't respectful to wait."

Faye didn't answer Joe, because she was busy. She would discuss this with him in a minute; he'd just have to be patient with her. She was wholeheartedly glad he knew how to treat this burial with respect. She may have become a common pothunter, but she was no grave robber and disturbing the dead chilled her bones. Joe's makeshift funeral rites assuaged her guilt a bit.

Still, she wished that he would hush for just a minute while she examined this skull.

The cabbage palms of Seagreen Island cast jagged shadows on the red-haired girl's face as she initialed her field notebook with a flourish. She ran her fingers through an inch-long crop of spiky hair.

"Done," she said. "I can't believe we finished before dark."

"Dr. Stockard would probably say 'Quick work is imprecise work.'"

"I don't care," was the girl's airy reply. "Let's go check the sample bags so we can eat supper and go to bed."

They crossed the crest of the small hill that ran down the spine of Seagreen Island. In their wake stood a tidy row of surveyor's flags, each consisting of a simple length of wire topped with a rectangle of orange vinyl. The flags marched straight toward a mammoth live oak tree and the last one stood in the shade of the oak's moss-draped branches.

Early the next morning, the rest of the field crew would arrive to dig a test pit at each spot marked by a flag. If they were to dig under the live oak, their shovels would turn over more than just dirt.

Faye picked up a twig and rested it on the bone that had once underlain somebody's upper lip. She tried to slide it into the skull's former nostril, but the twig butted up against a bony ridge.

"You're off the hook, Joe. There's no need for any mystic tobacco-and-corn ceremony. This is a Caucasian skull. I'll just cover him up and say a Christian prayer over him. If he was a European invader of the rape-and-pillage variety, even my puny prayer would be too good for him."

Faye traced her fingertips over the soil surface, looking for artifacts she might have disturbed while digging, and was rewarded with a clod of soil that was too heavy for its size. She worked the dirt away from the solid center of the clod while she listened to Joe argue his point.

"Everybody deserves a comfortable grave, Faye. Just let me go get my—"

Somewhere in the direction of Seagreen Island, Faye heard a boat motor turn over. Pointing at the sound, she barked, "Help me cover her up. Somebody's coming."

Joe tended to obey authoritative voices, so he dropped his argument and began shoveling dirt back into the excavation, but he didn't stop talking. "Why did you say 'her'? I thought you said 'him' before. How do you know that this was a girl?"

Faye kept shoving dirt over the skull without answering Joe. Getting caught would be an outright disaster. First, she was digging in a national wildlife preserve and removing archaeological materials from federal lands was a felony. Second, a brush with the law—and the fines and legal expenses that would accompany such trouble—would hasten the inevitable loss of her home. And third, the artifact in her hand suggested that she might be treading on legal quicksand far more serious than simple pothunting.

As they sprinted toward their boats, she held out her hand to show Joe the single item she had removed from the grave. "This is how I knew she was a girl."

A corroded pearl dangled from an ornate diamond-studded platinum earring. Her practiced eye saw that it was machine-made and recent, but no archaeological knowledge was required to date this artifact. Any woman alive who ever played in her mother's jewelry box could guess its age. The delicate screw-back apparatus dated it to the mid-twentieth century and the style pinpointed the period still further. The woman who wore this earring had wished very much to look like Jackie Kennedy.

Somebody had buried her in a spot where she was unlikely to ever be found. Most likely, that somebody had killed her.

Walking up the wooden stairs and onto the broad porch of her home never failed to settle Faye's soul. Even tonight, after violating her professional ethics, breaking several laws, and disturbing the dead, she was soothed by the gentle sea breeze that blew through the open front door.

The old house and its island had both been named Joyeuse by one of Faye's ancestors whose name she didn't know. The old plantation house on Joyeuse Island was more than home to her. It was a treasure entrusted to her by her mother and her grandmother and her grandmother's mother and, most of all, by her great-great-grandmother Cally, the former slave who had somehow come to own the remnants of a great plantation.

Cally's story was lost to time. No one remembered how a woman of color had acquired Joyeuse Island and held onto it for seventy years, but Cally had done it, and her descendants had preserved her legacy and her bloodline. Something of Cally lived on in Faye, maybe in her dark eyes or her darker hair, but another, essential, part of Cally survived in the home she fought to keep. Joyeuse was a decrepit relic of antebellum plantation culture, built by human beings laboring for people who believed they owned them. Even so, it was a calm, beautiful place and Faye had learned to live with the ambiguity of that. Sometimes Faye thought Ambiguity should have been her middle name.

If race is the abiding conflict of the Americas, then Faye considered herself the physical embodiment of that conflict. Her great-great-grandmother Cally had been born a slave on Joyeuse plantation, the product of the master's assault on her mother. Unprovable family lore said that the master himself was not as white as he might have believed; his grandmother was half-Creek. There were surely people who died on the Trail of Tears with no more Native American blood than he.

Faye's ancestors had sprung from Europe and the Americas and Africa and God-knew-where-else. The casual observer, noting her darker-than-olive skin, tiny build, delicate features, and stick-straight black hair, would be hard-pressed to name her racial affiliation. Faye was never too sure herself.

Settling herself on a ramshackle porch swing, she studied the earring in her hand. She couldn't call the law. How would she explain why she was digging on federal land?

Faye tucked one foot under her and pushed against the floor's cypress boards with the other, ever careful to maintain her balance. How many times in her childhood had she leaned back too far and felt the old swing dump her onto her head? Then, once she'd learned the trick, how many times had she done it on purpose because it was fun to fall, heels over ears, into a giggling heap of little girl? All those memories would be sand under the feet of anyone but Faye. There was no way in hell she was going to let Joyeuse go.

She swung herself gently back and forth. What harm would it do to forget she'd ever seen those bones? One more good hurricane and they would be swept away, anyway. She hated to think about someone getting away with murder but, in reality, someone already had. What was the likelihood that a critical clue had survived for decades under damp, wet sand? Still, her sense of right and wrong said that she ought to tell somebody. The dead woman's family would derive some comfort in knowing, with certainty, that she was never coming home.

Her sense of self-preservation wouldn't let her go to the police, but her conscience wasn't quite ready to let her destroy evidence of a murder. Keeping the earring at least gave her the option of doing the right thing someday. But where could she hide the evidence? There was no available nook in Joyeuse's above-ground basement. It was built of tabby, a durable concrete concocted of oyster shells, lime, and sand, and it would survive a direct atomic strike. After more than a hundred and fifty years, there were still no crevices large enough to serve as a hiding place in its rock-like surface.

She climbed the staircase tucked under the back porch roof, leaving the service rooms in the basement behind. The main floor sat a full story above ground level, a form of house design that was prudent in a hurricane zone. Faye wandered around the main floor, poking around in the ladies' parlor and the gentlemen's parlor and the vast room that had served as both dining room and ballroom. The fine furnishings and draperies were long gone and the cavernous empty chambers offered no nook to house the old pearl earring. There was really only one place in the whole house that offered hiding places which she didn't already use to store her everyday necessities, and it was two stories above her.

She climbed the porch staircase to the next level, which had housed the bedchambers and music room back when the house served as a home for a family and its servants. She'd converted the two largest bedrooms into her temple to legitimate archaeology, two treasure rooms where she stored artifacts that made her black-market customers sneer.

The walls of her own bedroom and the adjacent master bedroom were lined with glass-fronted shelves loaded with unsalable finds. Cracked pottery, broken bone tools, the bones and shell of a turtle—the discovery of each of these things was described in waterproof ink on the pages of the field notebooks stacked on the topmost shelf. Any of these shelves could have served as a hiding place for the earring, but Faye had another spot in mind. She reached in a broom closet for a long-handled implement tipped with a metal hook, but before she could use it, she heard Joe coming.

Faye listened to Joe climbing the spiral staircase that rose through the precise center of the old house, piercing the square landing that provided access to the rooms on this level. Joe's footfalls were quiet and fast. The ordinary listener wouldn't have heard him coming. His moccasined feet made no percussive tap as they hit the treads, but there was a faint creaking in the old wood that Faye, attuned to any disturbance in her cherished home, couldn't ignore.

Joe rose through the floor and stepped onto the landing, saying, "I made something for you, Faye. I was saving it for later, but I think you've had a hard day."

She took Joe's gift and turned it over in her hands, unable to think of an appropriate response other than, "You shouldn't have gone to so much trouble for me."

The workmanship couldn't be criticized. Joe was very, very clever with his hands. There was no way to tell him that it was wrong to alter something thousands of years old; she didn't intend to try.

Joe had used new materials to reconstruct fragments of an *atlatl* made by west Florida's Deptford people before the birth of Christ. Starting with a stone weight and a shell trigger that he'd taken from her display case, Joe had whittled and chipped the missing pieces of the *atlatl*, an archaic type of spear that was thrown by slinging its hinged spearthrower in a whiplash motion. The crowning glory of Joe's gift was a finely flaked stone point crafted out of chert, the same native stone Florida's original inhabitants had used in their tools. Given his penchant for stone tools and homemade glue, she couldn't hazard a guess as to how much of Joe's time she held in her hands. There was nothing Faye could do but thank him sincerely and resolve to keep her artifact cases locked in the future.

Joe, embarrassed by the encounter, disappeared down the stairs. Faye hefted the *atlatl*, choosing a prominent place for it in a display case in her bedroom, then she returned to the landing and lifted the hooked tool above her head. It grabbed hold of a recessed ring in the ceiling and she pulled hard. A hidden trapdoor opened, and she unfolded the rickety wooden ladder that dangled from the door. This was why she rarely ventured into Joyeuse's cupola. It was so dang hard to get up there.

Once she had struggled up through the trapdoor, she saw the cranny she'd had in mind. By standing on a windowsill and stretching upward, she could reach her hand into a gap between the top of the wall and the rafters. It was the perfect hiding place....

...And someone had found it before. There was a wooden box there, about the size of a shoebox, and she gingerly lifted it down to her eye level. Aside from an inch-thick layer of matted dust, the box was in good shape. Carefully dovetailed together without a visible nail, the box itself was an exciting find. She tucked the earring atop a rafter and sat down to study the box.

Faye knew how Howard Carter must have felt, clearing rubble day after day from the staircase leading to King Tut's tomb, knowing that wonderful things awaited him, but savoring the anticipation. She hefted the box in her hands a moment—it wasn't empty, she could tell—then she lifted the lid and her breath faltered.

It was an old book bound in leather and canvas, and handwritten across the cover were the words, "Journal of Wm. Whitehall, begun on 15 May, 1782, to commemorate the Birth of his Daughter, Mariah." William Whitehall had formed each *f* with a long, vertical curve shaped like an *s*. Time wrought changes in everything, even the alphabet, and that sometimes made manuscripts of this age devilish to interpret.

The penmanship made Faye think of John Hancock's unrepentant signature on the Declaration of Independence, and her breath left her again. A man who was an adult in 1782 was a contemporary of John Hancock and his revolutionary friends.

The journal was stuffed full of stray sheets of paper. A palm-sized portrait of a man in a powdered wig slipped free and drifted toward the dusty floor, but Faye, who had the instincts of a museum curator, caught it without so much as crinkling the yellowed paper.

She opened the journal and saw that William, like others of a time when paper was hard to come by, had inscribed each page in the normal left-to-right fashion, then turned the book a quarter-turn to the right and written another full page of text atop the first. No wonder neat penmanship was so valued in those days. It was going to take her quite awhile to decipher what William had to tell her.

◇

Excerpt from the journal of William Whitehall, 15 May, 1782

My Woman—that is to say my Wife, for we are as Married as two people can be in the absence of proper Clergy—demonstrated true courage today, whilst I cower'd in the meadow alone, except for my pipe & my tobacco. After the hard labour of the day had been done by others, I stood—hat in hand—outside my own home and humbly begged permission to enter in. The Creek midwife acknowledged my presence with a bare nod, as is her way, and I stumbled into a house of miracles. As I thanked the

Almighty for this hale and healthy Child, that most precious of gifts, the Sun lay lightly on my Susan's flush'd cheeks, and she lifted the Infant toward me so gently, so slightly, that the motion was hardly visible. I seized the invitation & I seized the child. "A girl," my Susan murmur'd. I would have known the Baby was female merely by the shape of her dainty face.

I search'd that face, endeavouring to assess the shape of the eyes, the colour of the skin, tho' unaware that I did it. Then Susan, who has attended the births of Creeks and of Whites and of Half-breeds like herself, said, "All Babies look the same, puffy and red. After a time, you will see whether she looks like you or like me, but you will have to wait." She looked strait in my eyes & I was shamed.

Chapter 2

The original roof on the big house at Joyeuse was made of slate, but it had been replaced with tin when Faye's grandmother was a girl. The patter of raindrops on tin was loud enough to disrupt conversation, but Faye lived alone, in silence. She found the chattering noise companionable, especially on nights like this when she couldn't sleep. It drowned the voice of the dead woman whose earring rested on a rafter in the cupola, high above her. It overpowered the melancholy voice of William Whitehall. And, if she put some effort into it, she could let the calming raindrops cover the voice of her conscience, which was aghast at the ethical boundaries she had violated.

The sound of the rain lulled her asleep so slowly that when she awoke to a cloudless morning, she was shocked to find that she had slept at all.

"I guess we were more tired than we thought last night, Sam," said the red-haired girl. "We'd better pull this last row of flags up and start over. Everything needs to be right when Dr. Stockard and the rest of the crew get here."

The boy regarded the long row. "Damn, Krista. Before breakfast?"

She grunted and he set to work.

Slack, lazy workers wouldn't have gotten up at dawn and they wouldn't have noticed that the surveying flags weren't quite where they were supposed to be. Suspicious people, on the other hand, might have wondered how the flags could now be misplaced when they had been so certain of their measurements the night before.

Their diligence and their accuracy and their naiveté were their undoing. The young woman slid the last flag into the exact place it had stood the day before under the ancient oak.

The young man approached with a shovel. "Let's get started now, while it's still cool."

His shovel hovered over the sandy soil, preparing to uproot something better left undisturbed. The vulgar noise of gunfire shocked the silent island and both budding archaeologists dropped to the dirt.

Faye was eating her usual Wednesday morning breakfast, a peanut butter and honey sandwich. Life at Joyeuse was a lot like camping. Refrigeration was a continual problem, so cereal and milk were out. Also, bacon and eggs.

Joe cooked supper every night, and he'd been known to flip a Saturday morning pancake, but the rest of her meals were peanut-based. Fortunately, Faye rather liked peanut butter. She'd been awake since sunup, but since it came early in August, she could linger over breakfast and still be at work by eight. Joe occasionally lingered with her, but early morning was prime fishing time. Usually she breakfasted alone and she didn't mind. Fried fish for supper was worth it.

On her way to the inlet that sheltered their boats, she met Joe, who proudly brandished a full stringer of fish. "I'll have these cleaned and in the ice chest, waiting for you until you get back."

Faye cranked the motor on her mullet skiff, opened the throttle, and pointed the craft toward Seagreen Island. The island, usually occupied only by Magda's archaeology crew, was a three-ring circus when she arrived. Some of the excess people were obviously reporters with their camera crews. Faye guessed that the others were campaign personnel and political hangers-on. All their attention was fastened on a man surrounded by television cameras and holding one hell of a press conference.

"Seagreen Island is pristine. There are precious few unspoiled spots on Earth and, when they are gone, there will be no more. Florida doesn't need another resort." State Senator Cyril Kirby spoke eloquently for one so recently drawn to the environmental movement. In his years in the legislature, he had supported his land development backers to the hilt. There was a time when it could be said that Cyril Kirby had never met a swamp he didn't want to drain.

"Let south Florida bury itself under pavement and strip malls," he continued. "We here in the Panhandle understand quality-of-life issues. Saving Seagreen Island will be an uphill battle against shadowy figures and their bulging bankbooks, but we must fight it. If we do not concede defeat, we can have this idyllic spot annexed into the national wildlife refuge, where it will be protected forever."

Senator Kirby delivered this ringing challenge directly into the maws of the television cameras belonging to three local broadcast channels. He had not even announced his candidacy for the U.S. House of Representatives and already he looked to Faye like a politician that plenty of voters could get behind. Time would tell, but his recent reversal on environmental issues might prove to be his shrewdest move yet, except maybe for recruiting Douglass Everett as a major campaign contributor.

Faye noticed that Everett was carefully positioned just inside the perimeter of the cameras' range. Senator Kirby was the star, but nobody could mistake the power of the man in the wings. Douglass Everett was the most influential African American in north Florida. He had accomplished much in his life, but then a man who managed to finish high school while helping his daddy sharecrop a few acres of sand is no stranger to accomplishment.

Douglass Everett owned a lucrative construction business, but he never forgot his roots. He was a deacon in his church. He provided sole funding for a homeless shelter. He had the black vote in his hip pocket and he was a handy man for any politician to have around. Faye noticed that Senator Kirby never missed an opportunity to share a camera with Everett.

Their mutual admiration society had kept local movers-and-shakers scratching their heads for years. Whatever their original motivations, the two gentlemen had both benefited from their relationship. Everett, who started life with exactly nothing, had amassed considerable wealth through state contracts. Kirby, an upwardly mobile redneck who was now a viable candidate for Congress, could count on his friend to deliver the black vote, no matter what. Their opposition to the resort on Seagreen Island was getting them media exposure worth more than all the paid political announcements that mere money could buy.

Faye leaned against a tree to watch a seasoned campaigner perform. Douglass Everett tried to catch her eye. She ignored him, even though he was her best customer. Rather, she ignored him *because* he was her best customer. Some of her best finds were on display at his privately owned Museum of American Slavery; he was willing to acquire unprovenanced artifacts with shady histories and he was willing to pay well. Her chronic need for money meant that she needed to talk to him soon—this week, actually—but that conversation would have to wait. This was no place to talk about the things they needed to discuss.

Chapter 3

Faye was idly watching the cameramen dismantle their equipment when she saw Dr. Magda Stockard approaching at great speed for someone with such short legs. Faye steeled herself. It was early in the day to be chewed out for lollygagging.

The older woman's words caught Faye off guard. They were not, "Get your sorry self to work!" Instead, she said, "Sam and Krista aren't here," in a tone that made Faye feel as if she should do something about it.

"Settle down, Magda. I'm sure they'll show up." Faye spoke quietly to avoid being overheard by her fellow workers or the television crews packing up their equipment. "They're usually so responsible that we forget they're just kids. Maybe they overslept."

"Just because it's early in the morning is no excuse for being stupid, Faye. If they overslept, then they'd be here. They slept here last night, remember?"

"Well, they were supposed to." Faye made an effort to add something intelligent to the discussion and came up with, "Is their camping gear here?"

"Yes, and their sleeping bags were obviously slept in. Everything's here but Sam, Krista, and the small workboat."

"Well, then, there you have it. They got up early and decided to boat in for breakfast at Wally's. They're undergrads, not even old enough to buy a legal beer. Wasting an hour for a stack of bad pancakes probably sounded like an adventure to them. Come to think of it, Wally would sell them a beer to wash their breakfast down."

Dr. Stockard picked at a ragged hangnail and said, "Yeah. Sounds plausible. Or maybe Sam finally decided to put the move on Krista."

Faye laughed. "Sam's scared of Krista. And it hurts his dignity that her biceps are bigger than his. But you have a point. Maybe they are right this minute sharing an intimate morning-after breakfast."

"Over a bad stack of pancakes." Magda's short bark of a laugh erupted once. "Okay, you're right. I'll drop my mother hen routine—although it's my most ladylike side—and go back to being a slavedriver. Get to work."

Faye found the area around the equipment shed filled elbow-to-elbow with student archaeologists gathering machetes, wheelbarrows, dustpans, trowels, brushes, dental picks—whatever it took to complete their assigned task for the day. The disarray drove Faye to distraction. She moved among them, helping this one arrange her tools in a plastic storage box, checking that one's field notebook to make sure he understood his assignment. She was an entry-level, minimum-wage employee like the others and, like them, she had completed less than four years of undergraduate study, but she was ten years older than any of them and advanced age gave her words the hard glint of authority.

As she organized her team for the day, Faye kept one eye on Senator Kirby and his ever-present friend, Douglass Everett. She had known Douglass for years, but Senator Kirby was an unknown quantity and she needed to learn more about him. Like so many politicians, the senator was tall and tan and his facial features were bold. Telegenic people are easier to elect than ordinary folk. It was startling to see him here, when she had an appointment that very Friday to meet with him in his Tallahassee office. If she hadn't already waited weeks for the appointment, she would have strode right over to him and, as a taxpayer and a voter, requested a few minutes of his time. Considering her appearance—olive-drab twill shirt, baggy khakis, ratty boots, shiny-bare face—it seemed wiser to wait until she looked older than twelve. He would take her more seriously when she was dressed like a thirty-four-year-old upstanding taxpayer. Not that she ever paid any tax she could avoid.

Keeping the senator in her peripheral vision, Faye herded her team toward their day's work. Most of her field crew preferred large-scale tasks: surveying, digging, and hauling away the dirt. Faye was glad, because she liked fine work. She loved to run a shovelful of soil through a sieve to see what stayed behind. The pottery sherds, flakes, and arrowheads that were frequently left resting on the top sieve would be exciting for anybody but, to Faye, even the small bones, seeds, and shells caught by the finest mesh were fascinating.

She was content to spend hours with a pair of forceps, separating scraps of bone from plant trash. Such work gave her time to think, or to listen to the other workers talk. Despite the fact that she listened more than she spoke and that they spent more money in an average weekend of club-hopping than she spent on food for a month, Faye had come to consider them friends.

She'd been lonely most of her life. Being born biracial in America in the late 1960s had naturally had that effect. She usually liked to hear what her new friends had to say, even their inconsequential nattering.

Today, she wished they would be quiet and leave her alone.

"Can you believe that Douglass Everett?" exclaimed Beth Anne, a tiny girl with her hair in cornrows. "He took me aside and asked if I had any artifacts to sell."

"Me, too," drawled slow-moving, quick-thinking Ted. "I think he tried it with all of us. He must think we're all common pothunters."

Faye couldn't shake her grandmother's old saying from her mind. *The hen that cackles laid the egg*. Being a certifiable pothunter herself, the safest course of action was to stay out of this conversation, but apparently her grandmother was right. She felt compelled to cackle.

"Maybe he's wrong to ask us to procure artifacts illegally, but look at the good his museum has done. He doesn't profit from his Museum of American Slavery, and think of the history he's passing on to people who'll never read an archaeology journal."

No one could refute her statement but, comfortable on the moral high ground, they resumed their condemnation of pothunters in general and Douglass Everett in particular. Ears burning, Faye picked up a paintbrush and concentrated on brushing sand from the design stamped into a pottery sherd, whether the task required her undivided attention or not.

Ignoring the discussion didn't help. Every comment jangled a different nerve.

"What kind of museum would display unprovenanced artifacts, anyway?"

"How could anybody buy a piece of somebody else's culture?"

The comment that drove Faye to the edge came from the privileged lips of a girl who drove a BMW to class. When she stated that some things were just more important than *mere money*, Faye, who had taken her first after-school job at fourteen to help pay her mother's medical bills, found that she needed to take a walk.

Seagreen Island lay shrouded in the canopy of an oak hammock, and the Gulf of Mexico was a stroke of seafoam green, barely visible through the trees. It drew her like a melody. Within seconds, Faye could no longer hear the students' incessant yammering, only the wind rushing through live oaks and cabbage palms. Someone had slashed a path to the water through the lush undergrowth just days before, but already the greenbrier reached for Faye as she passed. Intent on drawing peace from the ever-present Gulf, she pushed on.

Before she fought her way to the turquoise water she craved, she caught a glimpse of something hard, reflective, magenta. It was the color of Magda's workboat, and there was nothing that shade to be found in the natural world. Beached on a sandbar about a hundred and fifty yards off the coast of Seagreen Island, it rocked slightly with each passing wave. There were no passengers that she could see, although who knew what was lying out of sight on the bottom of the boat. Faye began to run before she let that thought crystallize.

Anthony Perez was renowned as a reporter with a knack for being in the right place when news broke. He never tried to figure out how he did it, because dissecting his gift of intuition felt rather like cutting open the goose that laid the golden egg, just to see what was inside.

His cameraman was working hard, knocking down the equipment and loading it onto a small boat that Senator Kirby had provided for the press. Anthony could have helped him, probably should have helped him, but he felt like taking a walk on this unspoiled island before somebody built a resort and spoiled it.

He paused under a tremendous oak tree to study how its dripping Spanish moss absorbed the sunlight. The stuff would be hell to photograph. The fact that he was standing still and alone and making absolutely no sound made the sudden frenzied crashing even more shocking.

It did not take a newsman of his celebrated intuition and undisputed good looks to infer that anything stimulating such activity might be newsworthy, so he followed his ears. A small, dark woman, dressed like one of the archaeologists, was running full-tilt for the water. His instincts were so good that he had already noted her singularly photogenic bone structure before he turned and ran for his cameraman.

Faye slogged through the swampy muck separating Seagreen Island from the Gulf, trying to come up with a happy ending that fit the facts. There, beached on a sand bar and surrounded by calm water dappled in more shades of aquamarine than even Monet knew, was the boat that should have been carrying Krista and Sam back from their pancake breakfast. If they were in it, then they were lying out of sight in the bottom of the boat.

Not liking that image, Faye tried another. Sam had fallen overboard, Krista jumped in after him, and the boat sped away out of control until it beached itself here. Two needles floating in a saltwater haystack—Faye liked that image even less.

The boat wasn't far away. She could swim that far. Hell, she could probably walk that far on the submerged sandbars peppering the waters around the Last Isles. Again, this did not bode well for Sam and Krista; they could have walked ashore as easily as she could walk to them. She let the gooey muck ringing the island suck the boots right off her feet and strode into the water.

Faye ran hard through the thigh-deep water until she hit a deep spot and plunged in over her head, driving saltwater into her sinuses. Aiming for the patch of water that was the greenest and therefore the deepest, she struck out swimming, using a flailing, slapping stroke in a futile attempt to minimize contact with the shallow bottom.

She swam until her knees scraped bloody on the sand, then she stood up and ran again. She had repeated this cycle three times before she reached the boat and dragged herself aboard. By this time, Anthony Perez and his cameraman had been standing in the muck for at least five minutes, filming every step of her race through the water and across the sand. They waited, ready to record her moment of discovery.

Faye disappointed them by finding the boat empty.

Chapter 4

Faye and Magda hunkered on the floor of the airless equipment shed, hiding from the media. Faye wiped the sweat off her neck and scanned the shelves. "You know there's a laptop computer and a couple of data loggers missing."

"Of course. I inventoried the shed as soon as you found Sam and Krista's boat. Either they stole the equipment, planning to sell it and run off with the money—"

"Not likely," Faye interjected. "They've been trusted with far more expensive equipment in the past."

Magda bristled. "They're good kids. They wouldn't steal."

"Well, you suggested it."

Magda spoke with her hands when she was nervous, a dangerous habit in such close quarters. "I didn't suggest it seriously. I was just getting to the point. Someone else took the equipment. Sam and Krista may have gotten in the way of a petty thief."

Faye gave a small nod. "So what's our plan?"

"The Marine Patrol has been called," Magda said. "If the kids are floating in the Gulf, they can surely find them better than we can."

"Their parents?"

Magda pressed her lips together and nodded. "And the sheriff."

"What'll he do?" Faye asked. "He'll search the island, but we can do that. We should be doing that now."

"It's a small island. If they were here—"

"They could be here, out of sight somewhere. The island is small, but it's overgrown. They could be hurt, right now, and we're not looking for them."

Galvanized, Magda said, "Yes. We can find them. What is archaeology if it isn't the science of finding hidden things? You and your crew can search the eastern half of the island. I'll take my crew west. Let's use the hill as a dividing line."

Faye nodded and took a first aid kit off the shelf.

Magda smeared a gob of sunscreen over her peeling and freckled nose—field archaeology is not an optimal career for a fair-skinned strawberry blonde—and the familiar activity seemed to help her reassume her familiar, cocky persona.

"A steak dinner says my team finds them," Magda asserted.

"Steak? At Wally's?" Faye asked.

"Better than Wally's. Lots better than Wally's."

Faye said, "Then you're on," and they plunged outside into a hungry pack of reporters.

The students in Faye's charge were calm, considering the circumstances, yet she felt that their composure would evaporate the second she displayed any emotion that wasn't ice-cool. They accepted her as a leader because Magda did. Faye was still amazed every time she found the skills to function in that capacity. Apparently she'd always had them, but Magda was the only person who'd ever noticed.

Faye divided her side of the island into three sectors and sent a pair of students to search each one. They fanned out from where she stood, atop the highest point. Her breathing controlled, Faye turned one step at a time until she had spun completely around.

Where were they? Faye was a finder, the winner of every childhood Easter egg hunt. For lack of a better idea, she decided to start in the area scheduled for excavation that morning. Neat rows of orange plastic surveyor's flags gridded over that piece of ground, evidence that Sam and Krista had been there. Faye walked among the flags like a slalom skier in slow motion, looking for a clue or at least a little inspiration.

Anthony Perez was enjoying his notoriety as the only journalist, on an island overpopulated by journalists, who had gotten footage of Faye's dramatic discovery of the missing students' boat. He was a small man, but his reputation grew larger all the time. Anthony stood again in the spot where he had seen Faye rushing away from her colleagues, drawn toward the water where her discovery waited for her. The woman had intuition. This was something he trusted.

He was not surprised to find her in the same spot, wandering around like someone who almost remembered where she had left her glasses. He would have been a fool not to hide and watch.

Crouching behind a live oak, he watched her move through the underbrush, stooping now and then to examine something on the ground. Footprints? Maybe.

When she squatted and started scraping at the pervasive mat of leaves and pine needles, he knew what she'd found, but still he waited to be sure. When she put her hand to her mouth and began digging with precise, rapid strokes, he got his confirmation. He hightailed it to fetch his cameraman, who was standing among all the other journalists waiting to find out where the missing kids were. Anthony Perez, ready to grab his second scoop of the day, knew exactly where they were.

Faye started at one end of the hastily covered grave, knowing she would find either faces or feet. It was a fifty-fifty shot and she was sort of hoping for feet.

Fate handed her a face, Sam's face, a broad, full-lipped face with a day's growth of beard. There was dirt caked around his eyes and mouth and she wanted to wipe it away, as if it would make him more comfortable, but she couldn't take the time. The grave was big enough for two.

She dug to Sam's right and was rewarded, if that's the proper word, with another face. Krista was barely recognizable, her freckles obscured by powdery white sand.

Faye screamed for someone to get Magda, then she kept screaming because it seemed the right thing to do. A rustle alerted her to the cameraman rushing up behind her and she threw her body over her dead friends, refusing to move aside so their fate could be recorded for the evening news.

She screamed for Magda, over and over, and the tough little archaeologist came running, yelling at the reporters, cursing them, whapping at them with a handy tree branch. Fearing for their equipment, Anthony Perez and his cameraman beat a swift retreat.

As they left, Faye unbuttoned her shirt, saying, "I'll be damned if those reporters will climb a tree and use a telephoto lens to get a picture of this."

Magda helped Faye spread her shirt over the spot where the students' faces peered up from the dirt, then, out of solidarity, laid her own shirt atop Faye's. The two of them stood vigil together, in their brassieres, until the sheriff came.

Chapter 5

The afternoon heat, the boat's side-to-side wallow, and the fact that she hadn't eaten since breakfast had combined to bring Faye to the point of seasickness. It had been an interminable day and it wasn't over.

Sheriff Mike McKenzie and his investigation team had worked efficiently through the morning, herding everyone on Seagreen Island onto a patch of sand near the dock before sending a search crew to fan out over the island. From her vantage point, she had watched technicians lifting fingerprints off the storage shed and searching Magda's crew boat.

Her nerves had stretched a little thin when they searched her skiff, not so much because she thought the killer might have concealed any evidence there, but because she had things of her own to hide. Would they wonder why she kept topographical maps of all the Last Isles stashed, along with her navigational charts, in coolers to keep them dry? Would they notice the shovels and trowels and sieves and brushes and dental picks stored aboard her skiff, and wonder why she didn't just use the tools the university provided? What if a tiny antique bottle or rouge pot that she'd dug out of the ground had rolled up behind the coolers and lodged there, waiting for the investigators to find it and wonder why she took her work home with her? It seemed that none of these questions struck the searchers. They poked through her skiff for a few short minutes, then moved on.

They had rifled through the audiovisual equipment on the TV reporters' boat with more care, then turned their attention to the sleek speedboat that had carried Senator Kirby and his entourage. Faye figured the searchers were focused on finding the missing laptop and data loggers, but they were empty-handed when they stepped onto the dock the last time.

About noon, she saw Sheriff McKenzie turn to the undersheriff and heard him say, "It'll take all day to do a complete search of this island, probably longer. We can't hold all these people that long, and it's ill-mannered to make them wait in this blasted heat. You take charge here. I'll take the witnesses back to the office and make them comfortable while they wait their turn to be interviewed. No way our boat can hold them all, so we'll use theirs."

Faye did as she was told, but it had felt wrong to leave Sam and Krista to the tender ministrations of the forensics investigators. It had felt wrong to allow herself to be herded onto the university's rented boat along with Magda and her coworkers and ferried back to land. The students accepted their enforced cruise easily, since they rode the same boat to and from work every day.

From its deck, Faye watched Seagreen Island and her skiff recede. Without her skiff, she had no way to get back to Joyeuse tonight, but she had ignored it. She didn't like to call the investigators' attention to the fact that she didn't ride to work with the others. They might then begin to wonder where she lived that made a mullet skiff more convenient for commuting than an oversized power boat.

Faye, Magda, the students, the sheriff, his chief investigator, and their staff overwhelmed the tiny convenience store and grill at Wally's Marina. The shabby little place was just the same, but the events of the day made its seediness surreal.

Faye had spent many hours at Wally's, but today the shiny colors of the potato chip bags hit her wrong. The greasy odor of the morning's bacon was off. The faces around her—Liz at the grill, the hobby fishermen poring over bait, the teenager eating a late lunch—were mostly familiar, but they were nonetheless strange. Somebody had shot two vigorous young people dead that very morning, and that somebody could be in this room. Or in any room.

Wild suppositions about why Sam and Krista were killed had begun fouling the air before their bodies were even found. Burglary had been dismissed as a motive within minutes. The killer didn't take enough stuff. Besides, a simple burglary gone wrong didn't set the imagination aflame. Most of the students leaned toward a botched drug deal. Many of them used drugs themselves and harbored a healthy fear of the people their habits forced them to deal with. And those who maintained a more chemical-free lifestyle were attracted to any theory that blamed the victims for their misfortune and fostered their illusion of safety.

Faye, who couldn't have afforded drugs even if she'd been attracted to them, had no illusion of safety. However Sam and Krista died, whoever did it, the fact remained that someone had committed murder. No matter the reason for the crime, no one was safe in the vicinity of someone who had once violated that taboo.

"The vans are here," the sheriff announced. "There's room for everybody. We'll bring you back here to your cars as soon as we've taken your statements."

As Faye allowed herself to be herded once again, she scanned the faces of the people she passed. They all looked so ordinary. If she had to guess which of them was capable of murder, it would be the black-eyed man in the corner. He was just standing there, waiting for the cashier to ring up a loaf of bread and a can of potted meat, but he stood out among Wally's rubber-necking patrons because he refused to rubber-neck. His casual stance was studied and he did not gawk at the grim-faced procession walking single-file and silent in the sheriff's wake. There was a stillness to his face that did not speak well of him.

Nguyen did not like the way the dark-skinned girl looked at him as she passed, as if she could hear what he was thinking and was appalled by it. He wished the cashier would quit ogling the sheriff's parade of witnesses and take his money. He needed to get back out to Water Island and dismantle his worksite before somebody stumbled onto it. Even though he was working miles away from Seagreen Island, the Marine Patrol and the Sheriff's Department would have cops crawling all over the Last Isles and he didn't want to abandon his equipment or his finds. If he got out there quickly, the search wouldn't yet have fanned out wide enough to catch him in its net.

He watched the cashier amble over to the redheaded hag working at the grill, probably planning to share a bit of gossip about the double murder. Nguyen had no time to watch a couple of rednecks jaw at each other. He walked out, leaving his potted meat and bread on the counter.

Stuart Sheffield was aware that his neighbors hated him. They hated his rusty singlewide. They hated the ramshackle roof-over that covered the trailer's leaking shingles and sheltered two porches, front and back, where he stored broken stuff that he didn't feel like hauling to the dump. They especially hated every scrap of trash that could be seen from the road (including Stuart himself, who sat drinking beer on the front porch with daily regularity), because they felt the condition of his home lowered their property values and made them look like rednecks by association. And they were right.

Nevertheless, Stuart liked his environment precisely the way it was. He lifted a beer can in tribute to every car that drove past his private paradise, listening all the while for the sound of real estate prices tumbling. He particularly enjoyed the fact that his choice of careers gave him plenty of idle time to annoy his neighbors, because a man in his line of work could afford to work very rarely indeed.

He would be working this week for a change and the anticipation vibrated in his chest, just as his cell phone had vibrated in his pocket not an hour before. It still tickled him to mate the tiny phone with his teeny palmtop computer, bringing the World Wide Web to his very own porch. E-mail was a beautifully anonymous way to deal with the kind of people who hired him and Stuart had just snagged himself a new client.

The job was practically in his backyard—he could drive there in a couple hours, easy—so tonight he'd be a guest of the Panacea Palace Motel, and his new client would be footing the bill. The household staff of the Panacea Palace would make his bed and cook his meals and swab out his toilet, while he focused all his attention on finding a tall, broad, ponytailed man with a tall, broad price on his head. The man and his companion—a slender, dark adolescent boy—had been seen digging in the Last Isles and, although his new client was stingy with information, Stuart inferred that the Last Isles weren't safe places to dig. With appropriate coercion, Mr. Ponytail would lead him to his young friend so that Stuart could conveniently kill them both and make enough money to forget about working. This job would pay him so much that he could look forward to simply sipping beer on his front porch every day for a year.

"I think Sheriff McKenzie was trying to get rid of us," Magda said, as she sat in her car in the parking lot at Wally's. She looked too tired to crank it.

"No. Not us," Faye said, leaning in the window to say good-bye. "He was trying to get rid of *you*. He's been trying to get rid of you all day."

"Well, I told him everything I knew about the kids and what happened to them. He was supposed to tell me everything he knew."

Faye rubbed at a stiff cord of muscle in her neck. "I don't think that's the way it works."

"The kids' parents aren't here yet. Somebody had to light a fire under the cops."

Faye grimaced, remembering how Magda had leaned over the crime scene tape all morning until they dragged her ashore, bellowing instructions to the investigators on proper handling of their forensics samples. "I bet those guys do a better job of tracking their chain-of-custody forms next time."

Magda shrugged and found the energy to crank the engine. "Where's your car?"

"My car's no help. I left my skiff at Seagreen Island when we came in on the sheriff's boat and I can't get back to the *Gopher* without it. I'm stuck ashore till morning. Maybe Wally will let me sleep on his boat."

Magda grunted. "Wally works his boat hard. It's dirty and it smells like fish guts. Want to grab a burger and bunk on my couch?"

"In Tallahassee?"

"No, genius. Even Dr. Raleigh, my department chairman, agrees a daily drive to and from Tallahassee would be a tough commute. The university keeps a few cottages and a trailer in metropolitan Panacea for researchers working at the marine lab there. The cottages were full, so I got the trailer."

"You say that as if it's a good thing."

"The trailer has a satellite dish."

Stuart circled through the parking lot at Wally's Marina, scoping out the territory. His new client had suggested that he begin his search for Mr. Ponytail and his young friend at Wally's. It was highly likely that the distinguished clientele would have information on every shady character in a thirty-mile radius. Oddly, the man had told him to scrupulously avoid Wally himself, describing him as both crooked and dull-witted. This was a combination that Stuart found useful in errand boys, but dangerous when the stakes were high.

It was nearly ten. Since fishermen like to have their bait in the water before dawn, perhaps to surprise sleepy fish, the marina parking lot was almost deserted. Left behind was a handful of cars belonging to people asleep on their boats or to the die-hard drinkers lingering at the bar and grill.

Stuart parked and went inside, ostensibly to take a piss but actually to see if anybody at the grill looked like a big Indian or a scrawny boy. Nobody did, and nobody would admit to ever seeing them, either, so he crawled back into his car and headed for the Panacea Palace. On his way out, he passed a parked car with a middle-aged, cranky-looking woman at the wheel. A younger woman, slightly built and dark, maybe foreign, leaned in the driver's window to speak to the driver. Stuart drove right past them.

Magda watched Faye use her last French fry to sop special sauce off the hamburger wrapper. Refilling their glasses out of a jug of cheap but decent wine, she blurted out a question that had bugged her for years.

"You were my best student. Why did you leave school?"

Faye looked thunderstruck. Magda saw that she had hit a nerve and, as usual, had done so with the delicacy of a butcher wielding a meat cleaver.

"What do you mean, I was your best student?"

This was not the nerve Magda thought she had struck.

"You were good in the lab. You came to class prepared and, judging from your essays, you read lots more material than I assigned. Speaking of your essays, they were grammatical—something that grows more unusual every day—and they were thoughtful. Occasionally, they were almost poetic. You loved the subject. My subject."

"But I struggled constantly to keep an A."

"Faye. Part of your grade came from class participation and you never made a peep. It made me mad. You had a lot to offer the class, but you kept it to yourself."

Faye wore the face of a snake digesting a mouse swallowed whole. "I'm glad to know I was a good student."

"So." The meat cleaver descended again. "Why did you leave school?"

"My mother was sick. My grandmother was sick. I took care of them until they died."

"I'm sorry, Faye. Don't you know they would have wanted you to finish your education?"

"Oh, yes. Yes. From the day I was born, Mama saved for my college. But it took me five years to pay all the medical bills. I think I'll always be behind on the bills I neglected so I could pay the hospital. School just isn't possible now. It may never be."

Magda respected the finality in Faye's voice enough to resist touting the possibility of grants and student loans. She said, "I understand, but I have always respected your drive to learn on your own."

Magda's office door opened directly across from the departmental library, giving her the poignant opportunity to watch Faye doggedly pursue the education she couldn't afford. She couldn't count the times she'd seen Faye in there, poring over the books. Not every day and not every week, but steadily, Faye was there, making better use of the school's resources than the students whose activity fees actually entitled them to the privilege.

After a time, Faye began requesting inter-library loans, apparently unaware that she didn't have official library access. Magda diverted the requests, approved them under her own account, and routed the books to Faye, who seemed oblivious to her machinations. One day, while cleaning her own bookshelves to make room for more stuff, Magda had a revelation. The armloads of journals she was casting aside were a few years old, but most of the material was still solid. She asked Faye if she would like to have them and was amused by how quickly the journals disappeared into the young woman's ancient Pontiac.

Years passed before Magda got her next opportunity to help Faye, but it came. The labor budget for the survey of Seagreen Island was generous. It would support fifteen field techs and she didn't have that many students. Faye had three years' credit toward an archaeology degree and her subsequent reading would have earned her a master's if she'd actually been a student. Faye was overqualified in some respects for the job Magda offered, but she accepted the temporary, no-benefits minimum-wage job in a heartbeat. Magda understood her passion to get in the field and do some real science. After all these years, she still felt it herself.

The cliché says that no good deed goes unpunished, but Faye proved it wrong. She was the best employee Magda ever hired. She had the life skills the younger students didn't, so she arrived on time, did what she promised, and gave some thought to her work. She was management material. Before the first week was done, Magda divided her staff into two groups, putting Faye in charge of the second team.

Magda managed her people by prowling constantly among them, silent unless she needed to chew somebody out for sloppiness or inefficiency. Almost immediately, Magda noticed Faye's comfort with the tools of the trade: shovel, trowel, brush, and sieve. Magda doubted skills like that could be gained from books, but she knew Faye's resumé was heavy on burger-flipping and retail sales, and absolutely bare of relevant experience. She began to wonder where Faye had been digging.

Soon after that, she began to wonder where Faye lived. She gave Wally's Marina as her mailing address, saying that she lived on her boat. Well, Magda had seen Faye's boats, both of them. One was a tiny mullet skiff that she used to get around in. Once, when the weather was too bad to trust her life to the skiff, Faye had arrived at work in a twenty-four-foot Trojan that she called the *Gopher*. Magda had seen it in a slip at Wally's a couple of times since, but she had no idea where Faye kept it ordinarily. While the *Gopher* was certainly bigger than the skiff, it was no more comfortable and much more mildewed. Magda refused to believe Faye's claim that she lived aboard the *Gopher*, but she had yet to catch her in an inconsistent statement that would reveal where she did live. Perhaps it was time to try again.

"So, you'll probably need to get home before you go to work tomorrow. Your car's at Wally's. Do you have much of a drive?" There. That was fairly subtle, for Magda.

"My skiff's at Seagreen Island, and I can't get to my real boat without it, so I'll have to hitch a ride with you. Can I borrow a tee-shirt and shorts and wash my work clothes here?"

Faye was smooth. She'd deflected Magda's question easily, without even saying where her "real" boat was, then ended the conversation by flicking on the TV, but she wasn't smooth enough to watch what the local news was broadcasting without flinching. Together, they watched Faye run, slog, and swim out to the empty boat, then they watched themselves stand half-dressed by a makeshift grave. The only good thing about this edition of the eleven o'clock news was the absence of Sam and Krista's dirt-encrusted faces. Faye and Magda had, through quick action, spared them that much of their dignity. When the newscast was over, Magda went to bed, saying nothing more to Faye but a simple, "Good night."

Chapter 6

Island dwellers sleep lightly. Some part of their conscious mind never switches completely off. Their dreams are littered with references to wind and water and wave. On the ordinary night, they rise out of sleep only enough to listen for an unexpected squall or the steady bumping of a boat whose moorings are no match for the weather. They toss around in bed. They disturb their sleeping partners.

But on the other nights, the not-ordinary nights, their hyperactive senses might register a drop in air pressure or a damp breath of wind through an open window or the electric smell of lightning. On those nights, islanders might owe the safety of their boats, their property, their very lives to their light sleeping habits.

Faye, who had lain awake on Magda's couch all night, customarily slept like an islander, but tonight she didn't sleep at all. This insomnia had nothing to do with an islander's alert senses and everything to do with her imagination. She was acutely aware that twenty-four hours before, one day before, Sam and Krista were still alive. As the night ticked away, she wondered, *What were they doing last night at midnight? At two?* Her imagination, being sly and malicious, let her dwell on impending death until she got used to it, then struck her with a sucker punch.

What were they doing last night at four? it asked. *And what would they be doing differently if they were aware that they would be dead by six?*

With that thought rankling in her psyche, she got up and fetched the morning newspaper off Magda's porch. The front page was blanketed with facts, near-facts, and rumors about the Seagreen Island murders. Her name and her picture leapt off the page. So she was to be denied the mindless daily escape of perusing the paper. She found a deck of cards in a kitchen drawer and played solitaire until the sound of riffling cards brought Magda from the room where she, too, wasn't sleeping. They played gin until it was time to go to work.

Faye and Magda walked into Wally's, where they found the rest of their crew sitting in the grill, each of them finishing up a plate of Liz's widely renowned eggs and grits. Faye was surprised to see Wally awake and sober. He was even working. He looked up from the SCUBA tank he was filling for an impatient-looking customer and sent a friendly half-wave in Faye's direction.

"I know that guy," Magda said under her breath.

"Wally?" Faye asked. "I know Wally. Everybody knows him."

"No," Magda said, "not Wally. His friend." She studied the patched linoleum floor, as if she hoped the impatient SCUBA diver wouldn't notice that she'd seen him.

"Who is he?" Faye said, trying not to stare. It was the grimly silent black-eyed man she'd seen brooding in the checkout line the day before. The day Sam and Krista died.

"I don't know his name, but I've seen him twice before, both times when I was working on a field survey way out in the sticks. It seemed odd to see the same guy hanging around the big towns of Vernon and Cross Creek. Especially since those two sites had something else in common."

"What?"

"Significant artifact losses. We never tracked down the culprit, but it was an inside job. One of my workers stole from both digs."

Faye frankly stared at the innocent-looking faces around them. "One of these kids—" she began.

"No, it happened years ago. But whoever the thief or thieves were, I'm sure they didn't have the connections to get rid of the loot. They needed a middleman, a fence. I've got no evidence, but we're looking at the only common denominator I ever came up with."

Faye gave the diver another corner-of-the-eye squint.

"Sam and Krista wouldn't steal," Faye said nonsensically.

"Maybe that's why they're dead," Magda said as she stepped into Wally's office without permission and flipped open her cell phone.

Magda was mightily tired of doing her civic duty. She'd kept her crew hanging around Wally's until an investigator arrived to talk to the suspect she'd turned up for him. Then she'd loaded her students onto the workboat and hauled them to Seagreen Island, all the while in touch with the Micco County Sheriff's Office by cell phone.

"His name is Nguyen Hanh and he's got an alibi," her new buddy, the sheriff's receptionist, told her. "He had breakfast yesterday at a diner way on the other side of Tallahassee. He's got witnesses, even a credit card receipt."

Magda, who was not easily convinced of anything, couldn't get her brain around the fact that they had let her suspect go. If the sheriff's people couldn't be persuaded to do her bidding, then why was she out here on Seagreen Island doing theirs? How could they possibly ask her to shut down her field survey?

She and her crew had spent the morning packing up the equipment that the undersheriff had deemed unnecessary to the investigation, trying not to think about what was going on behind the crime scene tape. At least the bodies were gone, taken ashore for autopsy. They were trying not to think about that, too.

Her workers, headed home to seek jobs at the mall or to do nothing, looked as gloomy as she felt. And Faye, who likely needed this menial, low-paying job more than any of them, still wore her usual serene expression, but her shoulders drooped.

Magda hurled a box of sample bags into the workboat. She had been packing up fragile, expensive equipment all morning and half the afternoon. Tomorrow—Friday, a perfectly good workday—would be wasted, and so would all the other perfectly good workdays between now and the beginning of the fall semester. Dr. Raleigh, who would be happy to see her production of journal articles dwindle to his own piddly rate, would make her time in the office insufferable. It felt good to use her pent-up anger to just throw something.

She would never get over Sam's and Krista's deaths. Alongside that enormity, her other concerns were, like Seagreen Island's remarkable population of mosquitoes, pesky but not catastrophic. Still, she hated shutting down her project so that the crime scene investigators could comb the island for clues. It had to be done, but what was she going to do with herself now, relegated to desk work in an antiquated building devoted to the study of a not-very-lucrative science?

Magda, while flinging another box of nonbreakable junk into the boat, caught a glimpse of something that surprised her ever-moving body into stillness. Striding toward the group of archaeologists was a huge, well-formed man who, in a single fluid motion, had navigated his johnboat close to the water's edge, cut the motor, hopped out, and hauled the boat onto the sand. Beneath his worn cutoffs, wet sand clung to muscled legs from his upper thighs down to his bare feet. Bulky arms hung easily at his sides and even his fingers looked muscular. His torso traced the triangle of the idealized male form and at the nape of his neck hung a long, black ponytail, carelessly tied.

Her entire work party was silent. The men assumed the head-cocked, puffed-chest stance of a flock of pigeons whose roost has been invaded. The women just stood like deer caught in the headlights of a Mack truck.

The man hesitated for a moment and let the sun glitter on the drops of water in his hair, then he said a single word. "Faye?"

Two students dropped what they were doing and rushed to find her. The rest of them continued to stare.

In the four months since Joe Wolf Mantooth had showed up at Joyeuse and, in a moment of weakness, Faye had let him stay, she had never seen him angry. She'd also never heard him string so many sentences together.

"You're always home by dark. I worried about you all night. Faye, you made me really mad. Why didn't you call me? Then I wouldn't have been so—"

Faye, growing ever more uncomfortable, said, "Joe. We don't have a phone. Besides—"

Logic was not Joe's strong point. He waved both hands, trying to quiet her because, even in this state, he was too polite to interrupt.

"I was worried about you after what happened to those students."

"How did you know about the students? We don't have a TV, either."

Joe continued talking with his hands. "I went to the *Gopher* and tried to raise you on the radio. You didn't answer, but I heard lots of people talking about a killer on the loose. Faye, I couldn't sleep all night."

Joe stirred the same tender spot in Faye that he always did. He was a simple man who would likely register borderline normal on an intelligence test, but he was the truest person she'd ever known. Joe could read a little and he could add a little. He was an expert boat pilot, but he couldn't drive a car. He could catch fish when they weren't biting, he could drop a deer with a homemade bow and arrow, and he could predict the weather simply by listening to birdsong and evening winds.

Had Joe been born two hundred years earlier, he would have been a man among men. In his own time, he was stymied by the intricacies of retrieving money from an ATM. Faye was glad that Joyeuse provided Joe a small piece of wilderness where he could thrive.

She took his hand, both to settle his mind and to lead him away for a private talk before he said more than he should about where they lived. They left behind them a crowd of young adults who would never ever have predicted that Faye—old, over thirty, and staid, in their eyes—went home every day to this half-crazed, fully-sexed hunk of man.

Sheriff McKenzie watched Joe's performance from his side of the yellow crime scene tape. This guy Joe had a temper. He was linked to the archaeologists and Seagreen Island, however tenuously, through Faye. And a crowd of witnesses had just heard him say that he had learned of the two students' deaths without benefit of telephone or television. Sheriff Mike wondered what he was doing the morning they were killed.

Deputy Claypool sprinted over the low hill separating the island into two distinct portions. Sheriff McKenzie could tell he had news that he wanted to deliver immediately, by shouting if necessary, and he was impetuous enough to do it. McKenzie took off running at a decent clip for a man sliding rapidly toward sixty, but nobody was quicker than Claypool's mouth.

"We found a campsite," the young man hollered. "Somebody was there all night, probably watching the kids. I bet the coroner says they died early yesterday morning."

McKenzie closed in on his loose-lipped underling, wrapped a big arm around the deputy's shoulders, and put his mouth directly on the young man's ear. "The coroner already did say so, you big-mouthed doofus."

Joe, Faye, Magda, and her students stood staring on their side of the crime scene tape. They were too shell-shocked to even pretend that they hadn't heard one of their public servants spilling sensitive information within earshot of the considerable crowd inhabiting Seagreen Island that day.

Faye was glad to be home on Joyeuse, glad to leave Seagreen Island and its grisly secrets behind. She had picked a likely spot to dig and she was turning over spadeful after spadeful of Joyeuse's dry, sandy soil. She found it amusing that her family had lived off the land, while she lived off the garbage they had buried under the land. *Come on*, she muttered to her dead ancestors, *you people were loaded. Why couldn't you just accidentally throw away a ruby ring so I could dig it up and pay my property taxes?*

Faye tended to talk to dead people when she was unemployed and she was indeed unemployed once more. The field survey on Seagreen Island was shut down while the murders were under investigation, so her itty-bitty paycheck wouldn't be coming for a while.

Faye was accustomed to having less income than outgo. Her net worth had drifted downward ever since she abandoned the mainland and human society, ever since she decided not to marry Isaiah. It wasn't that she didn't like people. She did. Her friendships were few, but sturdy. She would face down an alligator for Joe and Wally, and she believed they would do the same for her. Magda and Magda's archaeology kids were more than mere business associates; they were comfortable companions that she trusted.

And trust was the key word. Straddling the demilitarized zone of America's race wars, Faye had been walloped time and again by people who just couldn't get over their pigment phobia. Too much melanin. Too little melanin. Who really gave a damn?

On the day she had looked into Isaiah's eyes and saw that he, too, assessed the shade of her skin as part of her worthiness to be his bride, the seeds of her flight to Joyeuse were planted. It had taken time. First she'd had to sell her mother's house. Then she'd rolled a portion of that equity into a boat that she could live on, putting the rest of the money into CDs.

Actually, "subsist" was a more accurate verb than "live" for her life aboard the *Gopher*. It had the bare necessities—a head, a shower, a dinky and odorous refrigerator—and that was all. For two years, she'd camped on the *Gopher* while she patched Joyeuse's roof, ripped out rotting floorboards, replaced vandalized doors and windows. She spent nothing beyond her outlay on building materials, fuel, groceries, and taxes. Still, the CDs dwindled.

Pothunting had been a golden opportunity. Selling heirlooms from Joyeuse and from other islands her family had once owned had saved Joyeuse, pure and simple. She gave not a second thought to the fact that digging on islands that weren't precisely hers was legally unwise, particularly when some of them belonged to the federal government. The CDs continued to dwindle, but so far she'd staved off the end.

The sunlight faded, forcing her to quit digging for the day without uncovering the first salable find. The tree shadows reached for her like the specter of bankruptcy, but tonight there were other specters on the prowl.

Two days before, two young people alone on an island had met their end. And what were she and Joe? Two young—sort of young—people alone on an island. Was she a fool to stay? There was no way to know unless someone discovered why Sam and Krista were killed.

If the killer was motivated by theft, she felt fairly safe. She owned nothing worth stealing. The field survey had called attention to itself as a possible source of fenceable electronics in a way that Joyeuse did not.

Or maybe Magda was right. Maybe her black-eyed suspect Nguyen, or another antiquities poacher like him, had been rebuffed by Sam and Krista in his campaign to find someone who would sell him artifacts. This thought made her squeamish on several levels. She owned nothing that might attract an ordinary thief to Joyeuse, but an artifact poacher might find her home interesting enough to visit.

An uglier thought presented itself. If he had chosen to corrupt Faye, rather than Sam and Krista, she would have caved easily. No, she wouldn't have stolen from Magda's dig, but she would happily have sold him anything she dug up on her own. If he'd only approached her first, she'd have had a new customer and her more honorable friends would be alive.

Ugliest of all was the thought that there could be another pothunter in these waters, someone who didn't shrink from murder—someone who might not be pleased to learn that somebody else was harvesting these islands. Denial reared its self-protective head and said, *Don't be paranoid. There's a simpler answer and, when faced with a choice between a fancy answer and a simple answer, take the simple one. It's most likely to be true.*

The simplest answer was, in a word, drugs. Gossip among some of the field crew said that this wasn't the first time Sam and Krista had run afoul of a drug supplier. Other crew members denied it, saying that the two kids were straight arrows who wouldn't recognize a controlled substance if it jumped up and bit them.

Faye found both positions extreme. She knew Sam and Krista and she wouldn't have doubted that either of them were occasional pot smokers, but they were too serious about their studies, too gung-ho in their work ethic, to muddy their minds with any regularity. She couldn't see them being so deeply involved in the drug culture that someone would boat out to Seagreen Island, stalk them, and kill them.

But the thought was so seductive. Blame the victims. If they had attracted their killer to them, then now he was gone. She was safe. Joe was safe. At least they were safe until the tax collector took Joyeuse and left them both homeless.

The battery-powered lantern shed a more-than-acceptable reading light, and the fact that it was still shining at midnight was a fair measure of Faye's fascination with the journal in her hands. Faye wasted nothing: not batteries, not kerosene or gasoline or food. She had lived close to the economic edge for a long, long time. Sooner or later, she was bound to fall off but, when it happened, it would be through an act of God or through the malice of another human being. It would not be because she had failed to eke every bit of value out of everything she had.

Faye had yet to figure out who William Whitehall was. Finding his journal at Joyeuse suggested that he had some connection to her family, but she knew nothing about her ancestors prior to the Civil War, and two generations or more separated William from that period. Perhaps he was a friend of her ancestors or a business associate. She would not allow herself to assume that she was reading the words of her own flesh and blood until she knew it for certain.

She was scientist enough to ignore her romanticism—most of the time—but the act of reading a man's heartfelt thoughts recorded while Florida was still a pawn in the hands of the British, the Spanish, and the upstart Americans charmed both the scientist and the romantic in her.

◇

Excerpt from the diary of William Whitehall, 29 May, 1798

My Daughter Mariah has flourish'd these sixteen Years—her gracefull hands & expressive eyes would speak for her if she had not such skill at speaking for herself. God in Heaven forgive me, but she is the charming Woman that my Susan once was. Susan's step has grown heavy. She looks at me so seldom that it is clear she would prefer not to see my face at all.

Failure at love is not the same thing as failure at Marriage. We have a good, compleat life. Most days, the daylight outlasts the chores. This is a wellcome happenstance, for at day's end, we can rest while Susan stitches & I attend to Mariah's lessons.

How I chafed at my own lessons! Mariah drinks hers up. As the fifth son of an English gentleman of reduced circumstance, I saw my future in America; I found booklearning superfluous. Father insisted, so study I did and, as is commonly the case, on achieving his age I found him to be right. In the hard years, reading to Susan was our only pleasure between getting up & going to bed and now, in better times, I share my learning with my daughter. Susan never joins us, but when I tell Mariah a funny story in French, my Susan laughs.

My greatest concern at the present revolves around Mariah's future. She is in the peculiar position of being far better bred & educated than the few eligible young men in the area, yet they find her unsuitable because of her Creek blood. Susan has never once suggested that Mariah might marry a Creek man, but I see it in her eyes & there is contempt there, too. I cannot justify my preference for a White husband for Mariah. I wager there is no justification, but I desire it anyway. God has provided well for me in this life—I can only hope that He is as bountifull with my Daughter.

I have always believed in Divine Providence, because I was taught to believe in it. A fine man, educated & polish'd, knock'd at my door two weeks past, asking water for his horses & his servants. His name is Henri LaFourche & he says he is a Natural Scientist, who has come with a group of men to map the rivers & creeks in this Wilderness, while cataloguing the wilde beasts here. They seemed disappointed to see us, for I think they thought to find the land desolate of Humanity. Perhaps they forgot that the Indians live here & have done so for time out of mind.

I invited Henri LaFourche & his men to stay with us. I did not consult Susan before offering the invitation, but

I knew without looking at her that she wish'd I had not. I do not comprehend her attitude. Hospitality is the unwritten Law in these wilde lands, for one who refuses to shelter a Stranger might someday find himself without shelter. Providence tends to repay a man in the coin that he hands to others.

After each meal, Susan persists in enumerating every bite that Henri and his men have consumed. Their rate of consumption is indeed prodigious, but there are weightier matters afoot. Henri and Mariah leave each morning on long walks with the ostensible purpose of furthering Henri's knowledge of this Wilderness. He could have no better tutor than my Daughter.

No fool would believe that Nature is Henri's only interest. I too was once a young man, & I am not blind. Susan says his intentions are dishonourable, but her Prejudice against Henri is plain. "I have heard what he says to his men about her," she says, but she will not repeat what she has overheard. She only says, "He does not hide his words from me as he does from you. It does not occur to him that a Savage might speak French."

But Susan is wrong, and tonight she will know it. Henri Lafourche, a cultured & educated Gentleman, has asked for a private audience with me after the women are abed. Our Blessed Lord's Providence has provided Mariah with a Husband who is almost good enough for her.

Chapter 7

Faye moved around Wally's Marina as if she owned the place. She didn't, but her friend Wally did, and praise the Lord for that. He gave her a place to park her car when she was on Joyeuse and a place to tie her boat when she was ashore, and refused any payment other than her friendship—and the occasional jar of green tomato pickle made by her grandmother's recipe.

In gratitude, Faye had given him the use of an old tabby storehouse on her island, so he would have a place to keep the house goods salvaged from his divorce. It had been years, yet he'd never come back for them. Still, keeping Wally's stuff was the least she could do, considering what he did for her. Faye had a half-million other household projects to do before she renovated Wally's shed and she didn't need it to store surplus possessions. She didn't have any.

"Damn, Faye," Wally bellowed as he emerged from the men's room. "I didn't think you knew what pantyhose were, and here you are filling out a pair so nice. And lipstick does great things for those lips. Shit."

Faye blew him a kiss with the lips in question and said, "I didn't think you'd be awake yet. It isn't noon."

"An emergency rousted me out of bed. Beer's hell on the kidneys. Did you ride all the way over here in the skiff? Dressed like that?"

"Nope. I brought the *Gopher*. I gotta give it a shakedown cruise now and then."

He grabbed her hand. "No nail polish? I guess they don't make any that'll hold up while you're scratching around in the sand. At least you washed the dirt out from under your nails."

Faye gave a worried glance over her shoulder, but Wally squeezed her hand. "Forget about it, Faye. Ain't nobody in the room but us. You know I wouldn't tell your secrets."

Other than Joe, Wally was the only person who knew the particulars about where Faye lived and what she did for a living. He considered himself and his friends above the law—or beside the law or beneath the law, as the case might be. And that attitude appealed to Faye, whose relationship with the law was rocky at best.

Faye teetered toward the door in her unfamiliar dress pumps. "I gotta go, Wally, but how 'bout coming out to see me at Joyeuse sometime? You could visit your hide-a-bed. Say 'hi,' to your pots and pans. Relax. Go fishing. Dry out."

"You been messing in my stuff, Faye? I know you've got your eye on my electric skillet."

"Your electric skillet is safe with me. At least until I get electricity."

She waved good-bye to Wally and hustled off to her car without giving him his usual hug. The smell of Wally's breath didn't bother her one whit, but she didn't want to arrive in Tallahassee for a Friday morning meeting with a senator smelling of beer before the weekend even got underway.

She worried over Wally. Business was obviously slow. How else could he spare a boat slip reserved just for her? The grill did a decent business, but there was only so much money to be made on coffee, eggs, and grits. Maybe it was a good thing that Wally had few needs other than beer and a place to sleep, and maybe it wasn't.

Faye crawled into her car, pumped the pedal, held it down, and turned the key. Praise God, all eight cylinders were still capable of internal combustion. The air conditioner might have blown its last breath sometime during the punk rock era, but Faye's mother had known how to maintain an engine and she had passed her skills on to her daughter. The ugly rattletrap always cranked.

Faye's old Bonneville could have found its way to Tallahassee with no driver behind its wheel. Its parsimonious owner wished it could find its way to Tallahassee with nothing in its gas-guzzling tank, but she continued to feed it. Now, if the beast could be cajoled into an approximation of the speed limit, she would arrive in time to make a detour to the university library. Given an hour in the newspaper archives, she laid odds that she could identify the mystery woman buried alone in the Last Isles.

The fact that its archives were not available on diskette or on the Web was a fair indication of the size and circulation of the *Micco Times*. Searching its archives was a matter of sliding one piece of plastic after another into a microfiche reader. Still, when one is single-minded, an amazing volume of drudgery can be accomplished in an hour.

It only took Faye half that time to find the name she sought. That was one of the benefits of fishing in the small pond of a weekly, as the *Times* was in those days. She could place the age of the body within six or eight years, given the style of the earring. An unsolved murder in small-town Florida would have been big news, plastered on the front page over a period of weeks. And the value of the earring suggested that this was no unlucky prostitute who would go unmissed and unmourned.

Every front page printed in the Florida Panhandle during the summer of 1964 had devoted space to the search for Abigail Williford. In the half-hour left to her, Faye printed out every article she could. The microfiche printer was so slow that she had time to skim each article as it printed. Column inch after column inch was devoted to informing readers exactly who the missing girl was, though it was apparent to Faye that most of the newspaper's readership already knew more about her than the reporters themselves.

Abigail Williford was the eighteen-year-old daughter of the richest man in Micco County. He had inherited tracts of middling farmland so large that income from his sharecroppers and tenant farmers would have kept him comfortable for life, but he was not a man to be idly rich. He had built a thriving construction business and, by the time of his daughter's disappearance, he was a widower employing a goodly percentage of the farmers and day laborers in the area.

Each article was adorned with the same close-up photograph of Abigail. Clearly a senior portrait intended for the school yearbook, it showed a smiling dark-haired girl glancing at the camera over a shoulder draped in chiffon. Every newspaper printed the same photo, week after week, all summer.

Faye imagined the grieving father sitting alone in his home with the life-sized original portrait on the wall until the day he ripped it down, shattered the glass that covered it, and splintered the wood frame rather than look at his missing daughter's face any longer. Faye wished for a single glance at that original photograph, cursing the enthusiastic journalist who had cropped and enlarged the photo until Abby's face filled nearly the entire rectangle.

She understood his motives—*make the face prominent and find the girl while she's still wearing that untouched young smile*—but the search for the missing girl had been a failure. No one ever saw Abby again, not until Faye had dug her up. Even now, she couldn't be sure. The overzealous photographer had trimmed away the girl's earlobes.

The missing person's report stated that Abby was believed to be wearing her customary jewelry, pearl earrings and a silver necklace, but it gave no further description. Where was the silver necklace? She figured it was wherever the other earring was. And a simple mention of pearl earrings wasn't enough proof for Faye's tough brand of logic. Every girl of means had owned a pair of simple pearl earrings in those days. The jewel she had found was much more than that.

She kept feeding microfiche into the rheumatic printer, hoping that she'd missed something, that one of the articles she took home would mention the platinum and diamond settings from which Abby's pearls had dropped.

Right on time for her appointment, Faye wove through a warren of legislative offices. She brushed elbows with crowds of intense folks in expensive suits (lobbyists), busy folks who clearly had neither the money nor the time to dress that well (legislators' staff), and the jovial few who missed no opportunity to bellow "Hey! How you doin'?" to total strangers who might be voters (the legislators themselves). She stopped at an office marked by a sign proclaiming that its occupant's district was the zucchini capital of the world and asked for Cyril Kirby.

A big-haired blonde secretary pointed. "He's right next door, honey."

Entering Cyril's suite was like being transported seven hundred miles north into the very shadow of the Washington monument. The atmosphere was quiet, cool, and not particularly welcoming. Behind the receptionist, Faye could see two other women filing and making calls. She had no idea where these women got their clothes, because no store between Atlanta and New Orleans sold anything so chic.

She was ushered into Cyril's office, but he wasn't there and she was left to study a very dignified vanity wall. No honorary trade school degrees. No folksy shots with visiting elementary students. Not a single picture of a Floridian, not even the governor, graced these walls. Instead, there was shot after shot of Cyril with congressmen, senators, ambassadors, cabinet secretaries. Every molecule in the room said that this man wanted to go to Washington and that he was likely to get there.

Cyril entered and Faye found that meeting him indoors was a different experience from seeing him on Seagreen Island.

Nothing looms large out-of-doors, not compared to the sea and the sky. In Cyril's office, his physical presence pressed against the walls.

The senator was older than Faye, but he moved like a man who didn't realize that middle age was draping her cloak around his shoulders. Since he had forgotten his age, most people in his presence forgot it, too. His face was scored with rugged lines that photographed well, but it was equally appealing in the flesh. He was favored with a craggy profile and the real-person smile of a man who grew up before widespread orthodontia, but whose white, mostly straight teeth never needed fixing anyway.

He shook her hand with a knuckle-cracking grip and looked her in the eye. Faye—who trusted more or less nobody, particularly not politicians—heard him say, "What can I do for you?" as he had certainly said so many times to so many voters, yet she believed he wanted to help her.

"Thank you for taking the time to see me," Faye began. She didn't want to try his patience and she'd never been one to beat around the bush anyway, so she plunged directly to the point. "I've heard what you have to say about stopping the resort on Seagreen Island. I think I can help," she began. An innate need for accuracy nagged her and she clarified herself. "I think we can help each other."

"Please, sit down," he said, and she turned toward the visitor's chair situated the precisely correct distance from the senator's desk. "No, no, no," he said, gesturing toward the leather couch beside the window. "You have the face of someone with a more interesting tale than usual. Take a comfortable seat and take your time."

The informal gesture was so much more effective in dignified surroundings than it would have been in the folksy office of Senator Zucchini. Faye took a seat and started talking before she lost her nerve.

"Seagreen Island is mine," she said. "Well, it should be. My great-great-grandfather purchased Last Isle in the 1850s, back when it was all one island. Shortly after he bought it, the great hurricane of 1856 carried away most of the island, along with a few hundred planters and their families and slaves. There was a resort there at the time."

"I've heard the story."

The adrenaline was getting to Faye. She uncrossed her legs so he wouldn't see her dangling foot tremble. "Most people haven't," she said. "If a bunch of rich Astors and Vanderbilts and Roosevelts had been swept off Cape Cod, it would be in the history books."

"There was a war coming on in 1856, and the victors do write the history books." His eyes were hazel and their sharp glance gave Faye the impression that he was cataloging every detail of her face, down to the last pore and final eyelash.

"Yeah, but if somebody had bothered to write about what happened on Last Isle," she rattled on, "my great-grandmother might never have lost her land."

"So tell me what happened on Last Isle."

He was interested in her story. A second adrenaline rush threatened to give her the shakes.

"My great-great-grandfather owned Last Isle and he was an investor in the Turkey Foot Hotel—"

"Quaint name," Cyril interrupted. "I never knew the name of the hotel itself. I've always heard it referred to as the 'Last Isle Disaster.'"

"Well, that's what Grandma called it. It doesn't sound like the name of a luxury hotel, but tastes change. I've heard of places with names like Tater Island, Hot Coffee, Bowlegs Point, Cow Ford, even Hogtown. Anyway, Grandma said that when my great-great-grandfather died, the property passed to his daughter, my great-grandmother."

Then came the big question. "Do you have the deed?"

The deed. Such a pesky detail. "No deed has ever surfaced. And no, I don't have a birth certificate for his heir, my great-grandmother, Courtney Stanton Wells. I don't think she ever had one, since she was born during the War and her parents were never married. Oh, I forgot to mention that part." Faye studied the brown backs of her hands. "Courtney's mother was a slave. My great-great-grandfather owned my great-great-grandmother. If I dwelled on that too much, I'd spend the rest of my life on an analyst's couch."

"Well," Cyril said. "That answers some questions I've been too delicate to ask. The years during and after Reconstruction would have been tough for a biracial woman. Are you sure your great-grandmother ever held a legal title?"

"For years, no one questioned the validity of her claim to the remnants of Last Isle, probably because nobody else wanted them. I've found records showing that she paid taxes up until 1933, when some white men decided they wanted her land and a kangaroo court let them take it away."

"I don't suppose you even have a survey of the land your ancestors owned."

Faye restrained herself from calling him stupid. "No. Besides, it would be worthless. You've been out there. Every twenty years, a hurricane washes away some of what's left of Last Isle and resurfaces the rest. That's how they took her land. The adjacent landowners each laid claim to a few pieces of Last Isle and the jury wouldn't accept the word of a woman whose mother was a slave. She knew which land was hers; everybody in the courtroom knew it. She just couldn't prove it."

"This dispute is older than I am. Why are you coming to me now?"

Faye marshaled her wits. This man could help her. She just had to explain to him, in a way that made sense, why it was in his best interests to do so.

"Don't you see? Some of my land has been absorbed into the wildlife refuge. Let them keep it. It's not fair, but at least they're preserving it. Help me get Seagreen Island back. You—and your constituents—oppose the resort being built there. Get me my land back, and no tacky tourists will ever tear up the place. Your voters will be happy, and God knows that will make you happy."

"You make an interesting point, Ms. Longchamp." The hazel eyes were still sharp, but there was a glimmer of something else. "I will take your request under consideration."

Faye was glad to be alone in the elevator. Her guts roiled over the risk she'd just taken. She'd managed to keep Joyeuse out of her conversation with the senator, but anybody probing in court documents and tax records was going to find that her great-grandmother Courtney hadn't lost everything. The judge had ruled in her favor regarding ownership of Joyeuse because she could show more than a century of continuous occupation. Faye wasn't eager for Cyril or anybody else to ask any questions about Joyeuse, not until she could afford to answer them.

The elevator doors were opening, so Faye stopped leaning against the cool metal walls and pulled herself into a respectable upright position. Heaven only knew how she planned to pay the taxes on Seagreen Island, even if she did get it back. She couldn't even take care of Joyeuse. Nevertheless, she was going to regain what was rightfully hers before the resort developers ruined it. She owed that much to her mother and her grandmother and all her ancestors right back to Cally Stanton, the slave girl who had managed to hand such a legacy down.

Joe Wolf Mantooth was knapping flint, making a tiny bird point. He didn't plan to shoot any birds with it, but he enjoyed the repetitive work and the feel of the rock in his hand, smooth and sharp. The growing pile of stone flakes between his feet gave him a feeling of accomplishment. Truth be told, he would have enjoyed flintknapping even if he never got a useful tool out of the activity, simply because the cracking sound of rock striking rock was so completely satisfying.

Once, long before, Joe had listened as a friend tried to explain the concept of meditation, how it settled the soul and soothed the mind, how it even lowered the blood pressure. Joe had listened until he got tired of feeling stupid, then he'd gone home and flaked a chunk of flint while he studied on his friend's words.

Joe spent time chipping stone most days and sometimes he mused on things he didn't understand, like what "blood pressure" meant and how computers worked and why women wore silly shoes. He turned his questions over and over until they clicked together like hard cool rocks and made sense. Sometimes he knapped stone without thinking at all, but when he set down his tools he felt like something somewhere in the world made more sense than it had when he had sat down to work.

The sound of a boat motor startled him from his rhythmic chipping. Joe rose to greet Faye, as he always did. It would no more occur to him to stay with his work and ignore Faye's homecoming than it would occur to a child to stay with his crayons rather than greet his mother at the door with a sloppy kiss.

By the time he realized that this was not the sound of Faye's boat, the boat's sole occupant had seen him.

Joe raised a hand in greeting.

Wally cut his engine, looked Joe up and down, and blurted, "Who are you and what are you doing here?"

Joe, who always took the route to the truth that yielded the greatest economy in words, said, "I'm Joe. I live here." He didn't have to add, "What are you doing here?" The words were implied.

Wally sputtered something about checking on his stored furniture, but never disembarked. Instead, he cranked his boat and navigated it back toward open water at a rate of speed far too great for the shallow inlet Faye used to harbor her boats. Joe watched him tear away. Another man might have concluded that Wally was upset, even jealous, to find a man living with Faye, but such things were beyond Joe. He simply filed the encounter under "unexplainable." Joe found almost everything in the modern world to be unexplainable.

Chapter 8

Faye walked through the front entrance of the Museum of American Slavery like any sightseer looking to idle away her lunch hour. With a delicious sense of skullduggery, she browsed through the exhibits as if she'd never seen them. When she was certain that no one was looking, she slid through the door marked "Director" and took a seat at one end of a long conference table.

Douglass Everett took the seat across from her with a cordial, "It's good to see you again, Faye. I'm sorry we didn't get a chance to speak at Senator Kirby's Seagreen Island press conference. That was a terrible day. Are you all right?"

Faye nodded her head silently, unwilling to talk about something so painful when she was on such an important mission. She opened the large tote bag clutched in her lap and emptied it, one item at a time, carefully unwrapping each piece from its protective packing.

"Douglass, you're going to like what I've brought you today. Look, I've got a lace bobbin. Two thimbles: one china, one brass. Twelve buttons: eight made of hand-hewn wood, three that are plain and white, and one made of multifaceted jet. Three pipestems, two pipe bowls. Five handwrought nails: three rose-head and two T-head. A silver dinner fork. An iron pocketknife. Ivory ribs of a lady's fan. A horseshoe fragment. A chisel. A tiny porcelain horse. Two whetstones.

A battling stick for beating laundry clean. A pothook for hanging food to cook over an open fire."

She sat back and waited for the long, amiable haggling session that was an inevitable part of doing business with Douglass.

He fingered the corroded pocketknife. "Jesus, Faye. Where do you get all this stuff?"

"You ask me that every time, and every time I tell you the same thing. It's all mine. Do you want any of it?"

"You bet. If it weren't for you and your artifacts, wherever you find them, I wouldn't have much of a museum." He lifted each piece, gingerly separating her hard-won goods into piles of things he wanted and things he didn't. The pothook, the brass thimble, the battling stick, the whetstone, the chisel, the nails, and the wooden buttons went into the "sold" pile so quickly that she knew they would bring a good price.

The china thimble, the porcelain horse, the remains of the ivory fan, the silver fork, and the jet button went just as quickly into the pile of rejected goods.

"I found every one of those things in the ruins of old slave quarters. Maybe they were gifts, maybe they were stolen, but they were there." Faye pushed them toward his pile of acceptable goods.

"I can't display luxury goods in a museum of slavery unless I can prove a link to slavery. Can I reference your testimony about where you found these items?"

"Of course not."

He pushed the luxury items back toward her. "Then I can't use them. Where do you get this stuff, Faye?"

"I keep telling you. It's mine, every bit of it. I just prefer to remain anonymous."

"Fine. Then keep your fancy goods that you can't prove a slave ever touched—"

"Sure, they touched them. Somebody had to sew on the button. Somebody had to polish the silver and dust the little horse and clean the rouge off m'lady's fan."

"Sorry, Faye. By that logic, I'd have to buy everything you bring me."

Faye smirked. "And would there be anything wrong with that?" Her expression changed quickly when she saw him shove the lace bobbin into the pile of rejected goods. "No, you have to take that!"

Douglass' smile said that he had heard a sales pitch before.

"Really, Douglass," Faye said, "that's the most significant thing on the table. Slaves with lacemaking skills were rare and highly valued. It would have been quite unusual here on the frontier to invest in training someone in an art that was time consuming, yet put no food on the table."

Douglass raked the bobbin back into the pile of goods he wanted. "That's why I like doing business with you, Faye. My other suppliers are just pothunters. They dig up the stuff and bring me what they find. And it's all in execrable condition. Working with you is like having my own private archaeologist."

Having decided what he wanted, he turned each piece delicately in his hands, held it up to the light, ran his fingers over it looking for damage or clumsy repair. Douglass was a top-flight businessman. Beneath his poker face, Faye knew he was assessing the worth of each piece—not its worth on the open market and not the price an average antique dealer might put on it. Douglass would pay only what he felt the piece was worth to *him* and if that price were more or less than someone else might pay, it was a matter of no importance to him.

But it was a matter of significant importance to Faye. Her taxes were coming due, her boats wouldn't quit drinking fuel, her job was on indefinite hiatus, and she had a frenzied need for money. She had brought Douglass everything she had that might remotely interest him. Now came the true test of her sales skills. She had to sell him something truly expensive for which he had absolutely no use.

While her best customer fingered the merchandise, Faye reached back into her tote bag and drew out the most gorgeous things she had ever dug out of the ground, two matching tortoiseshell combs filigreed with finely carved scrolls and arabesques. They had been slightly etched by the sand that covered them for so long, but other than that, their graceful curves were unchanged since the day they had adorned the upswept hair of a great lady.

Douglass caught his breath when he saw them—the man had taste—but he started shaking his head before she laid them on the table before him.

"I've thought it through," she began, with her most persuasive smile. "You need a small display acknowledging the plight of the plantation mistress."

"What plight? She was waited on hand and foot."

"That's the stereotype, but time and again, documentary evidence shows that she worked from dark till dark, dispensing food and supplies to all the slave families, providing medical care, supervising food preservation. One woman wrote of using her spare moments to knit socks for everyone on the plantation—hundreds of people."

He was shaking his head.

"Listen to me, Douglass. Women, even white women, couldn't take a walk without a chaperone. They couldn't own property or vote or leave the plantation without an escort. They were half-slaves themselves. Document after document shows that many of them opposed slavery, but they had no voice, so they just fed and clothed and doctored their husbands' human possessions. Any drop of human kindness our ancestors received most likely came from them. They deserve a place in your museum, Douglass."

He kept shaking his head. "You make a good case, but it's too complex an issue to tackle during the forty-five minutes people spend with my exhibits."

"I can't sell them to any of my other customers. I won't. They'll turn around and sell them to some fat rich woman who'll wear them to cheesy costume balls. Buy them for your wife."

"She couldn't wear them. Her hair's shorter than yours. Keep them, Faye. Put them in a glass case and enjoy owning something beautiful."

Faye hated herself for pushing him so hard. Now she was going to have to close this deal through tears of frustration. She carefully replaced the combs in their box and laid them in the bottom of her tote bag.

She was reaching for the pile of goods that Douglass had rejected, but he caught her hands between his two huge ones.

"You really need the money or you wouldn't be selling those combs."

She raised her eyes, humiliated by the tears in them.

He gathered up everything on the table, the things he'd said he wanted and the things he'd said he didn't. "Keep the combs. I'll take all the rest. And I'll pay your asking price for every damn piece."

Douglass watched Faye drive away in her twenty-five-year-old car and he hurt for her. She had been too—too what?—too upset or embarrassed or desperate for money to stay for their usual post-negotiation chat, and he was sorry. He enjoyed Faye's company. After they concluded their business, he always poured her a glass of sherry—good sherry because he knew she couldn't afford nice things—but always in a tiny glass. She had to drive home, wherever home was, and he wanted her to be safe.

He looked forward to sitting with Faye, sipping sherry and enjoying a free-ranging conversation. She was remarkably well-read and so was he, considering that they didn't possess a college degree between the two of them, and she could be depended upon to view front-page events from a cockeyed angle that made him consider his own opinions all over again.

Faye had her secrets and he understood that, because he had his. She filled part of the hole in his heart that should have been filled by his own children. He wished her a safe drive home. He hoped her home was a safe place, too.

"Think," Faye said out loud to herself. "Where will the money come from?" The wind whipping through her open car window swept her words into the hot August air.

There was a simple answer: sell Joyeuse. Her island would make a better site for a resort than Seagreen Island. It was closer to land. It rose further out of the water. It had no beach to speak of, but that could be remedied with a judicious application of dredged sand. It was as safe from hurricanes as an island could be. Her home might be swept away by the next big storm—it was always possible—but the fact that it had stood for nigh onto two hundred years was undeniable.

If she sold Joyeuse, she could end the constant economic drain of property taxes. She could satisfy the bill collectors who had lost track of her when she sold her mother's house and fled to Joyeuse. She could have an apartment with electricity and air conditioning. She could go back to college.

But she would be alone in a world that showed its coldest face to a young woman who refused to call herself black or white, who refused to be anything other than who she was. American society had made great strides in tolerance during Faye's short life, but it would be a long time before she felt truly at home anywhere but at Joyeuse. If she sold it, she would have no place left to hide.

Okay, she wouldn't sell Joyeuse. Where else would she get money? What could she sell? She had no more artifacts of any value, except for a few broken pieces of jewelry. Her personal possessions were still more worthless. In subtropical Florida, an old Pontiac without air conditioning probably had a negative blue book value. Besides, she needed her car to deliver artifacts to her paying clients.

Her boats? The *Gopher* wasn't expendable. It was her cover story, the "permanent address" that staved off all the questions about where she lived. Besides, the skiff was only safe in calm waters. Jettisoning the *Gopher* would leave her trapped on Joyeuse if an unexpected storm blew up. She could raise a piddling amount of money by selling the skiff, but it would cost her in the long run. She used it to get around whenever she could because the *Gopher* simply slurped up fuel. The hike in her fuel bill would eat up any profit on the skiff within months.

What if she got another job, now that her work with Magda was on indefinite hold? Getting another job would be stupid. The jobs she could land with her puny high school diploma paid nothing and they would keep her from her artifacts business, which actually paid quite a lot when things were going well. Taking the job with Magda had been a stupid financial decision, but she had craved a chance to do legitimate archaeology. Too bad the illegitimate stuff paid so much better.

Pothunting was the only answer. It was like playing the lottery. Dig enough holes and you're bound to find something. Find enough stuff and you're bound to stumble onto something that makes you rich and saves your home and makes your mother, who is surely busy caring for all God's children in Heaven, proud of her earthbound daughter.

Sheriff Mike didn't mind spending his Friday afternoon waiting at Wally's Marina for Faye Longchamp. It wasn't like he had an appointment to talk to her. Patience was a virtue for a lawman hoping to "accidentally" bump into an important witness.

No, he didn't mind waiting for Faye, but he felt that he could easily grow tired of Wally's company. How convenient that Wally was one of those people who quickly found reasons to leave any room occupied by a law enforcement officer. The sheriff was left with Liz, Wally's hardworking short-order cook, a woman who could smile with her sweet eyes even when she was too busy to waste time smiling with her mouth.

Unfortunately, she was too busy to waste time talking about Faye Longchamp. After gesturing out the window and identifying a singularly dilapidated vessel as Faye's boat, she had returned to slinging grits for hungry mariners.

Finding Faye's boat, the *Gopher*, so easily came as no surprise. She claimed to live on it, giving Wally's Marina as her permanent mailing address. Assuming this cock-and-bull story was indeed true, then Ms. Longchamp should show up sooner or later.

The Coke he was sipping had done a great deal to settle his stomach. Sheriff Mike detested autopsy reports. Just reading them made him woozy. His fertile imagination easily conjured up the scenes described in the reports: scalpels slicing, forceps lifting cut flesh and moving it aside, out of the way. He could even smell the preservatives and the decay lurking beneath their cloying stench.

Years ago, he'd had a good long conversation with the Blessed Virgin. He'd asked her to put a stop to murders in his jurisdiction, mostly because murders are in general bad things, but also because no murders meant no autopsies and no autopsy reports. The Blessed Virgin had declined to answer his prayer. Perhaps coastal Florida was outside her jurisdiction.

For the second time since he had sat down, he updated his palmtop and checked his list of things-to-do. *Find a killer* was at the top of his list, and it would stay first until he'd done it. He'd spoken with Faye at length on the day of the murders, but that was before he'd laid eyes on her interesting roommate, so he added Joe's name to his suspect list and put Faye's name back on his list of witnesses to interview. Above Faye's friend Joe, the name "Douglass Everett" festered. The man's very name still made his blood boil.

Sheriff Mike was only on his third Coca-Cola when Faye walked in, dressed to the nines and looking nothing like a woman who depended on a shower fed from a tiny boat-mounted tank of stale water. He patted one of the bar stools beside him. Both were empty; Wally's patrons were also wary of venturing too close to the law. "Let's talk," he said.

She looked confused by his request, but she showed no signs of the run-when-you-see-a-cop-coming syndrome that afflicted Wally and his customers. Good. He rather liked Ms. Longchamp.

"You look nice," he said as a brief and inadequate warmup before he got to the point. "Tell me about this guy I saw you with—the one who put on such a performance over on Seagreen Island yesterday."

"Joe Wolf?"

"That's his full name?"

"No, his full name's Joe Wolf Mantooth. What do you mean by saying Joe 'put on a performance' yesterday? He was worried about me. What's wrong with that?"

"Maybe nothing. Maybe I just want to talk to him in case he knows something that could help the investigation. Tell me where he lives."

Her silence caught him off guard. He repeated the question. "So where does Mr. Mantooth live?"

She was slow in responding, although she did eventually respond. It didn't take a law enforcement officer of his experience to see that the witness was suddenly resistant. He wasn't surprised when she changed the subject, although the direction she took the conversation caught him with his pants down.

"You're about the age...." She pursed her lips a second, then asked, "Did you know Abigail Williford?"

Something in the innocence of Faye's question and the soft brown of her eyes conjured up Abby's face, and he felt a prickle of tears that he had thought were thirty years gone. He managed a quick, "Why do you ask?" and was surprised to hear his voice sound so casual.

"It's just that I'd never heard of her until just recently. It's hard to believe that I grew up thirty or forty miles away in Tallahassee and I've spent years down here, yet I've never once heard her name mentioned. I mean, she disappeared five years before I was born, but still you'd think I would have heard *something*. Anyway, I heard you were from around here and I'm guessing you're about her age. Maybe you were already doing law enforcement by that time."

"My deputy's badge still had its brand-new shine when Abby disappeared. There weren't thirty-five people in our graduating class. Of course I knew her." Seeking to regain control of the conversation, he gestured out the window. "By the way, no matter what you gave me as a permanent address, no way do I believe that either you or Mr. Mantooth live on that leaky bucket. A man his size would go stir-crazy on that boat. And you—you look like the type that likes to bathe more than once a week. So where does Joe Wolf Mantooth live?"

"He lives with me."

"On the boat?"

"On the boat."

"Is he on the boat now?"

"No. He's probably out on his johnboat, fishing."

Ms. Longchamp needed to shake her quiet wise-ass attitude, so he delivered the big question, the hard one, the one designed to make her think. "Where was Joe Wolf Mantooth on Tuesday morning, day before yesterday?"

He was unprepared for her expression of total shock. If she hadn't suspected where he was going with his questions, then what had caused her to turn into a wise ass when he started asking where she and Joe lived?

"You think Joe killed Sam and Krista? You're crazy. He'd never hurt anybody. The world should take care of people like Joe, innocent to the bone, instead of persecuting them. Leave him alone."

"Do you know a lot about him? Where he came from? Who his people are?"

"No. What's your point?"

Good. He had successfully pushed a well-bred, soft-spoken woman to the edge of rudeness. The truth would emerge any moment. "What's he hiding?"

"Nothing. Maybe he's just not a big talker." The words were clipped and her lips hardly moved. Angry people don't keep secrets well.

"So he hasn't told you where he was on Tuesday morning?"

Again, just when he thought he had pressed her closer to giving him a viable suspect, she graced him with an unexpected response.

"Why are you harassing me? I found Sam and Krista for you. If I hadn't been there, they'd still be lying under the dirt. After all these years, you haven't even found Abby Williford. Why don't you do your job and leave Joe and me alone?"

He had pushed her past rudeness, straight to cruelty. Surely she could tell that Abby's disappearance was an unhealed wound. With great discipline, he let the anger go and focused on his witness.

Sheriff McKenzie believed in the broken record technique of questioning. Keep asking the same question and, sooner or later, you'll hear something interesting. So he asked the question that bothered Faye so much, one more time.

"Where was Joe on Tuesday morning?"

"He was with me. On my boat. Fishing."

Troubles come in batches. Faye knew that. She'd lived this truth all her life. So she was absolutely not surprised when Wally took her aside after the sheriff left.

"A woman from the tax assessor's office was here asking questions. It seems there are rumors flying around about some scummy tax-evader living in a sumptuous mansion and defrauding the government of its rightful property taxes."

Faye felt her lips go pale. If she had to pay property taxes based on a livable house of more than twelve-thousand square feet, then she would be sleeping in her boat. No, the tax man would take that, too. She'd be sleeping on the street. No, not even there. If the Park Service got wind that she'd been excavating on public lands, they would see to it that she slept in jail.

"Wally, if they find out I'm living in Joyeuse, I'll lose everything. There's no way I could pay my taxes if they added the value of that house to my assessment."

"I know. So I told her I'd happily rent her a boat, so she could investigate the fraudulent piece of scum living out there, but she'd have to wait until tomorrow afternoon. I simply didn't have a boat of any size available at the moment. I bought you twenty-four hours, Faye."

Wally watched Faye hustle out to her boat. She moved damn fast for a woman in high heels. He hadn't a worry in the world. Faye would manage to fake out the inspector. She was gifted that way. That inspector would never get past Faye and her tricks to inspect the old house, much less the ramshackle storage building out back, the one where Wally had stored things that were far more valuable than a few ratty kitchen appliances rejected by his ex-wife. If Faye would only set her devious mind on thwarting the development of Seagreen Island, all of Wally's troubles would evaporate, and he and Nguyen could conduct their business in peace.

Cyril ushered his last visitor of the day to the door with the great relief that Friday brings to even the most powerful among us. It was important to be solicitous of voters and generous donors but, in the end, they were a monotonous bunch obsessed with personal gain. Faye Longchamp, like the rest of them, hoped to benefit from his influence, but she herself was absolutely unique, and so was the problem she wanted him to solve.

He had waited all afternoon for time to ponder Faye's visit. His first insight into her character was simple: she underestimated how very distinctive her appearance really was. He remembered seeing her during his visit to Seagreen Island on the day of the murders, so already he had a slight edge in their relationship. He knew what she did for a living and she didn't know that he knew it.

Cyril was acutely aware of the need to maintain an edge in any relationship. This awareness was the key to both his success in politics and his failure to construct any semblance of a personal life.

He thought about Faye some more. She was a pretty thing with those dark upturned eyes and that skin the color of tea with cream. She was intriguing, too, but absolutely not his type. He didn't go for close-cropped hair and he usually liked a softer, rounder figure. Still. There were changes afoot.

He'd soon be moving to Washington and starting everything over: house, business associates, acquaintances. He had no friends. Maybe he should put his ideals for female beauty in a compartment with the rest of his old life and lock the door.

He considered Faye's property dispute. It was probably valid, but she would lose in court without solid evidence. Ordinarily it was political suicide to back a lost cause, but African-American voters were going to eat this story up with a spoon.

His memories of the Last Isles stretched back to a childhood spent puttering around in boats, exploring uninhabited islands and claiming them as his own, if only for an afternoon. He would fight development of the Last Isles as long as he had breath and if doing so helped the lovely Ms. Longchamp, so much the better. If there was any benefit to leaving his youth behind, it was the acquisition of enough maturity, wealth, and power to fill the role of a shining knight. At least once in his life, every man should get the chance to rescue a fair maiden in distress.

Chapter 9

Faye was worn out. In a single day, she'd lobbied her senator, played hardball with her best client, and sparred with the law. All those activities, plus piloting the *Gopher* to shore and back and driving a car to Tallahassee and back, tended to make a girl tired. Then, after that, she'd spent hours making her cherished home look like an uninhabitable dump. She'd been successful, and that was depressing in itself.

This was the kind of day when she most appreciated Joe's culinary skills. He had no way to pay her rent. Besides, she would never have charged him for the square of ground beneath the one-man shelter he had built out of branches and palmetto fronds. Nevertheless, Joe paid his way, in his own way.

Faye hadn't cooked a meal since she met Joe, and her grocery bill had dropped precipitously, thanks to his subsistence skills. She hardly bought more than an occasional bag of cornmeal or can of shortening—Joe subscribed to the "fried is good" school of culinary arts—yet she ate like a queen. No one could catch fish more reliably than Joe, and he promised her oysters when they came back in season. Joe picked blackberries. He gathered hickory nuts and—she still found this remarkable—he brought down ducks, squirrels, and rabbits with his handmade bow and his chipped stone arrows.

He had pestered her to let him put in a garden, but she'd been reluctant, because modern property assessments are augmented by aerial photographs. The regular grid of a vegetable garden would be patently obvious from the air. She'd relented when he showed her how he could grow vegetables in tiny clearings that just admitted enough sun to support one plant. He had adhered to her rule that his unorthodox garden had to be in a part of the island far, far from the Big House. Even Faye had to admit that a single cucumber plant, when seen from the air, looked pretty much like the start of a kudzu infestation.

Faye tucked into her meal—fried fish, pink-eyed purple-hull peas, and sliced tomatoes—and her toes curled in pleasure. It was so satisfying to see the soil of Joyeuse feeding people after all the fallow years. Good food makes the eater feel cordial to everybody, especially the cook, and it occurred to Faye that the sheriff was right about one thing. She knew very little about Joe. When they'd first met, she had hesitated, out of good manners, to question him. Months had gone by and what had passed for good manners now bordered on unfriendliness.

"Joe," she asked, "where'd you learn to do all the things you know how to do?"

"My mama," he said, with the country boy's quiet assurance that his mama was the best mama of them all.

The silence hung there and festered while Faye wondered whether Joe had reasons for not talking about his past. The sheriff's suspicions nagged at her—how well did she know this man, really? She probed again.

"You hunt and fish better than any man I know. If you tell me your mama taught you to do those things, then I'm proud to be a woman."

"It was mostly Mama's doing. When I was little, Daddy thought I was slow and I am. I know it. I didn't like school and, after a while, Mama didn't make me go, but she said I oughta be useful, so maybe I could hunt and fish. Daddy was afraid I'd shoot somebody, or run a fishhook through my thumb, but he was a long-haul trucker and he was gone a bunch. Mama took it on herself to teach me to fish. One day after we'd practiced for months and months, I took my daddy fishing."

"How'd it go?"

"I handled the boat, picked out the bait, and set up my gear with the right hook and sinker and floater. I caught a stringerful of good-sized fish, cleaned them, and cooked them for his dinner. I was eleven years old." Joe paused to shake a drop of pepper sauce on his peas. "My daddy cried."

"Then did you go fishing with your dad a lot, after that?"

"Naw, Mama was the one that liked to fish. Daddy took me to Wal-Mart to get my first bow. He's the one what taught me to shoot."

Faye wished she could call up Sheriff McKenzie and announce that Joe was not secretive. He just didn't answer questions people hadn't asked. Sheriff McKenzie wasn't around, so she asked another one.

"It must have been hard to leave your mama. What brought you here?"

"She died a few years ago, when I was eighteen, and there just wasn't much in Oklahoma for me, no more. Daddy wasn't hardly ever home. So I told him I'd heard about somebody in Georgia who could teach me to knap flint the old way. He thought it was a good idea, so I left home."

A map of the United States flashed quickly in Faye's mind's eye. Try as she might, she couldn't make Oklahoma be any closer to Georgia than it was. "Joe. You don't drive. How'd you get to Georgia?"

"I'd walk a ways, then I'd find somebody who needed some work done. I'm not smart, but I'm strong."

"And you got here—"

"Same way."

Oklahoma to Georgia. Joe had walked the Trail of Tears. Backward. Each footfall echoed the mass removal of southeastern Native Americans to the Indian Territory in Oklahoma.

The forced exodus of the Cherokees known as the Trail of Tears—more literally translated as "The Trail Where They Cried"—had come to symbolize the experience of all Native Americans who were cast out of their southeastern homelands a half-century before the western cowboys-and-Indians conflicts immortalized by Hollywood. Lust for the gold under Cherokee lands prompted the 1838 removal of an estimated seventeen thousand people. They were herded, mostly on foot, more than a thousand miles. Nearly one in four fell victim to brutal winter weather, starvation, or the cruelty of the troops "escorting" them.

On his trek to Georgia, Joe had walked past four thousand graves.

Faye wondered if he had any idea of the significance of what he'd done. She suspected he might. No Native American grew up in Oklahoma without knowing about the Trail of Tears.

Faye was done with questions for the evening. She hoped the sheriff would give up and leave Joe Wolf alone. The idea of asking him outright, "Did you commit two murders day before yesterday?" made something inside her shrivel.

"I went this morning and consecrated the grave we found the other day," Joe said, picking up his last fish fillet and eating it with his hands. "It felt good to help the girl rest."

Faye didn't know where Joe learned the burial ritual he used. She'd never had the impression that his parents had brought him up in the Creek religion, or in any religion at all. It seemed to her that he'd asked a lot of people a lot of questions, then cobbled the answers together into a spirituality that was natural for him.

Consecrating a burial Joe's way required a pure body, a pure mind, and a substantial time investment. That morning, as she was just beginning her day of struggle—with the government, with the past, and with her conscience—Joe had drained a cup of ceremonial Black Drink.

Black Drink as Joe prepared it was no different than the Black Drink brewed by southeastern Indians hundreds of years ago. It was a noxious decoction that purified its drinker in several unpleasant ways. There was an excellent reason why the holly tree that lent its leaves to warriors needing purification was known to botanists as *Ilex vomitoria*.

After recovering from the Black Drink, Joe had returned to Abby's islet, bringing carefully wrapped coals from his own fire. After building a fire at the head of her grave and placing clay pots of food and tobacco beside it, he had sat with Abby. Just sat and kept her company for a while. Then he had rinsed his face and hands with water that had steeped all night in sacred herbs. Once clean, he had come home.

Faye studied Joe. He looked like a man who had purified himself, then done an act of kindness for someone who could never return it—someone who would never even know that he had done it. Someday she hoped to have a face so peaceful.

Faye was glad to think that Abby was resting easier. Sometimes she wished for a little rest herself.

Douglass Everett settled into his after-dinner routine—the *Wall Street Journal* and a cigar, followed by *The Micco Times* and a glass of brandy. The *Times* featured another front-page spread on the Seagreen Island murders and his name was listed again alongside Cyril Kirby's as a bystander to the discovery.

Seeing his name in the paper, even a low-circulation local paper, still made him feel like an impostor, an upstart sharecropper's kid. Seeing himself listed as a witness to the discovery of the Seagreen Island killings made him feel ill.

He studied the way "Fredrick Douglass Everett" looked on the page. He had hated his name since the day in fifth grade that he realized his mother's error. She had wanted him to have something to live up to, so she'd named him after the most famous black man she knew, but she could neither read nor write. She relied on the nurse to fill out her baby's birth certificate. The woman had left the second *e* out of Frederick, then, inexplicably, she got the double *s* in Douglass right.

On the day he learned who Frederick A. Douglass was and how his name was actually spelled, the former Fredrick became Douglass forever and ever, and woe to the person who forgot his new, true name. Except for Abby. She had called him Fred all her short life, and the hated word was lovely when it came from her lips.

For decades now, Douglass had had the wherewithal to correct the spelling of his name. He hated the fact that it displayed his mother's ignorance to the world, but correcting it would suggest to that same world that he was ashamed of her. Douglass lived with the name because he revered the memory of his parents. He would have traded ten years of his life for them to see the success he had achieved.

He sipped his brandy and pored over the details of the Seagreen Island killings, doing his habitual accounting. Two dead people, both white. A white sheriff, a black undersheriff. The witnesses were a small throng of fairly random racial makeup that consisted of archaeologists, reporters, and political hangers-on. And, praise God, the investigators treated everyone absolutely evenhandedly. When the sheriff and his coterie had arrived, Douglass had felt it again, the fear of being accused just because he was a black man and he was handy. No matter that he was middle-aged and respectable and wealthy, he still felt that shadow.

But this time he had been wrong. He'd been wrong a lot lately. Times change slowly, but they do change. He wished his parents were alive to see it.

It was dark before the dishes were done, and Faye wasted no time getting to bed. Exhausted from her efforts to deface Joyeuse so she could save it, she knew she should go to sleep, but she had a late date with William Whitehall. The fact that she had found his journal tucked into the rafters, the very bones of her home, made her feel a connection between the long-ago man and this very old house—a connection that she wasn't sure was real. Still, the adventure of reading his life story was worth wasting a few hours of sleep and a few dollars' worth of battery power.

◇

Excerpt from the diary of William Whitehall, 8 August, 1798

It has now been two months since Henri LaFourche, a cultured and educated Frenchman, gathered his men, his horses, one of my horses, & two bagsfull of horsefeed that belong'd to me. They were headed Southwest when they left and, had I so chosen, I could have track'd them down & kilt them. I have the skill to do it. I have Just Cause. No jury South of Philadelphia would convict me.

On his last night with us, the blackguard LaFourche sat in my house in front of my hearth & proposed an agreement—not a Marriage agreement, but a business agreement. He ask'd to buy my Appaloosa Horse. There is no place nearby for him to replace those he has worn out on his journey. In truth, I found his request a personal affront, for Henri knew full well that I needed the Horse & he knew full well that I could replace it no more easily than could he. He simply consider'd the needs of my Family to be unimportant.

After I declined his offer, he removed his ring, a heavy gold band set with a large ruby, & laid it on the table. I was befuddled. No man who meant to ask for a woman's hand in Marriage would begin the negotiations with talk of an insulting horse trade.

I watch'd stupidly as he rose from his chair, gestured at the ruby ring, and said, "Ten days' room and board for me & for my men. Here is your payment." Then Henri LaFourche walk'd out of my house & out of my Daughter's life.

Last week was consumed by a walk to Mr. Gottlieb's trading post. 'Twould have been easier on my rheumatism to ride, but the blackguard LaFourche left me short on horseflesh. Wisdom required that I save my remaining

Horse to pull an overloaded wagon on a long journey. I fear she was not bred for it.

Mr. Gottlieb was as excitable as ever, but this time with Cause, for a letter had come for Mariah, who never received mail in her life. He was anxious for me to open the letter so he could read it. I did not let him; I'd not have considered reading it myself, but the address was in the blackguard's hand. My actions that day depended on Henri LaFourche. There was no help for it. I open'd my Daughter's most private correspondence.

LaFourche begged pardon for his hasty departure & offer'd a miniature self-portrait as a memento. It flutter'd to the dirt. I would have ground it under my heel, but it was and is Mariah's. She may do with it as she pleases. The ruby ring, however, he gave to me. I have disposed of it as profitably as I could in order to provide for LaFourche's other memento. Mariah carries his Child.

Our possessions are loaded on the wagon & we are camp'd by a clear shallow stream. If the value of a homestead can be measured in sweat, then we are leaving behind a great estate indeed. Here in West Florida, a man can work up a sweat while eating his Christmas dinner, yet in such a climate, Susan and I forced the Earth to feed us. We are older now, but we are wiser too, so I suppose we can do it again.

LaFourche's ruby ring brought a fine price, as did our home & land. With the proceeds I have purchas'd a large piece of property—a Gulf Island, in fact—that will provide us with a livelihood & will someday be an inheritance more suitable for Mariah's child than our humble farm. It is fitting that LaFourche's ruby ring provides a future for his Heir, since he himself does not chuse to do so. Were I Mariah, I would sell the blackguard's portrait and add the proceeds to the Child's estate, even if it were worth no more than the paper it is drawn on.

Purchasing an uninhabited Island has the added benefit of giving Mariah a place to hide. Should she one day decide to move back to more populated Lands, her claims to Widowhood will be quite plausible, as there will be no witness to verify a wedding or its lack. After a time, even the Child's birth date will be arguable. Our exile need not be permanent. Yet, I find myself stimulated by the challenge of starting again, & I am not alone. Last night, my Susan took my hand as we lay side by side in our bed. Today as our wagon wheels stirred sandy dust & the branches of live oaks met in a canopy over our heads, she look'd into my eyes and smiled.

Chapter 10

Faye scrambled up the stepladder through the trapdoor and, once through, hauled the ladder up after her. She pulled the door closed, knowing that the enslaved craftsmen who built Joyeuse had fashioned it so well that, despite decades of neglect, it fit snugly and invisibly into its opening. A guest, invited or not, could roam the top floor of her house at will and never suspect that she was lurking above them in the cupola.

The tax inspector was willing to work on Saturday, which did not suggest that Faye could expect any mercy from that quarter. The inspector would arrive any moment to decide whether she should pay taxes on an undeveloped, uninhabited island, or on a twelve-thousand-square-foot island mansion. This day was bound to come. Now she would see whether she had planned for it successfully.

Her morning had been spent smashing each windowpane that wasn't original to the house, being careful to do it from the outside in, so that shards of glass scattered convincingly across the floor. Her roof was absolutely tight, but she'd painted spreading brown stains across the ceiling in several areas. Damp blankets festered under the ceiling stains and inside the broken windows.

Faye had removed pins from selected hinges, allowing shutters, casement windows, even the front door, to hang askew. Finally, she loaded her camp stove, generator, and personal items in a wheelbarrow and carted them to the *Gopher*, which Joe promptly piloted far out to sea with orders to return only when the coast was clear. The twenty-first century had been wiped away, and the twentieth century had gone with it. Only the great house remained on the deserted island, playing the role of an impoverished dowager lingering at death's door.

The work had been good for Faye. She was at her best when toying with bureaucrats, and mindless tasks were what she needed to drown out thoughts of the murders, of Abby Williford, of the goddamn taxes.

Faye's vantage point gave her views in all four directions. She could see the tax inspector approaching in the boat that Wally had considerately rented to her at his special government price, which was about twice the going rate. Faye was gratified to see that the narrow entrance to the inlet where she moored her own boats was as overgrown and easily overlooked as ever.

The intruder passed it up, anchoring her boat just off Joyeuse's tiny beach and hopping overboard. Faye focused her binoculars on the distant form and saw an intrepid-looking woman, wading ashore without giving her deck shoes or knee-length khakis a second thought. Damn. Faye had been hoping for a desk jockey in a business suit.

Faye watched the inspector walk slowly up the path, pushing back the weedy undergrowth. If it weren't for this woman and the flock of people like her who wanted to take Joyeuse away, she could trim the bushes along the path. She could paint her house and put a real roof on it, instead of patching it with pieces of tin salvaged from a junkyard so they wouldn't look too new. She could plant flowers in her own front yard.

The woman strolled into the dogtrot, an open breezeway that divided the aboveground basement into two equal halves. There was nothing to see there, just stone-like tabby walls that once enclosed the plantation office, the storeroom, the dispensary, and other service rooms a long-dead business had required.

Just as Faye was beginning to worry, the woman reappeared and stood studying the facade, clipboard in one hand and the other fist on her hip. The average bureaucrat would have given up at this point, because Joyeuse looked in no way livable, but this tenacious soul began climbing the grand outdoor staircase that had swept guests to the main floor to greet Joyeuse's owners.

At least she hadn't found the sneak stairs in the basement that had once brought servants to the dining room and, up another floor, to the master bedroom. It was vitally important that the inspection end before it reached the bedrooms.

It was in the bedrooms that the builders of Joyeuse achieved their highest art. They had ennobled every room in the house with moldings miraculously formed out of the materials available—mud, Spanish moss, horsehair, and Lord knew what else—and they had hung the hand-blocked French wall-paper on the main floor with delicacy, but the bedrooms flaunted Faye's favorite embellishment.

Each square inch of the bedrooms' ceilings and walls was covered with murals. Faye slept in a lavender chamber graced with swans and wisteria. A manly room across the hall, perhaps a guest room, depicted the climactic moment of a fox hunt. The master bedroom was a confection of flowers and painted lace, white on cream on ivory on gilded beige.

Faye's grandmother had showed her how to clean the murals with a fine, soft paintbrush, just as her own grand-mother had taught her. Five generations of care had left them marvelously preserved. Not content with merely keeping up the family tradition, Faye had gone the extra mile. She had taught herself to repair the cracked and faded areas of the paintings. Then, after studying *faux-bois* techniques, she had restored the painted wood grain to the doors, reversing a century of wear around the doorknobs.

If the tax inspector saw the bedrooms, Faye's goose was cooked.

Faye grinned maliciously as the woman yanked at one of the oversized front doors. She had gone to great pains to disguise the main floor as a former haven for the down-and-out. Dirty sleeping bags lay in every cranny. Those that lay under "leaks" were both wet and dirty. In spots, the sleeping bag covers were shredded and the stuffing pulled out by—what? Mice? Rats?

Faye was frankly stunned to hear a footfall on bare wood. Its hollow echo told her that the inspector had braved the staircase. Faye was hardly willing to climb it herself, preferring the sneak stair or the outdoor stairs tucked under the rear gallery.

Joyeuse's interior staircase was a freestanding spiral of singular grace, but it wasn't aging well. It shifted perceptibly underfoot and the plaster that coated its underside was flaking away, clear evidence of motion beyond the architect's specifications.

That very morning, Faye had removed several balusters to enhance its rickety appearance, yet the inspector was risking her life to climb it so she could harass Joyeuse's tax-dodging owner. Faye hoped it fell, because she had only one more trick up her sleeve.

The footsteps kept coming closer and closer, climbing further up the spiral. The treads creaked under the woman's feet and Faye could almost feel Joyeuse herself tremble and shift in sympathy. The footfalls stopped when the stairs ended at a square landing that served no purpose other than to provide access to the huge bedrooms hiding behind closed doors.

On this landing, Faye had pulled out the stops, evoking every stereotype she knew to convince the inspector that the tumbledown house was just a shell that luckless people used to keep the rain off their heads. Ratty clothes were tossed among discarded cans of beans and beer and Sterno. She hoped the inspector was writing "abandoned, uninhabited, and uninhabitable" on her clipboard. She hoped the inspector was doing anything other than reaching for the doorknob to one of the bedrooms.

For a long moment, there was no sound, no footstep broadcasting the intruder's inspection of the squatters' refuse, no turning doorknob, nothing. Then, there were quick footsteps as the woman stumbled down the deathtrap masquerading as a staircase, across the entry hall, and down the grand outdoor stairs.

Faye's final, inspired trick had worked. Joe had been instrumental to her plan. She had left him in privacy to do the task and she imagined he had performed it with the glee of a small boy. She hoped he was as gleeful when she asked him to clean up after himself.

The coast was clear and it was safe for Faye to laugh out loud. The intrepid inspector had been scared away by the simple odor of urine.

Stuart was tired of walking into bars and walking out again, still sober. It was not possible that his targets had lingered long in this area without being seen by somebody, especially when one of the targets wore a feather in his long black hair. Maybe the people who had the information he needed didn't drink, so bars weren't the best places to look. Maybe they were upstanding, churchgoing folk.

Tomorrow was Sunday. Maybe he'd find himself a shabby suit at the thrift shop and visit some churches. Nah. He shouldn't have to do anything that drastic. Bars are chockfull of churchgoing family people just looking for an hour's peace. Bars are full of people who filled their cars at service stations and shopped for groceries and picked up the weekly dry cleaning. How was it possible that no one in this lightly populated corner of the world had seen the Indian guy and his young sidekick?

Stuart could see only two possibilities: either they were drifters who didn't stay in the area long enough to make an impression on anyone but his client, or they lived someplace unusually secluded. If they'd drifted on, then they'd taken his chance at a fortune with them and he might as well go home and have a cold beer. It seemed more practical to assume that they were hiding in an extremely out-of-the-way spot and, if he could only find it, the money would be his.

Faye took a moment to enjoy being alone at the top of her home with a three-hundred-and-sixty-degree view of the Gulf of Mexico and its coastline. She didn't know when she'd last taken the time to crawl up into the cupola just to look around. The view was worth the climb. Her eyes were drawn to a scattering of dark patches in the aquamarine waters far to the southwest, like inclusions in an otherwise flawless gemstone. She'd had no idea that the Last Isles were visible from Joyeuse.

It was good to know that Joyeuse was safe and that she'd been the one to save it. Grounded by the feel of her home, old and solid beneath her, and soothed by the all-encompassing water, she sank down on a bench beside a floor-to-ceiling window.

When she felt rested, she stood up and looked down at the old storage bench where she'd been sitting. The words "old" and "storage" coalesced in her archaeologist's brain and she lifted the lid. It was stuffed with old dresses—Depression-era, from the looks of the fabric. Interesting, but not earth-shattering. She wanted something *old*. She pulled the dresses out and found nothing beneath them but broken glass. It was thicker and clearer than window glass, but no more earth shattering than the dresses. Finally, in a back corner beneath a broken teacup, Faye at last found something *old*.

Ten thousand years old.

It was a long, distinctively fluted piece of stone. Faye gawked at the Clovis-style spearhead in her hand. Implements from the famous Clovis, New Mexico, site had been found in association with Pleistocene species; the Clovis people lived so far in the past that they hunted mammoths and other Ice

Age animals. Could this point have been brought here by someone who bought it or collected it elsewhere? Or was there a Clovis site nearby? Artifacts of that age weren't unknown in Florida, but habitation sites of such great age had proven elusive so far.

Holding something so ancient made the great house on Joyeuse seem new, a frivolous whim built by someone who thought he needed a dwelling much more grand than the ephemeral hut of the hunter-gatherer. When this grand house blew away on a puff of wind and water, the artisan who made the thing in her hand would live on in the poetry of its form and function.

She couldn't wait to show this to Joe.

Stooping over, she pushed on the lever that activated the trapdoor's latch. Nothing. She tried again. The mechanism tripped properly, but the door didn't budge. Hanging on to a window sill so that she wouldn't drop through the hole when the door finally opened, she stomped on the lever with all her weight. Nothing.

This was a sorry state of affairs. Perhaps, in a single hour, humidity had caused the wood of the door to swell an extra millimeter. Perhaps the house had shifted and the trapdoor frame was barely out of square. Perhaps one too many coats of varnish had been applied to the door and its frame, and they had bonded chemically under pressure.

Joe wouldn't be back to the house until suppertime. Unless she planned to perch in the cupola until then, waiting for rescue like Rapunzel, she would be crawling over the roof.

Praying no one had painted the windows shut, she knelt by one and pushed up the sash. It rose easily and she leaned out to plan her escape. The roof descended at a sharp slant, but the tin roof's ridges and her rubber-soled boots would give her traction. Wrapping the still-sharp edges of the Clovis point in the silk remains of a seventy-year-old dress and tucking it inside her shirt, she stepped out of the window. It was a simple traverse, across the roof and down a little to the gable of her own bedroom window, which should be easy to open, considering that she'd smashed half of its panes.

Faye was in good shape and she was wearing boots with good traction. She should have had no difficulty sidling down the slanted roof. It would have been a lot easier if she'd made the trip in a single motion without pausing to think about the distance to the ground, and what a human body would look like once it had made that long trip. Three days ago, she'd seen two people with the life snuffed out of them. They'd been shot, whereas, if she fell, she'd merely break every bone in her body. Still, dead is dead.

Faye's crawl down the roof resumed, but her progress was painful. She successfully negotiated the roof and raised the window, then fell through the open bedroom window directly onto her bed. Very old swans and wisteria watched over her as she slept through the rest of the afternoon and into the night.

Nguyen had been watching the news and keeping an eye on boat traffic out of Wally's Marina. He and Wally had made a few scouting trips through the Last Isles. The coast was unquestionably clear.

The Marine Patrol boats and the Sheriff's Office boats and the Park Service boats had gone back where they came from, except for a few that carried investigators back and forth to the crime site on Seagreen Island. Nguyen's dig site was on Water Island, another of the Last Isles, miles away, and the cops hadn't been near it in days. Nguyen judged that it was safe to begin digging again.

It would take time to ferry their equipment back out to the island, but Nguyen figured that the rewards outweighed the effort. The riches buried under the sand and sea were more than sufficient to drive a man to extreme measures.

When Faye crawled out of bed on Sunday morning, she stumbled over a stack of papers. She had almost forgotten the newspaper articles about Abigail Williford's disappearance. Now that the government was off her back for the moment, she had time to read them.

She began with the earliest articles, which uniformly read: "Teenage Heiress Missing." Several of the newspapers printed special midweek editions, to avoid being scooped by their competitors who published on more fortuitous schedules.

As the weeks passed, the focus had shifted away from looking for a missing person or waiting for a ransom note. There were stories of human chains slogging through swamps, pictures of the girl's widowed father looking utterly alone, advertisements promising a sizeable reward for word of her whereabouts.

Bloodhounds were given Abigail's dainty silk slippers to sniff. Known ne'er-do-wells were brought in for questioning. As always in these cases, it was shocking to realize that, within twenty-four hours of a violent crime, investigators could list a few dozen people currently walking free whom they considered capable of a crime of any magnitude. And, it being 1964, a disproportionate share of those under suspicion were black men.

Faye's heart broke when she read that a young Douglass Everett was questioned repeatedly. His only crime was being employed by Abigail's father, who vigorously supported Douglass' claims of innocence. With no evidence and no support from the victim's father, who also happened to be the most powerful man in Micco County, the sheriff wasn't able to hold Douglass. But Faye was transfixed by a blurry newspaper photo of Douglass and a young deputy who would become Sheriff Mike McKenzie.

They were standing eyeball-to-eyeball, and Douglass was conspicuously not giving Deputy McKenzie the deferential gaze expected from black men. Deputy McKenzie was glaring at Douglass with the ferocity of a man who believes he is faced with a beast capable of slaying a fragile young girl.

Chapter 11

Nguyen considered himself a professional artifact poacher. He didn't mess around with peddling trinkets to hobbyists. Nguyen only worked for people who knew who the serious collectors were. His shadowy boss must be one of them since he had unloaded some powerfully expensive pieces.

The very fact that Nguyen was on tiny little Water Island signified that big things were afoot. Few non-archaeologists knew or cared that some of the very first Americans, known today as the Clovis culture, had spread all the way to Florida, and nobody knew that they'd been in this particular spot. So nobody would miss the spear points and bones that he was shipping to customers all over the world.

And there were more riches to be reaped under the Gulf's blood-warm waters. Not far from the beach where he stood lay a shipwreck reputed to be filled with uncommon treasure, and he'd found it. Retrieving those riches would be tricky, but with specialized diving gear, another diver, and a well-manned vessel to provide surface support, he'd have plenty of time to empty the wreck before the water cooled for the winter.

After fifteen years in the business, Nguyen had little fear of being caught, especially out here halfway to Timbuktu, but there was an additional layer of safety in this job. Wally said some chick, a real amateur, was working these islands. If the Feds started poking around, it would be easy to set her up to take the fall for their crimes. Nguyen felt it was always wise to have an emergency plan.

Because she was such a convenient part of that plan, Nguyen was willing to allow the amateur to continue burrowing for scraps in the sand for a while longer, but only as long as she stayed away from his dig site. If she came within binocular range of it, he would permanently remove her from the picture by any means necessary. There was that much money to be made.

"Listen closely," Magda said to a room that echoed with the racket of shuffling feet, whispered conversations, and giggles. Teaching freshmen was hard enough, but these guys weren't even freshmen yet. They were eighteen-year-old prospective archaeology majors, fresh out of high school, and this Monday morning lecture was the opening salvo of the university's week-long orientation program. Her assignment was to deliver an orientation speech that would enflame their desire to learn. It was probably not a good idea to tell them the truth, but, every year, she did it anyway.

"Nobody in this room, myself included, will ever discover a royal tomb like King Tut's or stumble onto a lost city like Machu Picchu. Few archaeologists are so lucky. We will spend our careers in the trash heaps, the wastepiles, even the latrines, of dead people. Among the waste, we will find the ordinary junk of day-to-day life, things that we will call artifacts. When we guess their purpose, we will be wrong."

They weren't listening. They were never listening, but she felt obligated to strip the profession of its pseudo-glamour. The students that remained would be worth keeping.

She forged ahead. "I see that you don't believe me. Consider this. About the time that you were born, soda and beer companies stopped making cans with detachable pull tabs. When I was in school, my friends and I tossed our soda tabs on the ground outside this very building. One day, archaeologists will find distinctive metal artifacts surrounding every door to every public building that was standing during the mid-twentieth century."

They were muttering among themselves, interested but still missing the point. "Soda tabs used to come off the can? Why?"

"Mark my words," she said, looking directly at the one student who appeared to be looking at her. "They will declare those pull tabs to be an integral part of our religious practices. How else will they explain the inexplicable? Remember this and be humble when you try to piece together the lives of people you have never met."

She dismissed the orientation class early so they could rush to the student union and confirm that beer was, indeed, actually for sale on campus before noon. Returning to her office, she found a soul-killing pile of administrative drudgery still festering on the far corner of her desk. It could stay there, even if Dr. Raleigh came and stood in the room so that he could watch her do precisely nothing. She had no stomach for academic tedium, not any more. She had had no stomach for much of anything since Sam and Krista died.

The telephone rang and she forced herself to let it ring twice so that the extent of her idleness wouldn't be obvious to the caller.

A cultured female voice said, "Please hold for Senator Cyril Kirby," and Magda did as she was told.

"Dr. Stockard?" the senator said in a low voice that commanded attention without resorting to the booming hyperemphasis used by most politicians.

"Yes, Senator, what can I do for you?"

"I called to offer my condolences on the loss of your students. I have already spoken with their parents but, having through coincidence shared the incidents of that terrible day with you, I felt that you, too, had suffered bereavement."

"Why, thank you, Senator, that's very thoughtful."

"Rest assured that I've spoken with the sheriff. He knows that if I have access to any resources that might help him solve this crime, then he should consider those resources his."

Magda thought that the senator displayed more social finesse than the typical backslapping politician, but, lacking a corresponding level of grace, she could think of nothing more intelligent to say than, "Thank you. I appreciate that and I know the families do, too."

"It's the least I can do. Now, I'd like to ask you a question about a tangentially related matter."

"Certainly."

"I've been doing business with a woman who, I believe, is an employee of yours. Attractive, petite, thirty-ish, dark-skinned—her name is Faye Longchamp. I've been trying to get in touch with her, but she forgot to leave me her address or phone number."

"Oh, she didn't forget. She lives on her boat and keeps to herself. You can't reach Faye unless she wants to be reached." Even if Magda had known Faye's address, she would not have given it to anyone without her permission—not a colleague, not a minister, and certainly not a minor-league politician. It didn't occur to her that she was giving out sensitive information when she said, "Faye will be in here to see me this afternoon. I'll ask her to get in touch with you."

He thanked her and hung up, and Magda didn't think about the conversation again for an hour, not until she saw the senator himself in the departmental library.

Faye sat across a library table from Senator Cyril Kirby. She would hardly have been more surprised if she had walked in and found a woolly mammoth awaiting her.

"Hello, Senator Kirby," she began. "I—"

He interrupted her with a warm, "Call me Cyril. Please. I had some questions about your property dispute, but my secretary said you wouldn't give her a phone number."

"I was going to check back in a week to see if you'd made any progress. I didn't expect such fast action. Or such personal attention."

"Your problem is an interesting and important one. If your claims prove true, then your family was defrauded of a piece of property whose value has appreciated significantly in the past few years."

Faye liked his smile. That fact unnerved her, because it was important that she develop a successful business relationship with this man and she had a distinct feeling that he had more than business on his mind.

"So what was the question you forgot to ask me?" she asked quickly, too uncomfortable to let silence linger long while he sat across the table and smiled at her.

"Do you know where the old Turkey Foot Hotel stood on Last Isle?" he asked. "No, that's not the real question. Do you know where its ruins are now? Last Isle is in pieces now, but it might be possible to find proof of your family's financial interest in the hotel. Then you could reclaim at least the piece of Last Isle where the hotel's ruins stand."

Faye shook her head. "I've thought of that, but no one I've talked to has ever seen even a trace of the foundation. It may be underwater."

Cyril looked disappointed. "It was worth a shot." He ran his fingers through his hair and she noticed that it was less stiff today, as if he'd left off the telegenic coat of hair spray. In his shirt sleeves, Cyril himself looked less stiff, more approachable. She wasn't surprised when he said, "I may be out of line, but would you like to have dinner with me?" but she was shaken all the same.

Surely his help with her legal problems didn't depend on her sexual acquiescence. Her female instincts were signaling a soft but insistent, "No," but she held back from turning him down cold. He was attractive and intelligent. He was also wealthy and influential, but those things didn't mean so much to Faye. She weighed the pros and cons for a minute, then came up with an inspired compromise.

"Why don't we meet somewhere tomorrow for lunch? I know a place that's charming. Unusual, too."

Chapter 12

Faye sat with Joe on Joyeuse's shuttered back porch, eating breakfast. It was Tuesday but, since she didn't have to go to work, Joe had fixed pancakes as a special treat. She was using her final bite of pancake to mop up the last drip of syrup while she blathered like a schoolgirl about her lunch plans. There was no reason to assume that Joe would be in the least interested to know that she had a date with a senator, but she had that adolescent first-date feeling. She wanted to talk about it.

Joe hardly responded, which wasn't unusual, so Faye talked to herself until she reached the climax of her story. "And the weirdest thing is this: I accept a date with this man, then I pick up the paper and his picture is on the cover. And he's going to be on TV this morning. Some kind of a press conference showcasing legislators who are opposed to the resort."

Joe just gathered their dirty dishes and headed to the cistern.

She wished he'd stayed and let her natter on about inconsequential things, like what she should wear. She'd rather pay no heed at all to the fact that this was her first date in two years. If she tried, she could ignore the fact that her date was a politician and, thus, unlikely to be trustworthy. She could even ignore the age difference, remembering instead Mother's sage advice: "Men are generally more trouble than they're worth, but sometimes they're downright entertaining. Besides, if there's any other way to get yourself a baby to love, nobody ever explained it to me."

She heard Joe crank his johnboat and wondered briefly where he was going. He usually fished at dawn and at dusk. It was unusual for him to leave the island in the middle of the day, but he was an adult. He could do as he pleased.

Deciding that Joe was in charge of his own whereabouts, Faye took a shower. Never one to waste a trip ashore, she needed to leave soon if she hoped to get a little research time before she met Cyril. She had a feeling the local library would have information on the disappearance of Abigail Williford that the larger university library had lacked.

Abby was a comfortable obsession. Her fate was distant and intriguing in a way that Sam's and Krista's could never be, and Faye was looking forward to delving deeper into it. Who would have ever thought that she'd be whistling happily, looking forward to a day that included an hour at the Sopchoppy Public Library, followed by lunch with a man probably destined to be her next congressman?

Joe found Wally's Marina deserted and he was glad. He'd successfully avoided the place, just as he'd successfully avoided all public places in the four months since he moved to Joyeuse. Crowds made him jumpy, and Joe Wolf defined a crowd as three or more people.

He paid the woman behind the counter for a cup of coffee and some chips then, after asking if she minded, he flicked the TV over to the Tallahassee channel. Cyril's press conference hadn't started yet, so Joe found yesterday's paper lying on the counter and focused on the front-page article highlighting the senator.

Newspapers are written at the eighth-grade reading level these days—slow going for Joe—but he learned that Cyril had entered public life as a county commissioner in his early thirties. A state representative at forty, he had moved up to the Florida Senate after a single term.

Cyril was a friend of the little man. He supported universal health care for children. He was in favor of an increase in the minimum wage. He co-authored a wildly popular bill that eliminated state sales tax on clothing the week before children started school in the fall.

Cyril's politics had not always sat well with the environmentalist factions. Everybody knew that most of his campaign money came from developers who thought Florida would be better off with no wetlands at all. This was not a problem in his job-hungry home district, but the congressional seat he aspired to would require support in more affluent, more environmentally sensitive regions. His political aspirations demanded that he lose the anti-environmental label. There was no other way to explain the sudden switch that placed him in the forefront of the "Save Seagreen Island" movement.

Joe understood about every third word of the article detailing this switch, but he persevered. When he reached the last sentence, he had come no closer to liking Cyril than he had been before he began reading.

Cyril's face materialized on the TV and Joe studied it, trying to figure out what he disliked about the man's looks. His hair was too "fixed." The short-sleeved sport shirt was just a little too casual in the way it revealed muscles that were just a little too well-defined to suit Joe. They were muscles purchased in a health club, not earned through meeting the burdens of everyday life.

Joe was too young, too content in inhabiting his own strong body, to realize that someday his own muscle-bulking testosterone would falter. He was years away from feeling empathy for Cyril or admiration for the man's refusal to go gently into middle age. And he was years away from cheering Cyril on in his pursuit of a pretty young thing.

Joe usually limited himself to one thought at a time and, as he studied the man on the television and munched on his Doritos, his current thought was uncomplicated: this old man was not good enough for his friend Faye.

The young man had said his name was Joe and the name suited him. Liz had been watching him study the newspaper for a while now and she'd been thinking.

Somebody had been in the marina, just yesterday, asking all the regulars about Joe—or somebody who looked like him—and a dark-skinned adolescent boy that he was known to hang out with. He'd been offering a pretty penny for information on their whereabouts, too. Well, nobody fitting Joe's description had sidled up to her snack counter in quite a while, so—adolescent companion or not—he must be the man in question.

It was puzzling. The guy had clearly been a goon, a human weapon working for somebody outside the law, so it was natural to assume he was looking for someone of his ilk. Yet this cute overgrown boy eating chips in front of the TV had none of the hallmarks of a criminal. Liz had encountered a few criminals in her day. Shit. She'd been married to one.

Stirring up a batch of waffle mix, Liz watched a scruffy fisherman in hip-waders shuffle into the room. He stood gape-mouthed a moment in the middle of the room, before fumbling in his tackle box and pulling out a cell phone. Her pony-tailed customer never looked up from the TV and so never saw the man who sold him out.

Stuart rolled over in the lumpy hotel bed and picked up the ringing phone, letting it crash back down without ever bringing the handset near his ear. Damn wake-up call.

It rang again. If he'd been suffering from his usual hangover, he would have buried his head under the stale-smelling pillow and let it ring, but he never drank when he was working. This time he lifted it to his ear. After a pause, he let it crash onto the receiver without ever having spoken a word.

He jumped into his pants, grabbed his room key and his weapon, and pointed his car toward Wally's Marina. Indian Boy had finally surfaced.

The grill was still deserted, except for one pony-tailed customer, and Liz leaned on the counter, waiting for something to happen. She'd sold the boy two more bags of chips, but that was probably his limit. He'd had to dig deep into the leather bag at his waist for the money, and he'd mostly come up with pennies. She noticed that the eight or ten pennies left over after he paid for the chips hadn't gone back into the bag. He'd put them in her tip jar, then settled back down in front of the TV.

Within fifteen minutes, the goon showed up, pretending to be a Fish and Wildlife officer. He stomped over to Joe and asked, "Been doing any fishing lately?"

"Yeah," said Joe.

"Got a license?"

Joe's baffled face broke Liz's heart. She wondered if the boy knew what a fishing license was.

"Come with me. Let's take a look at your boat and see if you've been doing anything else you shouldn't."

Joe listened, but he didn't have anything to say for himself. He was just going to follow the man outside. It seemed to Liz like the innocents of the world were the ones who got tangled up in life's cobwebs and eaten by spiders.

The cost of hiring a goon and paying for days of room and board while he located his quarry would be steep, and criminals were notoriously stingy with their money. Somebody wanted this boy bad.

Her heart went out to the young man as he threw his three empty Doritos bags in the trash and followed the so-called officer out, pausing only long enough to hand her his empty coffee cup and say thanks. Damn. Now she'd have to take action. In her day, she'd waited on thieves, wife beaters, and drug runners like her dear departed husband. She'd found many of them to be attractive and well groomed. Even polite. But she had never yet met a bad guy willing to bus his own table.

Liz dipped a big potful of hot grease out of the deep fryer and followed Joe and his escort out onto the dock.

"Where's your badge, Officer?" she asked in a voice that stopped just short of a bellow.

"You've got no authority here, lady," the impostor said, hustling Joe along.

"Your ID, your badge, your uniform, anything. Just show me and the boy here something that proves you have a right to treat him this way."

"You want ID? I'll show you ID," he said, reaching under his windbreaker.

Liz had never heard anybody say that Fish and Wildlife officers carried concealed weapons, but the action was unmistakable. With one foot, she swept Joe's feet out from under him. Once he had landed on his butt, safely out of range of her sizzling ammunition, she gave the pot in her hand an underhanded sling.

Hot grease slopped over the goon and his gun. It thumped to the dock and bounced into the water as the man staggered back and ripped at the soaked jacket and shirt holding the scalding grease to his body.

"Get away from here, boy," she said to Joe. "This place ain't safe for you."

She watched Joe navigate his little johnboat deep into the salt marsh, where no shooter would ever find him, especially not one nursing third-degree burns. Then she headed back to her kitchen to call the sheriff, swinging her empty pot and striding like a Valkyrie.

When he arrived, the man was gone.

Chapter 13

An anomalous low-pressure system hovered off the coast of Central America. It had dumped enough rain on Honduras and Nicaragua to generate localized mudslides but, because there was no loss of life, Americans had paid scarcely any attention.

When, at long last, the storm steeled itself for a move into the open waters, it was finally rewarded with an upgrade to tropical storm. Powerful things gestate slowly.

Faye had spent the last ten minutes perusing Wally's candy aisle, far more time than she usually spent in the presence of forty million calories. It wasn't that she never indulged in a little cocoa comfort; she just usually skated down the candy aisle and grabbed a Hershey bar as she passed. Anything more elaborate than a plain slab of milk chocolate was gilding the lily, as far as Faye was concerned.

But not today. Today, she needed to hide her face while Wally lied to the guy from the Park Service about the whereabouts of her friend Joe. So she listened to Wally swear he'd never seen a tall, dark man wearing traditional Indian clothing. Perhaps he wasn't lying; she didn't think Wally ever *had* met Joe.

The agent's sources had told him that significant artifacts, possibly excavated in this area, had shown up on the black market. The Park Service wanted to question any suspicious characters they could find, and the sheriff had told him that this new guy Joe looked plenty suspicious. And he'd been seen piloting a johnboat around the Last Isles.

Wally played dumb, making the man explain—at least three times—what a pothunter was, even though he knew exactly how Faye spent her spare time. Wally then denied (again) that he'd ever seen the man in question, proclaiming that he was absolutely shocked that anyone would do such a craven thing. In this case, he was surely lying. Wally was impossible to shock. Besides, pothunting was the kind of victimless crime that Wally could really get behind.

It took Wally a long time to convince the man that he was honest—no surprise—and that he'd never seen anybody who resembled Joe in the least, so Faye had plenty of time to study the nutrition label on each brand of empty calories. She learned a lot: for instance, twelve bars of milk chocolate provide a full day's quota of calcium.

Finally, the agent quit harassing Wally and left. Wally was in Faye's face before she emerged from Hershey heaven.

"You've got to send that Indian guy on his way. Now the government's looking for him. If they keep sniffing around, they're gonna find *you*."

So he *had* met Joe. Well, every once in a while, even nature boys like Joe got a hankering for junk food, and Wally's was the closest candy and chips dealer to Joyeuse, by far.

Liz's disembodied voice wafted out of the kitchen. "Hang the government. Goddamn taxes."

"Listen to the cook in shining armor," Wally said. "Did you know she saved your friend's ass this morning?"

No, nobody had told her a thing. Faye wondered why that surprised her. "Joe can usually take care of himself."

"Yeah, but he's gullible. He believed some thug who claimed to be a Fish and Wildlife agent and nearly hopped in the man's boat."

"What could Joe have done to cross somebody like that?" Faye asked. "He wouldn't hurt a fly."

Wally thrust himself back into the conversation. "Who knows what kind of trouble he was in before he ever showed up here? Women are stupid. You trust that man because he looks like a stud. He's nothing more than a vagrant, Faye. If he'd showed up at Joyeuse missing half his teeth and all his hair, you wouldn't have given him the time of day."

Wally had a point, but she didn't want to admit it, so she didn't answer. She just glared at him.

"You've got to send him on his way, Faye. He's not smart enough to keep your secrets. You've got a lot of them, you know."

Liz wiped down the bar while she watched Faye walk out. She knew Faye, because Faye spent more time hanging around the marina and jawing with Wally than most women who had good sense. And now Liz had met Joe, the studly innocent who'd just escaped disaster, thanks to her. It seemed that Faye and Joe lived together and that Wally knew it.

Liz studied Faye's back. She saw a slim body clad in a work shirt and khakis, topped with a head covered in short dark hair, and she remembered what she knew about the crook she had just scorched. He wasn't just looking for Joe, he was looking for his friend, a small dark adolescent boy.

Liz wondered how long it was going to take Wally to realize that, just a minute ago, he was talking to the missing "boy." She figured it wasn't her business to tell him. She wasn't sure he could be trusted with the information.

Faye's Bonneville was a slow ride and the short drive to Sopchoppy would take her twenty minutes to accomplish, leaving her time to stew. She even got angry enough to talk to herself.

"A vagrant," she fumed. "Who does Wally think he is, calling Joe a vagrant? He's got a lot of nerve, considering that he's the alcoholic owner of a business that's going down the tubes. He'd better be nice to me, because someday he may need a place to sleep and I may not be taking any more vagrants at Joyeuse."

As her car made its asthmatic way down the road, she worked at being objective. Was Joe a killer? No. Was he dangerous? Yes, in a way. Despite his personal loyalty, he was capable of serious lapses in judgment and, as Wally had pointed out, she had a lot of secrets.

Faye decided to deal with any problems Joe presented as they came. She'd sacrificed a lot to keep her home and she was probably going to lose it anyway. She drew the line at sacrificing Joe's friendship.

She reminded herself that she had a lunch date with a charming and powerful man who, inexplicably, seemed to like her a lot. And he was interested in helping her regain what was rightfully hers.

She pulled into the four-slot parking lot of the Sopchoppy Library. It was housed in a tiny building but it had Internet access, so it wasn't tiny at all.

Faye was proud her small-town library had Web access, but the Internet had proved to be singularly unhelpful in locating more information on Abby. There was no additional information to be had. The girl had simply vanished.

After a few months, the newspapers had dropped the story. Not a scrap of physical evidence had ever turned up. There had been plenty of news to report while the search was active, but it was all negative. The bloodhounds smelled nothing. The roadblocks uncovered nothing. Her father's offer of a $20,000 reward for information generated hundreds of crank calls, but little else. Dragging the rivers and creeks, searching the coastal marshes and offshore islands—all yielded no trace of Abby or her clothing or the jewelry she always wore.

And there was nothing else to look for. Her beach house showed no signs of robbery or forced entry. Her brand-new convertible still sat where she parked it. The rest of her jewelry still lay in her childish jewelry box with its dancing ballerina.

When, after fruitless months, the search was called off, there was nothing left for the newspapers to write about, so they stopped.

A collection of slender orange and black books caught her eye and she slid one off the shelf. This *was* a small-town library. The librarian allocated five feet of scarce shelf space to back issues of the yearbook for Micco County's combined elementary and high school.

1964. Faye picked up the volume documenting Abby's last year and enjoyed its old book smell. Individual pictures of the senior class were prominently displayed, the students' accomplishments listed below each of their photographs. They were arranged alphabetically, so Abby's "W" surname would have landed her near the end of the class. For the same reason, Douglass Everett was placed toward the front.

Faye read the list of honors beneath Douglass' face. They were short but choice: Summa Cum Laude graduate, National Merit Finalist, valedictorian. It seemed strange that titles like "Most Intellectual" and "Most Likely to Succeed" were beneath other faces with far paler credentials until Faye realized that Douglass' honors were all earned, not elected. His was the only black face on the page and any fool knew that, in that era, he would have won no popularity contests. Nobody could argue with his grades or his SATs, so he was, however grudgingly, allowed those honors.

Faye turned the page and found that Sheriff Mike had been class salutatorian, then turned it again and found that Abby, by contrast, was no scholar. Her achievements peaked when she was elected chaplain of the Future Homemakers of America. Apparently good at winning elections, Abby was also chosen Sweetest and Most Punctual. She peered at the camera over her shoulder in the same eerie senior portrait that Faye had seen on a hundred front pages, but this time it was uncropped. A single earring was visible and thirty-some-odd years in the ground hadn't dimmed its loveliness. Here was proof that Faye had found the woman who had been the focus of the largest search for a missing person ever seen in western Florida.

She flipped the page back to get another look at Abby's classmates. One of them, after all, might have murdered her but, to Faye, they all looked like children, not killers.

Then, dead in the center of the page, a face grabbed her attention. It was Cyril. Actually, it wasn't. Cyril was several years younger than these kids. The face that drew Faye's eye was Cyril's older brother, Cedrick. The family resemblance was strong. Even in black-and-white, Faye recognized the thick, fine hair that was light but not blonde, the sharp eyes, the square jaw. Brains also ran in the family, because the yearbook credited Cedrick as a Cum Laude graduate. He had Cyril's lean athletic masculinity, so she wasn't surprised to read that he was captain of the baseball, football, and track teams.

She flipped forward in the yearbook and found something that made her smile: a candid shot of the entire senior class clowning around for the camera. Abby, eyes crossed and laughing, was holding two fingers behind Douglass' dignified head in the age-old symbol for devil horns. Sheriff Mike stood behind a blonde girl who wore a bouffant hairdo and an effervescent smile. Grinning over her shoulder at the camera, he had both arms wrapped around her slender waist. Cedrick's yo-yo was in orbit around his own head.

Each student was identified by a nickname: Sweet Thang for Abby, Professor for Douglass, Criss Kross for Cedrick, Broomstraw for skinny Sheriff Mike. It was time to leave for her lunch date, but Faye wanted copies of this photo and of the individual portraits of each kid. She'd already gleaned all the information she needed, but the part of her that had grown up and grown cold wanted to document these children's last spasm of innocence. Abby would be dead before the summer was over.

On her way to the copier, she found a picture of Wally, who had been a strangely solemn-looking eleventh-grader that year. Flipping through the rest of the yearbook, she found

Senator Cyril in the fourth grade. He'd been a hollow-eyed boy, small for his ten years, wearing a dress shirt so small that its collar button wouldn't button.

His nose had been broken and a long ragged scar angled between his right brow and his hairline. A permanent front tooth was missing. It was not a face of privilege. He must have blessed the day he scared up enough money to get a nose job. Her opinion of the senator rose. It would be worth the effort to get to know anybody who could rise above a beginning like this.

Chapter 14

Bahia grass waved V-shaped seedheads in the muggy breeze. Faye inhaled its scent, like bread baking in the oven of a Florida noon. She was glad that the city of Panacea couldn't afford to mow this park on a regular basis. She liked its weedy, seedy ambiance.

There was a new sign standing among the weeds, impressive and expensive, marking the entrance to Panacea Mineral Springs Park. It was a monument to the governmental tendency to earmark plenty of money for capital expenditures and none for maintenance. Faye considered it a poetic place to bring a politician. She wondered how Cyril would like it.

Intrepid visitors who passed the fancy sign quickly found their cars jouncing over a rutted dirt road past aged brick and wooden pavilions on the brink of collapse. On her first visit to this park, Faye, being who she was, had hopped out of her car to see how old they were. She found that the pavilions were a century old and that they were never meant for picnickers; they were built to shelter invalids. Under each of the half-dozen roofs festered a stagnant pool of water, the remnants of a natural spring. These springs had lured the infirm here to dangle their weak legs into cold, healing waters.

At some point the water level had dropped or the springs had silted up, leaving nothing but murky holes—except for one. Walking over the grounds on that first visit, Faye had found a foot-wide hole where water bubbled out of the earth, still clear and still cold. The spring spilled into a creek skirting the park and, after passing through a culvert under Highway 98, flowed directly into the salt marshes buffering the little town of Panacea from the great Gulf of Mexico. Dipping her hand in the pure water, she finally understood why some fool had called the place Panacea, Greek for "cure all," a place-name that Faye considered as fate-tempting as calling a place Paradise or Shangri-La.

While Faye waited for Cyril, she sat happily at a picnic table and did nothing but just love the place. Even when he came into sight, she had to wait awhile for his white Lexus to bump slowly down the dirt driveway toward her. She hoped the potholes wouldn't harm Cyril's fancy car. When they had discussed this picnic, she knew he was thinking of a place more private and he'd been a good sport to go along with her warped sense of a good time. It was true that they had the small park to themselves, but the whine and swish of traffic on Highway 98 was everpresent. Faye's experiences with men had not given her a trusting soul. Yet here she was, playing with fire again. She welcomed the traffic noise and its constant reminder of nearby humanity, in case this date took a disastrous turn. Help was only a couple hundred feet away.

Would Cyril understand her affection for this park and its ruins? Would he be fascinated by the old mineral baths or repelled by the slime lining their walls? Would he be interested in the brick pavilion in the back that was sliding into the creek? Or would he be bored by the whole thing? Perhaps Faye was setting up too many tests for a first date, but she wasn't a woman with time to waste.

He unfolded his big frame from the driver's seat and flashed her an easy wave without checking his car for mud or scratches. Good. Then he reached in the passenger window and pulled out two Styrofoam food boxes.

Instead of "Hello," he said, "Barbecued ribs. Cole slaw—the good kind with lots of onions. Hushpuppies. And French-fried sweet potatoes. I hope you like it. It's what I always get when I'm in this neck of the woods."

Faye, who at the age of five had been labeled "Little Miss Standoffish" by her grandmother, heard herself say, "Anybody carrying food that good can come right over here and sit down by me."

The pine branches over their heads filtered out most of the sun and a sea breeze kicked up, taking the edge off the fact that both the temperature and the relative humidity had topped ninety. Faye was fairly comfortable, but Cyril was used to air conditioning. Suggesting an outdoor lunch in August was yet another test of Cyril's mettle.

After the initial food-related conversation—"Would you like salt and pepper?" "Is the tea sweet?"—ebbed, she said, "I'm glad you dressed for the weather. You would have died out here in a business suit."

Cyril glanced down at his madras shirt and tennis shorts and said, "The heat just keeps my sweet potatoes hot. People who can't adapt to the circumstances heaven throws their way don't get far in this world." He began to chuckle. "I'm having a vision of some of my esteemed fellow senators sitting at this table with us, keeling over one by one because they don't have sense enough to take off their suit coats and loosen their ties."

Faye lifted her tea and said, "A toast to your overheated colleagues," and Cyril lifted his. The Styrofoam gave an unsatisfying tap as the cups clicked, but they drank deeply anyway.

Faye said, "I can stand a powerful lot of heat if I have a good supply of iced tea."

Cyril nodded. "This is just the way I like it. Strong and sweet." After a sip, he added, "I bet that's how you like your men."

While his observation may have been accurate, Faye elected to sip her own tea without comment.

"I've got some aides looking into your claim to the Last Isles," Cyril said.

She had purposely avoided speaking of her legal problems. She would put Cyril through a gauntlet of tests before she was willing to date him; she would not base her decision on his ability to grant political favors. The idea of going out with him simply because of his clout had a whorish odor to it.

"What do your aides say?" she asked in a voice so studiedly casual that a bystander would have thought she had no more interest in regaining her family's lands than she did in daytime television.

"They think it's unlikely that we'll find evidence of property ownership so strong and so unequivocal that the courts will be willing to take the land back from a half-dozen owners—including the federal government—and give it to you."

Faye nibbled on her last hushpuppy and tried not to look crushed.

"But," Cyril said in a warm tone that made her feel a bit more hopeful, "race will continue to be a confounding issue in American politics for a couple more generations. If you're willing to live through the hoo-ha that will ensue when the press gets ahold of this...well, you know they'll love this story. A lone black woman fights the courts for her rights and loses to a bunch of cheating white men and a crooked judge then, seventy years later, her great-granddaughter demands justice. The government might give you some part of your land back just to shut the media up. It could work, Faye."

Not being someone whose private life could stand a media frenzy, Faye mumbled, "I'll think about it," and rose from her bench. Tossing her lunch trash into a bin, she ambled over to the one remaining clear-running spring, slipped off her sandals, and plunged her feet into the water. Cyril, passing his third test—or was it his fourth?—slid off his deck shoes and dipped his own bare feet.

They sat together, enjoying the contrast between their heat-addled heads and their icy-cool feet. Neither one spoke and it was okay. Faye figured that the ability to be companionably silent was important in a man and gave Cyril credit for passing a test she hadn't planned.

Why had her relationships with men been so uniformly abysmal? She liked men, even preferred their company to that of women, but her romances had always followed the same crash-and-burn trajectory.

In high school, she'd been a quiet, bookish girl who attracted exactly no male attention until, at sixteen, she suddenly and unexpectedly became pretty. Her grandmother had observed at the time that it was better to bloom late than never to bloom at all. In retrospect, Faye wasn't so sure Grandma knew what she was talking about.

Oh, it had been exciting, trying to decide whether she'd had more fun at the drive-in with Mark or the beach with Cary and worrying over whether Sammy knew she was also going out with Jon. Her sudden popularity with the boys did not equate to popularity among her female classmates, but Faye hardly noticed. She'd spent her childhood largely without friends, because God had seen fit to distribute racist ignorance evenhandedly. The white girls considered her black and shunned her accordingly, but the black girls, who twenty years before would have fawned over her creamy skin, rejected her as too white simply as a matter of black pride. Even from a distance of more than fifteen years, Faye couldn't blame her teenage self for flaunting every conquest in the other girls' faces.

Then, in May, it was over. The phone stopped ringing. No crowd of admirers waited at her locker after school. One day, instead of finding Sammy and Jon and Mark and Cary standing beside her locker, she found a circle of girls discussing their prom dates. The names Sammy and Jon and Mark and Cary were mentioned often and loudly.

Faye must have flinched as she stooped to twirl her combination lock. The hyenas smelled weakness and closed around her.

"Got a prom date, Faye?" asked a big-haired cheerleader. "Didn't think so. Wanna know why not?"

Being only a junior, Faye didn't rate an upper locker. Retrieving her books would have required kneeling before the predators and she refused to do it, so she turned and faced them.

"Going to the prom means having both sets of proud parents gush on about what a beautiful couple you make. It means having your picture made. Can you imagine anybody's parents being proud to have your picture on the mantel?"

Through her tears, Faye focused on the cheerleader's mouth and its vulgar ring of orangey-brown lipstick. It was spewing venom, but it was also speaking the truth. She had noticed that her dates were all white. Jon, who was more scholarly than the usual high school boy, had pronounced her looks exotic, while Sammy, who couldn't have been more average, had said she looked like Cleopatra.

She had known they were attracted to her because she was different. In that moment, she realized that none of the boys had ever introduced her to his mother. And none of them ever would.

Faye relived that moment for about the eighty-thousandth time, staring at her brown toes as the springwater washed over them. She looked over at Cyril, who was gazing at the creek running clear under its overhanging trees, and realized that she hadn't dated a white man since she was sixteen years old.

He saw her look at him and he said, "Did you know that the woods back there are full of springs and all of them feed this creek? Lord, I used to enjoy wading here, catching minnows and just generally having a redneck good time."

"You grew up around here?" she asked, knowing the answer.

"Yeah, until I was eleven." Something cast a shadow on his face. "That's when Mama and I went to Alabama and never came back. It was a brave thing she did, leaving Daddy, but she never quit being scared of him. Nobody could know where we were. She was adamant about that, even to the point of home-schooling me, and it worked. Daddy never found us."

"Did you have brothers or sisters?" Faye asked, oddly shamed that she knew this answer, too. All she had done was look at a few pictures in an old yearbook. Why did she feel like a voyeur?

"My older brother Cedrick stayed behind to finish high school. We heard he went to work in the oil fields. Mama did the right thing. Daddy was a mean man. I believe she saved our lives, but I still wish I knew where my brother was."

A breeze kicked up and spoiled the moment by riffling Cyril's hair back off his temples, revealing a fine white scar running along his hairline. Faye's heart gave a little skip at the thought of a damaged child making such good repair, not just of his psyche but of wounds to his body, although it argued a degree of vanity, of self-absorption that she found unseemly, particularly in a man.

To Faye, cosmetic surgery bordered on self-mutilation. She would never forget barging into the bathroom at her fiancé's house and surprising his mother, who was changing the bandages covering her recent nose job.

Embarrassed and nauseated, she had confessed her *faux pas* to her fiancé. "Isaiah, my roommate had her nose done and it wasn't anything like that. The surgeon worked from the inside and there were no scars at all."

Isaiah had stammered a moment before saying, "Well, Mama's a special case. She wanted him to narrow her nose and reduce the nostrils and—"

"And make her nose less African? More Caucasian?"

"I wouldn't put it that way." Isaiah hesitated. "See, Mama wants to be pretty and she thinks a few little scars are a small price to pay. Everybody's not lucky enough to look like you do."

Faye wished she'd been woman enough to break up with him on the spot, but she'd let the relationship rock on for another six months. Every time they went out in public, she watched for signs that he saw her as a light-skinned trophy who would be good for his career. They were all too visible. And when they were alone, she couldn't forget that this man thought his mama would be prettier with somebody else's nose.

A year after they broke up, she saw him at a nightclub with a sharp-featured trophy on his arm and telltale scars on his new nose. That was when she decided that it was time to move to Joyeuse full-time. Living among people was making her very tired.

So why was she sitting here next to this man fifteen years older than she was, a man she hardly knew? She'd been brought up to value family above all else, yet she had none. The loss of her mother and grandmother was an open wound. They would have wanted her to marry, to have children. She herself wanted a baby badly, probably more than she wanted a man. "You've got to go out to get asked out," Mama had always said.

Well, Mama, here I am, Faye offered, in the way of someone whose prayers were directed as much to her departed loved ones as they were to God.

She looked at Cyril sidewise. He was a nice-looking man, whatever his age—tall, rugged features, light tan, fine but still-thick hair without much gray. She catalogued his good qualities, most of which she had uncovered through her series of tests. He wasn't too snobbish to enjoy a picnic in a rundown park. His intellectual interest could be piqued by something as esoteric as the crumbling ruins of a third-rate resort. He was tough enough to withstand an August noon in Florida. He was capable of friendly silence. He revered his mother's memory. He liked barbecued ribs and good iced tea. And he seemed to like her.

"Sometime, we should revert to childhood and come back here to wade up the creek, just to see whether all those springs are still there," she said.

"Yeah," he said. "But first, let's do something more grown-up. Let me take you to dinner at The Pirate's Lair. How about Thursday?"

"I'll meet you there at eight o'clock," Faye said with a smile she didn't have to force. She could just hear her mama saying, "You're so pretty, Faye, when you remember to smile."

He rose and helped her to her feet. Older men had their good points. They remembered little courtesies that were unnecessary but pleasant. As if reading her mind, he opened her car door for her and extended a hand to help her in.

Faye used her car as a home away from home when she was ashore, and she was embarrassed for him to see its accumulation of junk. Predictably, the stack of photocopies she'd just made at the library reached its limit of stability as Cyril walked away, and the whole pile slumped over onto the passenger-side floorboard, leaving a single sheet on the seat.

Abby's face, looking coyly over one shoulder for all eternity, stared up at Faye as if to remind her that everyone turned to dust sooner or later. She might as well gather some good times, some friends, a lover, a family, something worthwhile to occupy her mind until the dust called her home.

Cyril shouldn't have been surprised to find Alice sitting at his breakfast table in his kitchen. The woman knew no boundaries, and he supposed that was a good thing in a campaign manager. She was a superlative predictor of human behavior and that was a campaign manager's single most important quality. She could predict how any given event would sway the voting populace and, apparently, she could also predict that, after two hours outdoors in August and an hour in the car driving back to Tallahassee, he would go home for a shower before putting in a late night at the office. The key question was how she knew that he'd been sitting outside sweating, when he'd been doing it in a miniscule town's deserted park, many miles away.

On cue, Alice said, "There are a negligible number of voters in the big city of Panacea, and they're all very, very loyal to you. Why waste your time there?"

Good old, single-minded Alice. No thought, no action, no breath was to be taken without considering its effect on the next campaign. And this time she was looking toward the United States House of Representatives. If Alice lacked a sense of humor before, she was positively funereal now.

"I felt like taking a drive. I think better behind the wheel."

"Do you think better in the company of a woman who could, with a single inopportune photograph, ruin everything? Being seen with Faye Longchamp could sink your campaign."

"Do you ferret out the names of all my dates?"

Alice gave him her patented you-idiot look. "Of course. And their addresses and phone numbers. But Faye doesn't seem to have those things. My investigator—"

"The one you hired to tail me, so you can make sure I date 'appropriate' women? Alice, that's sick."

Alice, who knew no shame, kept talking. "My investigator tried to follow her home, but it didn't occur to him that he might need a boat, so he had to watch her ride off into the Gulf without him."

Cyril opened his refrigerator and pulled out a beer. He didn't offer one to Alice. His rude gesture would have carried more weight, but for the fact that Alice didn't drink. "So she outmaneuvered your private eye. Big deal. You hire cheap help," he said, swigging a tremendous gulp of brew. Maybe if he made this bottle of hop juice look as completely satisfying as the beer commercials did, Alice would learn to drink and lighten up a little. "Why don't you go ahead and say it out loud? Why don't you want me to date Faye?"

"Come on, Cyril. It's hasn't been forty years since the Civil Rights Act passed. The bad old days aren't that long gone. Those people are not all dead yet. They're still out there and they still vote. You cannot date a woman of color and be elected. Not in Florida and not in most states in the union."

He had known from the outset that Faye was the kind of woman who would cause Alice to blanch. Actually, Alice herself would object to neither Faye's character nor her skin color, but she wouldn't hesitate to point out that he had constituents who would. Well, bullshit. A lot of his constituents *were* black, thanks to Douglass Everett's efforts. And another large fraction of his voters wouldn't bat an eye when their Congressman was sworn in with a woman of color on his arm.

"You love it when I'm seen with Douglass Everett. How is Faye different?"

"A black friend makes you look worldly and broadminded. A black girlfriend—" Alice responded to his impatient gesture, saying, "All right, a biracial girlfriend, then. It's immaterial. An inappropriate girlfriend—whether she be the wrong color or too young or married or an ex-convict—makes you look like a man who thinks with his penis."

Cyril didn't call her a racist, because he didn't think she was one. Alice judged people by only one criterion: whether they were useful or detrimental to the campaign she was currently masterminding. And she was probably right. Faye would not be an asset in an election. A relationship with her would cost him votes but, in his judgment, not enough votes to lose. And, if that relationship should evolve into something more, Faye had the beauty, the brains and, yes, the cunning, to be the toast of Washington.

Alice could natter on about this issue until the cows came home, and she was working on it, but Cyril wasn't listening. He knew she was too cheap to have him tailed indefinitely. Even if she did, he'd dodged her private eyes before. He refused to give up his dreams of electoral glory and he refused to give up a chance with the first woman he'd ever met who didn't make him impatient merely by the way she shifted her hips in her chair. When the voters of Florida saw Faye in a sweeping ballgown at the next presidential inauguration, they would be glad they sent Cyril and his inappropriate woman to Congress.

Faye's mind was chasing its tail as she sat down to supper with Joe. She'd had a day that left her with plenty to think about. Liz and Wally had been deliberately vague about Joe's trouble with the Fish and Game agent that morning. Joe himself wouldn't talk to her about it at all. And her library trip confirmed that she had indeed found Abby Williford's remains, but the question of who killed her was still wide open.

Her lunch with Cyril would also require some thought. Dating anyone seriously would, sooner or later, mean divulging the secret of where she lived, and she balked at going down that road. But the alternative was to spend her life alone. Was that what she wanted?

To clear her thoughts of that knotty question, she had spent the rest of the afternoon in her map room, a converted butler's pantry in Joyeuse's aboveground basement. It was one of her favorite spots. The thick tabby walls held out the heat and the casement windows funneled every breeze inside. Its walls were covered with built-in cabinets, drawers, and countertops designed as a staging area for serving tremendous numbers of partygoers in the ballroom overhead.

In this creaky old cabinetry, Faye stored maps of the area surrounding Joyeuse and the Last Isles. She had aerial photographs and topographic maps dating back to the 1940s. She even had copies of hand-drawn sketches from the latter half of the 19th century, but she had nothing that showed how Last Isle had looked before the 1856 hurricane blew it apart and washed away the Turkey Foot Hotel.

Faye adored poring over the raggedy old documents. They always gave her fresh ideas of where to go pothunting, but they never unveiled their big secret. Where did her great-great-grandfather build his hotel? If she knew that, maybe she could get his land back. Faye played with her maps until the scent of fish frying atop Joe's camp stove called her to supper.

Joe's plate was resting untouched in his lap. It was heaped with a working man's portion of food but, being well brought up, he was waiting for her to sit down before he lifted his fork. Sitting on a stump while he waited, he studied Joyeuse's back façade. She stood beside him for a minute, enjoying the sight of it. The house was impressive from any angle but the rear view, shaded by trees and protected by porches on two stories, had a homey feel. The dozens of wooden jalousies sheltering those porches added an air of privacy, even secrecy.

"How'd you come to own Joyeuse?" Joe asked, digging into his butterbeans as soon as her behind hit the porch step.

It was a reasonable question. She was surprised Joe hadn't asked it before. "My grandmother said that her grandmother was a quadroon slave girl named Cally and that Cally was the master's common-law wife. Remember, this is just family talk. I can't prove much of anything that happened in the 1800s. The master died young and, after the war, Cally raised their daughter and managed Joyeuse all by herself. Grandma said that Cally's daughter, Miss Courtney Stanton, was a great beauty with dark hair and blue eyes and dead-white skin, and that Cally sent her off to pass for white at a finishing school up north."

Joe chewed for a while, then said, "Did the master have any other kids?"

"Just Courtney."

"So if she went up north to live with white people, then how'd Joyeuse pass from Cally all the way down to you?"

Faye reminded herself never to underestimate Joe's deductive powers. Fishers and hunters aren't verbose people, but every day they outwit wild animals with millions of years of evolution on their side. "Courtney came home, duly educated, but adamant that she'd rather be who she was than sip tea with a bunch of vain, useless women. She married a field hand and they ran Joyeuse together until he died in the 1918 flu epidemic. With my grandmother's help, she carried on without him another thirty years, but they say she really died that day in 1934 when the judge took the Last Isles away from her."

"Judging from the size of those trees out back, this land ain't been farmed since then."

"My grandmother said the land was just worn out. When her mother died, she and Mama moved to Tallahassee and, being Cally's and Courtney's blood, they did just fine. Grandma was a secretary and Mama was a nurse, and we never had any extra money, but we never did without."

"Your father and grandfather—"

Faye smiled down at her plate and chewed a minute. Once Joe started asking questions, he didn't stop.

"Daddy died in Vietnam. My grandfather just left."

Faye picked at her food silently and Joe stopped asking questions. Whether through death or abandonment, the men in her family had only stayed long enough to give their women a single child, then they left. Her mother had never hidden her craving for more children. Faye tried to imagine living as a family with a man who didn't leave. How would she know when to stop having children? Sometimes her own baby-hunger was so bad she thought only menopause would end it.

"You come from a long line of strong lonely women, Faye. No wonder you...."

"No wonder, what?"

"Nothing. Just nothing."

Joe stared at the old house, though there was hardly enough light to see it. His eyes narrowed and his lips moved for quite a while. Finally, though Faye was still mad at him for his "strong, lonely women" comment, she couldn't stand it any longer.

"What on earth are you doing?" she snapped.

"I'm not good at arithmetic. I'm trying to figure out how much of your blood is white and how much is black."

"Cally's mother was mulatto. Her father was white and so was her so-called husband. That makes Great-grandmother Courtney almost all white. All my other great-grandparents were black, as far as I know. That makes me about one-eighth Caucasian."

"You look whiter than that, Faye."

"Probably my father had some mixed ancestry, too. And my grandfather. Who knows? And who cares? I can't reliably trace my ancestry back four measly generations and I'm an archaeologist. I live off the past. I have to think that it doesn't really matter."

Joe leaned toward her with a conspiratorial look. "Faye. I'm not a hundred percent Creek."

Touched by Joe's confidence, she stifled her amusement at his heart-baring revelation. Joe Wolf Mantooth's eyes were as green as the clear Gulf waters lapping at the shores of what remained of Last Isle.

Faye worked outdoors. She ate outdoors, she showered outdoors, she brushed her teeth outdoors, but she slept indoors. She loved her bedroom. Looking at its walls, festooned with painted wisteria, made her happy and ready for sleep. It was a safe place to commune with a dead woman.

Faye waved a torch in the face of her guilt, driving it back into a corner. Abby was dead, she reminded herself. Abby's father was dead, and her killer was long gone or reformed, for a forty-year crime wave would have been noticeable in this sleepy part of the world. It would be an injustice for Faye to lose everything tilting at an idealistic windmill. Even if her lance struck the mark, whom would it benefit?

Though she had renewed her resolve to keep secret her discovery of Abby's body, she still suffered a curious fascination with the girl's fate. It was likely that clues remained in the grave. She hadn't found Abby's silver necklace. She hadn't even found the other earring. Who knew what else might remain?

Tomorrow, on the off chance a physical clue had survived years and years in the most hostile of environments, she would finish exhuming Abby's bones. The idea would upset Joe, so she wouldn't tell him her plans. Once she'd finished the ghoulish task and neatly reburied the corpse, she would confess her deed. Joe would come back with his ceremonial fire and herbs and tobacco, but he would be spared the grisly details of what she had done.

Adrenaline pumping, she was ready to dig right away, but she had to wait for daylight. She dug through her photocopied newspaper articles and yearbook pages instead. They yielded nothing. Where else could she look? She wasn't a detective, just a black-market archaeologist; she delved into the lives of the long-ago dead and Abby had been gone a mere forty years.

The high-school yearbook gave her a handy list of people who had known Abby at the time of her death. The thought of cold-calling strangers to discuss murder made her introverted soul shiver, but perhaps it wouldn't be necessary.

Douglass Everett would talk to her about Abby. The nature of their business relationship gave them a camaraderie beyond the ordinary shallow salesperson/client link. Their every transaction breached one law or another, but they took the risk, time and again, out of passion for the artifacts. Shared risk fosters trust. Yes, Douglass would tell her what he knew about Abby.

Having decided to speak with Douglass, she didn't want to think about Abby any more, and she didn't want to think about Cyril and, God, she didn't want to think about money. She crawled into her bed, a simple but exquisitely wrought antique convent piece bought in Saint Augustine by her grandmother when the sisters' dwindling numbers forced them to divest themselves of excess earthly possessions. God only knew how many of them had died in Faye's bed. It was a good place to be haunted.

She thought of Sam and Krista. They'd been gone a week. What in the world was she thinking of, sleeping alone in this big empty house when there was a killer on the loose? And was Joe safe from the man who'd tried to lure him away that very morning?

Something, probably a squirrel, scampered over her roof. The house creaked around her, responding to the falling temperature.

Faye couldn't stand it any more. She gathered the journal, her pillow, her sleeping bag, and the lantern and hurried outside. With the lantern's help, she found her way down the lightly worn path to Joe's shelter.

Joe wasn't asleep. He was sitting on the ground watching the dying embers of his campfire hiss and collapse. He didn't ask her why she'd come, but fear made her babble.

"I got to thinking about the murders and all, and I got scared. Can I just put my sleeping bag right here on the other side of your fire?"

Joe nodded.

"And look what I brought. I found this old journal hidden in the cupola and the stories are fascinating. Can I read some of them to you?"

Joe smiled and said, "Yeah."

Faye knew that a killer with a gun could take them both out as easily as he had murdered Sam and Krista. There was no safety in numbers—not really. Still she felt safer here with Joe.

She opened the journal and carefully slid its ribbon bookmark from between the sheets. Turning the page, she was surprised to find that William Whitehall had put the journal aside without finishing his story. Someone else, with finer and more delicate penmanship, was reaching out to her across time.

William Whitehall had been dead more than a century when she began reading his journal. He was still dead, yet the fact that he had no more to say made her want to mourn him. First, though, she would see what his daughter had to say.

Joe watched Faye make herself comfortable. He was happy to watch over her tonight, just as he had every night since her friends had been killed. Tonight, though, she'd be in plain sight and his job would be easier.

◇

Excerpt from the journal of Mariah Whitehall Lafourche, 27 April, 1824

I should not have given my son LaFourche's name and I should not have assumed it myself. I most assuredly should never have created him a noble French father in exile from the post-Revolution Terror. I have made him arrogant.

My deepest regret is a sin of omission. My dear mother died when my son Andrew was but three. Neither I nor my father, also now departed, ever told Andrew of her Creek ancestry. It is incredible to me now, but I was ashamed of my mixed blood just as I was ashamed of Andrew's bastardy. Now I am too much the coward to remedy my error. I fear nothing so much as losing my son's love.

My pride has been my undoing, and my son's. I can accept that. Our lives are our own to ruin. I cannot accept the misery of others.

My son has begun to buy people. People! He bought four families of Africans to help with this year's planting. With their labor and God's beneficence in the form of good weather (How can He smile on such sin?), the harvest was bountiful. With the profits, Andrew plans to enslave more souls here on Catspaw Island. I mean, of course, on Joyeuse. Andrew felt the name given the island by the old settlers was coarse, but anything French is most elegant, so he named his plantation and his house—with all the luxurious furbelows he is forcing his people to add to our old dwelling—after joy. Now he has the effrontery to make it a place of misery.

After weeks of argument over this issue, this morning I tried a different tack. I argued business with him. How could slave labor be so much more profitable than that of free workers? Both have the same needs for shelter, food, and clothing. Why not pay the workers to cover their own needs and avoid the cost of caring for them himself, while saving a significant purchase price?

My only child gave me a soulless smile and reminded me that there were profits to be made from increase. "Increase?" I asked in my ignorance. When he explained himself, I knew that I had lost him forever. By increase, he meant the increase in value of his holdings generated by the birth of slave children. He sees no wrong in using human beings as breeding stock.

After this conversation, I retired to my sleeping room and I have not come out since.

Excerpt from the journal of Mariah Whitehall Lafourche, 3 August, 1829

I am comfortably settled in my own home and my son is fit to be tied, but I could live no longer in a house built by prisoners and paid for by the profits earned on their labor. When I told Andrew that I wished to build a small cabin in the woods behind the kitchen, his response was kindly, even condescending. "And how will you do that? There is no one on the island to build it but the slaves. You may as well live in the Big House with me."

I said I could pay them for their efforts. Andrew's condescension dissolved into outright mockery. He laughed at me, saying, "You don't own a thing in this world, Mother."

The most galling thing is that he is right. The law does not recognize a woman's right to own property. My father survived his last year by sheer obstinacy, determined to live until Andrew was of legal age. He managed to do so. He died believing that he had passed responsibility for my welfare to the one man he trusted with the job. The island, the crops, God help us, even the slaves, belong to Andrew. I am only his female dependent.

I removed a comb from my hair, and another, and another until my hair fell loose. I cupped my two hands together and held them out to him. The tortoiseshell ornaments glowed golden from inside. "Are these yours? And my jewelry? You can have that, too. Does nothing really belong to me?"

Andrew's face flushed. "Of course, your personal items are your own. Do what you like with them. Build a house. Build a hotel. I don't care."

So I did. I built a house, that is, not a hotel. I paid the workers with my mother's silver flatware, one fork at a time, until I saw that I had something they needed far more. Since May, I have paid them in learning. On Sundays, I sit on a slave cabin's porch. Anyone who comes to me can learn their letters. Some are quite bright; I think they will be reading by spring.

I am touched by their gratitude. They bring me gifts that I try not to accept. I emphasize that I *am paying* them *for their labor, but still they bring me things—fresh corn, hand-whittled figurines, aprons—that cost them time and goods I know they can scarcely spare.*

My favorite gift rests on my desk even now, beside my hand as I write. It is a stone spearhead longer than the palm of my hand. I pulled many a warrior's long-lost weapon from the soil during a childhood spent running wanton through the woods. This is like none I have seen. It is far larger. Its shape is more oval than the familiar three-cornered one and its coloring lacks the typical reddish sheen. My generous friend got it from a slave who found it while fishing on the far end of Last Isle. He says there are many such treasures to be found along the channel that last year's storm cut through the island. He also described a clearing west of the channel where, after a heavy rain, pottery with curious ornamentation surfaces. The spot can be found by a landmark thirty paces west of the channel, an old cistern cut into the highest ground on the island. The cistern, too, is said to be filled with curiosities. Perhaps I shall go there and see for myself. It has been a long while since I got myself thoroughly covered with mud for no practical purpose.

Chapter 15

It was Wednesday morning. Only a little more than half the work week lay ahead, and Kelly Bergdoll was glad.

Kelly had found that answering phone calls from people whose data didn't say what they wished it said was the hardest part of running the Florida Department of Law Enforcement's forensics lab. Her life had gotten considerably harder when Sheriff Mike McKenzie discovered that she came to work very, very early.

Kelly came to work very, very early so that she could accomplish something before her coworkers came in anxious to share the joke-of-the-day and, certainly, before her clients started bugging her.

Beep. On schedule. It was Sheriff Mike dialing in to her personal line, and damn the receptionist who let him bully that sensitive information out of her.

"Why is the fingerprint report blank?" he asked in lieu of saying hello.

"Because, Sheriff, no identifiable fingerprints were found, except those discussed in Appendix B."

"On the whole island?"

Kelly's voice rose a semi-tone. "The island is the *problem*. It's a huge murder site, compared to the usual apartment or alleyway. Where were the technicians going to lift the prints? Off the sand?"

"What about the storage shed?"

"The shed is thoroughly discussed in our report. As I said, check Appendix B. There were loads of prints, all of them traceable to the archaeology team, and I understand that none of them are suspects. We think the killer may have helped himself to the rubber gloves stored in the shed. Or maybe he brought his own." That was Kelly's personal theory. Criminals, on the whole, tended to be dumb and lazy, but this guy seemed to be plenty smart enough to take the negligible trouble of sticking a pair of surgical gloves in his pocket before he set out to kill.

"What about the bodies? We did that thing where you put them in a tent and fumed them."

"Glue fuming."

"Yeah, I haven't seen the glue fuming report yet."

Kelly waited a heartbeat before replying to prepare herself for the explosion. "The results are still preliminary, but—"

"But they're negative." The explosion didn't come. Sheriff Mike chose sarcasm for this rejoinder. "It was time-consuming and expensive. It put those poor kids' bodies through another round of disrespectful poking and prodding. Of course, it didn't work. I don't think you ever thought it would."

Pushed to the wall, Kelly said, "No, I didn't. The odds were low. The bodies were damp, they'd been buried, it's damn near impossible to get a print in those conditions. But we had to try."

Finally, she had said something the crotchety old man could understand.

"Yeah," he said. "We had to try. Thank you for trying."

Then Kelly remembered that she liked Sheriff Mike. She wished he were in the room, so she could give him a comforting pat on the arm, but she just said, "At least we have the bullets. Maybe they'll give us something we can use."

Sheriff Mike grunted and hung up.

Skimming across calm dawn-blessed waters in her battered skiff, Faye could forget her every trouble, but she didn't. Not this morning. She scanned the horizon constantly, because no one must see her today. She had an appointment with the remains of Abby Williford.

The sun had hauled itself above the horizon when Faye beached her skiff and unpacked her gear. Rain and wind had returned the sand to its untouched state and the tide was higher than it had been when she discovered Abby, but Faye's instincts rarely failed her. She found Abby's grave within ten minutes of beginning her search. Unfortunately, Abby was no longer there.

The smell of chlorine bleach was more nauseating than the grave had been when it was merely a pit of dried bones. The porous sand was saturated with it. Someone had pulled Abby out of the ground and made sure that no identifiable biological residue would remain.

Even Clorox couldn't keep a real archaeologist from digging when there was something she wanted to find. Faye donned a pair of sunglasses to protect her eyes. She covered her mouth and nose with the toilet tissue she carried with her everywhere, wrapping it around her head again and again to hold the makeshift mask in place. Her hands were already well-protected, since she always dug in rubber gloves.

In this outlandish getup, she probed further into Abby's violated resting place. The grave had been fairly shallow, so it didn't take her long to penetrate the acrid sand and reach soil that hadn't been touched recently, not by her and not by the bleach-wielding grave robber.

Faye was a finder, the sanctimonious child who found money dropped in grocery stores and handed it over to the lost-and-found department. This time, the finder hit pay dirt in a very real way, uncovering two disfigured lumps that looked vaguely unnatural.

Rinsing them gently, she found a heavily tarnished clump of metal that was barely recognizable as a medium-weight silver chain—surely it was Abby's silver necklace, just as the papers had reported in 1964. There was no time to gloat over this victory, because she wouldn't rest until she knew what the other lump of dirt contained.

It seemed big to be the missing earring. What else could have lain under Abby since she was buried, all those years ago? Perhaps her assailant had dropped something in the hole as he was digging. Or perhaps—well, there was no way to know until she cleaned the thing.

Layers of sand and gunk washed away, but a more thorough cleaning would have to wait until she got home. A good deal of corrosion remained, but the object's identity could be discerned. It was a pocket watch. Its catch was inoperable but Faye burned to open the case. The answer to Abby's mystery might lie inside.

Her impatience would not allow her to treat this artifact with due care. She took a tiny screwdriver, drove it between the watch and its cover, and wrenched the cover off. Picking up the pieces, she found that the inside of the watch was remarkably well-preserved. Much of the inscription was legible.

"D_ac_n Je__bo_m Ev__ett" had been presented this watch by the "B__s_d _ss___nc_ A_E C_u__h". The number "25" was still legible beneath the inscription. Filling in the missing blanks was easy. It was no big trick to discern that the watch had been presented by the Blessed Assurance AME Church for twenty-five years of service as a deacon and that the recipient was Jereboam Everett. These facts were easy to determine but hard to swallow.

Faye sat on the sand and stretched her legs out in front of her. She was having trouble making sense of what she held in her hands. She knew that old Jeb Everett died before his son Douglass finished high school in June of 1964. One would have expected his only child to be in possession of the watch by the time Abby disappeared in July. How did Douglass' watch get into Abby's grave?

The primeval, neck-crawling certainty that someone was watching settled over Faye. She wished for the binoculars she'd left behind in Joyeuse's cupola when the malfunctioning trapdoor had forced her to make a rooftop escape. Could someone with binoculars have lurked on one of the nearby islets and watched her dig up the old bones? Or might someone have been watching from a boat, maybe even the boat that had startled her and Joe into leaving Abby behind?

She'd been too obsessed with the empty grave to wonder why Abby's bones had gone missing after all these years. Why? Nothing had changed...except that Faye had found her. And, apparently, somebody knew it.

Faye left Abby's islet behind and radioed Wally's. It was her habit to call or radio the marina to check her messages about mid-morning every day. Sometimes Wally was awake by then. When he wasn't, Liz took a break from slinging hash and answered for him. Today, Faye got Wally. His hungover voice crackling over the airwaves did nothing to calm her nerves.

"Your rich friend, Douglass Everett, left an urgent message. He wants you to meet him at his beach house, right away. Watch yourself, Faye. He may be loaded, but he's married."

"Your vulgarity never ceases to amaze me, Wally. Out," Faye said, turning her radio off as if it, too, had offended her.

What could Douglass possibly want? He'd just bought her entire inventory and he knew she hadn't had time to dig up anything new. She fetched the watch from the pocket of her shorts and gripped it hard. Was it Douglass who killed Abby and desecrated her grave? And if he did do those things, and if he knew Faye knew about Abby, then was he calling her to his house to kill her, too?

That made no sense. Calling Wally to summon a prospective murder victim to his house, knowing that Wally was liable to blast the request over radio frequencies accessible to anyone, made no sense at all.

Something inside Faye rebelled at all the evidence. The Douglass she knew was not a murderer. He was her friend. The morning's turn of events meant that Abby's murderer was back in the area. She should notify the sheriff about what she'd found. But she couldn't throw a heavy pall of suspicion over a friend without allowing him to defend himself.

She wheeled her skiff westward and headed for Douglass' beach house.

Douglass paced the floor, clenching bad news in his hand. He had known that Faye needed money, but this was serious. He'd do all he could to help her, but his cash reserves were low. He couldn't even tell his wife where all their money went. Being no fool, she had long ago observed that their income and their outgo did not match, even given their fabulous lifestyle. She had reached the conclusion that he was supporting one or more mistresses and he had never told her that her suspicions were unfounded. The truth was so much worse.

Faye tied up to Douglass' spiffy dock, crossed the sprawling deck, and entered the living room where Douglass stood at a glass wall, gazing at the Gulf. Something was clenched in his left hand and there was a tall drink in his right hand. He gestured at the drink waiting for her at the wet bar. It was far stronger than sherry.

He greeted her with a blunt, "Are you crazy?" holding out the object in his left hand for her to see and explain.

It was a Clovis point. Faye didn't grasp his intent, saying, "You told me you weren't buying anything but slave artifacts."

"I bought this to protect you. I bought everything the man had, just to protect you. If the law gets wind that you've been robbing a site that's this old—spear points, mastodon bones, and all—they'll put you under the jail."

"I don't understand," she said, taking the point from his hand and examining it, muttering aloud about the kind of stone, its place of origin, the distinctive flutings, its probable age.

She looked up to find Douglass watching her with keen, assessing eyes.

"You've really never seen it before," he said.

"Why would you think that I had? I've never sold you anything pre-Columbian. Nothing in your museum is anywhere near this old."

"This is why," Douglass said, reaching into his shirt pocket and pulling out a tortoiseshell comb. It was smaller and flatter than the two combs she'd tried to sell him, but it was carved in the same lacy pattern.

Faye took it and cradled it in her hand. "Mariah would have worn it in back, to hold the hair too short to pin up. The other two combs were side combs. They would have held her hair out of her face."

"Who the hell's Mariah?"

Faye shook her head. "Never mind. Who sold you these things and where did they come from?"

"I don't think he knows where they came from. He was just an imbecile somebody hired to fence their goods for them, because it would be damn dangerous to be caught with all this stuff."

"All what stuff?"

He twirled the combination lock on a closet-sized safe hidden behind the wet bar. "I told you. I bought the man's entire inventory to get it out of circulation before someone else besides me connected it to you."

"I can't let you do that."

"You have no choice," he said, swinging the safe door open. "I've already done it and there's no safe way to get rid of it now."

They perused the things Douglass had bought and Faye saw his point. From the safe, he retrieved one fluted stone point after another. Mixed in among a number of much newer artifacts was a beveled ivory foreshaft, part of a composite spear point made from the tusk of a mammoth. And perhaps most significantly, there was a tortoise carapace with a Clovis spearhead protruding from its surface. A stone artifact in a datable context. Faye was thrilled, then the anger penetrated everything. These items might have taken proof of human occupation in Florida back thousands of years, if they'd been documented in context. As it was, they were a pile of really cool junk.

"You could give it to a museum and take a tax deduction."

"Fat lot of good a tax deduction would do me when they find out where this stuff came from. They'll put *me* under the jail."

"With me."

"Yes, with you."

It seemed a fitting moment to broach another issue that might well land them both in jail. She pulled the watch from her pocket.

"Tell me about Abby Williford."

Faye had never seen a black man's skin turn the color of ash.

"You've found her, after all this time," he whispered.

Faye noticed that he didn't ask where Abby had been all these years. She waited.

"I was a sharecropper's only son, his only child," Douglass said. He paused to drain the last of his drink. "My father farmed all his life for Irvin Williford. We lived in a house not a quarter-mile from the house where he raised Abby after her mother died." He retrieved a fistful of change from his pocket and worked the coins around in his hands like worry beads.

"It was a strange world," he went on, still clicking the coins. "In town, Abby and I couldn't swim in the same pool or drink from the same fountain. But at home, we played like brother and sister and nobody batted an eye. She taught me to ride a horse and how to swim. I hauled her home from the swimming hole the day she slipped off the swinging rope and broke her arm. When her father got me admitted to the white high school, Abby shadowed me for weeks, protecting me from her buffoonish classmates. I would have dropped out without her support. I will never stop missing Abby."

"What do you know about her disappearance? Oh, let's not mince words. What do you know about her death?"

Douglass answered without a moment's reflection. "I didn't do it, but a lot of people thought I did. Her father protected me."

Faye raised an eyebrow.

"He'd known me all my life and he knew I would never hurt Abby. He gave me an alibi. Nobody believed him, but when the victim's father is a rich, upstanding member of the community, nobody is inclined to argue with him, either. He was a good, fine man."

"Who did kill her?"

"Let her rest. She has no family to be glad you found her. Her friends have forgotten her. You stand to lose a lot if people know you've been digging around the Last Isles. Leave her where she is and protect yourself, Faye."

Faye almost believed him. After all, he had believed her about the Clovis artifacts.

The more she thought about those artifacts, the madder she got. There was nothing she could do for Abby. If Douglass was guilty, then he'd have to save his own soul. A Clovis habitation site—if that was where the artifacts had come from—was different. Such a site would be irreplaceable, but it was still possible that what was left of it could be saved if it could be found.

"I've got to get out of here," she mumbled.

"Can I have my father's watch?"

"I think I'll keep it for now," Faye said, and slammed the door shut behind her.

Running down Douglass' dock, Faye felt she couldn't get to her boat fast enough. Anyone watching her skim across the water in her mullet skiff would be astonished by how fast the ugly little boat could go. Faye enjoyed the hypnotic *slam*,

slam, slam of its hull crashing into one wave after another. They were only low swells, hardly ripples, but riding roughshod over her obstacles suited Faye's mood. She was maddeningly, blindingly, angry.

This was personal.

Somebody was trespassing on land that belonged to her by whatever definition she chose. It was hers by inheritance, if one ignored the thievery that took it from her great-grandmother. Even if she acknowledged that she had lost sole legal title to the land forever, it was still hers as a citizen of the United States, a country willing to purchase and maintain national seashores and wildlife refuges for the sheer beauty of them.

Sure, she'd skirted the laws protecting public lands to retrieve things she considered her family's buried heirlooms, but she'd done no great harm, not to the islands themselves and not to the archaeological record. She had dug up nothing of great intrinsic cultural value. She had seen to it that her most interesting finds were housed in a museum. And she had documented her every step in field notebooks, just in case she was wrong about a site's importance.

No, she had broken the letter of the law and the archaeologist's code, but she had preserved their intent, and she was hopping mad that someone else was raping the past.

On her skiff, Faye kept navigational charts, current topographic maps, and copies of the oldest topographic maps she could find, all stored in a watertight cooler, since nothing stayed reliably dry in a boat so small. She killed the motor and dried off a portion of the deck big enough to spread out her maps.

In her journal, Mariah had described a Clovis point brought to her by a grateful slave—maybe the very point Faye had found hidden in the cupola at Joyeuse—and she had described a cistern that marked the spot where it was found. Mariah had said the cistern was on the far end of Last Isle, presumably meaning the end farthest from Joyeuse. She had also said that the artifacts were found along a trench cut through the island by a hurricane.

Faye compared her copy of the topographical map printed by the United States Geological Survey in 1940 to a current one, pinpointing on the new map the location of the westernmost island pass in 1940. What were the odds that Mariah's landmark still survived? The map in Faye's hands depicted changes in elevation as small as five feet. She prayed that the old pit hadn't silted up completely, that there was at least five feet of topographic relief remaining in 1940.

And there was. The westernmost Last Isle was named "Water Island," probably a reference to the cistern dug so long ago. A small depression so nearly circular that Faye wondered why she'd never noticed it before decorated the east end of Water Island. It was visible on both maps.

She cranked the boat and pointed it southwest. The waves slapped the hull of her boat with even more jarring force, because now Faye had a destination and she needed to get there fast.

Chapter 16

Faye beached her skiff and struggled through the dunes of soft sand that kept Water Island from washing away with every wave. They were dazzling white in the noonday sun. Beyond the dunes, she saw the treetops of a small grove of sizeable live oaks and was encouraged. Their presence suggested that this spot of ground had poked out of the water for decades, possibly long enough to have been Mariah's high ground. Perhaps Mariah had made good on her ambition to come here and dig for curiosities. She would have worn her oldest clothes although, ever a lady, Mariah never would have allowed herself to be seen with her hair hanging loose. In the excitement and exertion of her amateur archaeological dig, however, she might not have noticed when a tiny comb dropped out of the hair at the nape of her neck.

Faye crested the dunes that Mariah might once have crossed and looked over a shallow lagoon separating them from the main part of the island. The destruction there sucked the breath out of her lungs. Litter-strewn pits dotted a clearing that was at least an acre in extent. In the center of the clearing, crude dikes and drainage ditches kept the old cistern dry and easy to loot.

Faye slogged across the narrow lagoon and picked up a good-sized chunk of pottery incised with lines and dots. It was of the type made by the Fort Walton culture in late pre-Columbian times. If she remembered right, artifacts found on some barrier islands in the Panhandle were as old as eighteen hundred years, long before the appearance of the Fort Walton culture, so the dates were plausible. But Fort Walton sites were typically pretty far inland. Did they live here on the islands too, or did this shattered pot belong to a member of another culture, someone who traded with the Fort Walton people for it?

She tossed the sherd to the ground. The artifacts, the soil, the strata of this site were completely churned, robbed of any useful information. She would never know how the Fort Walton pot got there.

The cistern's slopes had been chewed up by idiots armed with shovels, and the land around it was littered with sherds that were evidently too plain or too broken-up to bring a good price.

Faye guessed that this cistern had served as somebody's trash pit for many a day.

Here and there were pieces of bone. Outside of a laboratory, it was impossible to tell whether they had supported human or animal bodies, but a sloppy pile of SCUBA gear resting beside a crate of butchered mastodon bones, uniface stone tools, fluted stone points—virtually the entire Clovis tool kit—told her that the biggest tragedy lay beneath the water. It was the only place artifacts of that age *could* be. In the twelve thousand years since they were made, Florida had become a wetter place and the sea had crept in to inundate evidence of its coastal cultures.

But even the sea couldn't hide everything, not forever. Fishermen still found stone tools with distinctive Clovis fluting atop sandbars, their unchanged stone faces contrasting sharply with the mutable sand. And divers found them lying on the Gulf floor, their slender points aping roadsigns that might direct their finder to someplace yet unknown. Perhaps they pointed back to their source, the very spot where their makers lived, ate, slept.

Paleolithic occupation sites were notoriously hard to find, since humans in that era had lived biodegradable lives, leaving behind almost nothing but their stone tools and the bones of their prey. They even burned their own bones, leaving nearly nothing of themselves for their descendants to find.

Finding artifacts in such quantity and variety suggested that an occupation site was close enough to taste and smell. It might lie under the silty sediments of the Gulf. It might even lie underneath her feet. The island she stood on was thousands of years younger than the looted artifacts in the crate.

Maybe there was a drowned river bed beneath the silent, sunlit waters surrounding the island. Clovis people would have preferred to live on a bluff above such a river. Perhaps their home had been overtaken by water, then by sediments, waiting for the hurricane that peeled away a slice of the island and left the ancient site exposed to looting by anybody with a SCUBA tank. Maybe the looters had destroyed any chance of ever finding it.

Not three feet from her right foot, a gasoline-powered pump sat in a puddle of water, waiting for the perpetrators to return. The rainbow-slick of leaking fuel covering the puddle put Faye over the edge. She kicked the pump. She kicked it hard but, still, she was taken aback when it exploded.

A second ear-splitting noise corrected her misapprehension. The pump had been destroyed by a bullet, and there were other bullets on the way. She flung herself into the muck at the bottom of the nearest drainage ditch and lay there on her belly, listening to the nerves in her right leg scream and listening for another shot that might tell her where her assailant hid.

Stupid, stupid, stupid. It was stupid to come to a site of criminal activity and not expect to find criminals. Then, when she did find the place temporarily free of criminal activity, it was stupid of her to assume that criminals would leave their valuables unguarded. And that's what this site was to them: a repository of salable goods with a real dollar value, and nothing more.

Where was the gun? Faye had no idea of the actual orientation of the trench she was lying in so, for reference sake, she assumed that her head was north. She could tilt her head back ever so slightly and get a good line-of-sight up the trench all the way to its end at the lagoon, but she saw nobody and no tree or rock for anybody to hide behind.

Everything seemed clear to the north. She would try another direction. There were only three more.

She rolled carefully onto her back and the motion triggered another shot. Apparently, her nemesis was not worried about conserving ammunition. She lay there for a while, trying to discern motion or a human form in the woods south of her. There was none, but the clear view of the trees atop the lip of the far side of the pit was instructive. If someone were concealed there, he could see her just as well as she could see the trees, and he could shoot her just as easily. She wasn't dead yet, so he wasn't there. That left only west and east.

Faye considered a Hollywood approach, holding up a large object that wasn't attached to her body—a boot or a rock—and waiting to see which direction the shot came from, but she couldn't reach her boots without rising up out of the narrow ditch and there wasn't a rock in the ditch bigger than a grain of sand. Florida just wasn't a rocky place.

Then the sound of voices wafted out of the woods to her right. Slowly, she lifted her head, trying to raise an eye over the lip of the ditch without exposing any of the rest of her head. No shot erupted. The sniper was sitting high in an oak tree in a camouflaged deer stand and he had company. It was a tiny venue for a fistfight, but they were managing pretty well.

The gunman was as distracted as he would ever be, but Faye hesitated. It would take just about forever to heave herself out of the ditch, run across the lagoon and over the dunes, cross the beach, get into her skiff, and get out of range. The moment she cleared the dunes, she would be silhouetted against the sky. It would be a miracle if he didn't shoot her squarely in the middle of the back.

When she saw the rifle falling out of the tree, she found that she had underestimated her own speed. She was out of the ditch and running before the gun hit the ground.

Wally fell back under the power of a fist to his jaw, but he didn't quit. He was unaccustomed to playing the role of hero, but he had a vague idea of how it was done.

"Put down the gun," he barked. "Do you want to kill her?"

Nguyen's fist fell again. "Frankly, yes. I do. I like the money I'm making here and I don't think I would like prison. You've let her get away. Now she'll talk and this place'll be crawling with people who will want to lock our asses up."

Wally grabbed the other man by the shoulders and used his body weight to pin him against the trunk supporting the rickety tree stand. "And nobody will want to lock our asses up for murder?"

"*If* they found this babe's body, and *if* they traced it here, they would think the pothunter did it. The one who's going to jail instead of us for digging up this site. Hey, maybe they'll decide the pothunter killed those two students, too."

"You idiot. This babe *is* our pothunter. If you kill her, we lose our cover."

Wally released his partner and watched him yank a .38 out of his shoulder holster and brace his shooting arm against the railing of the tree stand. "Let her go. Even if we have to leave this site, it's nothing compared to the wreck. Besides, she won't turn us in. She has too much to lose. Either way, keeping her alive leaves us with a scapegoat if this thing goes sour."

Faye was still running for the dunes. Wally reached in his pants pocket and held up a small yellow box—a throwaway camera. "I'd shot nearly a full roll documenting Faye's tour of our island before you started throwing bullets at her. If we ever need a cover, a few of these handed over anonymously to the Park Service will make her their prime suspect."

Nguyen lowered his handgun and watched Faye sprint over the dunes, silhouetted against the sky. Wally breathed a sigh of relief.

Wally genuinely liked Faye, but he would let her take the fall for his crimes without a qualm, because that's the kind of guy he was. In the end, Wally looked out for Wally and no one else, but that didn't mean he wanted Faye dead.

His cut lip throbbed and his ears rang. Taking a beating from Nguyen just to save Faye's hide was the noblest hour in a life devoid of morality. He felt both proud and stupid.

Magda knew that the brave new cyber-world had finished dawning when archaeologists went on-line. A more hidebound, old-fashioned, technology-hating band of reactionaries than her colleagues was never born, but they had finally discovered the wonders of the Web. Some of them had been forced to give up their quill pens and learn to type.

Every day, Magda found that the chore of winnowing through her e-mail grew more difficult. No topic was so esoteric that it had no proponents to put on a conference and invite Magda to submit a paper. No academic rivalry could be allowed to fester on its own without both sides convening in private chat rooms to trash the reputations of their opponents.

But then, some of the information was useful, and so current that telephone and traditional mail were truly too slow to disseminate the message. Today, Magda's virtual mailbox was full, and much of its content was actually urgent.

Her colleagues were abuzz over a strange mixture of Native American artifacts, some ancient and maybe Clovis, and some far more recent, that had suddenly gone up for auction on eBay. The newer pieces were probably from west Florida, suggesting a similar origin for the Clovis artifacts, but none of her colleagues on the Internet could pinpoint a likely location.

The consensus was that someone had looted Paleo-Indian artifacts found in a datable context, maybe even in an actual occupation site. Humans lived lightly on the land twelve thousand years ago. No wonder the Internet was alight with archaeological gossip.

Magda signed off and brooded for a while. For years, she had overlooked her suspicions of Faye. Frankly, she couldn't believe that the woman she knew would loot a site of such importance. And the unsophisticated mixing of artifacts of such varied age didn't sound like Faye's work. Still, when solving a problem, she had to follow every possibility, no matter how unlikely, to its logical end. It was the scientific method in action. For years, she'd had clues to where Faye was digging. It was time to investigate them.

It was full dark when Faye awoke, lying on her bed, shirt sweaty, pants bloody, boots sandy. Her leg throbbed. If her memory could be relied upon, she'd gotten home sometime mid-afternoon, secured the boat, and hauled herself up two flights of stairs before collapsing into bed. She was hungry, dehydrated, and too depressed to appreciate how lucky she was to be alive.

If word of her black-market activities ever got out, she'd take the rap for everything those pothunting thieves had done to Water Island. She would lose her home, for sure. She'd go to jail, too, but that wasn't the worst part. The worst part would be knowing that people thought she was guilty, that she'd looted a site that might have yielded knowledge about the very first Americans. People would believe that she desecrated the past for money. People would think she was lower than dirt.

Wishing for a bit of the adrenaline that had powered her escape, she raised her carcass up out of the bed and lit the lantern. Her watch claimed that midnight was approaching. Slowly peeling off her rank clothing, she checked herself out. Some part of her had been bleeding and it might be an important part.

Faye's right leg was indeed important; she was attached to it. Three purple-black blotches and a not-insignificant cut, small but deep, decorated her thigh. Several flying pieces of the water pump must have struck her when the sniper shot it to bits. There was no money in her budget for medical treatment, so she found her first-aid kit in the dark.

Wet-wipes took off most of the blood. She couldn't think of anything to do for the laceration except treat it with an antiseptic. It was good that Joe was in bed, because she could just hear him saying, "She's treating a puncture wound with Bactine. And they call me stupid."

Using about twenty wet-wipes, she gave herself a spit bath, then put on a clean nightgown and fell back into bed. Bone-tired, but not sleepy, she could feel every speck of sand her filthy body had deposited on the sheets, so she got back up and fetched some clean linens. Still not sleepy after re-making her bed, she reached for the journal. Faye had nobody living and breathing to keep her company, but at least she had Mariah Whitehall LaFourche.

◇

Journal entry by Mariah LaFourche, recorded 15 May, 1832

I am fifty years old today. It seems a proper time to assess my life. The journey from my childhood home to this island is the only journey I have ever made. My human associations have been limited to my parents, assorted traders, my son, his wife, his slaves, the rich planters in his social circle and, finally, the father of my only child.

My father was never able to pronounce the name of Henri LaFourche in a sentence that did not also include the term "blackguard". This is almost fair, but not quite. My father was aware that I have always been hardheaded. I would not have yielded unwillingly to Henri. I was a strong, sturdy girl brought up in a wilderness; he could only have taken me by the most brutal force, and this was not the case. His dishonor lay only in his willingness to let me think he cared.

Henri's blood and his dishonor both run true in his son. Andrew showed his character long ago when he chose to keep slaves, but he shows the cruelty of his heart every day in the treatment of his wife. I do not know Carole well. She has, probably wisely, cleaved completely to Andrew. Befriending me would suggest that she was choosing my side in my constant disagreements with Andrew.

Still, I have eyes. I see that she is in every way the gracious lady that she was reared to be. Her grooming is impeccable, whether she is greeting guests or tending a slave dying of pellagra. I have never heard her raise her voice, not even when Andrew insults her in the presence of others, as he is wont to do. She lowers her eyes in the face of his spite, but her head is high and her back is straight.

He treats her so because she has not borne him children and, as men will, he assumes that the fault is hers. I grieve with her. I have reached an age at which I would treasure grandchildren, but it is not to be.

Journal entry by Mariah LaFourche, recorded 25 December, 1834

It is Christmas Day and my son has paid me a dutiful visit. To be fair, I should admit that his visit is more than dutiful. I do believe he loves me. Alas, this love is the only tender spot in an increasingly calloused heart and I do nothing to heal those callouses when I reject the largesse his riches allow him to bestow. But how can I do otherwise when his gift is a human soul?

Andrew stood there, holding a young mulatto woman by the hand. Plainly written across his face was a naked desire for me to spread my blessing over his sin. I had never seen such untrammeled rage as he displayed when I rejected his gift. He wheeled around and fairly jerked the girl off her feet. Fearing that he would break her arm, I called for him to stop. "Give me the girl," I said. "I will take her."

I stood between them. I believe she would have crouched down and covered herself in my skirts if her dignity would have allowed it. I asked her name. Her quavering voice was clear enough, but she said only, "Julia."

"Julia," I said, "you belong to me now. I set you free."

It is a perverse tribute to my son's love for me that he did not strike me. He merely bellowed, "She is yours to use as you like, but she is not yours to free. You know that, Mother," and walked out of my home. The Christmas sun shone on the golden curls that still tumble down his neck like they did when he was my little boy.

Journal entry by Mariah LaFourche, recorded 3 February, 1840

I know now why Julia has had so little to say over these past months. A woman's moods are not predictable when she is with child, particularly if the father is absent. After all these years I remember that. I would have shared Julia's heartache, but she would not even tell me the man's name. Andrew owns so many slaves now that I could not begin to guess the culprit.

I was greatly saddened by Julia's mental state, because her companionship has been a treasure since Andrew had the audacity to give her to me. Julia and I quickly dispensed with the nonsense of ownership. Somewhere there exists a paper giving Andrew absolute power over her existence, but my position as his mother shields her from this, or so I thought.

In our fantasy life here in my cabin, we are two women of independent means, free to live as we choose. We do up the housework together and if Julia, with her younger body, has found that her share of the burden was heavier, well, I hope she has found the learning I give her to be appropriate recompense. Her reading is improving apace and, though she is not yet ready to begin reading French, she speaks it quite prettily.

I looked forward to the birth of Julia's child, because I felt assured that she would be herself again once the necessities of maternity were behind her. And yes, I longed to hold a sweet-smelling infant again. My son is more than forty years old and I have been too long without a baby to love. I caught Julia's daughter with my own hands today, cut the cord, wiped her squalling face, and I knew. In the curve of Cally's cheek and the shape of her tiny hands, it was clear that Andrew had at last given me the grandchild I have so long desired.

Chapter 17

It would be no easy Thursday morning task to find Faye—she was a very bright woman and she didn't want to be found—but Magda had made a career of finding things. She flipped thoughtfully through the archaic filing system in the departmental library, an activity that was perversely appropriate. Archaeology was by etymology the study of the archaic, now, wasn't it? No quick computer search would answer her questions, but Magda had always found value in the kind of slow, mindless research that freed the mind to ponder more important things.

This was the wisdom of a woman who had done her time shoveling sand and sifting it for tiny clues. She had learned never to waste the minutes spent waiting for sand to fall through a fine screen. At such times, the mind opens wide like a loom opening to receive the next thread. Intuition is released and it can no more be crushed back into its home than Pandora's troubles can be replaced in her box.

Faye dropped Abby's necklace into a jar of dilute formic acid, hoping it would soak clean without too much rubbing. She'd hate to scrub off a layer of silver with the dirt. Douglass' father's pocket watch hadn't cleaned up easily, either. Maybe a visit to the library would enhance her jewelry restoration skills and she'd have better luck, or then again, the watch might already be as clean as it would ever get. After thirty-something years underground, dark and pitted corrosion might now be its natural state.

She filled a bucket with gloves, a hand trowel, a small sieve, and assorted dental picks and paintbrushes. She hadn't earned a cent in days and, while her leg throbbed and she felt awful all over, she couldn't afford to take the day off. Digging for the jackpot, the choice artifact she could sell for big bucks, was her only hope to avoid bankruptcy. Every turn of her spade was like entering the lottery and, on days like today when she couldn't get to her regular hunting grounds, she liked to buy lottery tickets in her own back yard.

There was no question that Joyeuse was well picked over. She'd found the old privies and retrieved all manner of goodies from them: broken bottles, whiskey flasks, even an unbroken tobacco pipe she imagined someone dropping as he buttoned his drawers.

Years before, Faye had stood at the back doors of the house, and the kitchen, and on the foundations of the slave cabins, and tossed a collection of cans, bottles, and apple cores into the woods. She marked the spots where they landed—the most likely spots for refuse pits—and spent an entire summer digging up Joyeuse's trash piles.

Despite the work she'd done in the past, there was still digging to be done on her island. Today, she planned to check out a shallow depression in front of the house where the gardens had once been. It might be the remains of a fish pond. It might even be the site of the old spring, the one her grandmother had heard about but never seen.

Either way, she would bet money on finding something there. In the days before weekly trash pickup, people were always looking for places to throw their refuse. A hole in the ground, a pond, a latrine seat—any of these places would be attractive to a litterbug looking to do some littering or to someone with a treasure to hide.

Every time Faye dug into a damp hole in the ground, she remembered her grandmother saying that Cally sank the family valuables in a water hole somewhere on Joyeuse to save them from the Yankees, then never found them again. This would be an excellent time for such a treasure to turn up.

Faye decided to treasure-hunt until noon, then quit for the day. Cyril was taking her to The Pirate's Lair tonight and, given her current bedraggled state, it would take all afternoon to make herself presentable.

Magda reviewed the list of titles that Faye had checked out in the decade since she had left school, paying particular attention to the interlibrary loans she had requested, because they were evidence of information she needed most. Most titles were predictable. Faye had read dozens of books on Native American cultures of the southeastern United States. She had also showed a distinct interest in archaeology conducted on old plantations, particularly in areas occupied by slaves.

An interesting and less predictable subset of her reading was in architectural preservation, actual how-to-do-it guides on the restoration of antique wallpaper and murals. Faye had researched methods for cleaning painted woodwork. She had even tracked down formulas for authentic paints and varnishes.

What in the world was she up to? No, that was the wrong question. The answer was obvious. Faye was attempting a do-it-yourself project of Biblical proportions.

Then what was the right question? Where was she working or, more specifically, where was the unrestored house that Faye was tackling by herself? Magda cackled, a habit she saved for times when she was alone, because she didn't like to reinforce her students' perception of her as an old hag. Far down the list of Faye's interlibrary requests, borrowed so recently that she had probably returned it on her last visit, was the book title that would give her Faye's home address.

Magda jumped up and hurried to the stacks. She didn't need the book to reach the next conclusion. She was just a bibliophile who wanted to hold this one in her own hands.

The book's loose binding spoke of years spent on a library shelf, jammed between other volumes on equally specialized topics. Knowing that the audience for this book was small but dedicated, its publisher hadn't wasted money on expensive cover art. People who needed this volume would not be seduced by a jazzy book jacket.

The cover read *Architecture of Late Eighteenth and Early Nineteenth Century Tabby Dwellings*. It wasn't an exciting title, but it told Magda what she needed to know.

Cyril returned to the legal briefs. The story of Faye's great-grandmother fighting for her land fascinated him. His life was bound up in the coastal area around the Last Isles, yet he never knew about this travesty. And the tiny little woman who took her losing battle to the newspapers was his key to understanding Faye—her reticence, her self-reliance, and her pain.

A random line jumped off the newsprint. "Mrs. Courtney Stanton Wells still owns and maintains her lifelong residence on Joyeuse Island. Ownership of Joyeuse is not in question."

There was no way on God's green earth that the descendants of a woman like Courtney Stanton Wells would let that land go. He would have his people check the property assessor's records, but he knew what they would read. Faye still owned Joyeuse. She had to. It was so useful to know the secret things that drove a person, especially a person you hoped to know very, very well.

Liz didn't like Wally's friend Nguyen, not even a little bit. Wally had a long list of crooked friends and, generally, they were charming people. Up to a point. They rolled into the marina and fastened their "please, like me" smiles on Liz. They admired her biscuits. They flattered her pretty red hair—which was dyed, for God's sake, and they knew it—and flirted until Wally appeared, then they forgot that she existed while they convened with Wally to discuss mysterious things in urgent whispers.

Nguyen was different. He had drawn Wally into many a corner booth for many an urgent conversation, but he had never once acknowledged that Liz was a human being who would appreciate at least a "Good morning." She knew he was a diver, because he always brought air tanks for Wally to fill, and she knew that he and Wally were up to something, because Wally never charged him for the refill. In fact, even if she'd never seen him near a tank, she'd still have known he was a diver by the way he walked, like he was wearing flippers. Something in the look of his motionless black eyes made her wonder whether Wally was stingy with the oxygen when he filled Nguyen's tanks.

Today was an extraordinarily unpleasant day in the marina, not just because Nguyen was visiting, but because about twenty hungover teenagers were sitting in her grill having their breakfast at noontime. The residual alcohol in their bloodstreams left them both loud and obnoxious.

"Sure there's a Wild Man. My cousin Bill saw him when we were kids," said a young blonde man perched at the bar.

"Well, my granddaddy says *his* daddy saw him when he was a kid. How old could this Wild Man be?" came the rejoinder from a young woman with the face of someone not to be messed with.

"I hear he's probably about seventy by now," the blonde at the bar replied. "They say a young mother took her twin boys for a walk in the woods near here and didn't get home before sundown. They were little, maybe two or three, and got too tired to walk, but she was too afraid of gators to stop and rest. So she'd carry one a ways, set him down, then go back up the path and get the other one, figuring she'd just leapfrog her way home."

"I've heard this," interrupted a young woman in a Sopchoppy High School T-shirt. "One time, she went back for the boy left behind and he wasn't there. Before the week was out, everybody in these parts had stomped through the swamp looking for the poor lost boy."

Liz sighed. This tale had been the catalyst for way too many drunken forays into snake- and gator-infested territory.

The blonde guy regained control of his story. "But they didn't find him. Not that day. Not till twenty years later, when the lost boy's twin brother went bear hunting and found himself face-to-face with him. He was naked and his hair hung down past his butt and his fingernails and toenails looked like bear claws, but the two men had the same face. Every hunter there saw it. Then the Wild Man followed two black bears into the woods."

"They say the bears raised him," came a voice from the corner. It was Nguyen's. "I've never seen him, but I've seen his tracks."

Wally looked at the man standing at his elbow as if he'd said the sun was blue. Nguyen's black eyes were cool and they said quite clearly that he didn't care what Wally or anybody else thought. He repeated, "I saw his tracks, just last year."

Nguyen scanned the kids' faces. "Aren't you folks about the same age as those kids that were shot last week? I've been wondering. Reckon the Wild Man can shoot?"

His question drew no response, so he continued speaking in his oddly deliberate way. "The Wild Man's tracks looked ordinary, like the footprints of a good-sized man, except you could see where his claws cut into the soil. Gave me the willies."

Liz felt a case of the willies coming on, herself.

A morning spent mucking around in Joyeuse's dirt was never a morning wasted, but Faye still wished she'd found something worth selling while she was playing in the mud. Joe, bless his heart, had come out to help her, and his company had made the fruitless hours pass pleasantly. They had chosen a spot within view of the great green-and-blue Gulf and the sea winds had brought the salt smell to them where they worked.

When she went inside, Faye decided it wouldn't be time-effective to primp for her date without simultaneously doing something productive. So while her facial mask dried, she sloshed Abby's silver chain around in the cup of formic acid that she hoped would soak off its encrusted grime. It emanated a chemical odor that made Faye think of two things: a manicure and another necklace she had found and cleaned years before, then stored away.

It was a pendant necklace and it was old, a hundred years or more, but worth no more than the current market price of silver. She had cleaned it, admired its delicate scrollwork, and wondered about the woman whose initials—CSS—were engraved on the back. Intriguing though it was, it hadn't been worth selling, so she had stashed it in her jewelry box and forgotten it.

Now Faye cradled it in her palm and put to sleep the ever-present appraiser in her head, the one who knew the street value of everything. She considered it for its aesthetic value. It was dainty, pretty enough to impress a senator, and broken. She debated whether to throw it back in her jewelry box, saving herself the trouble of dragging out her needle-nosed pliers and magnifying glasses, but she'd kinda been saving it for an occasion like this.

There was enough time before her date with Cyril to give herself a manicure or to fix the pendant, but there wasn't enough time to do both. Faye opted to fix the pendant. It was one-of-a-kind and having it around her neck would make her look a lot more distinctive than the same red-painted claws anyone else could buy and glue on.

Sheriff Mike was inexpressibly tired in body and soul. There was nothing much he could do about his body. If a case kept him awake nights, then he missed his beauty sleep. It had happened before. It would happen again. But he didn't often let a case rumple his soul like this one did. Maybe it was because the dead kids' weeping parents made him think of Irvin Williford.

Yesterday, he had excused himself from a pointless meeting in Tallahassee and gone looking for a heckuva big church, one where he could find a priest saying mass in the middle of a day that wasn't Sunday. And he had found one, too, but he'd left with his soul still rumpled, because the redoubtable Dr. Magda Stockard was there. The woman prayed as fiercely as she did everything else.

She had raised her head and conveyed, in a single moment of eye contact, her disdain for his failure to lock somebody up for the murder of her kids. Then she'd gone back to praying.

So here he was, trying to answer her prayers. The forensics lab report from the murderer's campsite was spread across his lap. It was thorough, but that didn't make it useful.

His detectives had found a few hairs, two of them gray, but none with root bulbs, so there would be no DNA evidence. They had overcome the devilishly difficult job of finding anything at all on a windswept, rainsoaked, outdoor murder site by locating a few fibers to go with the hairs. As luck would have it, the fibers were blue. They were cotton, for God's sake, nothing exotic. How was he supposed to convict somebody when he knew nothing about him except that he owned a pair of jeans or a cotton workshirt?

His investigators were doing a hell of a job. He would grant them that. In fact, he doubted that big-city officers could do as well if faced with a murder scene in the wilderness. But just having evidence wasn't enough. It had to be evidence that pointed to a single unique individual, or all this effort led to emptiness.

He was fighting like the devil to keep this case. Calls from the Feds grew ever more frequent. They were convinced that drugs were involved and they were itching for him to ask for their help.

He had fumed. He had spewed vitriol. Sometimes he could drive away pestering Yankees with a good old Southern tantrum, spiced heavily with nonsensical metaphors.

"Son, I wasn't born in the woods to be scared by an owl. The FBI cannot have this case and could not solve it if somebody gathered up the evidence and handed it to them in a Sir Walter Raleigh can. I'll make myself clear: the Federal Bureau of God-damned Investigation couldn't find the floor with their own two feet. Do you hear me, son?"

The young voice on the other end of the line hadn't quavered much as it said, "Yes, I do."

"Then don't call me back unless you want to be rowed up Salt River."

Then today, feeling merciful, Sheriff Mike had thrown the guy a bone. "Tell you what let's do, son," he said. "If you'll leave me alone for, say, three days, I'll give you something to do with your time. We had a little scuffle at a local marina. A man pulled a gun on one of the customers, and the short order cook settled things with a pan of hot grease. Unfortunately, when I got there, the assailant was gone and so was the victim. So all I've got is a gun and the cook's word that the assailant has grease burns all over his midsection. Think you could do something with that? Try to link the gun to some other crimes? Check the ERs for burn victims? You think so? Well, good."

Sheriff McKenzie thought maybe the federal agent had enough of a stick-to-it nature to do credit to the task. The boy had certainly been diligent in the thankless task of pestering him. Every day, he'd wager that the young man was completely cowed, then another call would come. The content of the calls never changed. The kid always pointed out that the location of the murders on an offshore island and the absence of a motive suggested a drug deal gone bad. Or so the Feds wanted to think.

He had pointed out their idiocy more than once. By that logic, any crime committed in his coastal jurisdiction could be declared drug-related. If mere location was enough to claim jurisdiction over a murder case, then he might as well close up shop.

The phone rang. Since he'd already heard from the FBI that day, he knew it was time for the other call he'd gotten every day since the killings. It was somebody's secretary, calling from Quin Land Development, wanting to know when he was going to release the island crime scene, so that pre-development activities could resume.

Every day, he said, "This investigation is unusual in a lot of ways. Any evidence left in such a natural, unprotected place is fragile. The crime scene will remain cordoned off until all the lab work is back." The secretary was beginning to sound bored with these exchanges. It wouldn't be long before Quin Land Development called in the big guns and he started hearing from their lawyers.

Lawyers made him want to heave, so he returned his attention to the information-free lab report. His field crew had lifted a print of a man's tennis shoe, cheap, size twelve, in the equipment shed. Dr. Stockard said that all of her site workers wore safety boots, all the time. Besides, even if they did wear tennies, he privately doubted any of those fashion-conscious kids would shop at Bargain Shoes-for-Less.

This is the culprit, he thought. But what did it really tell him? That the killer was a man. Well, he already suspected that, but now he knew. Half the human race was easily eliminated, unless a big-footed woman was running around in men's shoes.

The shoe size was a little large, even for a man, but still common. Casts of depressions in the sand around the bodies suggested that he was tallish and of average weight for his height. They already knew he had a least a few gray hairs. Reckon how many thousands of men fitting that description could be found in a five-hundred-mile radius of where he sat? Speaking of where he sat, he himself fit the description.

Magda thumbed through *Architecture of Late Eighteenth and Early Nineteenth Century Tabby Dwellings*. The title alone gave her the approximate construction date and the actual building material of Faye's mystery house and it raised an interesting question. Tabby was once used extensively as a construction material along the Atlantic coast of Florida, but there was no way that Faye was commuting more than a hundred miles to Saint Augustine. The only tabby buildings Magda knew of along the Florida Gulf coast were near the mouth of the Manatee River, more than two hundred miles away as the crow flies over the Gulf and double that by car.

Was there a house located a reasonable distance from Faye's stated mailing address, Wally's Marina, that was constructed all or partly of tabby? Not according to official records, but tabby was nothing more than concrete made with local materials—sand, lime, shell. It was often plastered and painted to mock a pricier material like stone or stucco or plastered brick. Maybe its humble origins had escaped the architectural historians.

Magda reached behind her without looking and grabbed her copy of the Historic American Buildings Survey catalog, Florida section. If the mystery house still stood, then it was standing in the 1930s and the dedicated public servants performing the survey had found a way to get there and document it.

Magda had long ago gone through this catalog and sought out as many of the buildings as she could find, marking "deceased" in the margins of the entries documenting structures which no longer existed. The few buildings she couldn't locate sported question marks in their margins. Surely a scientist of her caliber could quickly come up with a short list of candidates for Faye's tabby house. A scientist of her caliber could probably even find a photograph of it.

Faye hooked the repaired necklace around her neck, then went to check Abby's necklace. She swooshed it up and down in the solvent and was glad to see some of the crud rinse away. Dabbing at it with a soft brush revealed more of the original surface. Ignoring the ticking clock that said it was time to put on her makeup, she sat down and worked with the brush until she could rinse even more corrosion away.

The surface of the necklace's pendant was heavily decorated. She perched her magnifying glasses atop her nose and could immediately see a cross with four equal sides engraved on its circular face. On the right arm of the cross was the figure of a man bearing a child on his back that was oddly familiar. The words "Protect Us" beneath his feet helped her decode the words arching over his head: "Saint Christopher." Her knowledge of Catholicism was embarrassingly sketchy, but she had certainly encountered the ubiquitous Saint Christopher's medal that many faithful travelers trusted to protect them against storms, pestilence, and nose-picking kids.

There was a figure on the opposite arm of the cross, but it was unfamiliar and its caption was indiscernible. The image on the top arm of the cross was obscured by tarnish, but she could make out a heart in the center and the Virgin Mary on the bottom arm.

Faye had known more than one Protestant with an attachment to a Saint Christopher's medal that was more superstitious than religious, but this thing had the look of something that only the faithful would wear. It was unusual. Why hadn't the newspapers described it?

Another question surfaced. Had Abby been Catholic? She'd never thought about Abby's religion. Probably, she'd just assumed the girl was Baptist or Methodist or Presbyterian like just about everybody in that part of the world where the Bible Belt devoted itself to holding up the pants of a nation.

She flipped the medal over and found that its smooth back had yielded to cleaning much more readily than the front. As if in miraculous answer to the question she'd just asked herself, eight words appeared. *I am a Catholic. Please call a priest.*

Faye recoiled. Abby could have had a mass said over her bones if she'd called a priest that first day. Her fuzzy knowledge of Catholicism suggested that Abby would have wanted that. Now her bones were gone, and Faye had a feeling that the Pope himself would be ashamed of her.

She peeled off her gloves and found Abby's obituaries. The child in her felt like her sin of omission would be less severe if she proved to herself that the dead girl was just a Protestant whose faith didn't particularly care what was done with her body.

So there! that childish part of her exclaimed when she found the funeral notice crediting Rev. Devan Watts of the Panacea Springs United Methodist Church with Abby's memorial service. How hard it must have been for him, eulogizing someone when no one knew for sure that she was even dead.

So why was there a medal in Abby's grave that honored a religion that wasn't even hers? Unless....

She remembered the spot where she'd found the medal, assuming it was the necklace Abby was thought to be wearing on the night she died. It was in the grave, *under* the body.

Had the killer dug a pit to receive Abby's body, then brought her there to kill her so that her fresh corpse could fall neatly into its resting place? No muss, no fuss. Seeing the gaping pit, Abby would have had no doubt of his intentions. She would not have been granted the gift of denial, telling herself, "He only wants to rob me or rape me or beat me. I can survive this. I'm strong enough."

No, she would have known the stakes as she stood on the sliding, sandy lip of her own grave and clawed at her attacker. Her necklace could have been torn free in the melée, dropping into its owner's grave before she was even dead. That would explain its position beneath Abby's remains.

Pure, clean scientific reasoning prevented her from settling into a maudlin weeping session over Abby's long-lost necklace and her gut-freezing fate. No scientist worthy of the name seized on the first plausible theory that suggested itself without considering other options.

So how else might the necklace have come to be beneath Abby? Perhaps it was already there when her attacker shoveled a woman-sized hole in the sand and he didn't see it. Perhaps he did see it, but left it there. Or perhaps he put it there on purpose. She couldn't disprove those possibilities, but there was no evidence or human motivation to support them, either.

A more likely scenario insisted on replaying itself for her. She closed her eyes and saw Abby under attack, reaching up in panic and grabbing something, anything. Faye saw the chain snapping and the assailant's broken necklace falling unnoticed into the pit he had dug to hold his victim.

The scene reminded Faye that premeditated violent murder wasn't just a hypothesis to coolly examine and discard. It was a planned act that required the killer to disable key parts of a human body, stopping only when the body no longer functioned. Cries of pain, spurting blood, loosened bowels—these things had to be ignored until the deed was done.

Faye studied the religious medal in her hands. Perhaps Abby had indeed ripped it from her assailant's neck as she struggled for life. She liked to think that the girl had fought back, and this scenario fit the facts as well as any other.

Only one detail of the crime scene, as she herself had observed it, didn't fit. Douglass Everett's watch was also in the grave, under the body, and she knew for a fact that he wasn't Catholic. He was, in fact, a deacon of long standing in the Blessed Assurance AME Church in Panacea.

So what should she do? Turn over the watch and the medal to the sheriff? That would be tantamount to throwing Douglass to the wolves. The sheriff suspected him and he was handy, while the owner of the religious medal was nowhere to be found. She didn't feel good inside herself about doing that, because finding the medal reinforced her gut feeling that Douglass was innocent of Abby's death.

The sheriff didn't need to know about these things, Faye decided, as she tucked them in the display cabinet with her other artifacts and hurried to her bedroom to see whether the August heat had rendered her makeup unusable.

Hurukan is the Mayan storm god and it is fitting that his fearsome name is attached to hurricanes, the greatest storms on Earth. For all the death and havoc they wreak, it is important to remember that they are only heat engines, necessary to transfer energy from the tropics to regions that receive far less of the sun's heat. If humans didn't exist, hurricanes would simply be Nature's elegant means of taking from the energy-rich and giving to the energy-poor, wiping parts of the world down to a clean slate in the process.

But humans do exist and Hurukan recognizes that some of them desperately need to be wiped to a clean slate. And some places are just bad, provoking humans to be their worst selves. Last Isle was such a place. It was a haven for natives killing natives, then for Europeans killing natives and Africans and each other. Hurukan smiled when hurricane after hurricane took its toll on Last Isle, blasting it to pieces. Sometimes a place needs the cleansing only a mammoth storm can provide.

Sometimes, a lot of times, humanity needs cleansing, too. Evil can grip whole nations or it can nest comfortably in a single heart. In either case, human evil can only be cleansed by human beings. Even mighty Hurukan is impotent in the face of it, but somewhere south of Galveston a brewing storm waited for the chance, once again, to try to wipe the sullied world clean.

Chapter 18

The Pirate's Lair was one of those rare restaurants where patrons could arrive dressed elegantly, enjoy warmly efficient service and fine linen napkins, and dine well, yet leave completely relaxed. Housed in an actual refurbished pirate's lair, its well-polished floors bore scars that spoke of treasure and skullduggery.

Cyril strode out of the restaurant before Faye finished parking, in plenty of time to open her door and extend his arm to help her out of the car. Had he been watching out the front window? That seemed undignified. More likely, a discreetly placed gratuity had made sure he was notified as soon as a certain well-used Pontiac rolled off the highway.

She had brought a shawl, partly because the evening was unusually cool and partly because her dress was rather bare. Faye, like any woman reared by a mother who sewed well, appreciated well-made clothes constructed of good fabric. These days, she was appalled by what such clothing cost. On her budget, when she wanted something nice, she was forced to make it herself.

Another thing her seamstress mother had taught her was to never, never expend the effort to make a dress in the trendiest style. When Mama put days and days into a sewing project, she intended for Faye to get years and years of wear out of it.

As usual, Mama was right. Faye remembered making this dress for a party celebrating her short-lived engagement to Isaiah. Every pintuck in its strapless bodice was an old friend. The bias-cut skirt still clung where it should and floated free where it should. Best of all, it was flame red, and Cyril obviously liked it.

His admiration was apparent in the way he cupped her elbow in his hand, the way he helped her wrap the shawl around her bare shoulders. She let him guide her through the historical part of the restaurant out onto a newer open-air deck, where he had secured a choice table. They sat in comfortable wicker chairs with their backs to the other diners, facing the Gulf. The sky to their left was silver-black. To their right, the water still glowed orange where the sun had melted into it like a crayon.

Conversation came easily over an eclectic meal that featured Ethiopian-style vegetables served authentically on flatbread and without silverware. The inclusion of some inauthentically grilled shrimp and bay scallops reminded them that they were not actually *in* Ethiopia but, rather, were perched on the rim of the Gulf of Mexico, which was a damn fine place to be.

Pinot noir suited the spicy vegetables, and though their waiter delicately tried to guide them toward a rich Chardonnay to complement the seafood, they insisted on their wine of choice. Swigging the pinot and eating with their hands, they swapped garrulous tales of growing up in rural Florida. Cyril, of course, had her trumped. He was older and drew on memories of a time when nobody he knew had air conditioning and even indoor plumbing hadn't completed its conquest of the American South. He even remembered when saltine crackers came in big wooden barrels that sat next to grocery store cash registers for God-knew-how-long, yet the crackers never tasted stale.

Faye's city-girl childhood in Tallahassee hadn't been nearly so colorful, but she'd spent many a summer day at Joyeuse helping her grandmother make sure the old house didn't rot to the ground. She didn't bother to tell him about learning to replace termite-ridden clapboards at ten, then moving up to tin roof repair by age fourteen. Instead, they shared stories about cottonmouth sightings, and evaluated whether dewberries were best cooked in cobblers or eaten as soon as they were plucked ripe off the vine, if not before.

"But nothing could touch my mother's blackberry jam, God rest her soul," Cyril said, automatically tracing the sign of the cross on his body: forehead, sternum, shoulder, shoulder.

Faye was shaken to her bones. The pieces of the puzzle collided inside her skull and assembled themselves into a coherent, ugly whole.

If Cyril was Catholic then so, likely, was his whole family. Fragments of information leapt out of her subconscious. Criss-Kross, his brother Cedrick's high school nickname—for sarcastic, sadistic high schoolers, there could be no more perfect nickname for a boy so religious that he wore a cross adorned with Saint Christopher, the Virgin Mary, and all that other stuff Faye couldn't decipher.

Cedrick had been in Abby's tiny high school class, so he clearly knew her. Cyril had said something about his brother's last known whereabouts. What was it?

She fingered the necklace at her throat. Oh, yes, Cedrick went to work in the oil fields off the coast of Louisiana. She hadn't remembered because it was such a common ambition for young men who weren't college bound. The oil fields required no qualifications beyond the grit to work terribly hard for seven days at a stretch, spend a day driving home, enjoy five days there, then drive back and do it again. It was hard on wives and families, but it was a good living.

Cedrick had been gone from town for hardly more than a month when Abby was killed, but Faye was willing to bet that he had vanished from the radar of local law enforcement officers who were obsessed with proving Douglass Everett guilty. She would lay odds that no one had ever even bothered to find out who Cedrick worked for and whether Abby disappeared while he was working or during his week off. Seven days would give a man all the time he needed to cover his tracks.

She noticed Cyril studying her and she flushed, embarrassed by how she must have looked, staring off into space. She felt as if he somehow knew she was developing an elaborate scheme to prove his only brother guilty of murder. He reached across the table and took her necklace gently between his thumb and forefinger.

"Where did you find this?" he asked, turning the pendant over to examine the back.

"It's amazing, the things you can find in junk shops. And they're especially cheap when they're marked with somebody else's monogram," she murmured in the voice women once used to say, "You like my dress? This old rag?"

"Those places always make me sad. People die and their treasures become worthless. Instantly. I especially hate all the old photographs staring down at me. There hangs the face of somebody's grandfather, but nobody cares. Nobody even knows his name."

He released his hold on her necklace and took her hand. "Somehow, I think the woman who owned that necklace, the one whose initials were CSS, would be glad to know someone appreciated it enough to rescue it from the junk shop."

The moon had risen as they talked, and its calming light was telling Faye to keep her suspicions quiet. She could hardly give Cedrick's religious medal to the sheriff without also turning over its companion piece, Douglass' watch. The ensuing circus would hurt Douglass, who might not deserve it, and it would hurt Cyril, who assuredly did not. Why drag his family into the spotlight, with its violent father, runaway mother, and perhaps murderous brother? Abby was murdered when Cyril was a scrawny, undergrown little boy. His constituents shouldn't hold her death against him, but they would. No district could be expected to send the product of such an upbringing to represent them in Washington.

She thought of the face in his fourth-grade yearbook picture. That face had suffered enough.

The waiter checked their water glasses and deferentially asked, "Is there anything else, Senator Kirby?"

Faye froze and looked her escort up and down. He wasn't hiding behind a baseball cap or sitting incognito in a deserted, seedy park. He was in a public place, graciously nodding his head at other diners who felt that their social status was vicariously enhanced by the presence of someone a little bit famous.

He took her hand and she recovered herself. *He doesn't mind being seen with me,* she realized. *No, it's more than that. He likes being seen with me.*

Cyril casually caressed her hand as he stared out over the Gulf. The music was live. The wine was red. The evening star was sliding helplessly toward a horizon that had already swallowed the sun.

Faye was a smart woman who was well aware that, having lost her father at such a young age, she was over-receptive to the attentions of authority figures. And she realized that being rejected for her skin color made her vulnerable to just about anyone who accepted her as she was. These facts made it wise for her to fall in love slowly, but facts and red wine do not mix.

For history buffs, the Historic American Buildings Survey—HABS for short—was one of FDR's greatest New Deal investments. Jobless folk fanned out across the country, seeking old buildings, photographing them and sketching their floor plans. Many of the structures they recorded in the 1930s were caught in the act of falling down. Some of them were documented in no other place. Magda adored the photographs those nameless government employees took.

Magda used the HABS catalog frequently. It was useful, as far as it went, but it only told her which structures had been documented. Finding the documents—the photographs, the maps, the drawings—was a different story. It frustrated her that, to this day, no publication existed that gathered in one place photographs of all the structures documented by the HABS. Magda had never been one to accept the status quo. Over the course of her career, she had cobbled together her own compilation of HABS work in Florida. The resulting document was more of a scrapbook than a reference tome, chock-full of reprints and photocopies and scrawled marginal notes. She had pored over her collection of journals and exhausted the stores of more than one university library before ordering expensive photographic reprints. Compiling it had been costly work.

Those old buildings—houses, courthouses, general stores, barns—were hard-wired into her brain by now. She knew their front and rear elevations, their floor plans, every detail the HABS people saw fit to record. She loved them all, but she loved the houses the best.

It seemed like only minutes passed while she flipped through the scrapbook, searching for Faye's mystery house, but time is relative. The clock on Magda's wall stopped ticking when she opened the well-used book and its hands only rushed to their actual positions hours later when she smoothed her hand over a page and gave it a protective little pat.

The house itself told her she was right. There were no other candidates that met the criteria: early 19th-century design, never professionally restored, and within a reasonable driving or boating distance of the places Faye was known to frequent. Even in the faded photograph, she could tell that everything from the main floor up was of wood-frame construction, but the stuccoed ground floor could easily have been crafted of tabby. The ground floor looked old, relative to the style of the upper stories.

Magda guessed that a long-ago someone had built a one-room tabby structure on the site. Later, as his economic situation improved, he had built a second square structure next to it, roofing over the two tabby buildings and the space between them. This dogtrot configuration allowed for a covered breezeway that gave valuable outdoor living space in a hot climate, which was the prime reason why dogtrot houses dotted the American South almost until God created the air conditioner. The fact that this dogtrot was built of tabby made Faye's house a curiosity, a beautiful example of the adaptation of traditional design and native materials to a harsh climate. And the ostentatious palace that rose above its tabby basement was a textbook illustration of how a newly rich man might adapt an existing home to reflect his improved circumstance.

There were other houses with plastered exteriors that might hide tabby, but even if there'd been five hundred houses that could plausibly belong to Faye, she would still know that this one, Joyeuse, was the one. Now that she held its photograph in her hands, she could draw no other conclusion.

The old HABS photos occasionally featured the inhabitants of the historic structures. Sometimes they were the owners, but frequently the photographers had immortalized renters or squatters who simply wanted to be part of the picture.

Magda couldn't take her eyes off the figures posing on the front porch of Joyeuse. In two rocking chairs sat an old lady and another, truly ancient woman. Either of them might have been taken for white, but there was an obvious family resemblance between them and the darker-skinned woman standing between them. In this younger woman's arms was a beautiful toddler with dark eyes and long ringlets. Every one of the women had Faye's face, or the face she once wore, or the face she would someday wear.

Finally, Magda's suspicions jibed with what she knew of Faye's character. If Faye were indeed conducting digs on her own, even if she were selling the things she dug up, she, like Magda, would recognize a moral difference between doing it on your own land and doing it on someone else's.

Everything made sense to Magda, except for one critical thing. The Faye that Magda knew would not desecrate an archaeologically significant site, nor would she make the amateur's mistake of mixing artifacts of radically different dates. Maybe Faye wasn't the only pothunter prowling around those islands.

Faye brooded over the small cluster of graves in the grove beside the inlet on Joyeuse Island. Mother, grandmother, great-grandmother, great-great-grandmother, but no fathers or grandfathers. Somewhere on the island were Courtney Stanton, Mariah Whitehall LaFourche, Andrew LaFourche, even William and Susan Whitehall, but their graves had been lost when the two great Apalachicola hurricanes of 1886 reconfigured the island.

Joyeuse and the Last Isles were peppered with lost graves. Native Americans had occupied these islands since they had risen out of the sea. In the intervening years, all of them had died and some of them had been buried. Beside them were buried dead conquistadors who didn't survive the European invasion. Next to them were the unmarked graves of her ancestors, slave and free. And somewhere lay the unconsecrated bones of Abigail Williford.

When she got home from her dinner with Cyril, she had checked Cedrick's yearbook picture. There was something hanging around his neck that could only be the religious medal she had found buried with Abby. The presence of his necklace and Douglass' watch and the absence of other evidence made them equally likely to have murdered Abby, but human nature made her far more inclined to believe that Cedrick did it than to pronounce her friend Douglass a killer. But must she broadcast Cedrick's guilt to the world and ruin her new friend Cyril's life?

What would Cally and Mariah and William and Susan and all the others think of her for protecting Douglass and Cyril by keeping the evidence to herself? The law had been no friend to any of them—not to Mariah, a rich woman with nothing to call her own, and not to Susan, whose fellow Creek had been forcibly relocated to an inhospitable country. Cally could certainly have no respect for the law, not when she had quite legally been held captive for a quarter-century.

She wondered what her ancestors would have thought of her budding relationship with Cyril? They could not object to his race or hers. Each of them had carried some impossible-to-pinpoint mixture of blood, but they had lived and died in this world on their own merits. In the end, it just didn't amount to a hill of beans. Maybe it was time to bring Cyril home to meet the folks.

Because Faye had moved away from civilization and the need to wear makeup every day, she actually enjoyed the ritual of removing it at bedtime. Tonight, mindlessly rinsing off goopy mascara remover had the flavor of spiritual cleansing. No more guilt over Abby Williford. No more worries over whether Cyril was right for her.

"Things generally work out for the best," her mama had always said. "You just gotta trust in the Lord."

"Okay, Mama," Faye muttered through lips that still bore traces of the evening's cherry-red lipstick. "I'm doing the trusting. You and God better start working things out."

Faye generally washed her face in her beloved cistern-fed shower, but when she succumbed to the siren song of cosmetics that weren't water-based, the need for other equipment proliferated. She had an antique pitcher to carry the water in and a matching basin to hold it while she washed. Her battery-powered camping lantern provided the necessary light and a mirror provided the necessary assistance. If the sun hadn't heated her washing water so delightfully, she would have needed to warm a pot of water on the camp stove, too. Such labor-intensive toiletries were too much work for every day, but paying attention to her looks now and then made her feel like a girl.

She slipped out of girl mode only long enough to clean the wounds on her thigh. The purple-green bruises were hideous.

The control-top support hose she'd started wearing upon turning thirty had acted like a compression bandage—her leg had hardly hurt at all during dinner—but she was paying for it now.

Faye wrapped her battered but very feminine carcass in a cotton nightgown and soft slippers and shuffled to bed, casting an affectionate glance at the red dress hanging in her armoire. Fresh-scrubbed and damp-haired, she pulled out William Whitehall's old journal, one more time.

The fact that Mariah had closed the journal for the last time when her granddaughter Cally was born made Faye mad enough to spit. Finally, she had found the link between Mariah, her great-great-grandmother's grandmother and Cally, whose legends had been passed down to her through her own grandmother. Mariah was forever silent on the subject, but the journal's remaining pages were cluttered with several decades' worth of scrawled notes and recipes and planting schedules. Even if there were no more personal entries, surely there was a little more information to be gleaned.

Slips of paper poked from between the journal pages and she plucked them, one by one. A tiny drawing of a man in a powdered wig fascinated her. Could this be the miniature sent by Henri LaFourche to Mariah all those years ago? Could it really be her great-great-great-great-grandfather? It was unsigned. She would never know.

Obituaries of people Faye didn't know fell from between the leaves of the old book. Yellowed quilt patterns joined the pile. As the paper artifacts stored in the journal dwindled, she held onto twenty or thirty sheets of onionskin typing paper, folded and stapled. The bundle looked like her best bet for retrieving family history, so she superstitiously saved it until last.

Faye unfolded the papers and saw that they were a smeared carbon copy of a document produced by a bad typist. She skimmed the first few lines. Realizing what she held, she paused to offer up a history lover's prayer of thanksgiving. Then she added a few words of blessing for FDR and his inspired plan to keep unemployed writers busy. Somebody that the Federal Writer's Project sent out to locate and interview former slaves had found one here on remote Joyeuse. Cally was going to tell her whole story, in her own words, after all.

◇

Excerpt from oral history of Cally Stanton, recorded by the Federal Writer's Project, 1935

I've been a slave and I've been free. I've been mistress of a big plantation, and of its master, too. I was there when the water pulled itself far, far from the beaches at Last Isle and I saw the wind blow the water back. It rolled over Last Isle and washed away the big hotel and all the rich white people, and their slaves, too. Nobody ever gave much thought to the slaves that died on Last Isle, but I did. I was a slave on Last Isle and I was there when the big storm roared in and washed the whole island away.

You could say I saw the big storm twice. I saw it in my sleep a long time before it happened. I guess I should have tried to warn all those rich folks, but they wouldn't have listened to me. Still, I knew death was watching over us. My dreams ain't never once been wrong.

My worst dream came first, when I was a slip of a girl. I saw people sick and dying. Miss Mariah was laid up in the bed alongside the Missus, and my mama was tending them. Then Mama took sick and they laid her on the sleeping porch and there was nobody in my dream to tend them but me.

And that's just how it happened. When the fever came, I took care of all three sweet ladies, but the typhoid carried them away, along with half the slaves.

When the fever passed, the Master sent all the house slaves to the fields. 'Twasn't any other way to get the harvest in. My skinny six-year-old self wouldn't have been much good in the fields, so they gave me the whole Big House to dust and sweep and clean. I was so good at keeping house that I got to where I knew the Master wanted coffee before he did. I liked to bring him a hot cup in his office. He was a handsome man and I never, before or since, saw the like of his golden hair. I was about grown before I found out he wasn't nothing but a mean man.

Chapter 19

Faye knew she should be working. She should be looking for artifacts to sell to bolster her failing fortunes. She should be restoring Joyeuse, giving her the attention she deserved. Instead, she was sitting on the ground, watching Joe do target practice with his bow and arrow. Their conversation was punctuated with the pronounced *thwump* of stone arrows striking a rotten pine stump.

Instead of doing something constructive, she was talking to a man who had very little to say. "So, I had a nice time with Cyril last night. I think I'm going to tell him how to get in touch with me through Wally. Maybe even bring him out for a visit."

"You trust him that much? You could lose all this." Joe gestured at the wild beauty of Joyeuse. "I don't understand what you want with him." He let another arrow fly.

She could understand Joe's position. Living in a peaceful, beautiful place, untouched by the conflict that went hand-in-hand with human society, was seductive. She'd enjoyed that peace for years. Maybe someday Joe would get lonely and understand why she wanted something more.

"Cyril makes me feel good. Not just because he's some hotshot politician. He looks at me and listens to me as if I'm important, maybe even special."

"*Thwump*," said the arrow.

"This is why people vote for him," Joe said, showing marvelous political insight for someone who had never cast a vote.

"He seems to enjoy our time together," Faye babbled on. "He must, because there's nothing in it for him. He hasn't pressed me for my phone number or my address. He hasn't asked for sex. He hasn't even kissed me yet, though it's way past time. I wish he would." A "thwump" and silence. "He's older than me, but it's okay. I've never dated a grown-up before, Joe. Yet he still has the smile of a thirteen-year-old boy."

"He spends too much time at the tanning salon."

Joe turned and launched an arrow into the underbrush. Faye flinched at the ensuing squeal.

Joe stomped through the undergrowth to collect his kill. "No fish tonight," he said. "Rabbit."

It was Friday morning and public servants everywhere were trying to tidy up their work for the weekend. The sheriff knew Kelly had been at her lab since the sun had finished whiting out the stars. He knew she worked conscientiously, every day, trying to generate the kind of forensics data that solved crimes. He thought of calling her, but there was nothing to say. The data were all in and they told him nothing.

His investigators had uncovered nothing, no fingerprints and no witnesses. The few material clues to the murderer's identity were investigative victories for his staff and Kelly's, but they signified nothing. The shoe print, the hairs, the fibers, the bullet that had destroyed the boy's right ear before plowing into a pine tree. He could match it to a gun, if he had one, but in his gut, he knew that the gun, the cheap shoes, the rubber gloves, were all resting with the stolen equipment on the bottom of the Gulf.

His technicians had found the other bullet deep in another pine tree, where it had burrowed after passing through the base of the girl's skull. From its trajectory, they'd estimated where she had been standing at the time she was shot and the location of the shooter. Big deal. It was just another piece of data that told him nothing about why she was killed or who did it.

Nothing. He had no suspect. No one who wanted the two kids dead. No motive other than theft or drugs, which he personally found weak. And surely not even the biggest environmental nut would kill two innocent kids to stop the development of an island, no matter how pretty that island.

He himself hated the thought of constructing a winter playground for Yankees too dumb to move out of the cold. In his opinion, the Last Isles were some of the prettiest places left on Earth, but the resort people thought they could be improved by the addition of a couple of man-made beaches. He and his investigation had slowed that inevitable process, but he couldn't stop it. Nobody could. It was time to let the project go forward. There was no reason to let a couple of unsolved murders slow the progress of humanity.

Faye had been told she didn't have sense enough to know when to quit. She'd been told that more than once, and here she was demonstrating it again. It was a crystal-clear morning and she had a frenzied need for money, but had she done anything that might raise that money?

No. She had spent gasoline money by driving her car to Sopchoppy.

She wanted to find Cedrick Kirby, wanted it bad. What would she do if she found him? She didn't know. Turn him in and ruin Cyril? No. Hold his location in reserve in case she ever needed to protect Douglass? Maybe. Probably. Yes. That was what she would do.

Nobody could hide from the World Wide Web, not even Cedrick the murderer. Given a computer and time, he could be found, or at least that's what Faye had thought. Even now, she could hear the click-whirr-beep of a computer mating with the Internet and, Lord, she loved the Internet with all the passion of a lonely island dweller. If she could hook up with the Web from the comfort of her bedroom, she'd hardly want to come ashore at all.

Faye had learned a lot at the Sopchoppy Public Library's free Internet terminal. She'd learned that "skip trace" referred to a search for loan defaulters, deadbeat dads, and other missing persons. She'd learned that some missing persons searches could be accomplished for free.

Free was good. She'd perused the no-cost databases, but the result of her searches was cyberquick and brutal. No one in the United States had a telephone listed under Cedrick Kirby. No one in the United States had died while admitting to be Cedrick Kirby.

She'd never thought about how hard it would be to hide if your given name was as eccentric as Cedrick. Telephone records listed only three Cedric Kirbys living in the whole U.S. and not one Cedrick.

Having come to the end of her investigative ability fairly quickly, she steeled herself to spend some dollars. A low-rent private investigator located at wefindem.com offered only one service she could afford. It was titled simply "Real-time Name Search." Its cost, only $35, was probably a good estimate of its value in finding missing folk.

Faye pulled her credit card out of her wallet, the one on which she kept the annual fee paid but never actually used, the one that represented her final line of security. Nothing but insanity would explain her willingness to put thirty-five dollars on it for no good reason.

Wefindem certainly worked efficiently. After a quarter hour, the first message came through. "Got his SSN. I can't tell it to you, but he was born in 1946."

Faye nodded. This was her Cedrick.

Five minutes later. "No current telephone number. No current address."

Was he dead? Faye sorta hoped he was dead so she could let Abby rest and forget her. She leaned back and waited.

"No previous telephone or address," said the next message. "He's never had a magazine subscription, ordered anything by mail, or received a catalog."

After a twenty-minute wait, the detective gave the final report. "I've got no record of him living anywhere under his own name. And he hasn't renewed his driver's license since he got it in 1961. Dead end."

Faye was thirty-five dollars poorer, but she understood the value of negative information. Either Cedrick had changed his name or he had died about the time he left home, which was when Abby died. Suicide? Remorse? Who knew? Or maybe he'd been living in the woods since then, subsisting on roots and acorns. The notion reminded Faye of the Wild Man story, a tall tale passed down for decades to the gullible young of each generation.

The Wild Man was said to live in Micco County's abundant wetlands. The tale said that he'd gotten lost in the swamps as a young child, surviving only through the kindness of the native bears. If Cedrick was the Wild Man, Faye would eat her copy of *Beloved Southern Folk Tales*.

She signed off and headed home.

Her mind was fully engaged with the Cedrick problem during the drive from Sopchoppy to Wally's. She didn't feel like talking to Wally or Liz, so she skirted around the grill and walked directly to her skiff. She hadn't been underway five minutes when Wally's voice emanated from her radio, sounding remarkably unsullied for late afternoon. Maybe he'd taken a nap, giving his liver time to catch up with his morning six-pack.

"I see you out there, Faye," he bellowed. "Where in hell have you been?"

"I don't sit by my radio all the time. I don't even have it on all the time. The racket makes me nervous, especially when I'm working. Want me to spell it for you? W-O-R—"

"Shut up, dear. Magda's been calling me. All day. The phone is ringing off the hook and I really hate that."

"Disturbs your sleep?"

"Bitch. But yeah, I got things to do besides answer the phone when Dr. Famous Archaeologist wants to make it ring."

Intellectual jousting with Wally was a one-sided venture, so Faye got to the point. "So what did Magda want?"

"She has some paying work for you. Want me to spell that? P-A-Y—"

"Doing what?"

"The sheriff said they could dig on Seagreen Island again."

Faye cut the engine so she could sit in the quiet and take a deep breath before asking, "Does that mean he's found the killer?"

"No, it means he's giving up."

Wally's words made her feel heavy all over, despite her relief at being employed again. Krista and Sam had been dead for ten days. All that time, she'd been worrying about money and snooping around in a murder older than she was. Sheriff McKenzie had a good track record. She'd assumed he'd find the students' murderer just like he had so many others, but as far as Faye could tell, he'd never even had a real suspect. What had made her assume she and Joe could safely remain at Joyeuse?

Faye changed course, steering her skiff back to Wally's. She needed to return Magda's call.

Wally waved at Faye as she hung up the phone, waiting for her to leave before he went back into his office and closed the door. Nguyen sat in the chair where Wally had left him fifteen minutes before.

Nguyen waited better than most people—alert, ready for anything, but giving no sign of impatience. He worked with the same deliberation. Working with Nguyen was often a frustrating endeavor; sometimes Wally regretted going into business with him. Wally's usually flaccid body was capable of great bursts of activity. When he dug for artifacts alongside Nguyen, Wally always felt that he was working harder, moving more dirt, hurrying more to box up his finds and load them on the boat.

Yet at the end of the day, the pile of dirt Nguyen had shoveled out of the ground was always bigger than his. Nguyen's finds were more numerous and more valuable. His crates were more efficiently packed. His work was carefully thought out to minimize effort and so were his words.

"So what's happened to the cash flow?" Nguyen asked.

Wally squirmed. "I've sold everything we uncovered this summer. We've still got a warehouse full of things I stored on my friend's island east of here last year while we were looking for buyers, but I'm having some trouble this week, er—I can't get our goods out of storage right now." Nguyen drummed a single finger on Wally's desk.

How was he going to explain his dilemma to Nguyen? Faye's live-in stud might make life peachy for her, but he complicated Wally's life to no end. He needed to get into the shed on Joyeuse Island. He needed to get in there bad. But he needed to do it without anyone to witness what he pulled out of the shed and loaded on his boat. And as far as he could tell, the big Indian hadn't left the island since Liz scalded the phony Park Services guy.

Fate was conspiring against Wally these days. First, there was the resort being built in the Last Isles. It would bring tourists and heavy pleasure boat traffic to his marina, but Wally's more lucrative business thrived in the shade. It wouldn't survive the onset of civilization, although thanks to those two dead kids, civilization was being delayed a bit.

But there's never any rest for the wicked. The coming resort—and it would come, dead kids or not—filled Wally with an unaccustomed urgency. He needed to make money while he still could and that meant he had to get private access to Faye's island, which didn't used to be so hard.

For years, he had relied on Faye's hermit tendencies. He should have realized that even hermits need sex, as evidenced by the big dumb brute haunting Faye's island. Shit. He should have thought of it sooner. If it was sex she wanted, he could have given her that.

Nguyen's steely voice sliced into his sexual fantasies. "And exactly where are our goods stored?"

Wally, who was shrewd enough to know that the man who has no valuable secrets is expendable, avoided giving him a precise location. "On an island east of here owned by somebody I know. She doesn't know the stuff is there, but she comes ashore regularly. When she's here, she can't be there, so I get in my boat and pull some of our stock out of inventory. If I know the coast will be clear for a long time, sometimes I meet a client on the spot. They like that—it's too easy to be seen here at the marina."

"So why can't we go out there, right now, and pick up something worth selling?"

Wally chose his words carefully, but it was hard for him. Nguyen was the deliberate one. "My friend has a roommate now. I can't risk letting him know what we've got stored out there—he could clean us out—and he almost never comes ashore."

"I say we bribe him. Or we hurt him.

"He doesn't look like someone who cares much about money. And he's big, so if we go to hurt him, we better do it right the first time. Look at the size of him."

He fetched a stack of photographs from his liquor cabinet.

As Nguyen shuffled through the photos a second time, Wally said, "This guy's no rocket scientist. I can figure out how to get rid of him. Just give me a little time."

Faye's first aid kit was not well stocked. Band-Aids, generic painkillers, antiseptic spray—if it wasn't cheap and you couldn't get it over-the-counter in a small-town drugstore, then she didn't have it. She prodded at the wound on her thigh. It was surrounded by a hard red patch the size of her palm. No pus yet, but she'd bet the *Gopher* that it was infected.

Time to haul out the big guns. She reached for a tube of antibiotic ointment, the one with the label that said in huge print, "The strongest antibiotic you can buy without a prescription." Well, being as how she had no insurance to cover a prescription *or* the doctor who prescribed it, she slathered the non-prescription stuff on thick.

Cyril had mentioned going dancing sometime soon. She sure hoped she was able to walk. Gangrene was not an attractive quality in a date.

Faye was old enough to recognize the single-mindedness of someone enjoying the earliest stages of an affair, but no one is old enough to resist slipping into that giddy state. She had spent an embarrassing amount of time that day reflecting on Cyril's affable nature and fine intellect. She was thrilled that he enjoyed dancing.

Only someone very special could have risen so far above his miserable upbringing. Look what it had made of his brother: a probable killer. Her new friend's rise out of poverty was admirable and she liked spending time with people she admired. Faye hoped he found something admirable in her, but she didn't know what it might be.

She did have some admirable ancestors, no question. Thus reminded, she reached for the old journal, eager to continue Cally's story.

◇

Excerpt from Cally Stanton's oral history, recorded 1935

Lots of folks said the second Missus was stupid, but I knew her better than they did. She wasn't stupid. She was a Yankee.

She took to me from the start, saying I was pretty, and I had elegant bones. She said I was smart, too, and she wanted to teach me to dress and talk, so I could be a proper lady's maid. Maybe I'm smart. I think I am. But only a Yankee could look at my skin and my hair and, yes, Lord, even my bones, without wondering who my daddy was. I don't rightly know who my daddy was, but there was never but one white man on the place and that was her husband.

The new Missus kept herself busy by keeping me busy. I sponged her down with cool water—she didn't take to our weather—and I fetched her drinks. A little bourbon made her forget how the heat made her corsets stick to her skin. A little more bourbon made her forget that the Master married her for her money.

It wasn't hard work. The Big House felt cool to me, with the breezes coming in the tall windows and blowing the lace curtains around. There was just one bad thing about the Big House. The Master was there, and before long he noticed I was growing up.

I have lived a long ninety-six years. In all that time, I never hated anybody but one man: the Master, Andrew LaFourche. I never hated anybody in my life before the Master dragged me into an empty room and locked the door.

The Missus never noticed when my clothes was messed up and my mouth was bloody. Maybe my skin's dark enough so the bruises don't show. I don't know. But she never noticed. Or she made like she didn't notice.

Later on, he learned to hit me so he didn't leave marks. And I learned not to feel anything much at all. Time and again, I dreamed that he was going to come to a bad end and that I was going to make it happen. There was a heap of comfort in that.

The Missus always chirked up when her son, Mister Courtney Stanton, came to see her. Mister Courtney was a fine-looking man. His hair was even prettier than the master's, the color of sweet corn, more white than yellow. And shiny, good Lord.

Mister Courtney bought a fine plantation named Innisfree, slaves and all. It was near Quincy, right next door to one of the Master's tobacco plantations. And he bought Last Isle, too. First thing Mister Courtney did was lease half the island to one of his Yankee friends to build a hotel on. Next thing he did was set to work on the Big House at Innisfree.

Nobody had lived in the house at Innisfree for nigh onto five years—nobody except for possums and bats—and the roof had taken to leaking. Folks said Mister Courtney waded into his new house—right beside the slaves—to help shoo out the possums and mop out the mud. It was a scandal the way he acted, the white folks said. And their house servants heard every word.

Some said Mr. Courtney had bought a cobbler who did nothing all day but make shoes for the field hands. Some said he'd torn down the old slave cabins and built new brick ones. If all the stories were true, then Mr. Courtney had invited the black folk to come in the Big House and make themselves at home. And to help themselves to all his money while they were at it.

No, those were tall tales, but I knew a true tale and I wasn't telling. Mister Courtney was thinking about freeing his slaves. I heard him tell his Mama with my own ears. I didn't believe he'd do it, but the idea of belonging to somebody who'd even give it a thought made me dizzy. Thinking about my own Master made me dizzy, and sick to my stomach, too. He wasn't a man to set his slaves free. No, sir. I would belong to that man until I died, or he did.

Chapter 20

Faye was glad to have paying work on a Saturday, which was not surprising for a woman with no money and no social life. Some people might have been surprised to learn that the entire work team had been reassembled on one day's notice to resume the field survey on Seagreen Island—undergraduates usually plan their Saturdays around sleeping and beer—but not Faye. These kids loved their work, but it was more than that. Finishing this job and doing it well was something tangible that they could do to honor the memories of Krista and Sam.

Magda sat among them, hunched over her field notebook with her head cocked at an angle that suggested her shoulder was hurting again. Faye could sympathize. Field archaeology involved moving tons of earth and the first fact that young archaeologists learned was a simple one: dirt is heavy. And so is the equipment required to move it. And so are the artifacts of pre-plastic humans.

A single chip of pottery, a single stone spear point—these things are not heavy. But put them, carefully packaged, in a container for transport and you have a burden that will, over time, wreak havoc on the rotator cuff of the average shoulder. Neither Faye nor Magda was much over five feet tall in her stocking feet, so it was unreasonable to expect either of them to compete with the muscle mass and lever arm advantage of the full-grown men they worked with, but they were unreasonable women. Therefore, their shoulders were wrecked.

Faye laid a hand on the shoulder in question and said, "It's paining you again, isn't it?"

Magda looked up from her work with a weary nod.

"Naproxen sodium, over the counter. Double the recommended dose," Faye said with the authoritative tone of the fellow sufferer. "Get the generic. It's dirt cheap and Lord knows you'll go through a pile of it."

"What I need is a couple of Valium, but my doctor won't prescribe it. She says I have a hard-charging personality—and what the hell does that mean?—and might be prone to addiction. She says I should just get more rest, eat better, do some yoga. I'd like to see her stare into Sam and Krista's dead faces like you and I did. That's not something you get over with a few hours of extra sleep and some dopey breathing exercises."

Faye plopped onto the dirt beside Magda. She had not thought it was possible to be more depressed. "I can't get it out of my mind that we're here today because everybody's given up on finding Krista and Sam's killer," Faye said. "How is it possible that they can be dead with no reasonable explanation? We knew them pretty well and we don't have a clue to why they died. The sheriff knows criminals pretty well and he's stumped, too."

Magda doodled in the sand with a stick. "You want to know why this thing has left us feeling so off-balance? I mean besides the fact that we uncovered the dead bodies of two of our friends."

"Yeah. I do."

"Well, it's not pretty. If Sam and Krista weren't killed over drugs or some other kind of criminal activity, then it could happen to us. We're not safe and we never will be again."

Magda rose quickly, without giving Faye time to reply, without giving her time to think about it at all. "I want to go check on my crew. They're not used to working without having my crooked nose in their business."

Faye limped down the trail that surmounted the tallest part of Seagreen Island and descended toward the work site. She was glad nobody had asked what was wrong with her leg. Her prepared lie—that an old basketball injury had come back to haunt her—sounded weak even to Faye. She accompanied Magda, not just because she too needed to check on her workers, but because of Magda's newest safety rule. No one was ever to be out of sight of at least one person while they were on Seagreen Island and no one was to be there after dark.

The deputy that Sheriff Mike had sent to watch over them was constantly audible, stomping through the underbrush. He made everybody feel more secure, but his presence reminded Faye of Magda's premise: they were never really safe.

Faye and Magda stood in the shade of a tremendous live oak and looked down the line of the team's sampling sites. The surveying flags marking each site were the peachy color of orange plastic that has been faded by weather. These were the flags that Sam and Krista had set out the night before they died. There had been no reason to remove them. It would have been senseless and disrespectful to undo their work and then do it over again. So they stood as a last monument until, one by one, they would be removed and discarded when the spot they marked had been properly excavated.

The silent team members were working terribly hard, as if they wanted to finish the job and quit this place forever. Faye could see no sign that they had uncovered anything of significance. They were Seagreen Island's last hope. Unless they dug up something comparable to King Tut's tomb or Machu Picchu, this tangled spot of wildness would soon be a tamely exotic vacation destination. It would be gone, just like Sam and Krista.

They were digging in the wrong place. Faye couldn't have said how she knew it, but she was sure. Her intuitive sense—the one that told her where to dig when she was pothunting—said that the land beneath her feet was more interesting than the land her colleagues were excavating. The oak tree shading it had been there for centuries. It would have drawn human activity, simply by being there. There was no rule that said she couldn't dig there and, since she pretty much always had a trowel in her hand when she was working, there was no reason not to start digging right away.

She stooped down and cleared away the fallen leaves and branches that always litter the ground under deciduous trees of that age. Her trowel had hardly turned over a bucket load of earth before Magda dropped to her knees next to her and joined her in digging.

"Can you tell anything about the strata?" Magda asked.

"There aren't any. The layers of soil are all mixed up. Somebody's been digging here. And it looks recent to me."

Faye stopped digging and used her bare fingers to brush dirt away from a human femur. It was hardly longer than her forearm and a break near the knee had healed badly.

Magda made a choking sound. Faye looked up to see her uncovering an adult skull with an extensive, unhealed fracture.

"Somebody get the deputy," Faye bellowed. Her voice, usually so soft-spoken, cracked under the strain, but she recovered herself well enough to bellow again. "Get him up here now."

Faye stood with Magda on the floating dock that the university had installed to facilitate the project and watched Sheriff Mike and his forensic team disembark from their boat. Magda's students were gathered on the beach behind them, shoulder to shoulder. Together, they drew a line in the sand. They *were* a line in the sand.

"We will have an agreement with you before you set foot on this beach," Magda began.

"Let me list the laws you are breaking, right now," Sheriff Mike rumbled.

Faye would have enjoyed his discomfort more if she weren't having flashbacks. Sam and Krista's faces. Abby's bare skull.

Now, another skull, shattered, and the remains of a wounded child.

Magda continued, undeterred. "We have uncovered bones that are clearly not recent. Do they constitute evidence of a crime that's recent enough to prosecute? Or is the killer, if there even is one, long-dead, in which case this is an archaeological site that my team is trained and qualified to excavate?"

"I don't want to arrest you and your co-conspirators—I mean students."

"And we don't want to tie this site up in court while a bunch of lawyers get rich. We have one demand and it's simple. You will not exclude my team from the excavation of those bones."

Flashbacks or not, Faye was getting a charge out of watching Sheriff Mike squirm.

The Supreme Court. Sheriff Mike couldn't shake off the thought of nine black-garbed men and women peering over their reading glasses at him and asking, "You did what?"

What would he answer if this case survived appeal after appeal and reached the Supremes? "I was trying to expedite the investigation, Your Honors," seemed feeble.

Perhaps if he hauled Dr. Magda Stockard and her implacable companion, Faye Longchamp, to Washington with him, Their Honors would see his point.

The negotiations had been interminable, but the two women weren't entirely obstinate. They had agreed to his compromise and now they crouched just outside the yellow tape he had used to demarcate a ridiculously tiny crime scene. He crouched a few feet away from them, inside the tape with his forensic technicians. In a sense, he was supervising his technicians' work, but Magda and Faye were supervising them all.

The women had two distinct approaches to making him miserable, but they achieved the same result. Faye would gesture at a technician, reach over the yellow tape, and hand him an ax, saying only, "For that root."

Magda would squawk, "Jesus! If you pull that root any harder, the goddamn live oak's going to fall on all our heads. Don't you know what you're doing to the stratigraphy?" Then she would hurl a machete or a shovel in the offender's general direction.

How was he going to explain the sheer quantity of items that entered the crime scene from the hands of civilians, mere bystanders? And how would he explain the fact that those two civilians were making copious notes on every scrap of evidence he uncovered, all the while instructing his photographer on the precise angle from which she should shoot each bone?

For the evidence consisted entirely of bones, and there were a lot of them. They had been there a long time, maybe so long that the archaeologists were right to lay claim to the site. Maybe the Supremes would take that into account when they judged the detective work he was doing here.

A second small femur surfaced and he wondered again what had happened to the child. Everybody agreed that there was only one child in this hole, probably a boy of nine or ten. Nobody was willing to say yet that there was only one adult. The old tree had reached out for the bodies in the years since they were buried, entangling them in its roots, shoving them out of their original positions. And somebody, a human somebody, had come along later and dug the bodies up, reburying them and scrambling their remains even further.

The principal find of the day was a pelvis. When Sheriff Mike heard that it had belonged to a woman who had borne children, his first thought was *It's not Abby*. Then he thought of the two small femurs and shuddered, because there is no easier prey than a mother. Nab the child, and she will follow you anywhere to get it back. Threaten the child, and she will hand over her own life just to save her baby. Even if her baby's thirty years old.

Besides the adult skull and pelvis and the two little leg bones, a number of vertebrae and ribs had surfaced. People had lots of backbones and ribs, and it would take a practiced eye and skill with a cleaning brush to tell whether they'd uncovered one C4 vertebra or ten.

Early in the day, he'd assigned a technician to catalog those smaller bones and, for better or worse, the poor guy was getting plenty of help from Faye, who was leaning far into the crime scene to peer at the evidence. He had explained to both Faye and Magda that they should picture a humongous sheet of plate glass, starting at the ground, running through the crime scene tape, and extending toward the heavens. He told them to by God stay on their side of the glass. Faye seemed to have pictured in her mind a humongous sheet of Saran Wrap. She was stretching it with impunity.

Then somebody cried, "I've got another pelvis, but it's in bad shape. I'm not sure I should uncover it any more." Sheriff Mike watched in disbelief as Faye dropped to all fours and slithered under the tape. Magda hurdled it, crying, "Bless you for your responsible field technique. I want a look at that pelvis myself."

Sheriff Mike joined the huddle around the half-excavated pelvis. As one, Faye, Magda, and the responsible field tech said, "Adult male," and Magda looked the sheriff right in the eye. "You've got three bodies here."

Everybody has to eat, even the most frenzied workaholic. Even frenzied workaholics digging up dead bodies. By mid-afternoon, the excavators had washed dirt and death from their hands and dug out their sack lunches. Faye, for one, was mightily enjoying her peanut-butter-and-honey sandwich.

Even when hungry, Faye was a slow, meditative eater. As she munched, staring into space, her eyes focused on the pine tree directly in front of her, a few dozen yards away. There was an odd scar on its trunk. Glancing around, she noticed another scarred trunk, one tree to the left.

She rose, still gnawing on her sandwich, and went to see if she could tell how the trees got wounded. Sheriff Mike dogged her steps like he thought she was going to throw gasoline on his precious crime scene and set it alight. Something about the marks on those trees gave her the shivers.

"The bullets. The ones that killed Sam and Krista," she said, thrusting her fingers into one of the splintery cavities.

"That's where we found them," Sheriff Mike said.

Faye pulled her hands away from the living wood where traces of her friends' blood might yet remain.

"Could you tell where the shooter was standing?"

"Just to the right of that big live oak."

Faye faced the pine in front of her, braced herself against it, then leaned to the right. "So, if we assume a right-handed shooter, then we can assume he—"

"Or she."

"Yeah. We can assume whoever it was hid behind that tree—which would have been easy since it's at least five feet wide—then leaned or stepped out just far enough to get a clear shot at Sam and Krista." She eyeballed the two scars, extrapolating their trajectories. "It wouldn't have taken an especially good marksman to pull it off. They weren't standing far away from the shooter—just a few feet this side of the same tree he was hiding behind."

It only took a second for what she had just said to sink in.

She looked at the sheriff's face, where recognition was also dawning, and said, "When Sam and Krista died, they were standing smack on top of the mass grave. I can't believe you didn't realize this sooner."

Sheriff Mike muttered, "I've been working under duress," then stood silent for a full minute. When he spoke again, Faye wondered whether he might have cracked under the strain. Why else would he ask, "There's no need for Sandra Day O'Connor to know about this slip-up, is there?"

Faye, the sheriff, and Magda huddled over a communal bag of tortilla chips. Faye was half-listening to Magda expound on things metaphysical. She'd heard more than one of the professor's monologues on the convergence of destiny and entropy.

Magda must have moved on to more down-to-earth issues, because Faye's attention stopped wandering.

"Somebody shot those kids just because they were standing on top of an unmarked grave," Magda rambled on. "They needn't have died. We'd never have found those bodies with the simple survey we were doing. With ground-penetrating radar, maybe. Look at that line of flags. We would have passed ten or twenty feet from the bone pit without ever knowing it was there."

The long line of weathered surveying flags that Sam and Krista had planted on their last day on Earth seemed to stand up and wave at Faye.

"Where is the field notebook?" Faye blurted, jumping up and upsetting the bag of chips in the process. "Where's the notebook Sam and Krista were using that day?"

"In the shed with all the others," Magda said.

Faye headed for the shed as fast as her workboots would allow.

"Where are you going?" the sheriff asked sharply.

"To look for the killer's handwriting," Faye said, amused by how quickly Magda and Sheriff Mike got to their feet.

Faye deferred to the sheriff when it came to handling the notebook. He seemed to have forgotten his initial objections to letting her and Magda loiter around his investigation, now that they had proven useful. Besides, while she knew a few things about digging up secrets, she knew absolutely nothing about preserving fingerprint data.

They found the field notebook lying atop a short stack of identical books, which was only logical since it was the last one used. The sheriff donned gloves, then opened his pocket-knife. Leaving the notebook lying where it was, he slid the tip of the knife blade under the edge of each page and turned them gingerly, one by one.

"Find the last page they wrote on," Faye said.

The sheriff nodded that he heard her, but he didn't change his deliberate pace. Page one, page two, page three, page four. Seeing Krista's handwriting on each sheet made Faye so jumpy that she wanted to urge him to work faster, but she held her tongue because she didn't want Sheriff Mike to revise his new and improved opinion of her.

Halfway into the notebook, Krista's entries stopped. Faye studied the last entry. It was written the evening before the two students were killed, and Krista had recorded exactly what Magda had told her to record: the location of each of the planned sampling sites.

Not that those locations were meaningful, in and of themselves. They were recorded in relative coordinates, each one measured from a reference point. The first sampling point, for instance, was labeled "[12, 18]", meaning that it was twelve feet east and eighteen feet north of the reference point. Unless she knew the location of the reference point—and she was wholeheartedly certain that Krista had documented that point somewhere in this notebook—then this list of bracketed numbers could refer to sampling sites in Peru.

Faye didn't need the reference point and she didn't need to locate the actual sampling sites documented here. The fading line of orange flags that marked them quite well was still standing. But those flags couldn't tell her who had stuck them in the ground. This notebook could.

Someone had altered Krista's notebook entries.

The *y*-coordinate had been changed from 3 to 18, with three barely perceptible swoops of a waterproof felt-tip. The change from 13 to 28 was a bit more discernible, but the killer was deft with a pen. Changing 33 to 48 had required blotting out the three and starting again, but the purpose of data notebooks was to record science on the fly. Corrections were inevitable. Nothing on this page would call attention to itself unless the reader, like Faye, had some notion of what they were looking to find.

"He moved the flags. They're fifteen feet north of where Krista put them," she said. "Our archaeological survey would have found the bodies if we'd dug where we were supposed to. And I bet he tried to dig them up first, to keep that from happening, but he couldn't manage it because of the roots entangled in the bones. That's why the soil was recently disturbed."

"He killed Sam and Krista and moved the flags to keep us away from the old grave," Magda said. "They're dead because they were doing their job."

Faye and Magda allowed the sheriff to shoo them out of the storage shed before he hurried away to fetch his fingerprint technician.

Faye watched the sheriff's excavation crew dig bones out of the ground until the sun gave out. After reading Krista's notebook, she had taken a walk along Seagreen Island's waterfront, near where she had found the empty boat on the awful day Sam and Krista died. The tiny island where Abby had rested all those years lay just over the horizon.

It had taken a full afternoon of sitting on her butt and watching other people work, but she'd pieced the data together into a logical whole and she didn't like its shape. She and Joe had found Abby the night before Sam and Krista died. The sheriff agreed with her that Sam and Krista were killed to stop them from uncovering the mass grave under the oak tree. So one person was responsible for all five bodies found on Seagreen Island.

There was evidence that the killer had slept on Seagreen Island the night Sam and Krista were shot. It was possible (maybe likely) that the same person, while boating to and from the island, saw her dig Abby up. Abby's bones went missing within a day or two. Was the person who took them the same person who killed her? Did the same person kill Krista and Sam and the nameless people under the live oak?

Was the same person piloting the boat that had scared her and Joe away from Abby's grave?

The old murders and the new murders had tied themselves into a neat knot. The murderer was still loose and still killing people. Hiding what she knew about Abby was wrong, but it didn't cause anyone great harm. She could have gone on doing that forever and still have been able to live with herself. But she couldn't risk waking up one morning and finding that Sam and Krista's murderer had killed again.

She would give herself twenty-four hours to marshal her resources. That small delay could do no harm. Abby's bones were the most important piece of evidence and they were gone. She would need the time to gather the earring, the religious medal, and all her photocopies documenting Abby's life and death, because it was important that she be able to support her theory that Cedrick Kirby killed Abby and the people buried under the live oak on Seagreen Island. Even though no one had seen him in years, logic said that he had returned to kill Sam and Krista. She needed the sheriff to listen to her. He was going to think she was scum when he found out about her chronic withholding of information. She might as well get used to being treated like scum. She didn't imagine that bankruptcy court and prison were going to boost her self-esteem any.

Delaying her moment of reckoning by just one day would help her in another way. It would give her time to gather up as much money as she could. She would need plenty of money to pay a lawyer, to pay the fines, to maybe pay her taxes while she was in jail and out of the workforce.

Who was she kidding? She wouldn't need to pay her taxes. Joyeuse was as good as gone.

Faye was glad to go home and leave Seagreen Island behind her, and she was sorry for Deputies Claypool and Thornton, who were left to guard the evidence.

Rejecting Joe's offer of supper felt like slapping a puppy on the nose, but Faye had no appetite. Still, she wished she hadn't told him what they'd found on Seagreen Island before she dragged herself to bed.

"A man. A woman. A child. Dead and lying in pieces under the ground."

If she'd been speaking to a child she would have measured her words more carefully or said nothing at all. Joe's gentle soul deserved the same consideration.

Joe posed another problem for her. Could she steer her life into a controlled dive without taking him down with her? When she lost Joyeuse, he would be rendered homeless. But he'd been homeless before.

It was more important to protect him from the federal charges she would face for digging on public lands. Joe had kept a low profile; it was his way. None of her customers had ever met him, so there would be no one to testify that he had profited from her pothunting activities. If nobody knew that he helped her excavate Abby, she could face the charges for withholding evidence all by her lonesome self. That was the way she wanted it.

It didn't take long to box up the evidence supporting her suspicion that Cedrick Kirby killed Abby Williford. Sadly, it also didn't take long to assemble her few remaining valuables. Faye owned nothing worth selling, nothing but Joyeuse. But she was never without a plan. In the morning, she would call Cyril from Wally's and invite him out to see Joyeuse. He had money and good business sense, and he would understand the potential commercial value of her island. He would lend her the money she needed if she offered him Joyeuse as collateral.

There was no possibility that she'd ever be able to pay him back, but she preferred to lose Joyeuse to Cyril rather than to lose it for back taxes. She collapsed on her bed, surrounded by her gaily painted walls, and let failure hang in the air like a wet fog.

"I have failed," she said aloud. "I have let Cally down." Her days as mistress of Joyeuse were winding down.

◇

Excerpt from the oral history of Cally Stanton, recorded 1935

Going to Last Isle was Mister Courtney's idea and he always felt bad about it. He was visiting with his mama and she'd had too much bourbon. She was crying, like she always did when she'd had too much bourbon, and he asked her why didn't she go with him to the grand opening of the new hotel on Last Isle. I can still hear his sweet voice saying, "I hear it has every amenity."

When he said that, I stopped my dusting and leaned up against the window seat to free up all my strength for praying. *Please, Lord, let her go to Last Isle and let her take me.* I'd be out of the Master's reach for weeks. I held my breath.

The Missus kept sipping her bourbon, but she nodded her head yes and I was a happy woman.

It wasn't long before the Missus found a way to spoil my happiness. I remember the day, I remember it well. I was packing the Missus's things and loving my work. *I'm going away from this place*, I'd say to myself while the flatiron got hot. *The Master can keep his ugly face right here*, I'd say when I was laying her underclothes in the travel trunk. *I'll just keep the Missus drunk and have me a fine old time.*

But I should have got her drunk before we left, because when I went to heat the flatiron back up, I heard her talking to him.

"Really, dear, I wish you would go with me. How could I enjoy myself properly without my husband?"

The tears ran down my face. It surprised me. It'd been a long time since I took the trouble to cry.

I prayed a lot the whole rest of that day. *Don't let the Master go with us to Last Isle*, I prayed while I brushed the Missus's everyday poplin, and while I swept off the sun porch, and when I lay in my bed that night. *Don't let him go.*

I thought I'd hear those words all night—*Don't let him go!*—but I didn't. I slept a good sleep and I had a good dream and I woke up singing, because I knew the Master was going to die.

I didn't rightly see how it would happen. My dreams don't always come clear. All I could see was gray water and foamy waves, and somehow I knew I was on Last Isle, not on Joyeuse Island. The Missus was whinkering in my dream, because the Master was dead and I did it. And I wasn't afraid, no, I wasn't afraid any more. I wasn't afraid of being slapped to the ground. I wasn't afraid of a fist in my belly. I wasn't even afraid of hanging for murder. I was glad he was dead, glad I killed him. And I had a notion I wouldn't hang. I didn't know how, but I was thinking I might kill my master and walk free.

Chapter 21

If Joe Wolf Mantooth had been the kind of man who was in touch with his feelings, consulting them constantly in the self-conscious New Age manner, he would have known that, on this lovely morning, he was at peace in the world. This did not mean that everything in his world was perfect. He was troubled over the deaths of Faye's two friends and his soul hurt for the woman whose lonely rest he and Faye had disturbed. He didn't understand all of Faye's problems, but he was well versed in the turmoil associated with money and its lack. If he'd had a cent to his name, he would have given it to Faye, although he suspected that money might ease her troubles but would not solve them.

These concerns frequently occupied Joe's mind, but they didn't disturb the peace at his core. As long as he could be alive in a place where he could feel the gentle morning sun on his face and enjoy watching it blaze overhead before it fell cool again into the sea, then he would be whole.

He stood on the seaward side of Joyeuse Island, watching the cartwheeling dives of the sea birds catching their fishy breakfast. His ears hissed with the noise of a stiff breeze or he might have heard the interlopers' approach sooner, but instead an irate songbird was the one to tell the tale. At the unexpected sound, Joe wheeled around and saw what was bothering the tufted titmouse.

Two speedboats approached, hardly slowing to navigate the shallow waters ringing the island. Seven, eight, maybe nine teenagers hopped out in an area wholly unsuitable for landing boats and carelessly tied their crafts to some handy trees. Then they stomped into the marsh that dominated this side of the island, oblivious to lurking water moccasins, although they were making enough drunken noise to scare away any sensible predator.

"I been hearing about the Wild Man all my life and I'm ready to lay my eyes on him," said the boy in the lead.

"Sharon said she saw him right here, right on this island. Do you think he's really eighty years old, like they say?" said a younger boy, taking swig of his beer.

"Doubt it. Sharon said he was cute," said the only girl in the group.

Joe the Wild Man, who was indeed cute, could travel through deep woods without making a sound. While his hunters were busy thrashing around in the swamp, he had retreated inland to his camp with a clear idea of what must happen. They must not find him. They must not find this camp. They must, under no circumstances, stumble upon Faye's house.

His hands closed on his bow, laboriously crafted over a period of weeks out of wood he had gathered and bent and shaped. It was held together with sinew and glue made from the bodies of animals he killed himself. He fitted an arrow to the string, its arrowhead made of rock he'd chipped, held to its shaft with the same sinew and glue. He believed in fighting his own battles, using weapons that were integral parts of himself.

He watched the kids stumble forward. It had taken them a full night of drinking to get up the nerve for this sightseeing trip and the results were obvious. In this terrain, their gaits were uneven and unsteady, making it difficult to aim precisely. At last, he saw his chance and let the arrow fly.

It bit into a tree trunk after passing between the first two boys at shoulder height. They were walking so close to each other that they could have held hands if they'd been so inclined. The group turned in a single motion and fled, as Joe had intended. One of them paused and tugged at the arrow, as Joe had feared, but he couldn't free it, so he escaped empty-handed.

He heard them crank their boats and head for open water as he pulled his arrow from the tree. He pondered his options and saw only one: he had to leave Joyeuse, as soon as possible. He was endangering Faye's home with his presence. Unless he left, more thrill-seekers would come looking for the Wild Man and, one day, he might accidentally hurt somebody when he was just trying to get them to leave.

Being a man of action, not thought, Joe moved quickly to load his possessions onto his johnboat. Later, it occurred to him that he should have said good-bye to Faye.

The smell of smoke from Joe's ceremonial fire assaulted the nostrils of Deputies Claypool and Thornton, who had dutifully prowled the island all night long aided only by their flashlights. While some young lawmen easily rush into peril for the thrill of taking their quarry on its own turf, others are more sensible. Claypool and Thornton were two of the sensible ones. They wanted to survive the night, assemble the evidence, figure out who the killer was and get a warrant, then corner the creep with enough manpower and firepower to minimize the risk to themselves and their colleagues. Each of them silently welcomed the sunrise as an omen that they'd be living another day.

The flickering light of Joe's campfire was another omen, but not a welcome one.

Good training and a couple of years working side-by-side had eliminated useless verbiage. Communicating as much with a nod and a pointed finger as with words, they decided that Thornton would cover Claypool, and Claypool would do the talking.

Good training had not prepared them for the smell of herbs burning in a bonfire or for the torchlit sight of a dark-haired man sitting, eyes closed, beside the open grave. The man rose to his moccasined feet, and Claypool recognized him as the stranger who had appeared on Seagreen Island's beach the day after Sam and Krista were killed.

He drew his sidearm, knowing that Thornton had already taken aim at the stranger's sternum, and barked, "Drop everything and, very slowly, show me your hands." The stranger did as he was told and Claypool was slightly relieved. This was bad, because the relief brought on the head rush that so often struck when a crisis was over. This crisis wasn't over, but now Claypool would have to fight his own body chemistry—the muscle shakes that made his gun waggle, the cold sweat that dripped in his eyes, and the dry throat that made his voice squeaky when he yelled, "Did you do this?"

He gestured at the open hole where he'd watched people digging up pieces of a child, pieces of a man and a woman. "Did you do this?" he demanded again.

Joe was a simple man with a literal mind. He looked at the ceremonial talismans surrounding the grave and knew that he certainly made them, so he said, in front of Deputy Claypool and a witness, "Yes. I did."

Deputy Claypool could have slapped himself, but his hands were busy. He had just failed, in front of a witness, to advise this guy of his Miranda rights.

He chanted the mantra, the rosary, the creed, the TV script, the ever-familiar *You have the right to remain silent*, and all the rest of it, and he did it quickly. Then he asked again, "Did you do this?"

Joe remained silent, not because he had just been advised that he had a right to do so, but because he was unutterably confused and he wasn't sure exactly what the man in the uniform wanted him to say. He spent a quiet moment with his arms in the air, waiting for the men to put their guns away and tell him what to do. Even in such a situation, a part of him was aware of the wind's strength and its direction. Some part of his ear was monitoring the pitch and rhythm of insect song and how frequently waves broke on the nearby shore. Joe wasn't sure what the men with the guns were going to do with him, but his senses were telling him that something in the natural world was seriously off-kilter.

Faye had skipped breakfast and spent the first hour of the day combing her house for things to sell. The harvest was meager so she was taking her desperate inventory to the outbuildings scattered among the trees behind her home. She knew that Joyeuse's service buildings had once been confined in a courtyard that was always kept fenced and swept clean, because her grandmother had told her so, but nature can take back a lot of land in fifty years. Sizeable trees hung over the old sheds, and damp shade was hard on buildings of any age.

The condition of Faye's outbuildings depended heavily on their material of construction. Several small sheds that had served as corncribs and smokehouses were built of pine planks. They sagged at such discouraging angles that Faye had long since emptied them so that nothing would come to harm when they fell.

The kitchen, however, was stoutly built of cypress. Its long straight sills sat on cypress stumps. Cypress lasts well-nigh onto forever. Faye could have used the kitchen for its original purpose if she'd cared to cook in an immense iron cauldron suspended in a fireplace large enough to house her bed. Someone had years ago decided that the kitchen would make an excellent place to store old farm equipment. Faye looked it over. Some of the equipment might have value as scrap metal. She would ask Cyril if he knew anyone who would be interested in it.

Sturdier still than the kitchen was the barn she had lent Wally. It was constructed of tabby, the same shell-and-limestone cement that composed her house's bottom level. She had long suspected that the first settlers on Joyeuse Island, perhaps William and Susan Whitehall, had built a simple dogtrot cabin of tabby that was later converted into a basement for the current house. The ornate and ostentatious upper floors suited Andrew LaFourche's temperament perfectly. If her suspicions were correct, then the tabby barn would have been the original service building, so it was probably older than any other structure on the island, except for the first floor of the big house. That made it special, and she had been glad to lend it to Wally, whom she had long considered a special friend. Maybe he would miss her when she was in jail.

She hadn't been in the old tabby barn since she'd given Wally the use of it. She'd had no need to go in there, and she respected Wally's privacy. If her memory served, there was nothing of hers in there that had even as much dubious value as the farm equipment in the barn, but today was a day for pursuing long shots. She unlocked the padlock and went in.

It was dark, with only a single shuttered window. It was also cool, and the thick masonry walls would trap this morning coolness and use it to keep the building comfortable all day long.

Her eyes adjusted to the small amount of light coming in the door behind her. She was suddenly disoriented. The barn was jammed full of far more boxes than she remembered Wally bringing all those years ago. To her knowledge, he'd never come back. And some of the stuff she did remember—the couch, the dinette set, the well-used mattress—was gone.

There were only row after row, stack after stack of sturdy crates. Suddenly relieved of any high-minded desire to respect Wally's privacy, she tried to lower a crate to the floor so she could see what was inside. It was far too heavy.

Undeterred, she used the stack of crates next to the wall as a ladder and climbed up to open the shutter covering the barn's lone window, high in the front wall. Balancing atop the stack, she struggled to lift the lid off the top crate. The sun shone in the window, beautifully illuminating a treasure trove of rock and bone, packed none-too-carefully in wadded newspaper.

Just a glance at the top layer of artifacts in the crate yielded two Clovis unifacial tools and three pre-Columbian chert points. Her friend had stashed crates of stuff—some of it run-of-the-mill arrowheads, some of it irreplaceable museum-quality goods, and some of it junk—in her shed. Faye felt a girlish need to cry. Her backstabbing friend Wally was involved in robbing the Clovis site.

Oh, great. Now she was going to have to do the right thing and turn Wally over to the Feds. He would, no doubt, spill his guts about everything he knew about her black market dealings, but if she didn't do what she could to stop him and his grave-robbing, thieving accomplices then, once and for all, she would know that she was just as scummy as they were.

Wally tried to look assured as he sat down next to the boss, but it was hard, because he was so tired. The man liked to schedule these meetings at the last minute, in out-of-the-way places, and early in the day. If he had known the phone was going to ring before sunup, ordering him to get here by nine, he wouldn't have bothered going to bed at all.

Wally brought a battered briefcase full of sales records with him, as he usually did. The boss always wanted to know what artifacts Wally had dug up and what price they brought, and that was all that he had ever wanted to know, up to this point. Wally didn't have an M.B.A., but he'd kept the marina going for thirty years now. In the process, he'd acquired accounting skills that were at least marginal. He was prepared for the boss and his questions.

And then the man threw him a curve, asking him whether he knew that the Park Service was looking into possible artifact poaching in the wildlife preserve.

Wally was inordinately proud of the fact that he hit the curve ball out of the park. Digging deep in his briefcase he drew out an envelope full of photos. They were valuable and they would make him valuable.

"See these?" he said, fanning out the photographs of Faye touring the Water Island dig site. "This babe's an amateur pothunter, herself. If there's ever any danger of us getting caught poaching artifacts, we can use these to pin the whole thing on her."

The boss was silent, so Wally pulled out a second envelope. "And see these? I took them day before yesterday with a telephoto lens. They show her digging, and her boyfriend, some Indian-looking guy named Joe, is helping her. Now, she's digging on her own island, so she ain't breaking no laws, but you can't tell it in this picture. I zoomed right in where you can't see anything but them."

The boss was silent, looking at the second batch of photos, one by one. He pulled one of them out of the stack, a close-up of the man leaning over an excavation, while the woman—small, short-haired, with boyish hips—crouched with her back to the camera.

Wally was proud of his plan and the uncharacteristic foresight that had gone into it. He didn't understand why the boss, livid, kept shuffling the photos in his hand.

Chapter 22

The ride to Wally's was going to be a rough one. Faye had seen this kind of weather before when there was a hurricane in the Gulf. She felt bad for the people on the Texas coast, boarding up their homes and getting out. Her skiff was going nowhere today. It would take the *Gopher* to get her to shore in this mess.

Steering the *Gopher* out of its protective inlet and into open water, she steeled herself for the swells—evenly spaced and more than four feet high—that signaled misfortune for coastal Texans. Her own sky was steel blue and cloudless, so she reckoned she could weather a few swells.

She didn't, however, reckon she could stand to look at Wally, so she hoped Cyril would come quickly, before Wally woke up. She ran in to the marina—no Wally, praise God—and called Cyril at his Tallahassee office.

His secretary answered the phone, cool and business-like, but Faye simply blurted, "Can I speak to the senator? I need—just tell him that Faye would like very much to speak with him."

The secretary connected them so promptly that Faye wondered if he'd added her to his list, the list that all powerful men gave their secretaries. Cyril's list of people that he was always willing to speak to would be short. If she was on it, that was a sign that she hadn't imagined the things that had passed between them on that lovely evening when they shared a dinner and a moonrise at the edge of the Gulf of Mexico.

Popular wisdom said that sexual attraction was instantaneous but deeper feelings took time. Popular wisdom was usually right, but maybe not this time. Maybe he cared for her, and she needed to be cared for. Wally had betrayed her in a big way, so she could count one less friend. She had more or less accused Douglass of murder, so that cut out another. Joe was ever-faithful and she trusted Magda, but that was about it.

Today would be a day for her friends to stand up and be counted. It was time to find out where Cyril stood. "I'm in trouble. I need help, and I thought of you." She swallowed. "I want to show you where I live."

She had dodged his every delicate effort to worm her street address and phone number out of her. He would know the significance of her last statement.

He answered quickly, without bothering to ask what the trouble was. "I'll meet you at Wally's Marina in two hours."

Faye hung up the phone, feeling measurably safer. She dodged the mid-morning influx of recreational fishermen and walked over to the grill. As she plopped onto a counter stool, Liz leaned over the counter and whispered, "I've been waiting for you. Your handsome friend Joe called an hour ago, but I couldn't reach you. Don't you ever turn your radio on?"

Faye shrugged. "There aren't many people I want to talk to. What did Joe want?"

"He wants you to get him out of jail. You were his one phone call."

"Jail? What's Joe in jail for? Vagrancy? Building a campfire without a permit?"

"Murder. They got him for killing your two friends. And some other people. Three of them."

"Joe didn't..." Or did he? Where was he the morning that Sam and Krista were killed? Where had he been the night they had found Abby?

If Joe had done all five Seagreen Island murders, she could keep quiet about Abby. Cedrick was gone, dead or in hiding. If he had killed no one else since Abby, he couldn't be much of a danger any more. Let him rot, wherever he was.

It was so tempting to leave Abby to her fitful rest and let Joe answer for all the other killings. She would be back where she started, treading financial water and trying to save Joyeuse with nothing more serious on her conscience than poaching an occasional rusty artifact off the land of an American public that didn't give a damn. But she knew that the connection between Abby and Krista and Sam and the nameless three on Seagreen Island, though tenuous, was real.

Joe wasn't old enough to have killed Abby. And he wasn't old enough to have murdered people who'd been dead so long that tree roots had grown through their chest cavities. Her gut said that Cedrick had killed them too, then killed Sam and Krista to cover his crime.

Joe's plight didn't change her plans for self-sacrifice. It reinforced the need for it. She would go to Sheriff Mike, as planned. She would tell him about Abby, show him the earring, the religious medal, the yearbook photos. He would understand that the connection between all the killings was plenty real and he would free Joe. He would probably turn around and arrest her, which was why she still needed to take Cyril to Joyeuse for a fundraising drive. Lawyers could be fearfully expensive.

She had just one thing more to do and she could squeeze it into the two hours left before Cyril arrived. She said to Liz, "I'm meeting a friend. If he comes before I get back, tell him to wait here in the grill for me."

Faye thought she was prepared for the sight of Joe in jail. She was not.

An hour away from the sun had bleached the ruddy color from his face and bowed his broad shoulders. His jailers had taken the leather thong that graced his omnipresent ponytail, leaving his lank hair hanging around his face. Why? Was that tiny strip of leather a threat to Joe or the people around him?

He sat behind a sheet of safety glass and spoke meekly into the microphone. "I don't understand, Faye. I never said I killed anybody. I never did kill anybody. But they say I did. They say I said I did." There was a noise behind him and he looked surreptitiously over one shoulder at the sound of angry voices. Joe, who could face down a bereaved mother bear, was afraid of the men jailed with him.

Faye got through her allotted ten-minute visit with as few tears as she could manage. Above anything else, she couldn't afford to make Joe cry. The sight of his tears would finish her. Her impotent anger would drag her off the uncomfortable stool and make her put her skinny foot right through that pane of safety glass. Then they'd both be in jail and she'd have several dozen stitches down her leg.

"I'll get you out," she vowed before she left him, "but it may take me a little while. Be patient. And Joe—" His gaze, which had been wandering, focused on her again. "Please stay safe, Joe."

She left him and went looking for Sheriff Mike, but he'd gone to the forensics lab in Tallahassee. One of his deputies was tending the store.

"What will it take to get him out of here?" she asked.

The deputy was polite and well-trained. "Nothing short of intercession by the President, the Pope, and the Queen of England would get that man out of jail before he makes his first appearance in front of the judge tomorrow morning."

"Even if he's innocent?"

"They all say they're innocent and some of them are, but everybody has to go through a first appearance. That's just the way it is."

And so she left Joe with the criminals.

It was time to meet Cyril. The two-faced nature of what she was about to do struck her hard. She was going to hit Cyril up for money, then try to convince the sheriff that

Cyril's brother was a murderer. She hated like hell to do it, but Cyril could take care of himself. Joe couldn't.

When Sheriff Mike moved quickly, it was a sign that he was troubled in his mind. He was fairly well hustling as he entered the office where Deputy Claypool sat.

"Explain to me again why you arrested him," he said in an oddly gentle tone of voice, given his level of agitation.

"Who?"

"Who do you think? Joe Wolf Mantooth. How many arrests you made this morning?"

Claypool cocked his head and spoke slowly, as if he were explaining the obvious. "I arrested him because he told me he killed those people we found yesterday. Not many people confess to murder unless they did it."

"Not many, but it happens. You should be checking your facts, right now, instead of sitting there drinking your coffee. Hell, keep your coffee. You can drink a pot of it, as long as you're doing your job while you drink."

Claypool dropped his Styrofoam cup, still full of coffee, in the trash. "I'll be glad to do my job, if you'll just tell me what it is you think I should be doing."

"How old is your suspect?"

"He's a classic vagrant. No driver's license, no papers of any kind. We had a devil of a time filling out the paperwork to book him. No address or phone. His place of birth is just 'Oklahoma.' Couldn't even remember his birthday."

"How old do you think he is?"

Claypool pursed his lips. "Thirty-five? Forty?"

Sheriff Mike rolled his eyes. Claypool was no fool. He had five years of experience and he'd performed well, but there was no overcoming the handicap of being twenty-seven years old. Life experience was a complement to law enforcement experience and Claypool would accumulate both in time.

"Son, I've seen Mr. Mantooth. He's lived a hard life, but he moves loose and his eyes are young. I'll buy you a scotch-and-soda if that man's as old as you are."

Surprise was evident on Claypool's pale babyface. The boy needed a scotch-and-soda. He'd never known life without air conditioning and he'd spent his adolescence at the business end of a video game controller, rather than a fishing rod. Claypool's grandfather's face had likely worn a weather-beaten tan by the time he was twenty-seven but, for Claypool, the aging process would be a long, drawn-out affair.

"Say he's your age," the sheriff continued. "It took somebody man-sized to fracture that skull we dug up. And it took somebody man-sized to put those bodies in the ground. How old were you when you got big enough to do something like that?"

Claypool had committed thousands of video-game murders by the age of twelve, but his electronic victims had just fallen down and evaporated. "I don't know. Maybe fifteen or sixteen."

"So if Mr. Mantooth did it, it's been in the last ten years. How long you think those bodies have been in the ground?"

"Well, the flesh was all gone, so they weren't put there yesterday, but you can't always tell by the rate of decay. Bodies break down at different rates, depending on things like soil chemistry."

Sheriff Mike was pleased. Claypool never forgot anything he learned from a book. Life experience would sneak up on him and he'd be a real good officer.

"Then there's the roots," Claypool went on. "It surely took some time for them to disrupt the bodies that way. I'm not sure if they could do that in ten years or not."

The sheriff gave him an "Attaboy" nod, and said, "The coroner, the forensics people, and the archaeologists—they all think those bodies were buried before you and Mr. Mantooth were born."

"So we let him go?"

"You brought a trespassing vagrant with no proper ID in on murder charges, and now you want to let him go before he makes his first appearance before the judge? Hell, no, we don't let him go. It will not hurt Mr. Mantooth to spend a night in our air-conditioned jail and eat a few hot meals. Besides, I want to talk to him. You can sit in the room with us and listen to what he has to say."

Sheriff Mike hustled Claypool into a questioning room and had Mr. Mantooth brought in. The prisoner did not look good. Despair had drained the youth out of his eyes and anyone asked to guess his age might easily have made Claypool's error. He sat in the chair Sheriff Mike offered him and spread his hands out on his thighs. They were the hands of a man who made and fixed things. One of his fingernails was bruised black and all of them were broken. His hands were callused in odd places that had to be specific to a certain task.

"What do you do for a living, Mr. Mantooth?" the sheriff asked, hoping to figure out where he got those calluses.

"My last job was working for a flintknapper in Georgia. I ain't worked steady since then, but I still chip stone, when I got the time and the stone."

A bit of life glinted in the prisoner's eyes and the sheriff understood. Humanity had lived in the Stone Age far longer than it had enjoyed the Information Age, and the slick-sharp feel of a stone tool resided in the collective unconscious. He'd found few thrills in life purer than the act of pulling an old arrowhead out of freshly plowed soil. Like anybody who'd walked many miles behind a plow, he'd amassed a sizeable collection. It pleasured him just to look at the ancient things.

"You have the hands of a flintknapper. I wish I had your skill," the sheriff said before getting down to business. "Now here's what I want to know. Explain to me what you were doing on Seagreen Island this morning."

"It hurt my heart to think of those poor people lying for years and years in unholy graves. And your people left some of their bones in the cold ground and took some of them away. That can't be comfortable for them."

"And you know how to help them rest comfortably?" the sheriff asked.

"I do the best I know how, but I didn't get the feeling that I helped much this morning. Their spirits were just too stirred up."

The sheriff heard Claypool shift in his chair and, without turning to look at him, said, "Wipe that cynical look off your face, son."

"I didn't get a good feeling last week, either," Joe added.

Sheriff Mike considered this cryptic comment. "What happened last week?"

"Same thing. I tried to help a poor girl buried all by herself. I tried to consecrate her grave, too, but her spirit wasn't all stirred up. It just wasn't there."

The sheriff heard Claypool slide to the edge of his seat and hold his breath. Trying to keep the casual tone in his voice, Sheriff Mike asked, "What girl?"

"Don't know. Just saw her bones and a tiny little earring. That's how you could tell she was a girl."

Old tears rose in the sheriff's eyes, tears older than Claypool and Joe. "Tell me about the earring."

"It was silvery, with a screw on the back to hold it on and a little ball dangling off the bottom."

Sheriff Mike closed his eyes, to get a better look at his memory of Abby Williford's young face with her favorite pearl earrings dancing on either side of it. "Can you take me to her body? Please?"

Chapter 23

The sky was still clear, but the waves were rolling ever higher, complicating Faye's efforts to get Cyril to Joyeuse as quickly as possible. She needed to ask him for the loan before her dignity reasserted itself. She could not afford to be proud today.

The *Gopher* refused to slice through waves this size and the repetitive *thwap* as its hull hit the water after each swell passed jarred her wounded leg painfully. The windscreen wasn't doing its job, either. She could barely keep her eyes open in the face of the hot wind.

Faye was perversely happy to be uncomfortable. She was poised to use Cyril, then lay a pointy finger of suspicion on his long-lost brother. She hoped, for his sake, that the voters could be trusted to remember that being the brother of a murderer didn't make a man any less electable.

As if to make her feel even more like dirt, Cyril hadn't even asked her what her troubles were. He'd just cancelled his appointments for the day—appointments that probably included CEOs, other legislators, maybe even the governor. He was letting her take him into her confidence in her own time and she was grateful.

His concern was evident in the way he stood behind her as she piloted the *Gopher*, hands resting on the wheel beside hers, arms encircling her. It was a tender gesture but, damn her keen eyesight, it wasn't the most romantic position he could have put himself in. As she looked up at him in gratitude, she saw right to his hairline where the bright sunlight exposed the nearly invisible scar left by the plastic surgeon who had repaired the vestiges of child abuse.

She thought of Isaiah and his mother and their noses and the sad yearbook photo of little Cyril's battered face. Cyril was lucky that repairing his broken nose had left no scar. In fact, the adult Cyril had a nice nose, although the little asymmetric bump at its bridge perplexed her. She'd never heard of a plastic surgeon willing to give a patient a nose that wasn't movie-star perfect. Perhaps he'd broken it again.

She focused on the water and the image of Cyril's fourth-grade picture returned. The busted nose, the waifish smile, and the missing tooth tugged at her heart. There was no question that the man was a survivor.

She looked up at him again and he flashed her a smile. His teeth. They weren't unattractive. They weren't tobacco-stained and they didn't protrude. It was just that one incisor angled out ever so slightly, crossing the other incisor by the barest millimeter. They were the teeth of a real person, one whose mouth had never been perfected by dental science.

All the admiring observations she had made—how amazing it was that an abused child could have become the strong, graceful, competent, savvy Cyril that she knew—came back to her. There was no possibility that this man was the same human being she had seen in Cyril Kirby's fourth-grade photo.

There were no bones on the desolate islet where Joe claimed to have seen a woman's skeleton. Not even a fingernail. Sheriff Mike shrugged at the forensics tech leaning on his shovel and waiting for instructions.

"She was here," Joe said, the fear of returning to jail shadowing his eyes.

"Oh, I believe you, son. This soil's been turned over lately. More than once, probably. And don't you think it smells like bleach?"

Joe nodded.

"Well, somebody's been here trying to cover their trail and that's mighty interesting, because I'm thinking it's a real old trail. Looks to me like they somehow know you found this woman. Maybe they even watched you find her. Then they came and took her away, throwing a bottle of bleach in the hole to cover up the evidence."

"Do you have a suspect?" the technician broke in.

"Sort of. I wish to God I knew his name. I don't. But here's what I think I know. Years and years ago, somebody killed three people and buried them on Seagreen Island, right over there," he said, gesturing toward the horizon.

"A few days ago," he continued, "that person killed two people to keep them from uncovering that crime. He played it smart, manipulating the scene and the victims' record book to cover up his motive. And the forensics lab says he was smart enough to do it without leaving fingerprints on the record book, dammit."

He paced around the empty hole. "Now we have another person who was killed years and years ago and buried here. Did either of you know that this glorified sandbar used to be connected to Seagreen Island?"

Joe and the technician shook their heads.

"Well, it was. A big hurricane back in the Sixties rearranged everything in these parts." He jingled the key ring strapped to his belt. "So we have this body here and somebody, probably the killer, was smart enough to move her when people started getting too close. Six bodies is a lot of dead people for one little island. I'm thinking one person killed them all. Let's fill the goddamn hole and get back to land before this wind blows our heads off."

And the wind indeed was coming uncomfortably close to blowing their heads off.

"Radio says the hurricane's headed for Louisiana," the sheriff said, leaning back in his seat and letting the technician pilot the boat. "You can sure tell there's a storm in the Gulf. Look at them whitecaps." Wally's Marina was visible in the distance and, judging by the number of boats being maneuvered into slips, tropical storms generated a major peak in business. "We'll be lucky to get back in one piece."

Joe, who was sitting in the rear of the boat, directly behind Sheriff Mike, leaned forward and made a slashing motion across his throat. The sheriff gestured for the tech to cut the engine. The suspect—well, he wasn't a suspect any more, just a witness. The witness had something to say.

"You know I didn't kill those people," he began.

"I believe you, but we're going to have to keep you for a while longer. Murder cases have to be handled just so. You don't even have any identification. I need to talk to you about the body you found. Maybe you have information that you don't even know is important. Bear with me for a few more hours."

Joe was already shaking his head, but the sheriff held up a hand, determined to finish speaking his piece. "Mr. Mantooth, you and I both know that you withheld evidence important to a murder case. You're not in the best legal position here. By tomorrow, I may have helped your situation substantially. Today, right now, I'm going to talk to everybody I questioned in 1964 about the disappearance of Abby Williford, starting with Douglass Everett. I'll check them for alibis, then we'll see if they've been buying unusual quantities of Clorox. By the time I finish, the question of your innocence may be a moot point."

"But Faye needs me. She needs me now."

"How do you know?"

Joe leaned forward and pointed to the marina. "You know which boat slip is hers. Look. It's empty. That means she's not ashore. I've got to find her before this weather gets worse."

"That hurricane's headed for Grand Isle. This is probably as much wind as we'll get. Being east of the eye, we might see some rain. It depends. Faye's a smart girl. She'll be fine."

Joe gave a disgusted grunt and flopped back in his seat.

The sheriff had learned not to argue with a twenty-five-year-old wearing a sullen expression, so he told the technician to crank the boat. Nothing happened. He stood up, leaning over the tech, and opened the choke to offer the engine more gas. He was rewarded with a sound, but not the sound he was expecting.

It was the sound of Joe leaving the boat headfirst, diving into the five-foot waves. The purloined fuel lines tucked in the waistband of his pants flapped in the wind.

The sheriff would have feared for anyone's life but Joe's. His long arms and legs ate up the water as if the waves weren't there, as if he were enjoying his morning laps at the country club.

The technician rose from his seat and began ripping off his shirt.

"Sit down, son. Look at that water. Would you like to drown today?"

Sheriff Mike raised his dispatcher on the radio, saying, "I have an escapee and I'm floating in a disabled craft just offshore of Wally's Marina. Send some officers to patrol the swamp west of the marina. He may wash ashore there. And send somebody to pick me up."

Joe had already swum into the distance, swallowed by the rising and falling water.

The feel of Cyril's arms around her made Faye's breath shiver in her throat. No, not Cyril. This man was not Cyril. Could he feel her skin shrinking away from his touch?

What had happened to Cyril and his family? The official story, the one this man had told her, said the family had detonated in the mid-Sixties, flinging parents and children in all directions. The mother had left her abusive husband, taking the youngest son with her. The father, a renowned scoundrel, had run off, leaving older brother Cedrick to carry on alone until he finished school and took a job working offshore. Except maybe he'd come back long enough to kill Abby Williford.

So who was this man pretending to be Cyril Kirby? She'd never doubted he was who he said he was, because he looked so much like the pictures of Cyril and his brother, Cedrick. The plastic surgery scar now told her the tale. In 1964, Cyril was ten and Cedrick was eighteen. If Cedrick was masquerading as his younger brother, then he was now well over fifty. With every year, it had to be harder to hide his real age.

She tried not to moan as the man standing behind her leaned forward and brushed her back with his body. If she were only big enough, strong enough to throw him overboard, she would do it in a heartbeat, because she knew why he'd stolen his little brother's name. Suppose a man has committed a celebrated crime, a crime that every soul for miles around took to heart. What better way to evade retribution than to become simply too young to be a plausible suspect?

Say Cedrick killed Abby and fled with few possessions other than his brother's birth certificate, waiting for his alter ego to grow up. How long would it take? A decade? Could most people tell the difference between a twenty-nine-year-old and a twenty-one-year-old? Could she right now, today, distinguish between a fifty-seven-year-old and a forty-nine-year-old, especially if the older man had had a facelift? Apparently not.

A lean, powerful man strode along Douglass Everett's dock, dripping wet. Douglass watched him cross the very deck where Abby was beaten to death. He had the powerful sense that time was a circle, a carousel that no one ever got off. The man banged on the back door and Douglass felt he had to answer it. Otherwise the carousel would swing round again and again until the unfinished business of Abby's death was settled.

"Douglass Everett?" the young man asked.

"Who are you and why are you here?

"My name is Joe Wolf Mantooth. I'm here because Faye Longchamp showed me this house once and told me her friend Douglass lived in it. Well, Faye's my friend, too, and she's in danger. I need you to help me save her." He turned and pointed to a shiny white luxury cruiser resting on a mammoth boat lift. "What I really need is your boat."

"Faye thinks I'm a murderer. She doesn't want me to save her."

Joe cocked his head. "I don't think that's right. Faye goes by her own laws, but she wouldn't watch a murderer live this high on the hog." He gestured at the sprawling beach house. "If Faye really thought you killed somebody, she woulda taken her story to the sheriff, but she didn't. Besides, the sheriff don't need Faye's help to suspect you. First thing he said after finding Abby Williford's grave was that he wanted to talk to you."

Douglass leaned against the doorjamb and said nothing.

"Did you hear? The sheriff's coming for you. And we need to get Faye ashore while we still can. We can worry about the law when she's safe."

Douglass said, "It'll be rough, what with the hurricane heading for Louisiana and all."

"Might be bad," Joe observed. He didn't know that Douglass had spent the last thirty years indoors and had lost the connection to the natural world that he had once enjoyed.

Douglass didn't know that Joe didn't believe in wasting time on idle talk about the weather.

Chapter 24

The undergrowth reached out for Faye and Cyril as they approached the big house. No, not Cyril. Cedrick? He hadn't been Cedrick for decades. She couldn't think about him rationally without an accurate name and she was going to need every scrap of her rationality to get through this. She would think of him as the Senator. His title, at least, was the truth, no matter what other lies he might have told about himself.

So what had happened to the real Cyril, after his brother stole his name? Was he farming quietly in a rural county somewhere in the south? Was he in prison? The truth struck her so suddenly that she forgot to watch her feet and tripped over a briar. Cyril was dead. He had lain beneath the sand on Seagreen Island between his mother and father ever since his brother buried them there. This possibility had never occurred to her before. Until a few minutes ago, she had thought the Senator's missing family consisted of a man, a woman, and a grown son.

She remembered holding the broken femur. Coupled with the picture of young Cyril with a shattered nose and a missing tooth, it completed the picture of a short painful life quite different from the powerful destiny of his older brother.

In all these years, she had never brought a man out to Joyeuse, never revealed this part of herself to any lover. Now a man who had murdered many times over was walking up the grand staircase and into her home. Faye had always told herself that she chose to let people into her life based on cool, passionless skepticism. She had imagined herself as a woman who didn't trust easily, yet whom had she chosen to trust? Shallow, vain Isaiah. Backstabbing Wally. This man beside her, a murderer whose very name was a lie.

And Joe, the only man who had ever deserved the trust she gave him, sat in jail, accused of this man's crimes.

Faye knew she had to get back to shore in one piece. If she didn't return from today's outing with the murderous Senator, Joe would have no one to defend him. She had to survive this.

How was she going to do that? Her only plausible option was to pretend like nothing had changed. She'd have to carry on with her efforts to borrow money from this man, this killer, then hustle her butt back to land where she would be safe with Wally the smuggler and Joe the accused murderer.

Faye had showed the Senator almost her entire home, leaving out only the junk-cluttered cupola, the service rooms in the basement, and the sneak stairway built to bring slaves from the kitchen to the dining room without allowing the sight of them to offend anybody unnecessarily. He had made the correct admiring noises about the handblocked wallpaper and the handpainted bedroom walls and the handcarved railing running the length of the freestanding spiral staircase.

"I'm in trouble, Cyril." She choked on the name, but the break in her voice only made her desperate plea sound more sincere. "I've been selling artifacts I dug out of my old family land on the Last Isles and I'm about to be busted for it."

"You've been digging in the national wildlife refuge?"

She nodded.

"You know that's a federal crime and they prosecute it more vigorously every day?"

She nodded again.

"Let's walk out on the porch," he said. "I enjoy the wind."

There was a great deal of wind for him to enjoy. Each gust tore more Spanish moss out of the trees, rolling it across the ground like a southern version of tumbleweeds. The palms danced like windmills in the gale.

The Senator settled himself on the porch swing, patted the seat beside him, and said, "Come, sit down and tell me exactly what you need."

Douglass had long since turned over the pilot's duties to Joe. He knew where they were going and he handled the fifty-two-foot behemoth as if he owned one himself.

"Does Faye have a dock? Is the water deep enough for this thing?"

"She has a little dock way up in an inlet where nobody can see it. Her boat's pretty big, but it's got a shallow draft." Joe looked over Douglass' very expensive craft and said, "The tide is high. We can probably get it in there."

Probably. Such an encouraging term. Douglass wished the weather were as encouraging. One moment the skies were clear. Then a great band of clouds would rush in from the south, drop some rain on their heads, then rush on northward.

"I'd say the hurricane is passing close," Douglass said.

"Depends on what you mean by close," Joe responded with his accustomed verbal economy.

If pressed, Joe might have said that a storm passing directly overhead could be called "close."

"So," the Senator said, "you need money. How much for the pretty necklace you're wearing? I admired it when you wore it to the restaurant."

Faye fingered the chain at her throat.

"You're welcome to it," she said, "but it's worth no more than the silver in it. People don't buy jewelry with other people's monograms."

"And you bought it at a flea market? It's, what, a hundred years old?" He examined the pendant, front and back. "The woman who wore it is a mystery, isn't she? We know her initials, they're right here: CSS. But who remembers her name? Doesn't it bother you to wear a dead woman's treasure?"

Faye, leaning forward to get out of the swing, felt his left arm cinch around her neck while his right hand used the necklace to drag her face close to his. "She was wearing this when I put her in the ground. What kind of ghoul would dig her up and take her last possession, then throw dirt over what was left of her?"

"Her? Dig who up?" Faye sifted the possibilities. She was aware of only three dead women in the Senator's wake—Krista, his mother, and Abby Williford. She had indeed dug all three of them up. But who wore a necklace like this one? The initials didn't match any of the victims. Was it an heirloom?

The necklace had been stored in Faye's jewelry box since she found it five years before. Krista was a happy high-school girl then. She couldn't have been wearing it when she was put in the ground. Cyril and Cedrick Kirby's mother didn't come from an heirloom kind of family. That left only Abby.

It had never occurred to Faye that she already had Abby's silver necklace because she had expected it to be as contemporary to the dead girl's time as her earring had been. She had forgotten that Abby came from an heirloom-type family and might have had a grandmother or aunt with the initials CSS. She had also expected to find Abby's necklace near her body, not on Seagreen Island.

Her mouth hung open and her eyes rolled back in her head when the silver dug into her throat. She had some reservations about whether the fine chain was strong enough to serve as a garrote, but the Senator had decided to try and no amount of clawing at the chain could keep it from burying itself further in her skin.

She had a vision of the necklace slipping broken from Abby's breathless throat and falling to be trampled into the sand. She saw a rasp-voiced bird pluck it from the ground, adding it to the hoard of Christmas tinsel and soda pop tabs lining its nest. Later, much later, she watched as one too many tropical storms washed over Seagreen Island and a tiny islet was set free to safeguard Abby's bones. Her great-grandmother's necklace remained behind with the birds.

Reality had slipped so far from Faye that it was easy for her to believe that she had seen a vision through Abby's dead eyes. She could actually see very little through her own eyes, because lack of oxygen was making the sun go dark.

Nguyen was an experienced pothunter, but he was a landlubber. He had learned to SCUBA dive for this job and he did it well, but learning to pilot a boat had seemed like a waste of time. He had figured Wally might as well make himself useful, but now there was a great deal of money to be made if he could figure out how to get himself, alone, to an island called Joyeuse. Well, if Wally could get himself from Point A to Point B in a boat, Nguyen was sure he could do it, too. How hard could it be?

He'd been surprised to hear from the boss, who must have called him just as soon as Wally left their little business meeting. Nguyen was no accountant, so he was usually happy to leave the business arrangements to others, but it seemed that the boss felt there were some tasks that couldn't be entrusted to pea-brained Wally. He had offered Nguyen a small fortune to find two people hiding on Joyeuse and make sure they were never seen again.

From observation, Nguyen knew how to turn a boat key to crank the engine. He could steer the boat he "borrowed" from Wally because it had a steering wheel like a car. With the overconfidence of a man who did a lot of things well, he figured he could steer it east, find the secret island, do away with the boss's enemies, then come home and collect his payment.

The boss had given him the island's latitude and longitude, down to the last degree, minute, and second, but Nguyen had neglected to bring navigational charts, since he didn't know how to read them. Besides, the long chain of barrier islands was perfectly visible on the map he kept in his car. In fact, they were visible on the horizon. How could he possibly get lost? Wally had said his friend lived east of the marina, and only one barrier island extended east of the marina, so Nguyen simply pointed the boat's bow in that general direction. He would be a richer man by sundown.

He couldn't have known that his idea of an island was limited, that he was headed for a windswept spit of sand that could never have supported plantation agriculture. His targets, Faye Longchamp and her friend Joe and their hidden home, were not out there. Joyeuse Island was surrounded by water and accessible only by boat, but it was snugged up so close to the swampy coastline that, from the Gulf, it didn't look like a landlubber's idea of an island. Nguyen would never have found Faye, even in favorable weather.

The crashing, rhythmic waves only began to worry Nguyen when the first one splashed over the gunwales of his low-slung craft. Even then his faith in the slab of fiberglass beneath him didn't waver. Instead, he fretted over the wreck that still waited among the Last Isles to be looted. Who knew what this storm was doing to it? He would hate to think that the sunken drug-smuggler's boat would be silted over before he and Wally could pull all that plastic-wrapped cocaine out of its hull.

He was quite near the barrier island he had his sights on, the one that wasn't Faye's, when he steered broadside to the pounding waves and one of them tossed his boat belly-side-up. It would have been better if Nguyen had been knocked unconscious when the boat capsized. Then he could have drowned quickly rather than using his diving skills to fight through the debris trapped with him. He wouldn't have had to try, time and again, to overcome the powerful wave action slamming him into the wreck, so that he could swim down and escape his prison. He could have died easily rather than clinging to the upturned hull as it rose high on each approaching wave, then crashed into the trough that signaled another wave curling toward him.

Nguyen's death proved to be painful and protracted. Providence tends to repay people in the coin they hand to others.

"Here we are," Joe shouted above the wind. He cut the engine and let the boat drift into a shallow inlet.

Douglass saw that Faye's island was large enough to be heavily treed. It wasn't so very far from land, but the nearest shore was a long stretch of uninhabitable swamp. Besides, the true descriptor of an island's remoteness was the distance its residents had to travel to swap water transportation for ground travel. An island dweller didn't measure distance to land. No wonder Wally's Marina played such a central role in Faye's life.

Still, no matter how remote, this island was surely well-known to fishers and boaters plying these waters. That would explain the "No Trespassing" signs that decorated half the trees along the shoreline. At this moment, though, the thing that Douglass appreciated most about Faye's island was its solidity. He figured he could have withstood the bucking and swaying of about seven more waves, then he would have been forced to vomit.

"Do you think we'd be safer sleeping out here, rather than fighting this weather all the way back to shore?" he asked, thinking of his rebellious stomach.

He assumed he was wrong, because Joe's glare said he thought Douglass was a fool who didn't understand English.

Chapter 25

The necklace broke, as Faye had hoped it would.

She suspected the Senator had known it would, because he said, "I never looked forward to killing anybody before."

Faye tried to stop her head from lolling as she gasped for the breath he'd choked out of her. She refused to die until she understood. Why her? Why Krista and Sam? Why anybody?

"Never looked forward…" she wheezed. "You've killed six—" She let a long whistling breath interrupt her. "Maybe more. Should be enjoying yourself by now."

"No." He spoke quickly and precisely. "Only four."

"Only four?" Now Faye could breathe. She could almost think. "Does that mean the devil will assign you a cooler spot in hell? Are you trying to tell me you didn't kill Krista and Sam?"

"No, I did that. I had to do that. I couldn't let them—"

He hadn't let go of her neck and his face was a centimeter away from hers. She needed, really needed, for him to get out of her face, so she intentionally sprayed saliva as she hissed, "You couldn't let us dig up your family? Well, we already did that. Yesterday."

"No one will ever figure out who they are. My parents disappeared within two months of each other and the sheriff and his Deputy Mike McKenzie never doubted my story. They just figured that two no-account rednecks had shucked their responsibilities and run off to fornicate and birth another crop of mental defectives like themselves."

The anger boiled out of him and he shook her until the breath rattled in her throat again. Submission seemed appropriate, so she said, "You're right. Somebody should've looked for your missing parents. Nothing but prejudice prevented it."

"Of course, it was prejudice. I counted on it to cover up the killings, and I knew what I was doing. And I'm still safe. Nobody's going to suspect that those bones on Seagreen Island belong to my family. My parents were buried with a ten-year-old and, by golly, here I am. Cyril Kirby is all grown up. There is no missing ten-year-old. I'm not worried."

"You were worried enough to shoot two kids."

The Senator did not respond.

"You say you've killed four people. I know of six bodies. Why don't we take an inventory?"

Her challenge, to provide an accurate accounting of what he'd done, seemed to clear his mind.

"Abby was an accident," he said in a rational tone. "I'd just gotten paid for my first month on the oil rig, and I'd never had cash, folding money, to spend in my life. I wanted to spend it on Abby, because she was pretty and—all through high school—none of the boys had managed to get her attention."

The Senator's grip tightened on her arm when she taunted him with, "So your idea of getting her attention was to beat her to death?"

"No. No. I knew she was living alone for the summer at her daddy's beach house. When I knocked on her door, she didn't answer, so I walked around back to the patio and there she was at the wet bar, fixing herself a drink. She was dressed in a lacy dress with a tight waist and wide skirt. I didn't do anything wrong. I just asked her out to dinner. I was rough around the edges in those days, but my manners weren't so bad. I asked her nicely."

He didn't go on and Faye was compelled to prod him to finish his story. Somebody, finally, needed to know what happened to Abby that night and she was glad it would be her, even if she didn't live to pass the truth on.

"Did she laugh at you?" Faye asked. "Was she cruel? Is that why—?"

"Abby? Cruel? No. She was sweet about it. She said, 'You see I'm already dressed. Daddy and I are having dinner in Tallahassee. I'm going to college there in September, you know.' Then she offered me a drink."

"I'm not understanding this story," Faye said, feeling that the Senator had far better reasons to kill her than he had to kill Abby.

"You wouldn't. It's just this: At that moment, I understood that money wasn't going to fix what was wrong with me. The wad of money in my pocket was worthless. I could never have Abby or any woman like her, because they were going to colleges and cities and places where they could find husbands just like their daddies. The only women who would ever have me were cringing, stupid cows like my mother. I would have no choice other than to beat them, just like my father beat my mother, because what else can you do with a woman like that?"

He waited until Faye looked him in the face. "So I slugged her. That was how my father dealt with balky women. It seemed like the thing to do. Except, as she fell, she hit her head on the corner of the wet bar. It gashed her scalp to the bone and fractured her skull. There was blood everywhere and that nigra Everett came walking up her dock carrying a fishing pole while I was trying to wipe it up. He said he was going to kill me, but he changed his mind when I told him how things were going to be. Sometime while I was explaining why he needed to keep his mouth shut, she stopped breathing."

"How—" Faye groped for a word to describe a debutante with a bashed-in skull, overdressed and dead beside the patio wet bar of her father's beach house. "How ghastly."

"Yes. How do you like that? It took twenty years of beatings for my father to kill my mother, but I managed it on the first try. But then I always knew I was twice the man Daddy ever was."

"And little Cyril?"

"Oh, he killed him, too, same day as Mama. He beat my mother and brother forever, but if he ever beat me, I don't remember it. I don't know why not. Probably because I have never in my life looked or smelled like a victim. One day, I came home from football practice and found that he'd gone too far. I think he killed Cyril first. It was probably easy—there wasn't much to him in body or spirit—but then he had to contend with Mama. God, what a scene I walked in on."

"How ghastly," Faye said again.

"Yeah. I'd hated Daddy all my life, but that was the first and only time he ever scared me. He scared me enough to make me help him bury them, out in the Last Isles, then he told everybody nasty tales about where my mama was and people believed him."

Faye was doing the math. The Senator had confessed to killing four of the six bodies she'd found. If he didn't kill his mother or his brother, then he was responsible for all the others.

"When did you kill your father?" she asked.

"Baseball season. I came home from practice one day, still carrying my bat, and saw him sitting at the kitchen table. My hands just swung at his head without consulting my brain. One good lick upside the head with my baseball bat and Daddy wasn't ever going to bother anybody again. I buried him with Mama and Cyril, because I knew it would have made him mad."

"It was that easy?"

The Senator nodded. "I told the same story he told about my mama, that he'd run off with some drunken slut. Everybody was happy to believe me. I left town the day after I graduated and only came back to see Abby the one time. When

Cyril was old enough, I went to Auburn under his name. By the time I came back to this part of the world, fifteen years had passed and I had been Cyril for more than seven of them."

Faye knew it was unwise to bait a confessed killer, but felt she had nothing to lose. "And you're going to enjoy killing me to cover your tracks?"

"No, covering my tracks is just a necessary evil, just like killing the archaeology students. I'm going to enjoy killing you because you betrayed me. I cared for you, Faye. And all the time you were seeing me, you were carrying on with the young Indian, stealing from Abby, disturbing her rest, disturbing my mother."

Oh, Jesus, the garroting was just for fun. There was a bulge in the pocket of his khakis and he was going for it. Faye rammed the porch floor with her feet and achieved liftoff. The swing flipped backward, just as it had ever since she was a little girl. Faye hit the ground in a shoulder roll, just as she had done ever since she was a little girl. The Senator fell in a heap.

Joe led Douglass up the path to Faye's house. It was, as always, a faint trail through Joyeuse's lush undergrowth, but Faye liked it that way. She said it kept the paparazzi away, but she just laughed when he asked her what paparazzi were.

There was an odd rustling in the bushes to either side of the path, as if all the mammals on the island—squirrels, rabbits, rats, and more—were seeking cover at once. The birds and insects had been dead silent. Now, suddenly, they were making noise as loud and random as city traffic.

Joe stepped off the path, pushing vines aside and stepping under them. Something was bothering the animals. Perhaps it was just the weather, because the weather was certainly bothering Joe. But perhaps it was something more, and Joe wanted to know what it was. He pushed further into the tangled bushes, letting Douglass move ahead of him on the path, alone.

Douglass worked his way down an overgrown trail that Joe claimed led to Faye's house, shuddering to think what kind of tumbledown, vermin-infested cabin might lie at the end of such a path. He had known that Faye's monetary problems were mighty—that fact had been obvious in their every business transaction—but if he'd known she was virtually homeless, he would have adopted her and taken her home with him.

Joe turned aside, presumably to answer the call of nature. Not wanting to hover too close while the poor guy peed, Douglass plunged ahead. The path was faint, but it was clearly there. How lost could he get?

The trail ended in a clearing that was far too small for the building it enclosed. Faye assuredly did not live in a cabin. Her house might be tumbledown and it might be vermin-infested, but it was not a cabin. It had once been a mansion.

Massive columns supported a massive roof on all sides, their white paint fading to silver. A sweeping staircase rose a full story to a double door flanked with sidelights and topped with a graceful Palladian window that was miraculously unbroken. Sadly, many of the other windows had not been so lucky. The great house's decline was most evident in the corroding tin roof that capped its glorious bulk. No wonder Faye never had any cash. She lived in a money sink.

The house was too big to take in at a single glance. As he swept his gaze to the far right end of the main floor gallery, he saw color and motion. Faye was rising to her feet and somebody else was lying beside her with his arm upraised. As she bounded over the gallery railing, Douglass shouted, "Faye, no!" because she was headed for a twelve-foot drop. She hit the ground and scuttled on all fours into the open breezeway that divided the ground floor into two parts.

Her assailant was running down the staircase, which was wise. He would have been foolish at his age to take the fall Faye just took. Bones grow brittle with time. Besides, no one in their right mind would take such a risk while carrying a handgun.

Douglass stepped backward toward the well-camouflaged footpath, trying to reach cover before the gunman saw him, but he never had a chance. The man looked him bold in the eyes and Douglass recognized the face of his blackmailer, who coolly aimed and fired.

The bullet's momentum threw him to the ground. It had struck him somewhere in the chest. Shock blocked the pain, but he could tell that much. The shooter was coming toward him, coming to finish him off. Lord, he didn't want to take another bullet, but he'd been dying by degrees for forty years.

His vision was fading but he could see Faye hiding behind the house, peeking through the breezeway. His hearing was fading, too, but he heard what she did for him.

She cried, "Hey, Senator, you lousy son-of-a-bitch. I'm the one you're going to enjoy killing. Leave him to bleed to death, because you're going to have a devil of a time catching me."

And his blackmailer ran after her, taking his bullets with him.

How much money had he paid the man he'd known first as Cedrick Kirby, then as Senator Cyril Kirby? He'd looked Abby's father in the face every day, taken a paycheck from him every Friday, and stolen from him every chance he got, all because he was afraid of this man. Mr. Williford was never right in his mind after Abby's disappearance and he had trusted Douglass with his affairs. When the old man's will revealed that he'd left the construction business to Douglass, it eased a portion of the guilt. All the embezzlements that his blackmailer had forced him to execute were finally wiped away. Douglass had only been stealing from himself.

Irvin Williford wasn't cold in his grave when Douglass bought the old man's beach house from his estate. Controlling the site of Abby's death made him breathe easier. He remodeled the house before moving in—like any proud new owner who could afford it—and in the process sent the tiles from the patio to the landfill. He would never again look at them and remember the way her blood had looked, splashed across the gaily decorated floor. And he'd had the workmen demolish the outdoor wet bar with its wicked sharp corner. That corner had broken Abby's fall, caved in her skull, and ended her life. It was gone now, along with the clothes he'd worn that night and his junky fishing boat. And Abby herself.

Douglass wondered whether the wound in his chest was mortal and if God would let him see Abby when he died just one more time.

Faye figured that she and the Senator each had an advantage in this life-and-death contest. He had a gun, and she was on her own turf. She would gladly trade her advantage for his. She'd even move this chase to Mars if it meant she could have a gun, too.

Maybe Douglass was still alive. She liked to think she'd bought him another moment of life, but that's all she could give him. It was all she could give herself. She could only take one moment, then another one, all the while hoping for a miracle.

Joe, standing in the shadow of a pine tree, saw Faye jump and he saw Douglass fall. As soon as Faye, then Cyril, disappeared into the dense woods behind the big house, Joe stepped out of the shadows and pulled Douglass to his feet. The wounded man could stand, with help, but he couldn't walk. Joe draped Douglass' arms over his own shoulders, supporting him on his back. He hurried toward the house, with Douglass' limp feet dragging in the dirt behind his moccasins. Hauling Douglass into the basement, he stashed him behind the secret door that led to the sneak stair.

"I'll be back for you after I find Faye."

"The bullet?" Douglass wheezed.

"It went straight through. Must have missed your heart."

"I don't think it missed but one of my lungs," Douglass gasped, but Joe had already closed him behind a well-camouflaged door. If something happened to Faye and Joe, then he guessed he'd just become a grisly part of this grand house's historical character.

Hiding in a palmetto thicket had seemed like a good idea to Faye at the time, because her pursuer would never expect it. No one in his right mind would hide there. Palmettos, waist-high miniature palms, had stalks like serrated kitchen knives.

She had slithered on her side deep into the thicket, trying to ooze around each jagged trunk without jostling it. Waggling palmetto fronds would look like fingers on a beckoning hand saying, "Shoot me, please shoot me."

Every joint ached from her jump off the gallery but the old wound on her thigh was throbbing worse than that. The cool mud she ground into the wound with each movement was oddly soothing.

She had always believed she knew her island better than the markings on her own palm. She had eaten the squirrels and rabbits and birds Joe had shot here. She'd even eaten frog legs, fruits of his occasional frog-gigging ventures. Still, she'd had no idea that she lived in the midst of so many creatures.

Just since she'd crawled into this thicket, she'd seen a water rat, an armadillo, a lizard, and two snakes. She could hear the cries overhead of birds that should by rights have settled in for the fast-approaching evening. Could all this unusual activity be triggered by the Senator's mere presence? Could animals sense the presence of evil? If so, they were clearly smarter than she was.

A possum ambled by and she silently thanked him for making noise and disturbing the vegetation. Faye's critters were doing everything they could to make her hard to track.

A gunshot rang out and the possum dropped bloody to the ground, effectively removing any desire Faye might have to risk giving away her position by moving, ever again. There were no more shots. Faye realized that he was hoarding his ammunition, saving it for likely targets at close range. How much did he have? It only took one bullet to end a life. Could she wait him out?

The chittering screech of an enraged squirrel sounded in her right ear and she proved the power of the human mind over ancient animal reflexes by refusing to scream.

Then the squirrel whispered, "Faye."

She inched her head gingerly toward the right and saw Joe lying on his belly just outside the palmetto patch. He crooked his finger and she inchwormed her way toward him, sliding around one treacherous stalk at a time.

By the time she reached Joe, her hands were pinned to her sides and all she could do was incline her head toward him. He leaned forward, lips against her ear and murmured, "He doesn't know I'm here. I can lead him away. When it's safe, run to the house, all the way to the little room up top. I'll come for you."

She opened her mouth to argue and he covered it with his hand. Then he slid snake-like back to the woods and the path that led through it. She saw him sprint silently along the path, away from the house and toward the far shore. He stopped, ruffled the branches along the path with his hands and stomped down hard on a dry branch before disappearing down the trail. Hardly a minute passed before the Senator passed the same spot in hot pursuit. When he was out of sight, she leapt up, running for Joyeuse like a child taking a skinned knee to her mother.

Her thigh was swelling. It jiggled every time her foot struck the ground. She told herself that it wasn't infected. She told herself that Joe was younger and stronger than Cyril and that a fifty-five-second head start would negate the advantage of Cyril's gun. She told herself that Joe had a good reason for sending her to the cupola rather than to her boat, but all she wanted to do was escape.

She reached Joyeuse and remembered something she'd forgotten to worry about. There was a bloody spot in the grass where Douglass had fallen, but where was Douglass? She saw no other blood anywhere. Had he crawled into the woods to hide? Maybe she could spot him if she climbed to the cupola.

She rushed inside, instinctively avoiding the spiral staircase. It was too exposed and it took too long to climb. Any fool with a gun could pick her off if he caught her halfway up the spiral. She rushed to the sneak staircase and flung open the hidden door.

There, behind it, was Douglass and all the rest of his blood. The carpet at the foot of the stairs was soaked with it. When he saw her, he tried to use the arm on his uninjured side to push himself into a sitting position, but it didn't work. Bracing against the narrow walls of the closet-sized stairway for leverage, she wrestled him to his feet.

It took forever but she worked him up to the top floor and lowered the ladder to the cupola. With Douglass dragging himself upward one-handed and with her shoulder to his butt, she managed to get them both through the trapdoor, but she didn't dare close it before Joe came. What if it stuck again?

And she didn't dare let the sticky trail of Douglass' blood lead the Senator to their hiding place. Leaving Douglass sprawled on the cupola floor, she grabbed some rags out of the storage bench in the cupola and hurried back down the stairs. It was important to clean up the blood in the basement and especially on the landing beneath the cupola. Their trail must not be found because, from the cupola, there was no place to retreat.

She was wiping the landing clean when Joe bounded up the stairs and climbed the ladder to the cupola, extending a hand down to help her up. She kept him waiting as she ducked into her bedroom to salvage William Whitehall's journal. Armed with her most treasured possession, she climbed the ladder and helped drag it into the cupola after them. As the trapdoor closed, Faye watched a killer emerge from the woods and walk into her home, gun in hand.

The view from the cupola was surreal. It was her island, but it wasn't. The sea had pulled away, leaving immense wet beaches on the Gulf side and isolated pools of abandoned water littering the narrow strait between Joyeuse and the mainland. Looking toward the Last Isles, she saw that the Gulf had pulled away from their shores, much further than at low tide. All the pieces of Last Isle were nearly one again.

She felt a time echo, as if she remembered standing there before, long ago, watching as the Turkey Foot Hotel rose on Last Isle. That was silly. The outline of Last Isle was barely visible. Nobody could see that degree of detail from here. The chilly sensation of *déja vu* arose again and she sat down, weak and shaken. The polished pieces of old glass that she'd pulled out of the very storage bench she was perched on—they were the broken lenses of a long-ago pair of opera glasses. On the windowsill sat the pair of binoculars she had left the last time she hid in this tiny room. She lifted them to her eyes and saw, for the first time, the original shape of Last Isle. Projecting from its near shore was a large peninsula, from which three smaller peninsulas jutted into the water, looking for all the world like a turkey foot. She knew where the old hotel had stood. She would bet the farm on it.

She let the binoculars drop into her lap and studied the scene. There was no mistaking what the decrease in water level meant. The water had to go somewhere. It was gathering offshore, getting ready to roll over the island and wash them all away.

Faye felt the words. "Joe. The water. My God," leave her in a single breath, like a prayer.

She knelt beside Douglass, supporting him with her shoulder and her encircling arm so he could see out the window. He was too hot and his hands were dry. "What's happening?" he asked, and Faye wasn't sure whether delirium was speaking or whether he actually saw the landscape below them and wondered what it meant.

"The hurricane is coming," Joe said patiently to Douglass, as if it were something he had repeatedly warned him about, because he thought he had.

Joe, who just that morning had seemed so helpless when faced with jail and civilization and the law, was back in the natural world where his intellectual shortcomings hardly mattered at all. He sat cross-legged atop the trapdoor and opened the leather pouch that always swung from his belt, neatly arranging its contents over the floor like a little boy's bag of treasures. There were rocks and bits of leather. A skein of twine as fine as dental floss. A pocketknife. A handful of arrowheads, all different sizes.

"What are we going to do?" Faye whispered, afraid to speak aloud and risk giving away their hiding spot.

"We will wait for the storm to pass." It was amazing how quietly Joe could speak without resorting to a whisper. "This house has seen hurricanes before. Maybe it will survive this one."

Faye didn't wail. She didn't remind Joe that Joyeuse was old now, fragile. Faye herself had wounded her, just days ago. Windowpanes she had broken herself offered their toothy mouths to the storm. There would be water on the heart-pine floors, saturating the antique French wallpaper, dripping off the rosewood treads of the spiral staircase. These things would not be important tonight, when the only important thing in the world would be surviving the storm, but they were important now.

Could the old house stand the storm? The tabby foundation was solid. She'd found watermarks proving that floodwater had once risen a full story above the ground, completely submerging the aboveground basement, but the foundation had held. If the waves didn't undermine the basement and the wind didn't blow the hand-riven wallboards of the upper floors apart, they might survive.

"What about him?" she hissed pointing through the floor, down to where a predator was waiting.

"Is he a smart man?"

"Yes, very."

"Then he will think to search the house. We are well hidden here. Perhaps he won't find us before the storm strikes."

"And when the hurricane passes?"

Joe continued handling his treasures, holding each talisman up to the light. "Perhaps the storm will kill him for us. If he survives, we have an advantage."

"What advantage? Wherever he is in this house, he's still blocking our way out. And he has a gun."

"Yes. But he thinks you're alone."

Faye only had one talisman to comfort her. She hugged the journal to her chest.

Douglass was lying on the floor at her feet, stirring, moaning. If he cried out, they were lost. She laid her clammy hand on his hot brow and wished she knew the end to Cally's story. She was a mere four pages from the end of Cally's oral history, but she might not survive to read them.

◇

Excerpt from the oral history of Cally Stanton, recorded 1935

I'm a good liar. Belonging to somebody else can surely bring out the liar in you.

"Yes, ma'am, you are surely right. It's not fitting for a lady to go off without her husband to take care of her," I'd say when I carried their breakfast in. She'd straighten her bedcovers over her fat belly and cut her eyes over at the Master.

When the Missus took her nap, I'd find the Master and walk past him, swinging my skirts. "I never saw a hotel," I'd say.

"It's not a hotel. It's a glorified boarding house," he'd say, cutting his possum-eyes away from me.

I'd just swing my skirts some more and say, "I don't blame you for being afraid. A big storm might rise up and blow you to kingdom come. And your purty wife, too." There. I'd told the truth. If he didn't listen, it was none of my affair. "Folks say that Last Isle's a pretty place to take a walk."

I'd brush a piece of lint off his pants leg. "Sure wish I had somebody to take a walk with." Then I'd lean over and give him a good look down my dress. "Somebody handsome."

We kept after him, the Missus and me, until he packed his bags. Mister Courtney didn't care for the Master, so he didn't go with us, after all. Before long, the Master, the Missus, and me were on a steamboat headed for Last Isle.

The hotel there was even fancier than the Big House at Innisfree, and it wasn't snugged up under a shady grove, like our Big House at Joyeuse. It sat right out on the beach, plain as you please.

The sun shone funny that day on Last Isle, like it knew a secret. It made the real world look like one of my dreams. I was standing on the beach, afraid of the way the sun made my shadow look, when I heard an old man say, "I've seen weather like this. There's a hurricane coming"—he pronounced it 'hurrikan'—"I'd bet forty acres on it."

Another man said, "This is no place to wait out a hurricane. This island hardly pokes out of the water. I'm going home to Mississippi, where I can walk without getting my feet wet."

I watched those men head back to the hotel and set their slaves to packing. Both their families and all their slaves were off Last Isle that same afternoon. I have always prayed they were safe at home when the storm hit.

Not many had sense enough to leave. I had the sense, but I was bound to stay. This storm was gonna kill my Master for me.

The Missus heard talk about the storm coming, and she wanted to leave, but I shut her up. "Ain't gonna be no storm, ma'am. Look at that sun shine."

She kept up her whining, but the Master didn't say nothing. I think he had boat tickets to get us out the next day. I won't never know for sure, but he was a smart man. Those tickets didn't do any of us a bit of good. The storm hit that very night.

Now I've seen thunderstorms and I've seen hurricanes. Thunderstorms come up fast and loud and dark. They make plenty of light and noise, but unless you get lightning-struck, you'll get through a thunderstorm.

Hurricanes are different. I have never felt a building shake like that hotel did and I have never, before or since, heard the banshee cry in the wind. Before that night, I never saw a tree lean over side-ways and snap in two. When the water pulled back away from the island, I knew it was bad. The water was gathering together, so it could throw itself on us all at once.

Have you ever watched Death come for you? We were on the top floor of that hotel, so we could see the big wave coming a long time before it hit. The Master was standing at the window and I was behind him, looking over his shoulder. The Missus was curled up in bed, just crying. The big wave was gathering and the storm was shaking the hotel harder and harder when it happened.

The window busted right open. I hid my face in my hands and waited for the glass to hit me, but it never did. The wind hadn't blown the window in. It had sucked it out into the night. And the Master stood there, teetering at the windowsill.

Later on, I thought maybe I wasn't a murderer after all, because I didn't think about what I did. I didn't think to myself, *This man beat me and had his way with me and he deserves to die.* No, my hands just reached up by themselves and pushed him out of the broken window.

The storm swallowed him up. I turned around and there sat the Missus, looking at me. She saw what I did. I know she did. But she never said nothing, because that's when the big wave hit.

Chapter 26

In 1975, Hurricane Eloise was headed for Mobile Bay and, by midday on the last day before landfall, all precautions for a hurricane of middling strength had been taken. Most residents of the Florida Panhandle went to bed that night and slept soundly, unaware that the storm was strengthening and veering sharply to the northeast. By dawn, they were awakened by rescuers roaming the streets with bullhorns, urging coastal dwellers to seek high ground. Later that day, Eloise leveled their deserted homes with winds gusting to one hundred fifty-six miles per hour.

As recently as 1995, emergency personnel were caught flat-footed when Hurricane Opal, a mere Category 2 storm, blossomed over the brief course of an afternoon into a tremendous storm nearing the Category 5 mark. Its forward speed doubled during that time, bringing disaster closer, faster. The evacuation order came late, after most residents were in bed. As the warning spread, highway gridlock set in; the storm was moving faster than the traffic. Only a last-minute weakening of the storm—an act of God unattributable to science—averted great loss of life.

Since 1960, satellites and computers have decreased the National Hurricane Center's average twenty-four-hour forecast error only from one hundred twenty nautical miles to one hundred. Meanwhile, Florida's population has metastasized.

One day, a freak of nature will wipe a stretch of shoreline clean of its condominium fringe, and Nature will not deign to warn us.

Faye, Joe, Douglass, Cyril—not one of them had been in earshot of a radio since early morning. It was near sundown and, on a whim, the hurricane had spent that time churning their way.

The wind threw the first punch, slamming over the vulnerable Gulf islands and sweeping away anything that wasn't fastened to the ground. It erased large chunks of the sand dunes that protected the luckier islands, using the sand to fill the mouths of random inlets, leaving their waters cut off from the sea.

On a tiny piece of long-gone Last Isle, the wind scoured away the sand that had covered the foundation of the Turkey Foot Hotel for so long. The island under them held, for a little while, but the sea had its plans. Sooner or later, all the pieces of Last Isle would go under the waves, but for now the old hotel would have its time in the sun.

Sheriff Mike's late wife had dearly hated his job when hurricane season rolled around. He rode out every storm at his desk, because it was his job to be available in an emergency. She had known that, but it always griped her to think that if the house blew away, she'd have to call 911 to let him know. And she never let him forget it.

The phone rang and he snatched it up. It was Dr. Magda Stockard. "You've got to help me save Faye."

The events of the past couple weeks had eroded Sheriff Mike's people skills. He bellowed, "How'd you get through to this phone? Did you call 911?"

"I did what I had to," was the cryptic answer. "So listen to me. I know where Faye lives. She owns an island that hardly sticks up out of the Gulf, and she's out there in the storm. She has to be. I'm at Wally's looking for her right now. Neither of her boats is here, and one of them would be if she were ashore. I tried to get that bastard Wally to tell me where she was. He won't talk, but he knows. She's out there on her island. He's easy to read, for a dishonest S.O.B. So hurry over here so we can take one of your big official boats out to get Faye before it gets dark."

"The department has one boat, a small one. We work with the Marine Patrol for search and rescue."

"So call them," she said, and he would have been disappointed in her if she hadn't.

"You're aware there's a hurricane out there. Category 5."

"Yes, I know there's a hurricane coming. That's why we have to hurry."

Sheriff Mike's people skills were slowly returning. He fed her the bad news gently.

"This isn't an ordinary hurricane, Magda. It wasn't supposed to hit here, but the goddamn thing took a right turn at New Orleans and came up fast as blazes. And those extra few hours over warm water made it into a monster. I don't know many people level-headed enough to hear what I'm fixing to tell you. This is the big one, and we're not ready."

"So let's go get Faye."

"We'd have to swim. The Marine Patrol office in Tampa has suspended rescue operations in this area for the duration of—"

"Why? Because they don't work on Sunday?"

Sheriff Mike excused the interruption because he understood how she felt. "—For the duration of the storm," he continued. "In their judgment, and I think they're probably right, the risk of losing personnel and equipment is too high, and we're going to need every officer and every rescue craft they have when the storm passes."

"Cowards," Magda observed tartly.

"Be that as it may. And by the way—you're aware that Faye's friend, Joe Wolf Mantooth, escaped from my custody today?"

Magda sputtered. "Actually, no. But—"

"Well, I'd bet my arrowhead collection that he's with Faye. If you'd called me with Faye's location earlier, then I might be questioning Joe Wolf right this minute and Faye might be safe. Not many people play me for a fool. Believe me, I'll go get Joe Wolf Mantooth personally, just as soon as the storm passes."

"We'll go get them," Magda said.

Only then did Sheriff Mike realize his position. The deceitful woman had never given him the exact location of Faye's home.

"I can't take a civilian on a manhunt," he said flatly.

"How dangerous do you think Mr. Mantooth is?"

Silence erupted.

"That's what I thought. I'll be at your office as soon as the wind dies down. On second thought, I may have trouble getting there. There'll be trees in the road, power lines, things like that. Send an emergency vehicle to the hurricane shelter in Sopchoppy—that'll be my luxury suite for the night—and we'll head out to Faye's from there. And make sure you get a Marine Patrol vessel, not your little boat. God knows what'll be floating in the water. Their boats—ships, whatever—will be more suitable than anything you've got. No offense."

"None taken, ma'am."

"I'll be waiting for my ride."

"Yes, ma'am, Dr. Stockard."

Faye watched as great trees surrendered to the wind all over her island, taking down wide swathes of smaller trees as they fell. Pine trees rarely suffered the fate of less deeply rooted, less flexible trees. They swayed and bent at unnatural angles in the face of the hurricane's unremitting wind but they were bred to survive and most did. Still, more than once, a great crack echoed over the island as even the resilience of a pine tree was pushed past its limit. She wondered how much force it took to snap a tree trunk like a strand of dried pasta. How much could a tree endure?

And how much could a man endure? In the hour since he was shot, Douglass had slid rapidly downhill. He had been intermittently conscious for the past half-hour. When she pressed her ear to his chest, the sound was wheezy and wet. Was he developing pneumonia? Heart failure? Had his entire lung collapsed? She had no idea, but she was heartened to see him cling to life with the stubborn will that had turned a poor black boy into a wealthy and dignified man.

She huddled beside him and watched the sky. It was a luminescent gray-green, shading to orange in the west. When the sun set, they would be left with no light but the shimmering, ever-present lightning.

She wondered where the Senator was. Somewhere in the house below them, he was waiting, hoping that she was floating in the waters covering her island, hoping she was dead. He must wonder what had happened to Douglass. She hoped he believed that the wounded man had crawled into the bushes where he had bled to death or lay there still, waiting for the storm to drown him.

Wishing someone dead is powerful magic. She wished the Senator dead. He wished her dead, and Douglass too, but he thought Joe was safely imprisoned. Perhaps Joe was safe from the insistent magic pulling at her, at Douglass, at the man downstairs. Perhaps he was the one to free them from their interlaced bonds, from the net of hatred. Or perhaps the unremitting roll of thunder was affecting her mind.

She watched Joe work. She had left the shutters hanging by one nail apiece in her quest to make Joyeuse look uninhabitable but, with the windows broken, they would need the shutters to fulfill their original purpose: keeping the weather out when the windows were open.

With no hammer or nails, Joe couldn't restore the shutters to their original positions, so he leaned out each window, yanked each shutter free, and hauled it inside. They were just barely taller than the cramped room, so he rested the bottom of each shutter on the floor, slightly away from the wall surrounding its corresponding window. Slanting each shutter back toward the wall, he jammed their tops, one by one, into the angle where wall and ceiling meet. The makeshift screens wouldn't keep the water out, but they would provide some protection against broken glass and wind-blown debris.

Finished with the shutters, Joe spread the contents of his leather tool bag over a piece of plastic tarpaulin roughly the size of a desktop. Faye saw nothing among the twine, raw stone, and arrowheads that might save them from their pursuer or from the storm.

"When you get finished, Joe, can I have that piece of plastic? To protect the journal?"

Without a word, he nodded.

Douglass mumbled, "I'm cold, Faye."

She went to the storage bench and fetched the dresses she'd found on the day she discovered the Clovis point. She guessed by their style that they'd been made in the 1930s. Perhaps they had been Cally's or Courtney's or her grandmother's. She spread one over Douglass and let its wide skirt flare out over the floor. Then she wrapped another one around her shoulders, hoping that Joyeuse's ghosts would protect them.

◇

Excerpt from the oral history of Cally Stanton, recorded 1935

The big wave washed right up to the sill of that broken window. Folks on the bottom floors never had a chance. The wind was coming in hard, but I thought the building would hold. Maybe it would have, if that first wave had been the only one.

The Good Book says a house built on sand will fall and a house built on rock will stand. That worries me, because I don't think there's a rock big enough to stand on in all of Florida. There wasn't nothing on Last Isle to build on but sand, and I was there when it all tumbled down.

The hotel came apart, flinging splinters and boards far and wide. The wind was like a wolf breaking open a log to get at the little rabbit inside, and the little rabbit was me. The shrieking storm drowned out the Missus and her screaming. That was good, because it meant I could forget her and save my own rabbit skin.

The walls fell around me. As the water carried me off, two dresser drawers floated by and I grabbed one. I don't know why, but I shoved the other drawer over to the Missus and helped her grab hold. Then we floated out the window and watched the hotel pieces wash away.

The Missus hung on to that dresser drawer with more spunk than I figured. I knew I could get through just about anything, but the Missus couldn't get to the outhouse without a buggy and a span of horses. While we were trying not to drown, she rambled on about wanting to see her son one last time. She cussed the Master's dead body. She took on something terrible about what he did to me and to my mama. And he thought he was so smart and his wife wouldn't never know.

She cussed his dead body some more, but I hoped he wasn't dead. Not yet. I wanted him to float around in that black water, getting beat up side the head with floating tree limbs and trying to catch a breath that wasn't half sea water. The whole time we fought that storm, I hoped he was suffering, too. Then, when the storm slacked up, I went back to wanting him dead.

Chapter 27

There was no light but the incessant lightning. No sound could rise above the wind. There was a locomotive riding in that wind, and a banshee and a siren and the bone-shaking grind of a wrecked car sliding on its roof down a gravel road. Tree trunks popped like firecrackers and the massive piers that had supported Joyeuse all those years groaned under the shearing force of the wind. What were the swirling waters doing to the sand around the old foundations?

Faye's view of the ground below her was a shutterspeed illusion. Each lightning strike gave only a snapshot; the rapid flashes revealed a series of still scenes that blurred together like cinematic images, giving an illusion of motion.

It was less frightening to watch the world end this way, to see the storm surge approach in the jerky style of a music video, showing no discernible color other than shades of gray. The great wave was lit by strobe light as it crashed onto the land and through the trees and struck the long straight staircase that rose from the ground to the main floor, bypassing the ground floor service rooms where the slaves had tended their masters. Treads, risers, banisters, and balusters flew in the face of the wave, then fell to the water surface and were washed away. They did not fall far. In the aftermath of the storm surge, the water level was even with the main floor balcony, leaving the service rooms completely underwater.

The wind was loud enough to raise the dead and each wave lapped further up the walls of her home, but Joyeuse held.

Later, when the blasting wind suddenly ceased, Faye was wise enough to be wary. Many a soul had walked with desperate relief into the sudden eerie stillness of a hurricane's quiet center, only to perish when the eyewall's winds tore into them from a new direction. The setting sun added a faint glow as the gale died down and silence settled in, but only for a time.

Douglass was stirring and now, without the storm sounds to mask his moans, she needed to keep him quiet more than ever. Her voice quieted him. She should just talk, whisper anything to keep him still, but the storm had wiped her mind so clean that she could think of nothing to say.

"Have to tell you, Faye," he said, his voice rising. "If I die...want you to know."

She bent and whispered in his ear, hoping to quiet him. "What do I need to know?"

"Didn't kill her. She was dead—beaten to death—when I got there."

She gestured at the floor, pointing at their tormentor waiting below. "Was it him?"

Douglass nodded. "He made me help him bury her. Said he'd tell the sheriff I...killed...her. My word against his—"

"And he knew a jury would believe the white man." She stroked the graying hair at his temples. "Oh, Douglass. And your watch?"

"He took it, prob'ly while I was layin' her body in the grave."

Faye hadn't thought his breathing could get more ragged. She was going to let him say about two more sentences before she stopped him and made him rest.

"He put my watch in her grave...told me about it later. Said I could go ahead and talk to the sheriff, say as much as I wanted to, 'cause his testimony and my watch would put me in the electric chair. Then the hurricane came and we lost even her body, her grave...."

Douglass' racking sobs were punctuated with wheezes. She put her hand over his mouth. He had to lie quietly or die.

Joe was rummaging through his bag again. He cradled a stone loosely in the palm of his hand and struck it sharply with another rock, flaking off a sliver of stone that he handed to Faye. Roughly the size of her index finger, it hooked to one side in the shape of the number seven. He guided her fingers along the blunt outer edge, then showed her the inner edge. It was as sharp as a scalpel.

"To defend yourself," he said.

Faye tried to imagine getting close enough to the Senator to use this thing, but her brain wasn't up to the challenge.

The wind came back and it was stronger, though Faye wasn't sure how she could tell the difference. The flexible trees, palms and pines, had been blown out horizontal before. They were horizontal now. The booming reports of more rigid trees failing under the wind's assault may have come more frequently, but it was hard to tell. Perhaps the velocity of the rain spewing through the broken windowpanes had increased. It came from all directions now, hitting her like bullets, like great sodden bedsheets striking her from head to foot, again and again.

She clutched William Whitehall's journal, wrapped snugly in Joe's tarp, layer after layer, bound with twine. She wanted it to survive as much as she wanted Joe, Douglass, herself, all of them, to live through this. She tucked the bundle into her shirt, because she would soon need both hands. She clutched at Joe and Douglass and the three of them were huddled into a tight ball when, one by one, the remaining windowpanes pulled away from their frames and shattered.

Faye hoped that the destruction would stop, that a few broken panes would equalize the internal and external pressure, protecting the remaining windows that, in turn, protected them. When the glass settled, she looked up and understood why the windows had failed. The gaping holes where they had been were no longer square. The wood framing of the cupola was flexing with the pressure of the wind and the glass panes could not rise to the occasion. The framing itself would fail within minutes, blowing the cupola away.

Faye put her mouth against Joe's ear and screamed, "Trapdoor."

Joe shook his head and bellowed back, "Sitting ducks. Roof."

Perhaps he was right. She imagined dropping down through the trapdoor. Where would the Senator be? Huddled in a bedroom, deafened by the storm, unaware that they were moving through the house outside his door? Or standing, gun in hand, on the landing below, waiting to pick them off?

The roof was not inviting. She had been out there herself, quite recently. The pitch was steep and the tin roof was slick, even when it was dry and there was no wind. It wouldn't take much to send her sliding down the roof into the waves.

Joe and the wind and the rapidly dying sunlight were giving her no time to think. He had draped Douglass' good arm over his shoulder and walked him to a gaping window-hole. Faye was compelled to help him. Together, they sat on the roof facing downward, shoulder-to-shoulder and knees bent, working for traction against the ridges striping the tin roof. Douglass was half-lying behind them, resting most of his weight on their backs. When Joe gave the signal, they began inching downward.

Hardly capable of coherent thought in the face of the punishing wind, Faye was impressed that Joe had chosen the site of their descent so carefully. They crept downward till they reached a chimney to brace against, then they angled their path across the leeward side of the house until they reached a gable protruding through the roof. After draping Douglass across it, they straddled it themselves. This gable sheltered Faye's bedroom window and even though she knew it didn't lead to the warm, dry haven she had always loved, she believed that she would be safe if she could just get in there.

Impatient, she moved toward the gable, intending to crawl onto her windowsill. Joe grabbed her arm and shook his head, mouthing, "Check first."

Checking would be hard. She lay belly-down on the roof of the dormer, then crawled forward by inches until she dangled from the hips down. With Joe holding her legs, she peeked in the window. Someone had lit her lantern. Their tormentor lay on her bed, booted feet crossed at the ankle, staring at the ceiling. She retreated quickly.

They sat straddling the dormer, gathering their strength for one more leg of their journey. There was another dormer a room away, twenty feet away, a lifetime away. Faye and Joe inched toward it, butts and soles to the tin and Douglass draped across their backs. The maneuver couldn't be accomplished without sliding and Faye doubted they had the strength to raise Douglass higher up the incline. If they slid too far, too close to the edge, there would be no place to go.

They crept an inch toward the second dormer and slid an inch downward. An inch of slide was too much. They had to do better.

Creep. Creep. Slide. Creep. Slide. Stop and breathe and creep again. Slide.

The dormer window was an arm-length-and-a-half away, but they were too low. Faye looked up at the unattainable window and down over the eaves at the churning water. She wanted to shriek. She probably did shriek, but the wind was shrieking louder than she was.

Joe, who had been sitting next to her, shoulder-to-shoulder, suddenly wasn't there. She was left to support Douglass' weight alone, a situation that couldn't last. She looked up and saw that Joe had managed to stretch his long arms and torso enough to touch the panes of the window they were striving to reach, but there was nothing for him to grip. He lowered his hand to his waist, groped inside his tool bag, and pulled out a sharp-pointed hand axe. Pulling his arm back, he whipped it forward, breaking the remaining windowpanes. He whipped it again, knocking the frame free of panes and dividers, and again, driving the axe blade into the wooden window frame.

Using the axe for leverage, he shimmied himself upward until he could grasp the windowsill with both hands, hoisting his torso over the sill and throwing himself headfirst into the open window.

Joe was safe and Faye was happy about that, but she and Douglass were still trapped on the roof.

It didn't take Joe long to rip the sodden curtains from their frame and lower a rescue line toward them. It was only a sheet tied in a loop, weighted by shoes and lengthened by knotted curtains, but the loop fit nicely under Douglass' armpits. Faye steadied Douglass while Joe hauled him up, leaving her behind, alone with the storm. Even if she were tall enough to reach the windowsill, which she wasn't, she just didn't have the muscle mass to lift herself that far using only the strength of her arms.

Was it her imagination or did the wind pick up speed when Joe left her alone? It flung water in her face, her mouth, her nose, so that she couldn't even take the choking wet half-breaths that had sustained her since she crawled out onto the roof. Sitting there, twenty feet above the water, she was going to drown.

Afraid to raise her hands from the roof where they were bracing her against its sharp slope, Faye shook her head to drive the water out of her nose, her eyes, her mouth, but it was no use. Tucking her chin against her chest and hunching her shoulders forward, she used her own body to block just enough wind and water from her face to let her breathe a bit.

The tiny bit of oxygen fed her strength. Nothing but her brain could fight the panic, the racing pulse and heaving chest and trembling limbs that were adrenaline's gift to humanity. *You are safe,* she told her adrenal gland. *Joe would never leave you out here to die.*

Faye, who had always taken pride in her self-sufficiency, sat in the wind, talking to her autonomic nervous system and waiting for rescue. It would have been a humbling moment if she'd had a prideful piece of herself left to be humbled. In the first minute after she conquered the panic, three branches bigger than she was crashed into the tin roof and bounced off. When, not if, something similar hit her, it would knock her cold, shaking body into the heaving sea.

She could have kissed Joe when he reappeared and dangled the rescue line over the windowsill, reaching down to help her to safety. For a long while, she lay wet and spent on the floor of Joyeuse's master bedroom, listening to the storm and the throb of her tortured leg.

The Senator lay on Faye's bed and enjoyed the cheery light of her lantern. He had no idea how Faye had come to be outside his window, but he'd seen her there, peeking in, and he'd heard her struggle across the roof and crawl through the next window. She was right next door. This was going to be easy.

He had successfully contained his anger, bottling it up until he saw Faye again. So she was living with another man and seeing him on the side. She had been so sly and so good at hiding her duplicity. It was a relief to know that she and the Indian, the two people who posed the last remaining danger to him, and thus needed to die, were the same two people he most wanted to kill.

How strange that Faye would be the Indian's companion, the one he had been chasing since he dispatched the two archaeology students. He'd been confounded by his inability to find the Indian, understandably, as it turned out. Wally had described him as a hermit, more or less, a hermit whose only companion was a boy named Faye.

His fabled luck had brought on a howling storm to cover his crimes. When he had stepped onto Faye's boat that morning, he had planned to kill her and sink her body in the Gulf. Simple and neat. Given her secretive ways, it would be days before she was missed. With no body and no sign of a struggle, Sheriff Mike would, sooner or later, decide Faye had simply moved on. She did have a habit of making sure no one could find her.

The risk associated with killing Faye had been comfortably low when they had set out for Joyeuse that morning. Now that the hurricane had entered the picture, her murder carried no risk at all. After sinking her body, he could return to land and tell a harrowing story of survival with an unhappy ending. How tragic the headlines would be—Senator Risks Life in Futile Attempt to Save Woman.

And his luck had brought Douglass Everett to him. Now the body of the only witness to Abby's death was bobbing in the storm. Even if it should wash ashore with its inexplicable bullet wound, who could tie Douglass' death to him and his unregistered gun?

The only other soul who could hurt him was in jail. Once he dispatched Faye and returned to shore, the big Indian's days were numbered. Such an assassination was best done in jail, anyway. Beatings and killings happened in jail all the time. That's why those people were there. Joe Wolf Mantooth was as good as dead.

His secrets were all safe at last. He had never killed for pleasure before today, but putting a hole in Douglass Everett had given him great satisfaction. Killing Faye would be the crowning touch. Then he could lay down his gun and enjoy the life of power that he was meant to live. And no one would ever know what he'd done to acquire that power.

It was time. He opened the door to his room and stepped out onto the landing that encircled the staircase like a square doughnut. Rain fell on him so hard that it ceased to be individual drops, melding into sheets and masses of solid water. This was more than a roof leak.

Looking up, he saw that the entire cupola was gone, leaving a great open hole through the house that was broken only by the landing where he stood and the staircase that rose through the center of it all. When the joints in the wooden floor beneath his feet failed, he dropped to his knees and reached for the doorjamb of the bedroom door. Fear propelled him on all fours into the room he had just left. Behind him, the landing crumbled and dropped to the house's main level.

It was clear why the landing failed. It had been engineered to work in conjunction with the staircase. Should the staircase fail, the landing simply could not support itself. Sheets of wet plaster flaked off the dying spiral. A slow tremor shook the balusters out of their railings until, unsupported, the handcarved banister clattered down with a godawful racket, followed by the treads.

He was trapped in his room, but so was Faye. He could get to her only by taking her path over the roof, but that would put him at a disadvantage when he came through the window to attack her. Neither of them was going anywhere until the storm passed. He would wait until then for his chance.

Faye was encouraged. There were worse places to hide in the old house than in the master's bedroom. The sneak stair terminated there. As soon as it was wise to leave the house, they would be able to get out unseen. A moment's fumbling under the bed yielded one of the flashlights she had stashed throughout the house. It had been a prudent emergency measure for a woman who lived in a house without electricity, but she could never have foreseen this particular emergency.

The flashlight's narrow beam swept over their hideout. Each wall was lined with glass-fronted shelves, proudly displaying her heritage—the family garbage that she'd pulled out of the ground. When the storm hurled a piece of metal through the glass protecting one of the shelves, she shrieked and almost dropped the flashlight. Joe clapped a hand over her mouth, and he left it there for a long time while she sobbed. The wind drove water through the empty window frame as if it would never stop.

Faye knew they could survive this hurricane. It had been done before. Cally did it.

◇

Excerpt from the oral history of Cally Stanton, recorded 1935

It was dark when the wind died down, but the moon was bright and I could see a clump of trees. I set out swimming for it, dragging my dresser drawer behind me. I was glad for the Sunday afternoons when Miss Mariah took me swimming in the salty Gulf. I wasn't glad a bit for the Missus's company, because her spunk left her when the storm did.

She whined and she fussed and I had to just about drag her fat self through the water. Then she wouldn't climb up the tree. She was afraid to let go of the drawer, because it saved her life and she might need it again. I threw up my hands and left her, holding her drawer with one hand and a tree trunk with the other.

I sat in my tree and let the water drop off me. There wasn't a breath of wind and the moon shone like it had a secret. I wasn't surprised when the wind came back from the other direction.

I wrapped my arms and legs around the tree trunk and wished for my dresser drawer. The Missus was hollering for me, but I couldn't go to her. If I got down out of that tree, I would never see the light of another day. I didn't need a dream to tell me that.

The storm played out and the sun came up along about the same time. I could see a long ways from my tree, but there wasn't much to see, just a few other treetops. Last Isle was gone.

I figured rescue boats would come, since the hotel was full of rich people. There wasn't any other way I was getting out of there alive, so I figured I might as well stay in my tree and hope for a boat. I was hoping hard, because my dream said the Master was going to die. It didn't say anything about me or the Missus.

Maybe hoping works. When the boat came, I was hungry and thirsty and bug-bit, but I wasn't dead. I wasn't alone, either. When the sun got high on that first day, I looked deep into my clump of trees, deep where the storm had piled trash and sand and tree limbs. The Missus was laying there, pale and slack-mouthed. I felt like she still needed someone to fetch things for her. Just someone to take care of her. But I couldn't do her any good, not now, so I stayed put. We waited together, the Missus and me.

When the rescuers came, the captain asked me who I belonged to. I opened my mouth to say they were dead and shut it again. I'd lived through a hurricane, but I was scared to death of the auction. I opened my mouth again and said, "I belong to Mister Courtney. Mister Courtney Stanton. He's the master at Innisfree."

Chapter 28

Sometime before dawn, the storm broke. At first light, Faye and Joe executed their plan to slog through the floodwaters, dragging Douglass to his boat. Surely it had survived the storm. Or, if not, surely its radio had survived the storm. Plan B involved using the *Gopher* and its radio. There was no Plan C.

The sneak stairs were so cramped that there was no way for Faye to help Joe with Douglass, so she led, as if her slight weight would keep them from falling if Joe failed to support the wounded man's bulk. For just a few seconds during the escape, they would be visible from Cyril's window. If they could dodge him for that long and if one of the boats did its part, they would soon be headed for the safety of Wally's Marina. Or any portion of Wally's Marina that the hurricane had allowed to remain standing.

The Senator heard bumping and scraping behind his wall. He had spent the night comparing the eccentric shape of his room's interior with the shape and size of the house's exterior. The only rational explanation for the discrepancy between indoor and outdoor dimensions was a hidden staircase, and he knew Faye was using it. He had been waiting for this moment for hours, ripping Faye's sheets and clothes into long strips, knotting them together, knowing that a controlled slide down this fabric rope would take him to the ground faster than any cramped staircase.

He backed out the window and down the steep roof, then slid down the rope. The knots passed through his fingers, slowing his descent, and the water cushioned his landing. The look on Faye's face as she emerged onto the porch where he waited was priceless. He aimed and fired.

Faye dropped into the murky, hip-deep water. The shot had missed her, but there were no more. He was still conserving ammunition, waiting to shoot until he got a good look at her. Pressing her belly to the floorboards, she swam and slithered through the flooded dogtrot, hoping to get to the back of the house and some kind of cover before she had to breathe.

The dogtrot formed a bottleneck and he followed her into it, grabbing at her with his free hand. It shocked them both when she rose out the water and slashed at him with Joe's makeshift stone scalpel. She connected with his right arm. The damage was minimal—a torn sleeve and a deep cut about the length of his thumb, but the gun and the stone tool fell into the water.

It was a small victory, because he was far larger than she was. His fingers closed around her throat. She was bending backward, heading for the water, when she saw Joe behind him, silhouetted at the entrance to the dogtrot.

Faye hated to believe that her last thought was going to be a whiny, "Where have you been? I'm dying here." Then she saw where Joe had been.

In the left arm that was drawing back to deliver a killing blow, Joe held the *atlatl*, the spearthrower that he had reworked as a gift to her, still fitted to the spearhead and haft he made with his own hands. She pushed hard against the Senator's grip, trying to keep him standing as a more-or-less upright, unmoving target, and she was rewarded.

Joe let the weapon fly. The force of his muscles, amplified by the *atlatl's* whiplash action, drove the spear into the back of the Senator's neck until Faye could see the stone point protruding through his throat.

Faye rested on the floor of her bedroom, having insisted that Joe deposit Douglass on the bed and having refused to be left alone anywhere else. Joe had left them to look after each other while he went to check the condition of the boats and their radios. He also claimed to know some herbs that would bring down her fever, and Douglass', too.

Faye imagined that any herb on Joyeuse Island that had survived the storm was now underwater, but she didn't doubt Joe's word. If he could find the weeds he sought, she trusted that she would feel better quite soon. And she did feel terrible. Fever, chills, nausea. Her thigh was so engorged that she'd had to slit her khakis to give it room to swell. She pulled at the hole in her pants, trying to see whether the famed red streak of blood poisoning was crawling up her leg. If she found such a streak what would it mean? Amputation? Lockjaw? Death? God only knew the consequences of dragging an open puncture wound through mud and muck and floodwater.

"Douglass?" she asked, in a voice that sounded faraway even to her. "How do you think his necklace got in Abby's grave? Cyril's, I mean...Cedrick's...whoever."

"I decked him. Didn't I tell you?" The memory added strength to the wounded man's voice. "After we dug the hole. Abby lay right there on the dirt while I did it." He drew another labored breath. "Clipped him on the jaw. Knocked him down." It hurt Faye to watch him cough and wheeze again before he went on. "Straddled him. Did my damndest to throttle him."

"You broke the chain while you were choking him."

"Prob'ly. Shoulda finished the job. Would have, 'cept for what he said."

Faye wanted Douglass to go on, but she was afraid. He was breathing in such tiny gasps.

Douglass continued anyway. "Said if anybody come up right then—they'd see just two men and a dead body. Said, 'Who they gonna to send to the chair? Me? Or you, nigger?'"

Faye closed her eyes and watched two men lowering Abby's limp form into her grave. Covering her with dirt. Riding together back to shore in Douglass' tiny fishing boat, facing each other eyeball to eyeball, because each was afraid to turn his back on the other. Afraid for forty years to turn their backs on each other.

Partly to get his mind off forty years of slow torture and partly to get her own mind off her leg, Faye peeled the damp plastic wrapping off William Whitehall's journal.

"Want to hear a story?" she asked him.

Douglass shifted on the bed. "Want to hear a story, Faye," he mumbled.

Carefully unwrapping the journal, she arranged the clear plastic wrapping to protect its pages from her damp hands, her wet clothes, the sodden air. Her fever had risen to the near-delusional stage of garbled thinking and uncertain vision, but she needed to read for Douglass and for herself, so she pulled herself together and did it.

◇

Excerpt from the oral history of Cally Stanton, recorded 1935

Living in the Big House at Joyeuse after the hurricane and I killed the Master felt like I'd died and gone to heaven, but it didn't make Mister Courtney happy. Sometimes, he sat at his desk and unlocked the drawer where he kept his papers. Then he laid bills of sale for all his people across the desk, calling them by name as he sorted through their papers.

"Rufus. Sallie. Beau. Scipio. Ora." Then he would set one paper to the side, away from the others, and say, "Cally." After a minute, he'd go back to counting his people. There were plenty of them, because he inherited Joyeuse since the Master didn't leave any children. Well, he left me, but I didn't count.

Mister Courtney's Mama must have told him that his stepfather, the Master, was my daddy. Knowing that, a decent man like Mister Courtney couldn't treat me like a slave. He gave me a room in the Big House and, even though he never asked me to run his household I did, because it needed doing and I knew how. Once he told me he wanted to set all his slaves free. When I caught my breath, I asked why he didn't go ahead and do it. I can still hear what he said.

"Because I'm afraid." He fingered through the bills of sale laid across his desk and said, "I'm afraid of what will happen to them, and I'm afraid of what will happen to me."

It took a long time for the War to touch us at Joyeuse. Mister Courtney didn't go away to fight, on account of his lame leg. Truth be told, I never noticed his limp until I came to live with him, because he carried himself like a prince. When he spoke, he fastened his blue eyes on you so direct that you hardly noticed whether the sun was shining. You certainly didn't notice anything so paltry as a weak leg.

I know you can tell that I was in love with him. In the seventy years since, I never met anyone who could hold a candle to him, so I've been alone, but we had a few good years together, my Courtney and I. It took some time for us to forget that he was my Master. He surely forgot it quicker than I did. But we lived together in his house and I took care of things for him and I was the only person in the world he could talk to. I was his wife in every way but one, and in the end it was up to me to show him that I could be his wife in that way, as well.

I think it wasn't just Mister Courtney's leg that was weak. I think it was his heart, too. When he left us, it was sudden. He came riding in from the fields, holding his chest. I tried to help him off his horse, but he fell. I was a skinny thing in those days, but I'm proud to say I caught him.

I fixed him a bed out on the porch where it was cool and he was comfortable there, but right away he sent me inside to look for a box hidden in his desk.

"It's your Christmas present," he said, "but I think I need to give it to you now."

It was a chatelaine, all made out of gold. It hung at my waist and held my keys and my scissors and my thimble—everything the lady of a great plantation needed to get through the day. I said I couldn't think of any gift I'd like better, then he pulled a gold ring out of his pocket. He'd had it made with a funny little loop on the side.

"You can wear it on your finger when it's safe, but you know that little ring could put you in jail. The law won't let you be my wife. When strangers come around, you wear that ring on your chatelaine. You understand, don't you?"

His voice got stronger when he talked about that little ring, and I began to hope he would pull through. But when I said, "Yes. I understand," he settled down and got weaker again.

He put the ring on my finger and said "I do," and made sure I said it, too. Then he said, fainter still, "A wedding present. What shall I give you?"

The word "Freedom," came out of my mouth before I thought and he said, "Oh, Cally, I tore up your paper long ago."

"Not just for me," I said. "For everybody."

So I fetched the papers out of his desk and helped him write "Freed in consideration of years of faithful labor," across the face of every one of them.

The next day, my precious Courtney left me alone, five months pregnant and responsible for a hundred new-made freedmen.

Chapter 29

Faye closed the journal and closed her eyes. She was so very tired and so very proud of Cally.

She was startled awake by noises downstairs that couldn't possibly be Joe, because he never wore shoes with hard soles. It was over. No matter who owned the feet stomping up the sneak stair, those footsteps signaled the end. Joyeuse was gone. She had let the family down.

The door opened and Magda stood on the other side. She stood at the shelves of artifacts by Faye's bed, each of them numbered, labeled, and cross-referenced with a dated field journal—except, of course, for the shelf that had its glass and all the treasures hiding behind it blown away by the storm. Lifting a rusty flatiron, Magda examined it, and said, "This is professional-quality work. It would be a shame for the archaeologist who did it to go to jail. What are we going to do about it?"

Sheriff Mike was amazed and grateful that he and Dr. Stockard had found Joe and Faye and Douglass Everett, all three of them alive and, as far as he was concerned, innocent of any serious crime. After a night of emergency room commotion and a course of intravenous antibiotics apiece, Douglass was out of intensive care and Faye was laid up at Dr. Stockard's house, worrying over how she was going to pay the hospital bill.

Try as he might, Sheriff Mike had not been able to convince her to save her worries for later. Claypool was in the throes of organizing a county-wide fundraiser to pay her medical bills—an all-day bluegrass concert and fish fry, headlined by Claypool's mandolin quartet. Everybody for miles around would turn out and the money would be found. That was the way of things in this neck of the woods.

Sheriff Mike had grown up along the Florida coast. He knew the people and he knew the currents. He had been pretty sure he knew where Senator Cyril Kirby would wash up. Sure enough, after a few days of waiting, he had found him, lying on his back, with Joe's flint point still protruding from his throat.

It wouldn't do to arrest young Joe for this killing. Senator Kirby's deeds were already plastered all over the papers. Even if Joe were cleared of wrongdoing, as well he should be, the questioning, the lawyers, the reporters, the courtroom—well, it would kill the boy. Sheriff Mike had seen what a few hours in jail had done to him. Joe Wolf Mantooth could only thrive in fresh air. He didn't deserve to be dragged into the maw of civilization.

Sheriff Mike reflected that this case had induced him to take an elastic view of upholding the law. Sometimes the law fell short of ensuring that justice was done. Sometimes, fate or God or something past his understanding took care of things instead. Right now, a man lay in a Tallahassee burn unit, missing a couple of fingers and most of the skin on his chest. When the doctors got through with him, the law would deal with him for carrying a concealed weapon and impersonating an officer of the law, but Sheriff Mike wagered that the punishment he had already received was more appropriate for the attempted murder of an innocent like Joe Wolf Mantooth than anything the law might be expected to hand out.

The sheriff had come to the beach today prepared to do what needed to be done to the body of Cyril—no, Cedrick—Kirby. A pair of gardening clippers were stuck in his hip pocket. He used them to cut easily through the shaft of the spear, just behind the point, and pocketed the arrowhead. Then he rolled the body over, planted a foot between its shoulder blades, and yanked the shaft out of its neck. The coroner might wonder how a hurricane had put a hole through Senator Kirby's throat, but Sheriff Mike wagered the coroner had never seen a man killed by hand-knapped stone. He'd rule that the death had occurred by accident.

Now he could go home, burn the bloodied shaft, and return with witnesses to discover the body all over again—after he'd cleaned up Joe's spearhead and respectfully placed it in a velvet-lined box alongside the relics of ancient heroes.

Where it belonged.

Faye took a stool at the lunch counter at Wally's, waiting for Magda, who couldn't wait to ride out to Joyeuse and tour what was left of the house. Liz had told her that Wally, the prince of self-preservation, had disappeared the day after the hurricane. Faye looked around the convenience store for evidence that the owner had been missing for a week, but found none. Liz was running the place as if nothing had changed.

"I'm waiting for the taxes to go into arrears," Liz said, "then I'm going to buy this place at auction with the money I saved from my husband's life insurance."

Faye felt positively impish. "Listen close. Right before the auction, break this window and that one over there," she said with a careless gesture. "Even if it rains, they won't let much water in. Do you want to keep this floor?" Liz looked at the peeling linoleum and shook her head. "Then slop some hot grease on it. You know all about creative uses for hot grease, I hear. I can show you how to make the toilets leak and the doors stick. If we set our minds to it, I figure we can knock twenty percent off your purchase price. Maybe thirty."

"Faye," Liz said, "you have always got a place to park your boat. Count on it."

"Good, because I'll need one round-the-clock from now on. I think I'm going to be moving to town."

Magda was already talking when she walked through the door. "One of my colleagues is a lithics specialist. He's chomping at the bit to hire Joe as a lab tech, so Joe can teach him everything he knows about ancient toolmaking techniques. The pay is low, but how much does Joe need? And he'll get the use of the school's infirmary and catastrophic health insurance."

"Joe's going to have health insurance?" Faye asked, incredulous.

"Sure, as a student, you'll qualify for the same deal. You are coming back to school, aren't you?"

"I'm going to have health insurance?" Faye asked, the incredulity in her voice cranking up a notch.

Magda had taken on Faye's future as a personal project. On the day after the hurricane, while they waited on Joyeuse for the Coast Guard to get paramedics to Douglass and Faye, she had sat cross-legged on Faye's wet floor, brandishing a waterproof pen. The act of initialing every page of Faye's field notes, sheltering years of pothunting under the umbrella of her Ph.D., had made Magda chuckle. No, cackle was the right word for the sounds that had come out of her sturdy chest.

"Now," Magda had said, "you've got enough material for your dissertation and I've got fodder for years of academic publications. You have to come back to school now, Faye."

Recklessly confident that the funding would materialize, Magda sat sipping cocoa at Liz's lunch counter and chattering about Faye's research assistantship.

Faye waited until Magda stopped to breathe, then broke in. "I won't be needing the research assistantship. I'll be able to fund my own studies. During the hurricane, Douglass offered me a job curating his Museum of American Slavery. He may have been delirious, but I've accepted the offer anyway."

It felt good to know that she could pay her tuition, get an apartment in Tallahassee, go to the movies now and then, but these things would cost her dearly. No research assistantship or museum curatorship was going to generate enough income to allow her to keep Joyeuse.

The water birds were gathering in their rookery and Faye could hear their evening cries from the back porch of her ancestral home. Sheriff Mike, Magda, Douglass, and Douglass' wife, Emma, were digging into heaping plates of Joe's barbecue, and Faye felt quite the hostess. She had never thrown a party at Joyeuse and this first one would also be the last. She knew it was healthier to let the bitterness go, and she was trying.

Joe was sitting on his favorite stump and he looked comfortable, because he was outdoors. Douglass and his wife sat side by side on the ground, companionably together after thirty years of marriage. She noticed Sheriff Mike and Magda looking pretty comfortable, too, sitting next to each other on the porch steps and wolfing down Joe's famous corn and crab soup. And Magda had thought she was too scary for any mortal man. All the coziness made Faye lonely, but a consolation lay buried beneath it all. If there was a man out there for Magda, there was surely a man somewhere who would love Faye.

She poured the sheriff a second glass of iced tea, then replaced the pitcher in her cooler. Sheriff Mike was a notorious history buff and that had given her the impetus to throw this party. She knew he'd get a charge out of touring the place, even in its current condition. She had talked Joe into showing the sheriff how to knap flint, and the older man's effusive admiration for Joe's skills had made him blush. A taste for mischief had prompted her to invite Douglass and Emma, because Douglass deserved an apology for living a lifetime under suspicion. Sheriff Mike delivered.

He raised his glass of tea and said, "Here's to Abby, one last time. Her killer has found justice and there's nothing more we can do for her but remember her beauty and her tender soul. And here's hoping that everyone here can forgive me for all the mistakes I made during all the years I looked for the man who took sweet Abby away from us."

After everyone drank to Abby, he said. "I guess you folks have heard about the bones that keep washing ashore on Seagreen Island."

"Are they Abby's?" Magda asked.

"Maybe. It'd be hard to prove. Maybe if we got some DNA out of them and if we could coerce some DNA samples from her fifth cousins in Austin. Not likely, I figure."

"Do you have the arm bones? The right upper arm?" Douglass asked.

"Well, yeah," Sheriff Mike drawled, interested. "Why do you ask?"

"Because I was there when she broke it. A compound fracture, right there," he said, pointing to a spot just above his elbow. "I've got a picture of her in the cast."

"It's circumstantial," the sheriff said. "Reckon it would be enough to get the trustee of Mr. Williford's estate to release the reward money at this late date?"

"I imagine so," Douglass responded, "considering that I'm the trustee."

Sheriff Mike, who knew the answer to his question before he asked it, said, "Reckon who you'd be releasing the money to?"

Everybody looked at Faye, who didn't want to be crass and ask, "How much?" She stifled the "how" with a loud exhalation.

"Don't know how much, exactly," Douglass said. "I don't check regularly because it just sits in the bank and earns interest. The reward was twenty thousand dollars in 1964. Reckon it would make a regular person rich, but you're gonna blow it on this house. Reckon it'll just make you comfortable."

Faye wondered how long it would be before she was able to breathe again.

"How's it feel to be a rich woman, Faye?" Joe said. He was lying on his back studying the summer stars and he looked like a man who owned everything he could see.

"I don't feel richer, exactly. I feel like I already had everything I could ever want, but now I get to keep it."

"Can I stay?"

Faye let the question hang in the air, because she didn't understand it. Finally, she said, "What?"

"When I came to Joyeuse, you said I could stay a while. How long is that?"

It seemed like a long time since she'd lived alone on the island, with only its ghosts for company. The old house loomed over them, silver-white under the moon. The dim light hid most of the storm's damage and some of the ravages of time. She had the money to make her home beautiful and livable again, as she had always dreamed of doing. It would feel like an empty shell if Joe left.

"You can stay, Joe. You can stay."

They watched the moon slide past the million stars studding the dark sky over Joyeuse and they didn't talk any more. That was the best thing about Joe. He knew how to let things be.

It was late when Faye crawled into bed, but she left her lantern burning. She was nearly finished reading Cally's story and nothing short of a hurricane would stop her from finishing now, tonight.

◇

Excerpt from oral history of Cally Stanton, recorded 1935

I saved my favorite story till last. I always laugh when I remember the day the Yankees came to liberate the slaves on Joyeuse. They were naturally more gape-jawed when they found us already free.

Mister Courtney always said I was a charming liar. Well, I did him proud that day. I knew it wouldn't be safe to let anybody, not the Yankees or anybody, know that we didn't have a master any more. The laws weren't good back then and the courts were even worse. Somebody was liable to come take the land—*my* land—and make my workers farm it for just about nothing.

So I told them the master and his wife had gone to Tallahassee that very day to pledge their allegiance to the Yankee flag. Then I showed them young Courtney, my baby, and made sure they knew that my job was to take care of the master's heir. I forgot to mention that young Courtney was a girl and not entitled to own anything in her own name. I also forgot to mention that she wasn't white, so she wasn't entitled to anything in this life at all.

I practiced that lie on the Yankees, then I told it to the people who wrote up the deed. By the time Courtney was bigger and people noticed she was a girl, nobody gave the deed much thought again until just last year when they used my old lies as an excuse to take part of her inheritance away. Courtney fought them. She fought them hard, because the women in our family are tough. We could chew the heads off a barrel of nails if we had to. We lost that land, but we'll get it back.

And we'll always have Joyeuse. Men come and go. They go to war and die. They get diseases and die. They meet other women and leave, then you wish they would die. But home is forever.

Mark my words: Take care of your home. Keep its roof fixed, and the taxes paid, and never mortgage it. Then you'll always have a place to go.

And let me tell you another thing. Don't ever hide anything so well that you can't ever find it again. When the Federals came, I sunk my chatelaine and all the table silver in a cow pond because I was damned if I'd see the Yankees get it. I have shed many tears over my treasures ever since then, because I never found them. Sometimes I send my little great-granddaughter out to dig for the precious wedding ring that Courtney gave me. I think I'll send her out there now. It's always good to keep little folks busy.

Chapter 30

Faye was on fire to dig in a brand-new piece of ground. The hurricane had left more sand on her shore than it took away, closing the mouth of the inlet where she moored her boat and reducing an area that had been inundated all her life to a low, marshy spot.

As soon as she read the last entry of Cally's memoirs, she knew: that swampy pit was the pond, the spot where she hid the family valuables when the Yankees came.

Sifting through the muck, Faye uncovered a tiny golden thimble crafted with a minuscule eyelet that was obviously designed to attach it to something. She documented its location in her waterproof field book and dug with renewed purpose.

She couldn't wait to show it to Joe.

Author's Notes

There is no Micco County in Florida. As far as I know, there has never been a Joyeuse Island or a Last Isle there, either. They exist only in an imaginary segment of the Florida Panhandle coastline in the general vicinity of Panacea and Sopchoppy. There were a number of island plantations along the southeastern Atlantic coast, and Joyeuse is modeled in many ways after them.

There really was a Last Isle in Louisiana, however, and it really was the site of a resort frequented by wealthy planters and their families. When I read about the hurricane that destroyed the resort and the island, I found that the reported mortality varied widely, from less than two hundred in one source to more than five hundred in another. As I wondered whether the variance might be explained by the possibility that only some of the sources counted the slaves who were surely there, the seeds of this story were sown. It is written in respectful memory of the people who died on Last Isle—all of them.

To receive a free catalog of other Poisoned Pen Press titles, please contact us in one of the following ways:

Phone: 1-800-421-3976
Facsimile: 1-480-949-1707
Email: info@poisonedpenpress.com
Website: www.poisonedpenpress.com

Poisoned Pen Press
6962 E. First Ave. Ste 103
Scottsdale, AZ 85251